I0664278

DAY
OF
RECKONING

JEFFERY L. CHENEY

CRAIG J. CHENEY

JARED L. CHENEY

ISBN-10: 1939223008
ISBN-13: 978-1-939223-00-5

DEDICATION

To Gienah, Pam, and Patti:
For putting up with us

CHAPTER 1
28 June, 2787

Ensign Monica Samuels dispassionately watched Clint Morrison in his engineering enlisted uniform tap the butt of his pistol on the door frame before quickly bringing his prisoner back in its sights. The hatch opened and he eyed the young officer as she passed into her own quarters. The barrier closed again, and the metallic click indicated that it would not open again until someone on the other side came for her.

Finally alone, she dropped the brave front she'd maintained since she had reentered the ship. Her impassive face slid away, to be replaced by a snarl of anger. She looked about for something she could kick without breaking her toes, but there was nothing that fit the bill. Navy beds, navy footlockers, navy doors. If this were one of her own family's ships, at least there would have been carpeting!

Blast it, what did the captain mean? Is it possible that he knows why I'm here? Is that why he told me to stay? Uncertainty clouded the young officer's expression as she looked into the navy mirror secured to the wall above the room's sink. The mirror held no answers and offered no solace to her personal pain. Instead, it showed the bunk belonging to her missing roommate, Ensign Jherri Roberts which just accentuated her own situation. Jherri had been one of the officers who had been exiled to Antoc-A3 with Captain Brighton aboard the shuttle *Vanguard*.

Samuels grabbed the rim of the sink, and closing her eyes, leaned forward to rest her head lightly on the mirror. *Man, what a mess I've gotten myself into now! I finally think I have it all worked out, I know where my duty lies. I get on board* Vanguard, *and then Captain Brighton sends me back! Why would he do that? Does he feel that I belong with the traitors?*

1

How could things have gone so horribly wrong so quickly? she wondered.

Six hours ago, her world was precisely what she wanted it most to be. She had been a newly promoted ensign posted to one of the most sought after position in the fleet, serving a tense watch on the bridge under the exacting scrutiny of her captain. Well, perhaps not precisely what she wanted. If it were a perfect universe, when she had graduated from Warner Naval Academy six months before, she would have gone straight back to school for Advanced Cyber-Warfare. Rules were rules, though, and a "middy tour" was mandatory before she could apply for further study.

Going back to school was not likely to happen now, any more than she could change the last six hours. She was done as Officer of the Deck on Captain Brighton's third watch. The odds that she would ever see Captain again, or any of the eighteen others exiled with him, were vanishingly small.

Monica Samuels opened her eyes and leaned away from the mirror. There were tears threatening to spill over, and the weakness they represented embarrassed her, though no one was there to see them. She wiped the moisture away and put her hair back in place where the mirror had disturbed the laser line of her black bangs. Next, she willed her pale face back into its calm mask; she was getting good at living behind a mask.

Samuels found that putting herself physically back into good order was helping to restore her mental and emotional equilibrium as well, which she desperately needed. She continued her efforts, removing the hair clip that held her ponytail, shaking out the hair that didn't quite reach her collar, and then clipping it tightly back in place. She still had on the officer's uniform of a Warner Space Navy ensign that she had donned for her rotation on the bridge that had started at 0000 that morning.

Unbidden, the morning scene replayed itself in her mind.

* * * * *

Ensign Samuels looked around the bridge. The captain was occupying the astrogation console. Tim O'Neill had moved around to the scan board on the port side of the bridge just aft of the Environmental station manned by Drew Le Vesconte. Everything was quiet. She turned to walk toward the unmanned cartography console on the other side of the bridge, but she never made it there. The bridge hatch slid open and two engineering crewmen jumped through, holding pistols. Samuels knew that she should do something, but she stood frozen in place. She watched Captain Brighton hit a button on his console then he stood to face the threat. He stopped suddenly, as frozen as Samuels, when Lt. Commander Teach, the man who the captain thought was his friend, came through the hatch behind the crewmen, Kasdorf and Morrison she thought their names were.

"Everyone, sit back down," Teach ordered, waving his pistol. Just then the ship was shaken by several small jolts.

He stood there and looked at the captain. Indecision showed plainly on his face. He had not expected the explosions so he appeared unsure.

Samuels herself was not sure what the jolts were but they felt like very small explosions in multiple points on the ship's surface. She briefly considered whether she were about to die but Captain Brighton stood there, unfazed and patient, so she calmed her quavering stomach and tried to follow his example.

"I said to sit down, Captain," Teach repeated finally, and waved his gun at the watch crew. Samuels took the last few steps to the cartography console and sat down slowly, never taking her eyes off the captain. He would know what to do.

Brighton folded his arms across his chest and stared at the renegade officer.

"What was that noise?" Teach asked as he moved over to stand in front of Captain. The captain made no reply, but the fury in his expression was strong enough that she was surprised that Teach didn't recoil.

Getting no answer from Captain Brighton, he turned to the bridge crew. "I am taking command of this ship. All officers and crew who wish to stay on the ship will be welcomed and receive the respect they deserve. I will no longer allow the kind of abuse and harassment that has been the norm under the previous command," he said.

Samuels sat back in her chair, stunned.

She wasn't sure to expect, but she certainly had not imagined mutiny. The comments about abuse were also confusing, Captain Brighton was an intimidating presence, especially to an Ensign just out of the academy, but he had never been abusive to any of the crew in her presence.

Teach grinned at the captain as if he had scored critical points in some game. Samuels remembered wanting to scream at him. She wanted to pound her head on the console, anything to make this nightmare end. Instead, she sat frozen and silent in her chair trying to decide what to do.

Captain Brighton stepped forward quickly and slapped Teach hard enough to make him stagger back a step. The two startled crewmen raised their pistols but took no further action nor did Commander Teach move to use the weapon held loosely in his hand. The captain took a step back and said to the bridge crew, "Take no immediate action. Do as you're instructed. Loyal members of the crew will no doubt be here soon to collect these misguided lunatics."

The watch standers visibly relaxed as they received their instructions, but Teach seemed to swell with rage and his eyes flashed.

"You are no longer in a position to give any orders on my bridge, Willy," he said, before turning to face the helm.

"Ms. Williams, you will set a course to Antoc-A3," he said to the helmswoman. She never made any response.

"Did you hear the order, Ms. Williams?"

"I heard some noise come out of your mouth, but I haven't heard any orders. Orders come from the captain," she said, with insubordinate venom.

Samuels watched with horror as the rage exploded across Teach's face and he swung his pistol around to fire at Williams. Captain Brighton lunged after the weapon but he was grabbed from behind by crewman Morrison who was standing just behind him. Williams threw herself out of the chair as the flechettes tore a large hole in the seat back.

Teach didn't fire again, even though the pilot lay on the deck beside her chair staring daggers at him. Samuels shivered as if ice slid down her spine at the XO's sudden mood shift. *Was he even sane?* she wondered.

He turned calmly to Morrison and said, "Take them down to the shuttle bay. Put the captain on one of the lifeboats and don't let him talk to anyone."

"Aye-aye, sir."

The armed crewman nearest Samuels, Kasdorf his nametag read, grabbed her by the arm and yanked her to her feet while motioning to Le Vesconte and O'Neill with his pistol. He held his weapon pushed into Samuels' head while the rest filed out of the hatch and then pushed her through to follow them.

Exiting the bridge, she watched as Major Chowdhury, the head of *Pathfinder's* Marine security team, was marched down the central passageway in front of them. She had both hands manacled behind her back. Crewmen Trendle and Green were behind her with drawn pistols trained on her head. As she went by, Samuels could see that her uniform was covered in blood. *How had they gotten so many of the crew to go along with this insane mutiny?*

They were followed by two other engineering ratings carrying the unconscious form of Sergeant Burton, one of the other Marines. Her right side was blackened from some sort of blaster fire, but Samuels could not tell if she was living or dead from the brief look she had. Two other engineering crewmen followed them all with weapons drawn. Both were also covered in blood. They all continued across the main walkway toward sickbay.

Similar scenes were repeated as far as they could see along the corridor, as crew and officers were being herded down to the boatbay, already filling with tense, angry men and women.

The captain was pushed in first, followed by Morrison, who seemed have become his personal guard. Kasdorf pushed Samuels to the starboard corner away from the captain.

Morrison tried to undog the seal on the access hatch to lifeboat nine but found that it would not unseal. It was only then that he noticed the red light on the side panel indicating that the pod was no longer there.

The bay was noisy and all the rest of the crewmen and officers were moved to starboard, completely isolated from the captain. Elle Williams looked at the cluster of mutineers and shook her head. She moved from her group toward the captain. There were murmurs among the pirates, but no one moved to block her way. Drew Le Vesconte followed her after a slight hesitation. Both moved to stand next to Captain Brighton and glared at their captors.

As the doors opened again to admit Teach, the room quieted slightly in anticipation. He surveyed the bay and singled out Dr. Ward who was standing with the other loyalists. Ward looked disoriented and stunned as he moved hesitantly to stand near Teach when instructed to do so. The Executive Officer said something to him that Samuels could not hear. They stood and looked at each other and Ward clearly answered. Teach looked stunned, barked some orders to one of the guards, Simon Chin, and Ward was escorted out into the starboard corridor.

Once the assistant medical officer was accompanied out of the bay, Teach seemed to collect himself and turned to address the larger group. As he did so, more crewmen and officers were pushed into the bay to join the huddled group with Samuels, nearly doubling its size. She saw her friend Jherri Roberts at the front of the group, but was too far away to dare trying to speak to her. Amber Sullivan was standing next to her with fear and confusion covering her thin features. At a quick glance, it looked like nearly all of the crew was assembled.

"Respect is a hard thing to earn," Teach said in a voice that brought the attention back to himself. "It is also impossible to live without. For the last nine months we have been working as slaves to the ambition of a heartless captain without any proper respect, recognition, or acknowledgement. That ends now!" He stood and surveyed the group as if waiting for applause. None arrived.

Samuels snuck a quick look at the captain to see how he was reacting to this slander, but he acted as if he could not hear what was being said. For herself, she wasn't sure what she was hearing. Just like the pronouncement on the bridge, Teach's claims didn't seem to have any basis in fact. Had she been that isolated from what was going on in the rest of the ship? Had there been abuses she was unaware of?

"Soon you will be called upon to make one of the most important decisions of your lives. Brighton will be sent down to a nearby planet. He will have food and water enough to support life. Those who will not acknowledge me as rightful captain of the *Pathfinder* are welcome to join him there. You can stay here and be free of the tyrant, or you are welcome to share his meager existence. You must choose now. Those of you foolish enough to reject my generosity, please join him. If you wish to take part in this venture as free men, stay where you are."

Monica's mind raced as she considered what she had just heard. The venom in Teach's pronouncement left her wondering if he would really allow Brighton the chance at life that he had claimed. It felt more reasonable to assume that he was lying to cover the murder of the captain and all those who followed him. Samuels realized that to follow him would mean her death as well. This thought froze her in place just as the pistols had done on the bridge.

The group shifted uncomfortably on their feet but no one made a move toward the captain. Finally, the large bosun, Derrick Mackey, took two steps toward Teach and spat on the deck plates at his feet. He continued to stare at the traitor as he moved purposefully to join the captain's small group. He stood in front of him and snapped a parade ground salute. Nearly two thirds of the remaining people, led by Lt. Fyonna Johnson and Major Chowdhury, her hands still handcuffed behind her, quickly followed him. Only Samuels and eight other people were left in front of Teach. Next to Monica, Sullivan started to cry and fell to the deck.

The young ensign looked at the captain, trying to evaluate where her duty directed her. She had a duty of loyalty to the captain and to the Warner Fleet but she had other responsibilities, and other loyalties, as well.

If she went with the captain, she might die and fail in her ultimate responsibility to her parents and immediate family, but if she stayed she would be numbered as a traitor and a thief and would never have a career in the Fleet. Then she would have failed both duties.

The captain looked back at her with the first compassion that she had ever seen him show. He looked into her eyes and nodded as if in agreement with her decision to stay.

She knew she could delay her decision no longer. She hung her head as she contemplated the death of her career and her dream of helping her family and she began to cry softly along with Sullivan, as she made the hardest decision of her life. With that decision made Monica Samuels threw her head back and acted.

She reached down and grabbed the hand of her friend and whispered, "I can't protect you if you stay." Sullivan came to her feet and they both walked over to join the captain.

There were seven who chose to remain behind with Teach; one officer, Ensign Omundson, and six crewmen.

Teach sent those seven to their quarters, under guard. He then approached the remaining group standing loyally with the Captain.

"Each of you crewmen will be allowed to return to your quarters to grab clothing and whatever personal items that you cannot live without. You will be guarded at all times. If you come to regret your rash decision, simply inform your guards that you wish to stay and you will be allowed to remain in your quarters. All officers, security and bridge crew will remain in the boatbay."

The nine loyal technicians and crewmen departed, guarded by Trendle and Green.

When everyone had returned to the boatbay, Teach began the unlock sequence on the nearest lifeboat. The hatch stayed closed, and the indicator stayed red. The lifeboat was gone. Not believing the evidence of his eyes, he had his toadies check each of the other lifeboats. All of the lifeboats in the bay were gone. Samuels knew this had been the cause of the small explosions she had felt just after the pirates had entered the bridge. She remembered that she had seen Captain Brighton activate a switch as soon as he had seen the two crewmen.

He had planned for this, she realized.

We may survive after all.

Teach's reaction was very shocking to Samuels. He stood there and ranted and raved at his crew, at the group of exiles, and at Captain Brighton, specifically. Throughout the take-over Teach had remained calm. *Well, except when he shot at Williams*, she thought. Now, however, he was completely out of control.

At one point, he had to be physically restrained by the crewmen standing next to him. The chief engineer, Katherine Leung, had a haunted look on her face as she pocketed the pistol that her engineering crewmen had taken away from him. Samuels could not feel sorry for her.

Teach finally seemed to regain some control. "Bezates, Danis," he called. "Get into *Vanguard* and disable the long range transmitter. Jettison the communication pods and pull enough batteries to disable the jump engines."

The crewmen assigned to disable *Vanguard* returned quickly. They did not carry any batteries or equipment, so doubtless they had simply sent it all out the launch's starboard airlock. Dr. Ward returned to the boatbay with medical boxes and carrysacks loading him down. He was added to Brighton's crew and they were all marched at gunpoint to the deck hatch and down the ladder that led to *Vanguard*'s port airlock. The gunmen soon returned for the officers and they were all secured behind the inner airlock door.

Teach stepped forward and offered one last time for anyone else to save themselves from the fate that awaited them.

"I need you to stay aboard. I'll be back for you," Brighton said quietly to Samuels. She was stunned. It was like a reprieve at the foot of the gallows. She had been ordered to stay. She stood quickly and pulled Sullivan back out of the hatch without ever acknowledging the captain's remark or looking back at her abandoned fellows. Aichele stood from his seat next to Chowdhury, and moved out of the hatch with his head down, as if in shame. They didn't look at each other as they made their way back into the boatbay and under guard back into the main living section of the ship. Samuels was separated from Aichele and Sullivan and Morrison took her to her quarters.

* * * * *

She tried not to think of her fellow officers and crew who had been abandoned to their fate, but with limited success. Abruptly, she realized that Brighton was the only one who knew she had been ordered back. If he didn't survive, she would still be branded a traitor. *Why did he order me back?*

She had lost track of the number of times she had made such an evaluation while leaning on the meticulously clean fixture.

She had been in her quarters almost five hours now, with nothing to do. She had talked to no one. Her only contact with the outside world was a muffled sobbing from the quarters just forward of her own. It sounded like Amber Sullivan, even though those were not her assigned quarters. This brought another wave of guilt. *Poor Amber, I should have left her with Captain, but I thought bringing her back with me would look less suspicious.*

Samuel was beginning to go stir crazy. She threw herself onto her bed, as she had several times in the last hours.

She stood again after a moment, unable to hold still. Her black ponytail spun behind her as she began the pacing that was the next step in her personal frustration cycle. Her mind continued to churn out the questions that had been plaguing her during her hours of isolation.

"Stay," the captain had said. *What did he mean? Did he mean that he didn't want me?* She thought for the hundredth time since her incarceration. *Was it an instruction simply to stay on the ship and nothing more? What was his expectation? Does he know?* she asked herself again. *If he knows, it would change everything. Should I be trying to delay the theft of the ship? Obstruct their attempts to leave the system? If only Captain Brighton had had more than a few seconds to give me orders, then I might know what the blazes I should be doing right now.*

What if he's aware of my history and he's already reported me to Warner?

That could make this a very sticky situation. If he did, I am better off throwing in with Teach at this point. That is definitely the second best option, though.

I have to know for sure and there is only one way to do that, she decided. *If I have enough time, that is,* she told herself, arriving at the mirror once again.

She moved quickly to the nearest of the two computer interface modules. She glanced at the hatch nervously, as if, after remaining shut for the last five hours, it would choose this moment to open and betray her.

She sat at the desk and logged into the terminal. After inputting her codes she was shocked to see the level to which the system had been locked down.

And locked down by an expert, it appeared. After twenty minutes of trial and error, using everything Commodore Wellesley had taught her in Advanced Cyber-Structure, she finally got access to her own files. Once she had those, she had what she needed to invade the captain's personal correspondences. She didn't have access to any of the ship's systems from her cabin, those were part of the main computer on the bridge and only terminals physically connected there could do anything with them, but she was able to get far enough into the system to verify that the only messages to Warner Fleet Headquarters from Captain Brighton had nothing to do with her. With that knowledge, she knew that her only course of action was to complete her original mission. The only way to complete her original mission was to get help to Brighton, who was the only witness to her having been ordered back to *Pathfinder*.

As soon as she had made up her mind as to what to do, the impossibility of the task nearly overwhelmed her and she flopped back onto her bunk. *How am I supposed to do that?*

Certainly, the odds were stacked heavily against her. Her ship, WNS *Pathfinder*, had been taken over by Commander Teach, the executive officer, and others that he had convinced to support him. She didn't know precisely why he had done this, nor anything about what he planned to do now.

Any people that might have helped her in reaching her goal had been forcibly removed from the ship, including Captain Brighton and eighteen officers and crew. That left more than thirty supporting Teach against her solitary self. There would be no help coming from outside the ship either, since they had just completed a test jump into an uninhabited system.

Samuels rose once again and retraced her circuit of the room, analyzing what she knew and trying to formulate a plan that might allow her to provide some assistance to Brighton. Some chance of rescue had to be created for those who had been ejected from the ship, as well, if she could manage it. For all the confident claims to the contrary, the captain and her friends might never return from their exile. She could think of nothing, but that did not diminish her resolve to find a way. She would have to be vigilant for opportunities to communicate what had happened here to the Warner Naval Board. Likely, she would have to manufacture such an opportunity herself. Once word got to them, a force could be assembled both to rescue Brighton and to reclaim *Pathfinder*. The difficulty would be in getting word out quickly enough that it would make a difference. She knew that only a limited supply of food and water had been provided to Brighton, so rescue had to arrive before that was gone. The other time constraint was that with her prototype engines, *Pathfinder* could move anywhere in the galaxy without leaving a trail to follow.

Once Teach could control the ship completely, they would disappear without a trace. Delaying that time had to be one of her primary objectives as well.

Commander Teach had said that anyone was welcome to join with him but obviously anyone who signed on at the point of a gun was not going to be completely trusted. She could still see the scene in her mind's eye. Commander Teach had been ranting to the crew. Crewmen with guns pointed at everyone else. Everyone had been looking at each other and trying to figure out what was going on. Mostly, to her shame, she remembered the gripping terror in her belly that told her that if she went into that launch, she would die. Even though Commander Teach had said the exiles would have food and supplies enough to survive on the planet that was their destination. It had taken everything she could muster to make that decision to join the captain. It shouldn't have, but it had. *Had the captain been able to see that? Was that why he had ordered me off the ship? Did he know that I was not up to the task?* she asked herself as she landed on her mattress again.

All through the academy, the Leadership series had been the most difficult courses for the young ensign. Math, Computers and Astrogation had come easily. Most were second nature, having spent considerable time aboard ships in her life. Only the decision-making skills had been difficult. Monica Samuels knew this about herself. She had studied Captain Brighton on watch and envied the easy manner in which he gave commands and dealt with problems. He was an officer and a leader and he *led* his crew. He never over-analyzed the situations the way that she did as a matter of course, he simply acted. What was it that her command instructor had said? "It's usually better to take the wrong action, quickly, than to make the best possible decision, too late."

She realized that she not only had to make up her mind quickly, but she had to have a plan in place from which she could act.

Sitting up and taking a deep breath, Monica once again tried processing the information at her disposal into a course of action.

Trust was going to be the most important element, she decided. Without the trust of the other crew, she would be watched constantly and would never have the opportunity to do anything. Obviously, she was not trusted yet. *How could she be?* she thought. She had had no opportunities to prove herself. She had been escorted here directly from the boatbay and had had no contact with any of the mutineers since. *No, I can't call them mutineers,* she thought to herself. *That is not how they see themselves, regardless of the facts of the matter.* Now she was, technically, one of them. And there were still no answers to any of her questions.

Finally, she saw the answer. She had to *become* one of them. She knew that she could fool anyone with her ability to play a role. Wasn't the fact that she was here on this ship proof enough of that?

She would need to blend in with the crew. She must do whatever she was required to do to make them trust her, and then take any chances that came along for covert action either to delay the theft of the ship or to get help for the exiles. Of the two considerations, helping the exiles had to be of secondary importance, regardless of her personal feelings on the matter.

Pathfinder was too important to the survival of the Warner Family as a viable government to allow its theft. *Pathfinder* was a one-of-a-kind prototype that would revolutionize space travel. The ability to bypass jump points and jump from anywhere to anywhere else without going through established jump gates was too valuable to lose to another Family. If necessary, she would have to destroy the ship to keep it away from the mutineers – *current owners*, she corrected herself.

She began to move along the well-worn track from bed to mirror again, this time with a purpose in mind; to school her appearance to that which the others would expect and to formulate her plans.

Secrecy would be the key to everything. If she were discovered, it could mean her imprisonment or possibly even her death. Of course, that could be what the mutineers had in store for her anyway, regardless of how cooperative she had become.

The continued sobbing from the berth forward reminded her that she had to keep this secret even from Amber, who was her closest remaining friend. Amber was not built to handle this kind of high-stakes game, and any further stress might well push her over the edge, if she hadn't already gone over on her own.

Once again, she felt regret for dragging the girl back into this death trap with her. She sat on her bunk and let out a deep sigh.

I don't have time to just sit here, she chided herself. The ensign stood and moved to the desk once again. If she was to stay alive, she had to take control of *Pathfinder* away from Teach, Leung and Lamont. In order to do that, she had to have control of the computer. She didn't know how to accomplish that yet, of course, but that only brought

Commodore Wellesley's favorite quotation to mind: "Do not let what you cannot do interfere with what you can do."

After four grueling years in the academy she had learned a number of those things about herself. One of these things was that she was most comfortable when she could work outside of the spotlight. This was probably logical due to the number of activities in her life which wouldn't stand up well to the scrutiny of the spotlight.

That wasn't to say that she folded under pressure. No one could survive the academy, let alone finish second in her class, with that sort of flaw, but she preferred not to attract notice.

It was also a fact that she was very good at what she did.

With that thought in mind, she went to work.

CHAPTER 2
28 June

"We're going down in flames. You know that, right?" Lt. Commander Katherine Leung said acidly to the present captain, Edward Teach, as he entered the bridge, without taking her dark brown eyes off her work. Instead, she turned casually to her right in the command seat of WNS *Pathfinder* only after he approached her position. She was small in stature, but her intense personality tended to dominate any gathering where she found herself. Her long dark hair was pulled back into the traditional navy ponytail, but it was starting to be streaked with gray as a reminder that she was closer to the end of her career than she was to the beginning.

Her face radiated the frustrations and anger that had been building over the last several hours as their well-planned takeover had fallen apart in the face of application after application of Murphy's Law.

Everything that could possibly have gone wrong, had. "Brighton and his officiousness," she fumed as she pounded a fist into the arm of the command chair. "Everything would have gone smoothly if he hadn't had to stick his nose into everybody else's business." She finished with another curse under her breath.

"It is common courtesy to stand as a senior officer enters the bridge," Teach stated. "Because we are alone on the bridge, I will let it pass this time, but I will not stand for any laxity in my command." He stood ramrod straight and his near-ebony eyes radiated an almost palpable intensity.

Leung stared at him as if he were some interesting specimen that had crawled in under the door. He was short, barely 165 cm, but still taller than her own 157 cm. He also had an intensity that belied his small stature. He had cultivated that domineering attitude for many years to help overcome his insecurities. The bushy beard added to the menacing appearance he wanted to project.

She began to protest. This was her ship now, she thought. She had created and executed the plan that had put them in charge of *Pathfinder*, a ship that would no doubt change the future of mankind. She had done the work. She had taken the risks. She was the one who had killed the ship's first captain and others to make this theft possible. Why should she turn it all over to Teach, just because he had outranked her in their previous employment? She had foreseen more of a joint, relaxed command structure and had failed to take into account Teach's need to dominate.

She studied the bridge as she struggled to control herself. It was odd to see the command deck bereft of people, of the sound of information being passed back and forth, of the hum of electronic systems. If only Teach hadn't come to interrupt her solitude.

She didn't want to act too quickly, however. She may still need the temperamental commander as a front for the rest of the crew. No one knew the extent of her complicity in the piracy. Well, no one who was still alive, she corrected herself absently. She had even manipulated Teach into believing that most of the plan was his own. She was an engineer by temperament as well as vocation so she always felt more comfortable when she was able to plan all of her actions ahead of time. Did she really need Teach around anymore? She'd have to think about that.

Where Brighton had been a capable and intelligent captain since taking over for the murdered Vanderjagt, Teach was an idiot. Now that she had control of the ship, there was very little need to keep him around. She ran through the ship's status rapidly in her head.

The four consoles in front of her were dead. They represented the communications, weapons, cartography and survey controls for the ship. All the other consoles around the bridge were equally inoperable; a casualty of Brighton's hastily improvised destruction. She wasn't sure how Brighton had figured out that the take-over was coming but somehow he had figured out enough to set up a lock-out on the computer which blocked all access. They would need bridge officer overrides to regain control. She, Teach and Lt. Lamont were the only officers left on the ship with those codes. If Brighton hadn't changed the parameters for a standard lockout, they would need all three in order to override it. She would need Teach for a while longer then, as well as Lamont. Finally, she stood and feigned contrition. *I'll let him have the headaches for a while longer,* she thought.

"Of course, you are right, sir. We must maintain the proper courtesies at all times," she said before her pause became noticeable. *As long as you are useful,* she added to herself. She composed her features and continued her report quietly, as if there had been no interruption. "I'm locked out of the computer up here as well as the one in Engineering," she said as she stood and moved over to the astrogation computer that sat behind and to the left of the command chair she had just abandoned. "If you wouldn't mind trying your codes, Captain," she added the title deliberately, "we might be able to restore power and control. As things stand, we are drifting at our previous speed, which I cannot determine, on an unknown course that will most likely take us beyond the Antoc system if we are unable to gain control quickly. In essence, we are a 'Flying Dutchman'."

Teach blithely pushed past her and took a seat in the captain's chair she had just vacated. Her jaw clenched as she was casually shouldered aside, but she said nothing. Teach began to input his codes and became more and more frustrated as his codes obviously did not work either.

"Blast him!" he yelled as he slammed his fists down on the arms of the chair, all semblance of calm evaporated in the furnace of his sudden rage. He shot up and flew to the astrogator's console, where Brighton had been seated less than two hours before. A quick series of keystrokes momentarily caused the screen to illuminate. His smile at this momentary success was immediately wiped away and he leapt backward as the console erupted in a shower of sparks. "What the--?" he spouted as he slammed the red emergency button on the top corner of the console to kill power to the circuits. The console continued to smoke, but no further eruptions were forthcoming. He turned back to Leung and the look on his face made her hand shift involuntarily to the pocket which held the gun she had taken from him earlier. He was clearly on the verge of losing control again. "Where is Lamont?" he bellowed in rage.

"I don't know," she said quietly, trying to calm him down by example. "I searched the ship for him during the takeover, but I couldn't find any trace of him. You know how he is; he's probably off sulking somewhere."

"Search the ship again. He might be injured or incapacitated somewhere. We will need all of the command officers' codes to override whatever Brighton did here." He waved his hand to indicate the smoking ruin next to him. "We'll lock the bridge and gather a search party. We're not doing any good here," he said with abrupt calm. He moved over to the communications console and tried to give the necessary orders. He found that console equally useless and stomped out the bridge hatch without another word.

Leung watched him with growing consideration. These sudden switches between rage and reason were unnerving and potentially dangerous. She knew he had a great deal of resentment about losing command to Brighton but she had never seen this level of wildness. If he couldn't be controlled, his usefulness was minimal. She shuddered involuntarily as she followed Teach off the bridge. She realized she was squeezing the gun in her pocket and made herself stop as they gathered the first six crewmen they encountered.

After collecting the light weapons they had removed from the arms locker before the takeover, they split into three groups. Teach took Danis and Bezates and followed the central corridor. Leung sent Martin Terry and Lenore Chandler down the port corridor with instructions to secure everything and do a thorough search for any injured or missing crewmen. She never mentioned Lamont by name, but Terry would understand. This was the same assignment she had given him immediately after everything hit the fan at the end of last shift. She then took the two remaining crewmen, Eric Goesch and Simon Chin, and followed the starboard corridor down the right side of the ship.

There were surprisingly few people out and about. From the state of her thoughts and emotions she had somehow expected chaos everywhere, but she found this was not the case.

Most crewmen seemed to be doing their jobs, taking refuge in the familiar routines of their normal duties, but there were still many worried, furtive glances at the armed group moving down the corridor. There were small items lying on the deck where people had evidently dropped them or let them slip from their grasp in their haste to exit the ship. They had few choices while being marched to the boatbay at gunpoint.

Most of the rooms off the starboard corridor were offices and storerooms and the group found nothing out of the ordinary in any of them until they reached the medbay, which was the last series of cubicles on the interior side of the corridor. As they entered, it was obvious that this was not a routine day here.

Meghan Johnson, the senior medical officer on *Pathfinder*, was just emerging from the operating room. Dr. Johnson was a tall, striking woman, despite the fact that she was nearing her seventieth year. Her hair was still dark brown and cut short. She was dressed in her surgical garb and her round, kind face was haggard and worn. She was clearly exhausted and struggling to function. Leung found this to be confusing. *How could she have gotten that tired in just a couple of hours?* As Leung looked past her into the operating room through the observation glass, the answer became obvious. Jill Burton, one of the Marines assigned to *Pathfinder* as security, lay unconscious or dead on the operating table. From the plethora of bandages on her right side, she guessed the former. Burton had been the only major casualty on the loyalist side during the takeover.

"How is your patient?" Leung asked quietly.

"She will live. She may retain the use of her arm. We'll have to wait and see on that." Johnson replied with an overtone of formality despite her obvious exhaustion as she began to remove the bloody apron she had been wearing over her working clothes. "Frankly, I'm surprised she made it through. She lost a lot of blood and will be weak for quite some time."

"It would serve her right if she died," Goesch said quietly from behind the engineer. "She and that witch, Chowdhury; they killed Morales and Brandon. If you ask me, we should put her out an airlock."

Johnson started to bristle at the tone and thought that had been expressed. It was a Doctor's instinctive reaction to protect her patient. Leung was quick to notice this and jumped in immediately.

"It's a good thing that no one asked you, then," Leung snapped. "We are neither murderers nor brigands. She defended herself and did her duty as she saw it. No one will ever be punished on this ship for doing their duty. AM I CLEAR?" she asked, disregarding the inner twinge at her hypocrisy.

"Yes, ma'am," Goesch said as both he and Chin unconsciously straightened to a posture of attention. "I'm sorry, ma'am, but Brandon was a good friend."

Leung watched the doctor out of the corner of her eye and tapped her finger on her lips as if weighing alternatives. The doctor had not been a part of their conspiracy but had apparently remained on the ship in order to tend those injured during the takeover. She would turn out to be useful if she could be convinced to refrain from actively fighting the takeover.

Turning back to Doctor Johnson she said, "That being said, Doctor, I cannot allow her to do her duty at our expense." She moved to the pile of discarded clothes on the floor near the operating room door and, rummaging through them, came up with a set of handcuffs and a key. "How long will she remain sedated?"

"She will probably be coming out of it in about six hours," the doctor replied.

"I want you to keep her sedated and unconscious unless there is a medical need for her to be awake. Any time that she is alert, she will be secured to her bed and only released under your direct supervision and only for medical necessities. Is that clear?"

"Yes, ma'am," the doctor replied with distaste. "I don't like it, though."

"Noted. Have you seen Lieutenant Lamont in the last two hours, by chance?"

"No, no one has been in since Dr. Ward left."

"Very well, we'll leave you to your work." Leung then moved into the operating room and snapped one ring of the handcuffs on Burton's left, undamaged, wrist and the other end of the handcuff onto the metal side rail of the moveable bed. Leung handed the key to the doctor and continued out the door.

After completing their search of the last storeroom in that corridor, they moved into the boatbay, which had access to most of the cargo holds. Staying along the starboard side of the cavernous bay, she entered the first hold. There she found a crate labeled "Computer Spares," so she ordered it moved to the doorway.

They had just finished their search of that hold when Teach, with his two cohorts and several others, entered the boatbay with the same goal of searching the holds. On seeing her and her group, he ordered her to take the computer parts and begin building a new astrocomp. She bristled at the condescending tone that he used and she jerked her hand out of her uniform pocket to keep from rubbing the gun she still carried there. She grabbed several of her engineering techs and began moving supplies to the bridge. Even if she was successful in rebuilding the computer, she knew, they were still missing vital data from the main astrogation data files. They would still need access to that data or the ship couldn't be successfully jumped out of the system to their planned rendezvous. Such forethought never seemed to occur to Teach. *What an idiot,* she thought.

Soon she would have no further need for the irritating little man and then … she grinned as she contemplated that future.

Teach took all the remaining crewmen and continued aft into Engineering in a vain search for the lost lieutenant as *Pathfinder* continued at 81,879,337 m/s past the orbit of the outermost planet in the Antoc system with no one at the controls, oblivious to his danger.

CHAPTER 3
28 June

There just aren't enough people to get everything done, Lieutenant Commander Leung thought to herself as she unsealed the hatch to Monica Samuels' berth. There was a faint sobbing coming from the berth just forward, which should have been empty. *Who was in there?* she wondered irritably. *I will have to check it out,* she thought. She added one more item to her mental list of things that needed to be taken care of immediately.

She brought her thoughts back to the task at hand.

Lamont was still missing and the chances that he was still on the ship were almost nonexistent. Two complete searches had been done and the entire interior of the ship had been scrutinized repeatedly. In his absence, or, more correctly, in the absence of his computer codes, command and control systems would have to be physically bypassed to get around the lockout that Brighton had managed to throw in their way.

In order to accomplish that, they needed help.

They needed bodies.

They needed to be able to assign tasks to crewmembers for computer repairs and expect that the jobs would be done. Unfortunately, that meant that they had to trust, to some extent, all of those who had stayed behind.

This is what brought Leung to Ensign Samuel's hatch. Leung had worked with Samuels on engineering projects for the last several months as they prepared for the test jump into the Antoc system.

While she was young and inexperienced, Samuels had shown an ability with computers.

Monica was lying on her bunk staring at the ceiling as the commander entered, but she jumped up quickly at the sound of the hatch sliding open.

Neither said a word for several seconds until Commander Leung said simply, "Follow me." The commander then turned on her heel and left the room, leaving the hatch open behind her.

Ensign Samuels was happy to do as she had been instructed. Finally, to be let out of her quarters was a gift she had just about given up on ever receiving. She had worked out a plan to delay the removal of *Pathfinder* from the Antoc system and had begun to implement it. There were several items that she could accomplish from her quarters, but they were a very small part of her list. She needed access to the rest of the ship, and she needed access to electronic components, so she followed the older officer willingly. Anything was better than being stuck in her room.

They stopped at other crew hatches and collected a small group of crewmen and then, Ensign Omundson.

Omundson was the only other officer in the group, with the exception of Commander Leung, who had retrieved them. Monica Samuels studied him carefully as they were herded aft toward the boatbay.

She knew him as well as any of her shipmates. They had completed the Academy together, as all of *Pathfinder*'s ensigns had. In fact, the five ensigns on *Pathfinder* represented the top five graduating cadets of her class. There were few similarities beyond the academic ones, however. Her thoughts brought a pang as she realized that she might never see the other three again.

Jherri Roberts had been her roommate and her closest friend on *Pathfinder*. Quiet and cheerful, she would struggle with the enforced hardships of an unimproved planet. As far as Monica knew, Roberts had never lived outside the Quito complex on Earth before attending the Academy on the Warner Headquarters Station. The other two Ensigns, who accompanied Captain Brighton, Jordan Hayes and Josiah Mitchell, were another proposition entirely; they would probably treat the wild planet as a great adventure and run off a cliff without noticing that it was there. The thought struck her with more weight than she had expected. They were her friends, and the thought of their hardships or possible deaths hit her especially hard. She struggled to bring her feelings back under control. She would need to be clear-headed to get through this.

She studied Omundson again. He was the only one of the ensigns who hadn't been part of her social group. He had always been apart from the rest, even at the academy. At 1.85 meters in height, he was not immediately noticeable in a crowd, but he had an attitude which colored all of his contacts with his fellows. As the nephew of Gerry Warner, the CEO of the Warner Family Board, he knew his place in the world. He was condescending and supercilious with all of those around him. His uniforms were impeccable, and each one would probably cover the cost of Monica's entire wardrobe. His sandy blond hair was styled and worn just slightly off the collar, longer than was strictly allowed under the regs unless it was queued into a ponytail. He had made no attempt to get to know any of his classmates and he often looked as though he were merely enduring the riffraff around him, but he certainly would never stoop to their level. It was no surprise that he had remained behind. He would never put himself at risk by leaving the ship or endanger the brilliant career that he expected would be his. Odd that he didn't think that joining thieves and pirates might be something of a blemish on his résumé.

His career could, quite possibly, survive even that taint. There seemed to be two navies within the WSN. There were those who moved ahead on merit alone, and those who had the right connections. Stuart Omundson was firmly in the second camp, despite the quality of his Academy scores. Or perhaps those scores were more evidence of the same problem. Who could say? As she watched, he had a posture that seemed to indicate that those around him were simply escorts.

In time, they came to the end of the central corridor and stepped through the main hatch into the boatbay.

This was where the nightmare had begun for her several hours earlier. As before, there were people standing there under guard.

Monica Samuels scanned the area and took note of those around her. There were now a total of ten in their group, guarded by five crewmen under the direction of Commander Leung.

Samuels recognized all the guards as members of the engineering crew. Samuels thought that made sense. If Commander Teach had brought Leung into the mutiny early enough, she would have had a chance to recruit her crewmen.

"We have repairs to make," Leung said when they had all collected in the aft section of the boatbay. "Computers are our first priority. I am going to divide you into three groups and we will search the port storage holds. Most of the parts that I need should be in these three holds. I want you to pull any electronics or computer spares out into the main bay to be sorted. Samuels, Goodwin, Semrad; you have hold nine. Samuels, I'm going to put you in nominal charge of your group. Terry, you watch them," she said, motioning to one of the armed men at the back of the group.

"Crowson, McGough, Calvi; hold seven. Crowson, you are nominally in charge. Chandler, you watch them," she continued. "Omundson, you take hold five with Fields and Jenkins. Goesch, you watch that group. I want everything usable out of the holds by 1500. If you can prove yourselves to be trustworthy, then maybe we can dispense with the guards."

Monica Samuels took control of her group and worked them hard. They were the first group to complete their task. Samuels immediately had her group begin to separate the components that were accumulating on the boatbay deck. She really wanted the mutineers to believe that she was trustworthy, but not for the reasons they were hoping for.

She couldn't believe her luck. She needed access to the electronics components to move forward with her plan and her enemies handed her the opportunity on a platter. She was very careful to avoid notice as she created a third pile of components that she surreptitiously slid into an empty container. As soon as she could get back here without a watchdog, her plans would begin in earnest.

* * * * *

At precisely 1700, Ensign Samuels strode through the hatch into the galley. The officers' and junior officers' wardrooms had been shut down since the majority of the cooks had chosen to accompany Captain Brighton. These closures necessitated an exacting schedule in the galley to be able to accommodate those who had remained behind. Her time had been written on a slip of paper stuck to her door when she had returned from her work shift. She had been surprised to be allowed to wander free, without a guard, so quickly.

It was an unusual assortment of officers and enlisted personnel that crowded the space. Ensign Samuels moved to the food line at the forward end of the room and grabbed a tray from the rack. She wiped her hands surreptitiously on her pant leg as she realized the tray was still wet from the cleaner. She regretted the action immediately as she noticed Commander Teach and Lt. Commander Leung in the queue in front of her. She didn't want to draw any attention to herself. She needn't have worried, they were completely absorbed in their conversation and they acted as if they weren't aware of anyone else around them.

"I tell you, sir, there is no sign of him anywhere. He must have left with Brighton," Leung said in a tone that indicated this was not the first time she had made this observation.

"Lamont hated Brighton, the only reason he would consent to be with Brighton is if he thought he would have a chance to kill him," Teach replied. "Besides, I checked who was aboard *Vanguard* myself before she launched. No, he's here somewhere."

Samuels focused her attention on the conversation while acting exhausted and distracted.

"Sir, we have been through every meter of this ship. If he's here, there is no evidence of that fact."

Samuels slid her tray onto the counter as the two officers moved off to a table to continue their discussion. She looked up and for the first time noticed what was available. The unappetizing selections looked haphazard, as if the galley techs had just grabbed whatever was most convenient. She took a plate of some kind of potato hash and a slice of cream pie and headed to a table.

She saw Amber Sullivan sitting alone on the far side of the room. She was staring down at her plate and sobbing quietly. The others at surrounding tables were talking quietly and leaning unobtrusively away from her, creating an island of isolation in the middle of a crowded room. She reluctantly headed that way.

Monica had met Amber during the transit from Earth to *Pathfinder* when they both had first been assigned. *Pathfinder* had been undergoing an increase in personnel as it shifted into its final phase of trials. Amber had just been assigned from one of the deep space patrol ships in the Idyll system and didn't know anyone on *Pathfinder*. Despite the fact that she was only a specialist/technician and Samuels was an officer, they had developed a friendship during the trip out from Earth.

Monica had liked the calm self-assurance that Sullivan had shown and the warm welcoming manner she displayed. Neither of those qualities was in evidence now. Sullivan sat at her table with a fork in her hand staring at her still full tray. A glance at Amber's tray showed the same hodge-podge of food as her own. Although, the aroma of her baked beans made Monica wish there had been some of that left when she went through the line. Sullivan didn't move or look up as Samuels set her tray down in front of her.

"How did today go for you, Amber?" she asked quietly.

Sullivan jerked her eyes up to look Samuels in the face. "Terrible. I was locked into a room that belonged to someone else and left there until someone remembered to let me out for dinner," she said between sobs.

They probably just decided you weren't much of a threat and unlocked your room, she thought. "I'm sorry, Amber, you weren't acting like yourself and I thought that if I brought you back on board I would be better able to protect you, but now I realize I have very little ability to do so. I'm sorry for dragging you into the middle of this."

"I didn't even get lunch," Sullivan complained as if she had not heard a word of Samuel's explanation and apology.

"Well, eat now," Samuels said motioning with her fork to the pile of scalloped potatoes on Amber's plate. "We don't know how often we'll get the chance."

Samuels watched Amber start mechanically eating her dinner when her features glazed over once again. *I guess I won't be tempted to share my secrets with her after all*, she thought.

When both of them had finished, Samuels made sure that Sullivan got back to her proper quarters and then hurried to her own. She barely had time to shower and make it to the bridge for her watch. Leung had been explicit in explaining that she needed to be perfect in her duties if she wanted to be trusted.

As she left her quarters on the way to the bridge, she slipped a chip that contained her morning's work into her tunic pocket. It was a risk. If she were searched, it could mean her continued imprisonment and possibly even her death. For an instant she stood frozen as solid as she had been when the mutineers broke onto the bridge. It was one thing to intellectually decide on the proper course, and quite another to picture the faces of your family as they received notification of your death. She shook herself and continued to the bridge. She had made her decision this morning. It was still the right one for many reasons. And besides, the snippet of conversation she had just overheard gave her a great idea that she could only execute from the bridge. If only she could make her hands stop shaking.

CHAPTER 4
30 June

Gunnery Sergeant (Warner Space Marine Corps) Eric Aichele stood ramrod straight and looked down at the inert form of his fallen comrade. Rage filled him at what he saw, but there was no trace of it on his silent features. His eyes appeared calm, his well-muscled body relaxed. Perhaps his jaw was held closed a bit more tightly than was normal, but not so much that a casual observer would note it. If anything unusual could be said of the way he looked, it would be that his very lack of expression carried the impression that he had been sterilized of all emotion.

He fit in quite well with his surroundings. The recovery room of the medbay practically screamed sterility; stainless steel counters, cabinets, and beds, pristine white bedding, everything. There was also the distinct smell of bleach in the air, which added to the impression of cleanliness. The lone break in the dead white and metal landscape was Marine Staff Sergeant Jill Burton lying before him. His friend.

Even there, however, the pervasive color scheme had invaded. The white sheet and blanket had been pulled up above her shoulders, but it could not hide the white bandages on the right side of her neck, face, and head. Her dirty blonde hair could only be seen on the left side. The rest was shaved clean.

Earlier that day, Sgt. Burton and Major Chowdhury had been ambushed just outside the security office. Neither of them had any reason to suspect anything was amiss, but they had still reacted to the threat with the speed drilled into them over the course of many years of service. Aichele had been off duty at the time, unconscious to the events elsewhere in the ship. He didn't know any of the details of what had happened, but some facts he had been able to deduce by simple observation. Glenn Morales and Carl Brandon were laid out next door, in the morgue. He recognized Sheli Chowdhury's oak-handled knife as the means of his demise. Nothing was immediately obvious as the cause of death for Carl Brandon, on the adjoining table. McIntire had recently developed a limp, and Green was not currently able to use his right arm. Eric had waited for those last two to leave the medical area before he came in.

He didn't trust himself around them yet.

During the fight, Burton had taken a blast from an energy pistol at close range. He didn't know which one of his crewmates had fired that shot, but it was a good thing for Burton that he or she was not a marksman. Most likely, it had been Morales. Whoever was best armed would have been Chowdhury's primary target. To Major Chowdhury, "target" and "deceased" were all but synonymous.

Now, Jill Burton was unconscious after six hours of surgery. She might never wake up. Even if she did, she might never use her right arm again. Maimed and in critical condition, at least she had survived and continued to do so.

The fury he had been containing struggled to free itself. Muscles tightened under his graying temples, but a deep breath was enough for him to reassert control, and his handsome features resumed their placid inscrutability.

Unlike Samuels, Sergeant Aichele had received specific instructions from his superior. His primary assignment from Major Chowdhury had been to protect Burton. It was such an ingrained part of any Marine not to leave a comrade behind that, once the offer was made by Teach, the only question had been who would go back and which would provide security for those leaving the ship. Chowdhury had reasoned, and almost certainly correctly, that she would never have been believed as a turncoat. And so, Eric had undertaken this part of their joint duty.

But like Samuels, he could not discharge his orders if those in control of the ship suspected where his true sympathies resided. Trust would have to be earned from them, and that meant that he could not do anything to arouse their suspicion. He must appear natural and at ease around them, and avoid saying anything that would not fit with the new image of himself as a trustworthy compatriot.

This new image of himself would not include visiting a recuperating friend, who was definitely on their "not to be trusted" list. This would have to be his one and only trip to see her, for both their sakes. He would need some way to inform her of his status if, no, *when*, he corrected himself firmly, she recovered. Most likely she would be able to understand what he had done and why, but perhaps his behavior would still cause her to have her doubts. He needed some way to make his position clear to her, without risking further contact.

He could wait, he decided, for an idea to come to him or an opportunity to present itself. She would be a long time mending. He would have to protect her from afar to avoid bringing her the very trouble he was trying to protect her from.

Dr. Johnson approached the bed and excused herself to cut in front of him. She quickly took several readings and marked them in a log. Eric waited patiently until he could see that she had completed her task.

"What is the prognosis, Doctor?"

She studied him intently, as if deciding how to answer. She wasn't sure which side of this conflict he was on, so she hesitated lest she cause trouble for herself or her patient. There was no clue in his expression one way or the other. Finally, she decided that she would answer truthfully, but offer nothing more than clinical details. It was unlikely that would provoke either side of the issue, and it would allow her to maintain her neutrality.

"She will live, almost certainly. A 90% chance that she will regain at least basic use of her right arm, 30% that full use will be restored."

"I'm glad to hear that," he said. "Jill is my friend."

Dr. Johnson relaxed the muscles she hadn't realized she had tensed. Aichele's keen hazel eyes noted it, however.

"If you had not been in surgery, would you have left with the captain?" the Marine asked, seeing an opportunity, deciding that he couldn't waste time beating around the bush. The doctor was not so quick to respond, taking several long moments before giving a reply.

"Yes, I would have," she said quietly but firmly.

"Would you give her a message for me, when she wakes?"

"You could give it to her yourself. She's not going anywhere, after all. Leung has seen to that." She rattled the chain of the handcuffs, pointing out what the sergeant had already seen. "Leung has also seen to it that she won't be allowed to wake up until I receive new orders, either." This part he hadn't known, but it didn't change what he was thinking.

"No, I won't be back. It is too much of a risk, for both of us. If you could give her a message, though, it would be appreciated."

"Certainly, then. What is it?"

"Tell her, 'Rio Bravo'."

"That's it?"

"Yes."

"I don't understand."

He grinned then, the first expression she'd seen. "That's because the message isn't meant for you."

She didn't argue or complain. She simply nodded and went back to her office.

Jill would understand. The code word 'Rio' would indicate that she was released for independent operations. 'Bravo' would tell her the orders came from the second in command, and not from Chowdhury. When she could, she would do whatever she was able to do, without waiting to hear from her superior first.

That accomplished, he turned sharply and stepped to the hatchway. He glanced both ways and, seeing no one in the corridor, strode purposefully back to his own newly assigned quarters. He would miss his old quarters in the security suite with the access to all of his gear but Teach had been adamant about not letting him back into that area.

When he had gone, Dr. Johnson replayed the strange conversation in her mind, attempting to find hidden meaning. Eventually, she gave the task up and returned to her medical logs. She could see that *Pathfinder* was still not a united ship, and that conflict between the two opposed groups must inescapably come. It would be a challenge to remain neutral but it was necessary. She had taken an oath as a doctor before taking an oath as a military officer. In order to be able to help people she needed the freedom to act, and she could not maintain that freedom if she participated in the coming quarrel.

She would deliver Sergeant Aichele's message, and keep his trust, but that was as far as she would allow herself to become involved.

CHAPTER 5
1 July

Exhausted and sweaty, Lt. Commander Katherine Leung climbed up the portside rear stairs from deck one to main deck to find Captain Teach waiting for her. Equally exhausted was any possibility that Lt. Neil Lamont remained on the ship. The fourth complete search of *Pathfinder* was finished, and there was no longer any room for doubt. Lamont was gone.

"Well, did you find anything?" Teach wanted to know.

"No, Captain," Leung responded, amazed at her own ability to find patience enough for courtesy at this early hour of her morning. With only two available rated command officers, she and Teach had been standing watch and watch on the bridge for the last three days. Of course, that did not excuse her from maintaining command of the engineering section, a full-time responsibility by itself, with the damaged and locked systems of the ship that still needed rebuilding.

Leung's hair, normally worn clipped up out of the way, had come loose and tickled her neck annoyingly. Her round face was pale from lack of sleep. The ageless look that was her Asian heritage seemed to have lost its hold on her features, and she looked every one of her 74 years.

"I think we are going to have to face the reality that he is no longer among us, sir," she told him. She fervently hoped that he would indeed accept that and allow her to get some sleep before she was due on the bridge in three hours.

That thought gave her pause. *Why is he so insistent that I remain on the bridge during my watch when he is down here in the engineering section looking for a report during his?* She knew better than to question him on it, though. He seldom had rational or consistent explanations for his actions when she did. "Command Prerogative" was his favorite justification of late.

Not that it truly made any difference whether there was a bridge watch or not. If there were a planetoid directly in their path, they were powerless to move the ship to avoid it. And equally powerless to detect its existence to know they needed to move. *What a filthy mess*, she thought.

A grim frown appeared on Teach's face, partially obscured by his bushy beard.

"He must be dead," Leung said. "He is not on the ship anywhere, and we never saw him enter *Vanguard*, either. If he were alive, we'd know where he is." She stood waiting for some response from Teach; hopefully a dismissal so she could collapse into bed.

None seemed forthcoming. Teach continued to frown, his eyes unfocussed while he gnawed on the enigma in his mind. Distracted as he was, he took no notice of Leung's impatience to depart. For her part, she was practically dead on her feet already. Her desire to maintain an amicable relationship with the prickly commanding officer was the only thing keeping her from simply walking directly back to her quarters. Lamont's fate was already decided, and in the larger scheme, there were too many things that needed to be done to fix the ship for her to spend much effort trying to figure out what had happened. While his disappearance would eliminate the possibility of overriding Brighton's lockout, she would be happy to deal with only one irritating officer instead of two.

When she caught her eyes beginning to droop, she started a bit, but Teach was still looking away and didn't notice. She tried to bring him back to the here and now, hoping to end this as quickly as possible.

"Orders, sir?" she prompted.

"Huh?"

"Do you have any orders for me, sir, or may I be dismissed?"

"I was just thinking about what must have happened to Lamont," Teach responded distractedly. "If Brighton was on to us, just before the liberation of *Pathfinder*, he must have sent someone else to get Lamont for him. He never left the bridge during that time. I'll bet it was Chowdhury," he finished with an involuntary shiver.

"Likely true, sir," she responded, though in truth, she didn't care in the slightest to know how the arrogant twip had met his end. All she cared about now was finding the most efficient means of dealing with the mess his disappearance had left them.

"Repairs should be our first priority, Captain," she continued, moving back to a productive topic. "Without override access to the locked down systems, we're facing a major delay to our plans. The sooner we can establish an independent control system, the sooner we can get things back on track. I have submitted a written summary to you, but I haven't seen it since. Have you had a chance to review and approve my schedule?"

The very fact that she had submitted her proposal in writing, on actual paper, was testament to how fouled up the ship was. She'd only found paper and pencils by accident while going through the inventory case by case. Without any sort of computer access, there was no inventory listing, no way to submit an electronic proposal to the commanding officer, and especially no ship's controls.

That had to change. It was time to drop the Lamont issue and move on to the next step. Teach seemed to be having difficulty with that concept.

"Maybe someone else did him in, and there is still a murderer at large on the ship," he said now. "The rest of the crew could still be in danger. I'm going to begin a full-scale investigation tonight!" He stroked the black bristles on his chin; she presumed he was thinking about how this investigation should be organized.

"If you say so, but it would seem certain that the person or persons responsible are no longer on the ship. You may use up a lot of man-hours looking for information that can't be found anymore."

That topic closed for now, she tried to bring Teach back to more important subjects. "Now, in the matter of replacing our command computer, I'd like your permission to take the medical database system and use it. Since it is not connected to any other system, it was unaffected by the lockout. We do have a replacement command system in stores, but it is completely disassembled and I would need two weeks just to put all the pieces together and test it. Normally, it makes sense to keep replacement parts on hand, since it's rare to need a whole command and control system replaced. In our case, though, assembly of the replacement unit will be slower than converting the already working system to handle new functions. Would that be all right with you, Captain?" she finished, again amazed at her own display of patience.

Teach watched her intently as she made her request. His features got more focused as she spoke, but his eyes suddenly drifted away and he seemed lost in a world of his own. He paused a few moments, then nodded as if making a decision and asked, "Did Lamont seem overly upset the last time you saw him? I mean, more than normal? He was agitated, sure, but that was hardly an uncommon state for him. I was just wondering if possibly he took his own life. Do you think that likely?"

Leung stood in front of her commanding officer as if she had been hit with a length of pipe. Before she could recover her senses, she gave in to her frustration and released the thoughts that she had not even allowed herself to think.

"Will you shut up about that conceited snot? We'd be better off without him if we had his codes!" Her voice reverberated off the unadorned metal walls of the stairwell. All restraint was gone now, her nerves frayed past the breaking point. She let her frustration and exhaustion have free rein. A small part of her recognized that there would be a price to pay for her outburst, but that part was just as tired as the rest of her and went unheeded.

"Can't you get it through your thick skull that Lamont is gone and we have other priorities to deal with? We can't even maneuver the ship! If you can't give me a simple yes or no when I make proposals for getting us out of this mess, then just stay out of my way and let me do my job!"

Once the incriminating words were out of her mouth, Leung's rational mind asserted itself again, and she knew she had put her foot in it. The enormity of her misstep turned her red-hot rage into an icy chill at once. The one thing that you were never allowed to criticize about Teach was his ability to lead. The captain's eyes narrowed and she abandoned the idea of sleep.

"I know I have been pushing you hard these last few days, Kate, so I'll let that pass tonight," Teach said in a mild tone. Leung, tensed and expecting the worst, slowly allowed her shoulders to relax.

"Thank you, sir, I apologize. I won't let it happen again."

"I understand, Kate. We'll speak no more of it." He smiled. "As for orders, I'd like you to focus on replacing the command computer, by rebuild or replacement, whatever you think is best. I'll see what I can do about replacing the astrogation data that we're going to need."

The engineer was completely caught off guard, but she kept her face neutral so as not to give further offense. *Finally some useful directions out of him,* she thought. *Maybe I should yell at him more often. No,* she concluded, *that innocent smile is harder to take than his one-track mind.*

"Time enough for that tomorrow, though. You should turn in," he finished.

"Thank you, sir, I believe I will."

He motioned for her to precede him into the main engineering section, but before she could move, Samuels entered the space and interrupted.

"Sir, ma'am, you should come with me. There's trouble in Engineering," the ensign reported gravely. Leung searched for signs that Samuels had heard too much, but there were none that she could spot. That was one problem she wouldn't have to deal with, Leung was thinking, but it still left another before she could turn in.

When they arrived, there was indeed a commotion in Engineering. Not a large one, in Leung's estimation. *Can't this girl handle anything on her own?* she wondered. It wasn't fair, she knew, to expect such a young officer to be able to deal with every situation, but her fatigue interfered with her compassion, what little there was to begin with, at the moment.

"McGough, I'm telling you, it had to have been you," Young, the engineering lead on this shift, loudly proclaimed. Leung turned in time to see McGough's curly-haired and grease-stained head emerging from under the power converter console.

"And I'm telling you again, with all due respect to your extra stripes, that I don't know what you're talking about." Nick McGough sounded as tired and frustrated as Leung felt, but his shouted reply was the equal in volume to Young's, and seemed completely lacking in all due respect.

"The cooling monitor station is dead. You were the last one working here, so what did you do?"

McGough pulled himself up off the floor and took the several steps he needed to cross from one work area to the other. "I haven't been over there for an hour, at least. Don't look at me." Upon arriving at the station, he pressed a few keys experimentally to try to wake the system. His actions elicited no response. There was no on/off switch for the monitor, since it was designed to function constantly, so he resumed his now accustomed position on the floor to check the wire traces for a loose power connection. As soon as he was horizontal, he let out a startled shout. "What the blazes...?"

35

Teach and Leung, led by Samuels, had approached undetected, and they were right next to McGough when his disbelieving outburst escaped him. "What is it, Crewman?" Leung asked, in a voice that said she didn't care.

McGough peeked out to see his department commander awaiting the bad news, and he would have sighed in dismay if the shock of seeing the captain there as well had not brought him instantly to his feet saluting. He wondered idly why no one had called out the 'Captain on deck' warning when he had entered.

Teach returned the salute brusquely and demanded, "Well, we're waiting for your report, Crewman."

The hapless man gulped, wishing abstractly that the money Leung had offered him to help with the takeover had been just a little less enticing. He knew exactly what was going to happen when he answered the question the captain had posed, yet he had no alternatives to answering. Nothing for it but to do so as quickly as possible. Delaying the bad news would only make it worse.

"Captain, Commander, this station has been intentionally disabled by person or persons unknown at some time in the last hour." There. He had said it, and hopefully in such a way that none of the blame would fall on him. Young had already singled him out as the last one working there. He just hoped that either the captain would not remember, or else that he was able to see his surprise was genuine. He remained stiffly at attention, and took advantage of the silver lining that with both commanding officers in front of him, he could direct his gaze at the wall in the distance between them, and didn't have to look at either of them directly.

His line of sight was not far enough from Teach, though, that he didn't see the explosion coming. The commanding officer's face flushed, making his black beard more pronounced, and his eyes narrowed with menace. "What do you mean, McGough?" His voice was not the raging sandblaster Nick was prepared to face, and the unexpectedly soft words caught him off guard. He was a few moments responding, and realized immediately that this, too, did not put him in a favorable light just then.

"See for yourself, sir. Someone has literally ripped out half of the power and data feeds," McGough said while stepping out of the way so the two could take him up on the offer.

Nick hadn't expected that they really would, but Leung lay down and rolled onto her back, looking upward at the mangled ruin that wasn't visible from eye level. She found everything as McGough had described it. Someone had torn out a good portion of the wires and data leads of the system, including the main power input. Someone strong might have done quickly by yanking out two handfuls. Then again, any person could have done it by pulling a little at a time. Not a smart idea though. Pulling the power line would have been enough to disable the monitor. The more that was done after that would have increased the chance of discovery without much further gain. Probably, they were looking for someone strong enough to have done it all at once, she decided.

She pulled herself out from under the machine and stood. "The damage is definitely deliberate," she reported. "It could have been anyone on duty here, though I may be able to rule out quite a few with a little more investigation."

"There are also the work crews that have been in and out all shift," McGough added helpfully.

"I want to know who did this!" Teach yelled. He turned to face the entire engineering compartment. Everyone on duty had gathered around to see what was going on, and all eyes were on the raging captain.

"Who did this? Tell me now!"

Nervous glances were fired back and forth among the group, but no one spoke. The lack of results infuriated Teach even further. "I gave an *order*, and I expect it to be obeyed! Tell me who damaged this system, or there will be unpleasant consequences for all of you!"

Leung moved closer to avoid anyone overhearing her and tried to calm the man down. "Captain, if you'd allow me to do my own checking, I might--"

"Belay that!" he bellowed. "I will teach these miscreants the consequences of disobedience!"

Everyone in the area had gathered by then, and the glances had changed from nervous to suspicious, and in some cases accusatory. Still, no one uttered a word. Teach grew visibly more angry with each passing moment of silence; his jaw muscles clenched beneath his ebony whiskers. The steely gaze he leveled at each person grew more and more heated.

"Very well," he finally announced. His voice was not loud, but still held unmistakable scorn. "You are all assigned double shifts for ten days. Also, half rations for the same period. If, at the end of that time, I have not learned the name of the responsible party, further punishment may be warranted."

Amber Sullivan's eyes had gotten bigger with each sentence and she looked around wildly. When the captain announced that perhaps more would be added later, she began crying.

"That is enough of that!" Teach declared. "Back to work now, all of you."

Sullivan shuffled off with the others, but her shoulders were shaking and audible sobs continued to escape her. Teach was disgusted at the display and moved off hurriedly toward the exit into the boatbay. Leung did not catch up with him until he was halfway across the expansive bay. She wanted to try to mitigate the severity of the assigned discipline by pointing out the disastrous effect it would have on morale. If she could only get him to see reason, she was thinking.

Teach spoke first when she approached.

"We need to do something about Aichele," he stated.

The statement was so far from where her thoughts were that she couldn't think of any response to it immediately. After a moment she asked, "What did you have in mind?" She thought this was sufficiently bland that it might give her some clues as to what the topic of conversation was without letting on that she was lost. Hopefully, she could quickly deal with whatever this problem was and move the conversation back to the crew's punishment.

"That Marine uniform he always has on, it's… disconcerting. I want him in Navy undress the next time I see him." Aichele had been given assignments to work parties, but Leung had not seen him among the crowd a moment ago. What had prompted this subject in Teach's mind? Who could tell what the man was thinking most of the time?

"I see," Leung replied. It seemed a frivolous item to be worried about just then, but one that was easily accomplished. Still, there was one detail about it that she should clear up before moving back to the punishment issue. "And at what rank should we transfer him from one service to the other, sir?"

"Just transfer him at his current grade," he directed absently.

By this time, they had reached the hatch to Leung's quarters. Both stopped, expecting the remainder of the conversation to be brief.

"Yes, sir. But, if I might point out, Gunnery Sergeant Aichele is grade eight, enlisted, which would correspond to the naval rank of chief petty officer."

"Yes. So?"

"That's the same rank held by CPO Young," she hinted.

"And?"

Leung was perplexed that she should have to spell this out for him. The man had been the executive officer, responsible for everything to do with personnel, for most of the last two years. Maybe he was just tired, as she was.

"Aichele has more time in grade than Young, which would mean that if we take him out of the Marines, where he is not in the chain of command, and place him in the Navy, he would be taking on the position of Bosun of the Ship. If that's what you had in mind, sir, that's fine with me," she lied smoothly, "but I'm not so certain about where his loyalties truly lie. He may just have wanted to take the easy way out."

"Hmm," Teach commented, "I hadn't considered that. I think he did opt for the easy way out, but that doesn't make him disloyal. Besides, now that he's made his choice, it's in his own best interest to work with us. He's old enough that he was probably having the same thoughts about a meager retirement that you'd had. Still… giving him a position of authority may be a bit premature. Just make him a crewman instead, until he proves himself."

"Very well, sir. So you want me to name Young as the Bosun?"

"No, we don't need a Bosun. We'll all be turning this ship over for a profit in a couple of weeks. No need to bother about that."

Leung's anger started to rise, though she was trying hard to remain patient. "Then why does it matter what—"

"Are you questioning my orders?"

She straightened erect without thinking. "No, sir."

"Good. Oh, I did have one other item I'd like you to handle for me," Teach said in an abruptly genial tone.

"Sir?"

"I want you to reprogram *Pathfinder*'s ZFlash beacon with dummy information to report our destruction and launch it, if you would. Also, change the guidance system so that it passes A3 before it looks to orbit a planet, so that when it is found, Warner will start looking in the wrong place."

Leung couldn't help but grin as she thought of it. "Yes, sir," she said with some enthusiasm. "Smart thinking, Captain."

Her exhaustion suddenly reasserted itself with a vengeance, and she couldn't keep herself from yawning. Gone from her memory, at least for the moment, was her desire to broach the subject of crew discipline. Teach left her there before taking the few additional steps needed to bring him to the bridge hatch. He raised his hand to enter the unlock sequence but froze before beginning. He could feel himself being watched from somewhere. His neck hairs tried to push his tunic collar away.

He spun to face his attacker, but empty corridors in three directions were all that met his fevered eyes.

* * * * *

Leung's automatically closing door cut off the last second of the odd scene, but she saw enough to get her mind churning anew.

Teach's behavior the last few days, perhaps even going back before the takeover, had been more than a little odd. Revisiting just the last hour showed numerous examples of the inexplicable.

What a mess, she thought. *I wish I didn't need him around. It would be so much simpler not to have to ask permission for the most basic things.*

Abruptly, she realized what she was thinking. She *didn't* need him anymore. When there was still a chance of finding Lamont alive, she needed Teach for his bridge officer's codes. With three valid codes, she could unlock the command and control systems of *Pathfinder* and jump directly to where they were set to turn over the ship to the Forrest Family and complete the deal that would make her a rich woman. But without Lamont's access, Teach's did her no good at all. *Maybe I can use his erratic behavior to my benefit,* she thought.

Leung poked her head out of her hatch to scan the area before leaving her room. Teach was not in sight; hopefully he had returned to his duty station on the bridge. She walked past the heavy blast-proof hatch at which Teach had paused a minute before and then aft down the portside passage to the galley.

The large display opposite the entrance said 05:20 when she entered, and the dining area was understandably deserted. Almost deserted; Crewman Green was sleeping on a bench against the forward wall. She almost went and woke him on general principle, but decided against it before the impulse was fully realized. With only two cooks left on the ship, Green and Trendle were facing the same on and off rotation that Leung and Teach were dealing with.

She wouldn't know what to complain about, either. The space was perfectly clean, there were pre-made sandwiches available for anyone who came in, and coffee and tea were accessible from piping hot cisterns.

She decided waking him would not serve any purpose. The only result would be a tired cook who was angry with the new XO. Decades in the navy had proven the old axiom that the only enemy worse than the captain on a long deployment was the cook. They had so many ways to make your life miserable that you didn't want to mess with them. Besides, good food was good for morale.

That wouldn't have stopped Teach from punishing Green, had he been the one to walk in. That brought her back to the reason she was still up instead of catching some rack time herself.

Leung crossed to the metal containers and filled a cup with tea. She added two sugars and stirred them in as she sat at the nearest table. The scalding liquid did wonders to burn away the drowsy fog in her mind and clear the way for some deep thought.

Leung always thought deeply before acting, especially for serious matters, and this was definitely a serious matter. She was not convinced that leaving Teach in command was, of itself, a bad thing. But she was certain that Lamont was gone; alive or dead, he was no longer on *Pathfinder*. That fact removed the primary reason to keep Teach around, and she needed time to map out the new state of affairs to determine what would be the most beneficial course of action at this point.

Mentally, she started two lists and labeled them positive and negative. Under positive, she considered her other reason for leaving Teach as captain. She had liked being number two on the totem pole during the planning stages of the takeover. Had things fallen apart, she could always sue for leniency by claiming that it had all been Teach's idea, and that he had coerced her into going along. The need for such a contingency plan was very real, especially after Major Chowdhury joined the crew. Leung shivered at the thought of what would have happened if the Marine had gotten any clue as to what had been going on.

Still, that need didn't exist anymore. There was no chance that anyone from Warner could catch them now. So what did that leave on the positives side?

Nothing else came immediately to mind.

She shifted over to the negatives side and several problems jumped out at her. Apart from the fact that she personally loathed his pomposity and condescension, his arrogance and the need to intrude in her areas of responsibility were hampering her efforts to get the ship running again. He was dragging morale down, which slowed the work even more. He insisted on manning a needless bridge watch that sucked up precious man-hours.

And, of course, there was the money. Without Teach, she wouldn't have to split the officer's share with anyone. Her original cut was enough to disappear to a quiet retirement. With Lamont and Teach gone she would get three times that share. Three shares was enough to do anything she could imagine.

She supposed that having him in charge freed her up to focus on Engineering. That was one for the positive side.

She added a few more items to her mental balance sheet, but when she was done, the outcome remained the same; her life would improve without Captain Teach in it.

The next portion of her analysis was to sort out what problems might arise as a result of moving forward and removing Teach from command. She saw many problems here, too.

First, since she had wanted Teach to be a potential fall guy, all the crewmen that were in on the takeover before the fact looked to him as the leader. If she were to remove him by force, would she have the support of the rest? Most of Engineering would back her, she believed, but that wasn't quite a majority, and a move that dangerous wasn't something to leave to chance. It would be better to be sure of the crew's backing before she took any further steps.

Second, plotting *another* takeover would draw her focus away from fixing the ship, which was the whole problem she wanted to avoid.

Third… she knew there had been a third but she was having a hard time recalling it. Her empty teacup prompted her to refill it and get another mental jolt. She resisted the desire. She needed sleep more than anything, and she had come to a conclusion of sorts. Teach ought to be removed, but only when she was sure she could do it without adverse consequences. She needed support from the rank and file before she could safely act.

And there was no time like the present to start working on that.

She put her cup in the used dishes bin and walked over to where Green lay motionless and gently nudged him. "Alex, wake up," she said, just above a whisper.

Green started, looked up, and then had to try keeping from falling over and getting to his feet at the same time. "Ma'am, I—"

"Easy, Crewman. You're not in trouble. There clearly isn't anything pressing for you to do right now. I just wanted to warn you on my way out not to let *Teach* catch you napping on duty. Maybe from now on you should nap in the back room, where you're not so obvious."

"Uh, thank you, ma'am," Green stumbled, more than a little surprised that she didn't seem upset.

"As you were, Alex," Leung said cheerfully on her way out the door.

A small seed, Leung thought, but who knew how much it might affect things later on? She had a few other ideas along similar lines; ways to make Teach look like more of an enemy than a friend.

The engineer was all the way back to her quarters and disrobing for bed when she remembered what the third thing was.

In order to remove Teach from power, she was going to have to kill him. She yawned and climbed into her bunk.

Her last conscious thoughts were that she'd rather not have to do so, but if that was what it took…

CHAPTER 6
4 July

Eric Aichele yawned expansively. He hadn't meant for it to expand quite so much. Just a little yawn to make Sullivan and Giannini believe him when he said he was going straight to bed. The first rule of misleading others is not to oversell. Stick to subtle clues rather than grand expressions. The problem was that he really was as tired as he could remember being since boot camp, and once he started his little fake yawn, it grew on its own, increasing in size and volume as it went.

"Pardon me, ladies. It's not the company, I assure you," he excused himself with a grin.

"Didn't think it for a min--," Crystal Giannini almost managed to finish before Aichele's contagious yawn spread and claimed her. Amber Sullivan said nothing, but offered a hesitant smile to acknowledge the apology.

When her jaw muscles were once again her own to command, Giannini said, "Well, I think that should do it for today. There's not enough left of this watch to start somewhere else. Why don't you two turn in a little early, and I'll go report to Commander Leung."

"Thank you, ma'am, I will do just that. I'm getting too old for these double shifts," he said.

"You're not old, Gunny," she disagreed.

"Wrong on both counts."

"Huh?" Sullivan asked. It was the first word she'd uttered in hours, if it even qualified as a word.

"I mean, yes, I am old, and no, I am not 'Gunny' anymore. Crewman Third Class Aichele, at your service," he finished with a smiling half-bow.

"Oh," Amber said. That would definitely qualify as a word, even if the other didn't.

"Sorry, I hadn't thought about you losing your rank, Gu-, uh, Crewman," Giannini finished lamely.

"Oh, for heaven's sake, call me Eric, even if I am old enough to be your grandfather."

"Fine. I'll call you Eric if you'll stop exaggerating. You can't be more than, what, fifty, maybe fifty-two."

Aichele laughed. It wasn't a chuckle, but a full-throated belly laugh. Crystal and Amber got puzzled looks on their faces and when Eric saw them, it set him off again. When his laughter subsided, he finally said, "Bless you, child. That was quite a compliment. I haven't seen my fifties for a long time now. I turned eighty-two four months ago."

"Nuh-uh," Amber disbelieved.

"Marine's honor," Eric said, placing his hand over his heart, then letting it drop to his side. "I guess I am going to have to find a new phrase. But it really is true. Eight more years and I would have retired, anyway. With a lot less money, of course."

"But you don't even have a gray hair!" Crystal said.

"What do you call this?" Eric asked, gesturing to his temple.

Giannini looked closely at the side of his head. "Huh. Your hair has always been shaved so close on the sides, I hadn't noticed. But your face certainly doesn't look old."

"I grew up on Fairfield in the Centauri system, so I had access to the latest antiagathics as soon as they came out. Plus my family has a history of long life. My great-granddad always tells me so, anyway."

Crystal looked dubious. "Now you're pulling my leg."

"Nope. I went to his 160th birthday party the day before I shipped out to *Pathfinder*." His right hand rose for an instant, but then returned to his side. "Honest," he concluded.

"Anyway, we've gabbed away the last of second watch. Why don't you two turn in so I can report back and do the same," the attractive, dark-haired Giannini directed.

"Yes, ma'am," Eric agreed, and headed off. Amber left without a word, in a different direction, apparently headed for the mess rather than her bunk.

45

When Aichele arrived at his quarters, he moved about the room as if he were preparing to turn in, while surreptitiously checking for any electronic signals that didn't belong. Finding none, he changed quickly into his Marine class C uniform, and snapped open the quick release tabs on the ventilation cover that he had rigged the day before. He stepped onto his bunk and used the extra elevation to help launch his body up and into the ductwork that ran between main deck and upper.

He didn't have to worry about the duct being strong enough to support his weight. Warships, as *Pathfinder* began her life to be, are built to take a lot of punishment, built with the expectation that they would take damage. That is why each compartment of the ship was built to be airtight when sealed off, and designed to automatically seal if the air pressure should drop suddenly. That meant that the air circulation system also needed to be able to seal itself, to keep the ship from losing air if it became punctured due to battle damage. So the materials from which it was constructed had to be able to hold in at least one atmosphere of pressure. 100 kiloPascals was more than enough to support his weight so that wasn't an issue. The problem was that he didn't fit, or at least not very well. Aichele was built like a prototypical wrestler, broad at the shoulders and narrow at the hips, even before the Marines had added 15 or 20 kilos of muscle. In order to get his shoulders in, he had to keep them diagonal to the cross-section. *It's going to be a long trip*, he thought, inching his way forward.

A jolt of claustrophobia hit him, and he wriggled backward a half meter before he could stop himself. He closed his eyes and shook for nearly a minute before he had himself under control once again. His mental equilibrium reestablished, he caterpillared ahead, wondering what kind of crazy world it was that had him owing his altercation with Tommy Knives for preparing him for this day.

At the corner of his room, the shaft branched to the right and left. Negotiating the turn was difficult and time-consuming, but eventually he took the right turning and headed aft. It was marginally less constrictive here. He could lie flat now, and use his elbows for support and locomotion. Dust covered everything about him, and he was going to have to be careful to see that he cleaned his clothes and himself before anyone was in a position to notice how dirty he had become.

Tommy Knives was a name he hadn't thought of for years. Long enough, in fact, that Aichele could no longer remember his last name. Regioni, maybe? It started with an R… Well, that tidbit was floating around somewhere amid his many years of acquired knowledge.

No matter. Knives was the name he had earned, and that was the only name the rest of the company had used after the first three weeks of boot camp. Back in those days, the Corps had still accepted "coerced" volunteers; those who were given a choice between military service and prison time. That policy had changed back in the forties, while Aichele had been a drill instructor, and that had been good for both the Corps and Aichele personally.

Aichele moved silently past a vent that led into someone else's quarters. Sullivan's, he deduced, though it was unoccupied. She must not be back from her dinner yet. There were still two more vents ahead before the next turn, so he maintained his stealthy crawl.

Anyway, Knives thought he was pretty hot stuff when he hit dirt at Camp Hogan. Rumor had it that he had run a street gang in one of the Warner enclaves, and he was used to people jumping when he said, "Frog." Aichele had discounted that notion as soon as he met Tommy. It takes brains to run an organization of any size or description, and Knives was as dumb as a sack full of hammers.

Eric came to a tee, but instead of a left-right option, this offered only up and down. The vertical shaft was quite a bit wider, which in this case made things more difficult. There were no handholds or deep seams to aid in climbing, either up or down. He eased out beyond the edge, holding himself in place by pushing against the opposite wall so that his hands and shoulders were pressed tightly to each side. There wasn't enough room to pull his knees up to his chest, so there was no convenient way to use his legs to help support his weight.

He felt the unaccustomed strain on his arms and, looking above him, judged how difficult it would be to climb up and over the boatbay area. Really hard, he decided, but he knew he could do it. His shoulders would likely ache for a week, though. There was no help for it; he couldn't stand by and do nothing.

That was how he clashed with Knives, as well.

When Knives was packed off to the none-too-tender mercies of the Corps, part of his gang came with him. With muscle to back him up, he figured he'd be running the place within a month. Clearly, he was not the brightest bulb in the pack.

Aichele had not been aware of any of that when he first met Knives; that had come later. His first meeting with Knives was while the whole company was out on maneuvers. Aichele came upon him threatening Jepsen. He didn't know what it was all about, since he hadn't actually heard what was said, but something was clearly not right. As now, he couldn't stand by and do nothing.

As Eric had approached, Tommy had backed away, looking all around to see who was near. There was no one else in the area, meaning no witnesses to corroborate anything Jepsen might say.

"Everything all right here, Jepsen?" Aichele had asked.

"This don't concern you, Boy Scout. Why don't you just move on?" Knives had said flatly.

"That right, Jepsen?" Aichelle asked.

Jepsen didn't make a sound, but the panic and fear in his eyes was answer enough. "Well, you and I have to be on the other side of that ridge in fifteen. I think you and Ricaterra will have to finish your business later. Come on." Ricaterra, That was his name. Tommy Ricaterra.

"I don't think so, Boy Scout. Jepsen and I got an arrangement to settle before he goes anywhere. You know what's good for you, you'll make yourself scarce," Tommy said with a leering grin.

"Look, buddy, I don't know what area you were assigned, and I don't much care. But if Jepsen and I aren't where we belong in time to support the rest of the team, we're going to catch extra duty. I don't see that your business or you are worth that, so back off and get to your own position."

"And I'm telling you," there was no trace of a smile now, "you don't stick your nose someplace else, I'll reach down your throat and pull your lungs out for you."

Aichele didn't threaten easily; never had. Bullies had always seemed the lowest sort of life to him, and he wasn't about to back down to this one.

"Don't let anything but fear and inability stand in your way," Aichele said quietly.

Tommy was livid, as Eric had intended. A pair of knives suddenly appeared in Tommy's hands and he took up a street fighter's stance. "Gonna cut you some, Boy Scout!"

"Try it if you want to. Just remember that self defense makes this justifiable homicide," Eric had said with a taunting grin. Eric assumed the ready position he'd been practicing in hand-to-hand combat training for the last few weeks. "And I have a witness, right, Jepsen?" Jepsen made no answer from behind Aichele, but he didn't dare look back to see what the other man was doing. Perhaps he had no witness after all.

"Ain't you gonna pull your stick?" Tommy used one of his own knife to gesture at the combat knife still in its sheath on Eric's belt. The street tough had lost some the sneering arrogance he had shown earlier. Eric was not following the normal script bullies depended on; he was neither afraid nor indifferent. Tommy was less sure how to handle the rapidly escalating situation, and he was not very good at disguising that fact.

"No. I don't need a weapon to squash a little bug like you," Eric said. "But hurry up and make your move, if you're going to. I still have work to do today."

Perhaps Eric had not given him enough credit for his intelligence. There was a long pause with each recruit eying the other. Finally, Knives arrived at a logical conclusion and opted to retreat in the face of a superior force. "Ah, you ain't worth the effort, Boy Scout. Just stay outta my way, or else."

Once Eric was sure the other was truly gone, he turned to gather up Jepsen and get moving to their assigned stations. Jepsen was nowhere to be seen, but there were muffled sounds coming from the brush. Eric headed off, and thought nothing more of the incident at the time.

Aichele had made it to the top of the shaft while reminiscing and had begun crawling down the relatively roomy conduit above the boatbay's enormous expanse. The vents in this stretch were no longer in the sides of the ducting as they had been before. Here the openings were on the bottom, and Aichele had occasional views of the floor twelve meters straight down with only a thin sheet of metal to support him. Fortunately, heights had never been a particular problem for him, and his trauma-induced claustrophobia he had learned to control.

When he had crossed that space, he had the option of stretching across the opening to another horizontal shaft to move into the engineering section's upper deck or else to head down to the main or lower decks. His arms could manage another descent, but he chose the straight path anyway. He had planned this excursion in advance, of course, and he had three potential targets in mind. The question was whether or not he would be able to find access to any of them from the air ductwork.

The conduit had squeezed down another couple of sizes again, and he fought to keep a chokehold on his fears. He tried taking a deep breath, but found that led to a constricted feeling that was counterproductive.

Unbidden, his mind slipped back to basic training once again. To Aichele, his run-in with Knives had not seemed to be an event of any great importance. Aichele knew what Tommy was, and Tommy knew that Eric was not going to be bullied. Once that was firmly established, he had believed the issue was resolved. Had the matter remained simply between the two of them, that might have been true.

Unfortunately, Knives had been a little too good at intimidating others. Jepsen was well and truly scared by the thug when Aichele had intervened. While the two potential combatants had focused all their attention on each other, he had run for help, fearful that Aichele had bitten off more than he could chew.

The delay that Knives had instigated meant that the rest of the squad, for whom Jepsen and Aichele had been acting as scouts, had all caught up, and within a minute the cavalry had arrived, though unobserved by the two opponents. Marshall, the squad leader, had made a different assessment of the probable outcome and, instead of stepping in, had waved his men into concealment.

So, rather than the forgotten incident that Eric had believed it to be, it soon became known to everyone in the whole camp what had happened. "Knives" was Ricaterra's only appellation from then on, and his ability to intimidate evaporated into thin air. No one would take him seriously after that, even the three young men from his own gang.

Humiliated beyond enduring, he plotted his revenge on his tormentor. Had he not made two critical mistakes, it might have meant Aichele's doom.

Knives had seen his opportunity three weeks after the initial incident, when the training exercises had added powered armor to the weapons list. Using his familiarity with breaking and entering, Tommy managed to get his hands on a drill instructor's control wand, which allowed them to control a recruit's armor remotely to simulate damage during a mock battle.

That day's orders had the company working in the mountains that Camp Hogan was famous for, practicing power-assisted jumps in Armor. Of necessity, the recruits were spread out as much as possible. Each leap covered a good deal of terrain, and you didn't want to slam into your neighbor unexpectedly, armor or no armor.

Knives had to have been watching Aichele all morning in order to get himself into a position to strike at just the right moment. That opportunity came while Eric was traversing a deep fissure in the rocky ground. Without warning, the boot jets shut off and the suit became completely immobile. The horrible sensation of falling was made worse since Aichele was unable to move.

Aichele slammed into the rocks of the near side, bouncing and continuing to fall. Finally he came to rest at an awkward angle, on his back. He landed with his head much lower than his feet. The armor had fulfilled its primary function; Aichele wasn't dead, but he was bruised and broken enough that he almost wished he were. His head was the only part of his body that he could really move, though his temples throbbed when he did so. The movement at least confirmed to him that he hadn't broken his neck.

As Eric was assessing the damage to himself, he saw the tiny black and red form of a practice suit peering over the edge 120 meters above. The sense of relief that he had been spotted and help was on the way turned to an icy lump in the pit of his stomach as he heard in the radio earpiece that was miraculously still working, "So long, Boy Scout. See you in hell."

That had been Knives first mistake, though neither he nor Aichele were aware of it at the time. For Aichele, it was the start of a long day of suffering, both physical and mental. His injuries were agonizing, but he could do nothing to alleviate the pain. His radio transmitter appeared to be functioning, but the signal was unable to pierce the solid rock and his repeated cries for help went unanswered.

After ten or fifteen minutes of futility he gave up and spent his time panicking. It wasn't a planned transition, of course, but the conflict between the need to stay alive and the inability to do anything to ensure that result has often led to panic in even the best trained men.

Twenty minutes of staring at the brownish gray rock with a stripe of light blue sky in the middle began to disorient him. All the blood rushing to his head certainly hadn't helped matters. He thought that he could *see* the walls drawing closer together, seeking to crush him and grind him into nonexistence. He began yelling, screaming, and crying into his radio again, though not nearly so coherently as before.

Closing his eyes did not help at all. Once the image of constricting stone was in his mind it seemed nothing he could do would remove it. It took more than an hour before he was even thinking straight enough to try.

The human body has its limits, and there is only so long that a person can scream before all physical and emotional energy is depleted. Once Aichele's body had reached that point, his mind was again able to begin asserting control. He began by simply concentrating on his breathing and eventually he was able to slow his heart rate and calm himself down. The logical portion of his brain tried hard to convince the rest of the body that since the walls hadn't already squashed him, odds were that would continue to be the case.

The suit's heads up display had died along with all of the control functions, so he had no way of marking time. It seemed that he was in that pit for an eternity, but five hours was the actual span. By the time Marshall and Li spotted him, he was having a hard time staying conscious, and he didn't recognize the radio transmissions for what they were. A few more minutes, half an hour at most, and Eric would have passed out, likely never to awaken. He slipped in and out of consciousness anyway while they were getting him out of the fissure, and he wasn't really aware of things until he woke up in a hospital bed two days later.

The first mistake that Knives had made was in not knowing everything about the tools he had. Plugging the command wand into his suit had indeed given him the ability to shut down Eric's suit. It had also given him much broader communication ability, which he hadn't known about. While he thought he had been speaking suit to suit with the line of sight components, he had actually been broadcasting to everyone in the company. The fact that all were aware of the event and began the search for Aichele at once was a saving one.

The second error was Tommy's belief that he knew his way around the legal system, and a slap on the wrist was all he should have expected. Unfortunately, the leniency of the civil courts that had punished him by giving him a job with the Marines bore only a passing similarity with a Warner Space Marine Corp court martial. That mistake had proven fatal for Knives.

Still, because of Knives, Aichele was now aware of his fear of confinement, and also knew that his will was strong enough to do what needed to be done regardless of how it made him feel inside.

Aichele folded himself around a corner at the rear of the engineering section and struggled both to move forward and to remain silent. He could hear the voices of at least two people working in that area, though the hum of machinery and power made their words indistinct and helped to conceal his own movements.

Aichele had planned on disabling some of the engineering machinery required for ship operations and he could only think of three things that wouldn't be immediately repairable. He had already checked the first two items on his list, and discarded them as impossible. Both were on the engineering section's upper deck, where the air vents were all near the ceiling, away from the equipment resting on the floor. Target number three the jump engine field generator was down on main deck, and the duct openings were all at the base of the walls there.

As he pulled himself into position he found a home run rather than the strike three he had feared. The vent grate was exactly facing the rear access panel of the main field generator's housing. There was space between the wall and the massive machine, but he could still reach everything without even exiting the ductwork.

Reaching into his sleeve pocket he pulled out his field multitool and began removing the screws from the cover plate, which was a slow and awkward endeavor while reaching fingers through the narrow slits. It took more than half an hour to remove the grate, and Eric began to be nervous about being able to get back to his bunk before his next shift started. It was almost certain at this point that he was not going to have any spare time actually to sleep today, but being late for duty, with the questions that would raise, would be stressful at best and potentially lethal.

The rear cover of the generator housing came free much more quickly and easily, now that he literally had some elbow room. Once clear, he examined the interior briefly, looking for the more sensitive components within easy reach. He found what he was looking for almost at once. There were several control circuits not far from a main power coupling. It was not inconceivable that a power surge might damage or destroy those delicate data pathways. If he could make it look like a random occurrence rather than sabotage, no one would come looking for a saboteur, which would suit Eric Aichele just fine.

Gently, he extracted his prepared package from a thigh pocket. He had yet to liberate any actual explosives from the locked-down security section, but there were other tools in other locations on the ship that didn't have anyone watching them. His package was one such, and while it wouldn't go boom, it was still amazing what kind of damage a self-destroying fuse timer and primacord would do to delicate multistate electronics.

A quick check of his chrono told him he had only two and a half hours left before he was due to report to his work party. He set the timer for five, and resealed the back of the generator. Closing up the duct grating was again a laborious chore, and Eric was sweating by the time it was completed.

He pulled himself forward then, intending to loop back around to the main shaft that would lift him over the boatbay again. There was not enough room to turn around and backtrack, and he would prefer to see where he was going, so forward it was. The tight fit of the duct made corners especially difficult to negotiate, and each one slowed his progress. He checked his chrono again nervously as he approached the last turn before the vertical passage. Only an hour and a half. *Time to get your tail in gear, Marine*, he thought.

When it came time to climb back up, Eric wasn't as sure about his ability to do it as he had been, but he wasn't going to waste time debating.

He made it, but only barely. His shoulders burned and his arms shook from the immense effort. He didn't have the energy to go on, but he also didn't have the time to rest. Lessons from Camp Hogan came back to him, and he thought of a way to do both at once.

Rolling onto his back, he could use his legs to slide himself along while his arms could rest. He needed to be on duty in twenty-two minutes when he reached the downshaft. Did he have time to make it? Should he crawl out here and trust to luck to make it back without being spotted? No, he decided. Late for his shift was less dangerous than being spotted where he didn't belong in a dirty uniform he was no longer allowed to wear.

He tried to use his legs a little in his descent, but it was problematic. He really couldn't support his weight with them, but he did manage to use them to slow his rate of descent, which otherwise would have been dangerous. He had to slide down quickly, both because he was out of time and because his arms wouldn't take a slow and gentle pace.

He dropped below the opening and then had to climb back up in order to be facing forward. The ducting in this section was too small to allow him to lie on his back the way he had while crossing the boatbay, but he still tried using his legs as much as he could.

Finally, dropping into his quarters, he wished he could drop straight into his bunk. He'd been up and working for a full twenty-four hours, and he still had sixteen to go before he could rest.

He had to get cleaned up to remove all the dust and grime he had collected first. The Marine uniform couldn't go in the laundry or it wouldn't come back, so it went in the shower with him. In four minutes he had himself cleaned and dressed, his quarters ship shape, and all evidence of his activities of the past eight hours removed.

It was more time than he had available to use, though. He was two minutes late reporting in to the chief engineer. He didn't think she even noticed, since he was far from the last one to report for duty. Most had clearly foregone a shower this morning in exchange for a few extra minutes of sleep. Danis looked like he had slept in his work uniform.

It was twenty-five minutes past watch change when assignments were handed out and Aichele headed forward with Goodwin and Chandler. With a minimum of conversation, they began laying replacement communication and data lines in the conduit beds just under the decking. They started at the junction box which butted up against the bridge bulkhead and were working their way aft, testing the connections at each successive junction.

Eric checked his watch only a few times that morning, but he was aware of when his timer went off. His mental countdown told him that the moment had arrived and there was...nothing.

No alarms, no shouts, no anything. Perhaps he was simply too far from the right area to have noticed anything. Even though it was certainly better for him that no one had noticed, it was incongruously disappointing not to have to pretend he didn't know anything about what was going on when he was questioned. Especially after all the mental preparation he had put into being ready for that potential threat.

It wasn't until almost three hours later that it occurred to him that the field generators had not been activated since the takeover had happened. There had been no way to control the engines with the destruction of the control lines. The local control lines in engineering had been replaced, but there was no point in driving the engines when you couldn't see where you were going to begin with.

His carefully laid alibi was useless. He might as well have eliminated the timer and blown the electronics while he could be sure of their destruction. Since the field generator wouldn't be needed until they were actually ready to test the engines, it might be weeks before anyone noticed that *Pathfinder* was again lame.

CHAPTER 7
5 July

Eric Aichele yawned expansively. This time it was completely unintentional.

He was again paired with the same two young ladies for this watch, but all three of them were more listless than the previous night. There was none of the casual conversation they had enjoyed before. In fact, there was little more than the bare minimum of speech required for completing their work. That was not unusual for Amber Sullivan, but represented a drastic change for the normally garrulous Crystal Giannini.

When their shift ended, all three returned to engineering to report on their work. None of them made an audible farewell, only an exchange of nods before heading to either the mess or straight to their bunks.

Aichele opted for food first, but simply grabbed three of the waiting sandwiches from the platter Green had prepared and began consuming them on his way back to his quarters.

Aichele found his quarters as he had left them. *Exactly* as he had left them, noting that none of his three telltales had been disturbed in his absence. One of these warning signs was electronic rather than physical, and it indicated that the surreptitious surveillance feeds still had not been activated back in the suite of rooms that had housed *Pathfinder*'s security team.

Losing his former bunk in the security suite had turned out to be a step up for him. He and Burton had shared a common squad room which was designed for four occupants, but with little in the way of luxuries or privacy. With half of an already small personnel detachment, there were only a couple of dozen people on a ship that was originally designed to hold eighty or a hundred people. He now found himself quartered in a four-bunk room all his own. The community head which adjoined the bunk room was just as private.

That was good, both for personal and professional reasons. It certainly made it possible to skulk around the ship without anyone being the wiser.

All three of the sandwiches were gone before Aichele had undressed, and he briefly considered going back for more. It was a brief thought because he immediately decided it was a good one, and was on his way back. This time he grabbed water and two desserts as well. Both of those items could be stored for later, and he berated himself for not having a store of emergency supplies handy in case he needed to hide himself on the ship at some point.

With his caloric needs met by the five sandwiches plus one of the desserts, he peeled out of his work overalls, socks, shoes, and skivvies and bundled all of them into the chute. There was a clean set in the return slot, which he tossed on an empty bunk so the system wouldn't wake him when the fresh ones tried to return and found the opening blocked.

A piping hot shower relaxed him, but the forty plus hours on his feet started gnawing at his consciousness before he was done. His body was exhausted, and his mind was not as clear as he needed it to be, so sleep was a necessity he could not postpone much longer. Still, he couldn't allow himself as much as he would like.

Since there was no alarm raised during his work shift, no one was looking for a saboteur yet. There was lots of talk about the damage to the monitor station in Engineering, but most agreed it was an isolated incident. Eric wished he knew who had been responsible for that bit of sabotage; any ally would be welcome; but it could have been any of a dozen people, and there was no way to narrow it down. Once the disabled field generator was noticed, it would take almost no time to figure out that the damage had been done from the rear, and the logical leap from there would be that the air circulation system had been the means of approach.

Once that was known, it would no longer be safe to use that means of transport. Aichele could not afford to sit back and wait for the traitors to catch on to what he was doing. He needed to take advantage of the free travel pass he currently enjoyed to cause as much damage as he could. He also needed to do things that would not be noticed immediately.

So he had more plans for tonight. But not right away.

He climbed into his bunk and set his chrono to wake him in 34 minutes. One of the things he learned in his Security training was how to mentally program his body to deal with the effects of limited sleep. This ability was going to come in quite handy in the coming weeks, Eric predicted.

He mentally recited the poem he'd learned way back then, and had never heard anywhere else. The hypnotic programming activated and Eric Aichele fell immediately into REM sleep. Thirty-three minutes was the time Aichele's mind took to complete a full cycle, and the quiet chime from his wrist had no trouble bringing him back to full wakefulness.

He felt refreshed as he rose and pulled out his old Marine fatigues. He knew the feeling was deceptive and he couldn't fool his body indefinitely, but it was certainly better than having his mind and reflexes dulled by fatigue. Lying down to get a nice comfortable sleep while there was urgent work to do simply wasn't an option.

He checked the video bug one more time before standing on his bunk and launching back into the constrictive ducting. The expected claustrophobia attacked, and he threw it back and lashed it into its proper place before moving on. He headed the opposite direction from the previous night's excursion, heading to port first.

He had a target in mind already, one which was both more conveniently located and should have been the first target on his list all along. However, other work crews had prevented him from getting near the jump engines without being seen until now. His top priority had to be to keep *Pathfinder* out of the hands of whomever Teach was working for. The functioning Improved Jump Engines that *Pathfinder* contained would change interstellar travel forever. The purpose of the *Pathfinder* prototype was to test those improvements to the existing engines. Those improvements had allowed the ship to move from the Betre system to their current location in the Antoc system without the use of a Jump Gate. Possesion of *Pathfinder* would allow one of the other Families to jump without using the Jump Gate system and could potentially allow them to invade a Warner system undetected. In addition to the security implications, the Jump Gates were a Warner monopoly and created a huge revenue stream for the Family. In order for Teach and the other traitors to give the ship, with its secrets, to anyone else, they would have to jump it out of the Antoc system. No exit gate was in existence here, so no one would be coming here after it.

It followed, then, that the jump system should have been his first target. Especially since it would be a target not likely to show any damage until they were ready to try using it, and that might still be two or three weeks, at the current rate the repairs were being completed.

He still had to climb up and over the boatbay, but his destination was just behind the port stairwell at the front end of the engineering section's upper level. With his practice moving through the shafts and the shorter distance, it was only a little over an hour until he arrived, six hours before he had to report for duty again.

Eric dropped silently to the floor of the unoccupied jump engine control room. He went quickly to the door and tried it. Already locked.

Perfect.

He had no more primacord, so he did things the hard way, opening up the console and disconnecting crucial circuit pathways. A short here, a clipped wire there. Some were random, since he didn't have the schematics memorized, but others were very specific.

He took his time, working silently, and when he was done, there was no visible sign that anything had changed. He had even rewritten the internal programming so that running a system diagnostic, either remotely from the bridge or engineering control or locally from the machinery itself, would show that all systems were working to specification. It was a simple bypass that wouldn't fool anyone for very long but it was the best he could do. No one was likely to notice anything was amiss until they tried to power up the jump engines themselves.

That completed, he headed back into the air vent and retraced his path to his quarters. The trick he had played on his body to make it believe it had slept more than it had begun to come apart with the enormous strain of descending back down to the main level on the other side of the boatbay. He was again filthy, shaky, and sweating when he climbed back into his own room, but he still had over an hour to clean up and slip in another sleep cycle.

His last thought before reciting more poetry to himself was that he was going to be really short on sleep if no one caught on to what he was doing.

Another of life's mixed blessings, he drowsed.

CHAPTER 8
7 July

Intense white light reflected off the sterile metal fittings that composed most surfaces of *Pathfinder*'s meticulously clean medbay. The same light shone on the face of the Chief Engineer and Executive Officer as she strode quickly in the front entryway, showing reddened eyes inside dark circles on her normally cheerful face.

Dr. Johnson looked up as Leung came in and the doctor was startled at the changes since Leung's last visit. Leung's hair was unkempt. Spots of grease and dirt could be seen in several locations of her working uniform. Her face seemed thinner and more drawn than it had just over a week ago, before the mutiny.

Leung turned right to enter the doctor's office, which lay down a short hallway past the operating room and a medical supply room, but looked left into the recovery room and noted in passing that Burton was still secured to the frame of her sick bed, even though she had not yet regained consciousness. *One more item on my list of things to keep track of*, she thought.

Tired as she was, Lt. Commander Leung did not feel overwhelmed. Work was proceeding on her assignments at a slow but reasonably steady pace. The ship's crew was shorthanded, but everyone was putting in extra effort to restore manual and automated control to the myriad systems needed to operate the ship.

She realized that she couldn't continue to live on stimulants and three hours of sleep indefinitely, as she might have in her younger days, but she also knew herself well enough to know that sleep would be elusive so long as there were things on the ship that needed fixing. If all went according to plan, *Pathfinder* would be fixed before she herself was broken.

"Something I can do for you, Commander?" the woman at the desk asked pleasantly.

"I need your computer, Doctor."

"Well, let me just gather my things, and you can have the whole office for however long you need."

Announcements like Leung's tend to start arguments, and that was the reaction she had resigned herself to. The doctor's nonchalance seemed incongruous, but not unwelcome. After butting heads with Teach over every choice for the last week, simple acceptance by others felt refreshing. Johnson collected the items she had been working on in silence and was almost out the door before Leung's overworked mind recognized the reason for her calm demeanor.

"Doctor Johnson…"

"Yes, Commander?"

"You're not going to get your computer back."

"I'm not--?"

"I'm sorry I wasn't clear at first," she said tiredly, "but this is the only working computer on the ship. I need to move it to the bridge in order to control our ship's systems. I'll have a team in here in a little bit to--"

"What's going on in here?" Teach demanded angrily, his sudden appearance catching both women off guard. Dr. Johnson, who had turned back toward Leung and thus had not seen the man approach, jumped at the sound of his voice and nearly lost her grip on the stack of datachips she was holding.

She stepped quickly out of the captain's way to allow him to fully enter the small office. It was clear that dark storm clouds were trailing in his wake, but Leung couldn't imagine what the problem was this time.

"Good morning, Captain. I was just explaining to Dr. Johnson why I need to take her computer away from her and move it to the bridge," she explained calmly. Leung felt that she should expound on the brief description, but there really wasn't any more data that needed to be shared.

Teach countered immediately, "I thought I ordered you to do that days ago. What have you been doing all this time instead?" The new captain's gray eyes narrowed.

The engineer nearly snapped back at him, but managed to stifle her natural reactions. "No, Captain, you gave me permission to proceed several days ago, but what you actually said was to do what I thought was best. When I studied the specs on this system, I realized that it would have to be rebuilt to expand both processing and memory capacity. I ran a thorough analysis to determine if it would still be a more efficient choice than building the command unit from scratch, which it will be.

"As for what I have been doing with my time, the captain is certainly aware that replacing the bridge command unit is not the only item currently on my repair/replace list. Nor is engineering my only duty, since the captain requires that I spend half of each day in command of the bridge watch."

Leung winced mentally at her rash comments. Her lack of sleep was beginning to undermine her control. She eyed him critically, and could see that his face had reddened with anger, but she plunged ahead before she could stop herself. "And who, may I respectfully ask, is in command of bridge watch now? Sir?"

Startled by the engineer's words, Teach's jaw worked for several moments before he spoke. "It is not necessary for you to know what arrangements I have made on my watch, and it is not your place to question me, Commander." It was a lame defense, and both knew it, but at least it provided the illusion that he had not cornered himself with his own requirements.

Johnson looked from one to the other, and clearly wished she were somewhere else. Seeing her pained expression, Leung felt inwardly glad. Once again, Teach was making a spectacle of himself in front of the crew, and Leung was sure the scuttlebutt about this latest event would make its way around the ship in no time. Still, she didn't want to seem to be contributing to his behavior. She should tone down her own language, so that the scuttlebutt would show her in a favorable light. She needed to play the peacemaker if she was going to keep the crew on her side and against him.

"Of course, Captain. I spoke out of turn and I apologize. If there is nothing else, I will return to my duty here."

"Very well, then, see that there is no recurrence." The captain's words were hard, but his hand on her shoulder softened it somewhat. Leung flinched away from the contact, but eased her stance when she could tell what he was doing. Teach seemed not to notice, spun on his heel and left, turning forward as he passed the hatch, to follow the port corridor toward the bridge. Leung watched him go and suppressed a sigh of relief. *That was a near thing*, Leung thought.

She turned to the doctor and smiled. "I am sorry, Doctor, but as I was just telling the captain, appropriating your computer is really the quickest way to get the ship operational again."

"I understand, Commander. Whatever I can do to help."

"Do you have a backup of the medical database, or should I create one before reprogramming?" the XO asked then. "We have a replacement for this unit in stores as well, and eventually, when things settle down, we can restore it for you."

"Don't worry about that. I have more than one, actually. My portable unit has all the information I have ever had to use."

"Very well. I'll have a team in here in a few minutes to start dismantling and removing the computer. I'll ask that they not disturb you, as far as that is possible."

"Thank you, Commander. I think I will take advantage of the interruption to go get my breakfast, finally. Burton's monitors are linked to my pad, so you can tell the crewmen that I will handle any emergency."

"That will be fine. Thank you for being so cooperative."

"Not at all, Commander," she smiled. "I understand that these are not normal circumstances, and, as I said, all the information I generally need I still have at hand."

The two left together, Dr. Johnson heading to the galley and Leung moving aft to the engineering area. Orders flew about as soon as she had cleared the hatch.

"Young! I've got a job for you. Giannini, Bezates, Goodwin, Chin, front and center!" When they had assembled, she passed out their new assignments. Young was to be in charge of the group, with Goodwin handling the electrical connections. She told Young to disassemble the unit, but not to take it to the bridge until it was her watch again. She wanted to be there to supervise the installation, or at least as much as she could. A second team; De Saumserez, Sullivan, and Beacham; were instructed to bring the additional parts that had been pulled from stores to the bridge when next watch began.

Duties performed and crew organized, she headed straight for her quarters to get some much-needed rest. Her uniform was a mess, but she didn't have the two hours she needed for it to return from the laundry before she was due on the bridge - again. She searched through the pile, though, and took the time to find her two other uniforms.

One of them was cleaner than what she had on, so she kept it out, hanging it over the back of her desk chair to minimize the wrinkling, and put the other two into the laundry chute.

Rather than collapsing into her bunk, as she wished to do, she lay down on the edge and rolled into the center to avoid the overhead storage bin. If she ever found time to move into the executive officer's quarters that was one annoyance she would be pleased to dispense with.

Sleep rapidly overcame her, the thoughts and plans of the day receding to nothingness.

A knocking at the door interrupted her sleep, polite at first then a bit more insistent. She rolled carefully upright, then leaned forward and held her head in her hands. It pounded in time with her heart, and almost masked another round of knocking from outside.

"Commander Leung? Are you awake, ma'am?" It was Ensign Omundson outside, who had been standing bridge watch with Teach, leaving Ensign Samuels to assist during Leung's watches. That suited Leung just fine, since Samuels was easier for her to work with. Omundson's behavior and attitude reminded her of the unlamented Lt. Lamont.

"What is it?" she growled harshly, and immediately wished she hadn't as a wave of pain squeezed her forehead.

"Ma'am, I'm sorry to disturb you, but Captain Teach requires your presence at once on the bridge."

"Is the ship in danger?" Sudden panic hit her and she was wide awake and standing.

"No, ma'am, not that I am aware of. He was speaking with Chandler at the comm station and then he sent me to get you."

Her head tipped again into her hands, which did their best to hold her fatigue-induced throbbing to a minimum. "Couldn't this have waited? I'm due on the bridge in…" A glance at the chrono showed that she had been in bed for only sixteen minutes, bringing renewed anger. "…another eighty minutes."

"I'm afraid not, ma'am. Captain Teach said immediately." He didn't sound very apologetic to her.

"All right. Tell him I'll be there in a minute," she said, crossing to her desk to put her clothes back on.

"Ma'am…uh…the captain asked me to escort you to the bridge." He did sound apologetic now, but Leung's surging anger did not let her recognize it. *That arrogant prig*, she railed silently. *How dare he summon me like a serving girl in my few off hours, and* then *not even trust me to follow orders. He deserves everything that's coming his way!*

Anger was still swirling around in her core but she pushed any trace of it off her face as she dressed and exited her quarters. If she let it out, there would be unpleasant consequences, she knew. Omundson was waiting just to the side of her door. He did not salute, but did dip his head and say, "Ma'am," as she went by, not waiting for him.

She walked the short distance to the bridge quickly, and Omundson struggled to keep up without actually running. When she reached the bridge, she entered her code and the hatch swung over to admit her.

Glaring with an angry fire of his own, Teach turned his center seat to face her. He remained seated and waited for her to approach him, a pointed reminder of who was in command. It was dangerous for Leung to take offense at such things, but she did anyway. Perhaps if she had had a full night's sleep it might have been different. Perhaps if she had had a full night's sleep since this mad enterprise had begun...

"Why can't I send a message to our Forrest contact," he demanded loudly.

Leung considered asking him to find a private location for this meeting, but immediately dismissed the idea. It hadn't worked any of the previous times she'd suggested it, and it suited her purposes to have witnesses.

Impatience colored her response, at both the man and the situation. "I don't know why you can't send a message. Someone probably crossed a wire during repairs. I'll add it to my list of things to check, right after the four hundred or so more important things to fix, like being able to steer the ship! Did you ask Young to look into it? He is manning Engineering this watch, you know."

Teach's eyes narrowed under his bushy black eyebrows. A dim part of her brain registered that he would soon explode into another rage, but she was too tired to try to prevent it. "Look, Captain, I know that there are things that don't work. Most of the ship is in that state. The crew and I are fixing things as fast as we can, but I also need to get some sleep occasionally! Why is it necessary to get me out of bed just to add one more thing to my workload? This could have waited until I came to relieve you, surely!"

"No it could not wait, *Commander!* This is another case of deliberate destruction of the ship's systems."

Leung knew the captain had been acting a little paranoid, so she had made allowances in her own mind. In this case, however, perhaps her caution was misplaced. It was possible that Teach was right and someone had acted to take away their ability to communicate with Forrest.

"I apologize, Captain. I did not realize the seriousness of the problem. Where is the damage located?"

"How the blazes should I know where the damage is? You're the engineer, you tell me!"

"Excuse me, Captain, but are you saying that you have not actually seen the damage to the communications system?" She was confused now, and her face showed it. Controlling her features at this point was beyond her fatigue-impaired capacity.

"No, of course not. I tried to call Forrest and the system failed to respond properly. It's your job to find out how the saboteur did it." His bearing and tone of voice suggested that a child of five should have understood this without the need of an explanation.

"I'm sorry, sir. Maybe I'm too tired, but I don't follow you. If you haven't seen any damage, how do you know that it was done deliberately and that it is not simply a glitch or some other problem?"

Teach looked confused for the briefest instant before his confident and somewhat arrogant carriage returned. The pause in the conversation was long enough for Teach to undergo a complete reversal of tone and volume. "I suppose I don't know for sure, XO, but it is still a possibility that we should explore. I might have overreacted, but better that than to ignore a potential problem until it is too late."

Leung had a nearly irresistible urge to yawn, and only by locking her jaws closed was she able to stop herself. When the urge passed and she could trust herself to speak she said, "I'll have someone start looking into it immediately, Captain." She tried to project an air of efficiency and competence, but she wasn't sure how well it would come off when she was having a hard time remaining upright. "I'll report anything unusual I find immediately, sir."

"We need to take some precautions also, Leung. I think we need to have two of the crew assigned to security detail as well. Not Aichele, though. Is there anyone else who has any training in that area?"

"I don't think so, but I can check the personnel fil--" No, she couldn't check personnel files without a working computer and restored crew database. "I'll ask around, Captain, and submit a recommendation by the end of my watch."

"That will be fine," he said with a conciliatory wave. "Why don't you turn i--?"

"Energy discharge!" Amber Sullivan sang out from the cartography monitor station which was linked directly to the sensors and thus had not been disabled by the loss of the computer. "Bearing…"

"Bearing where? What sort of discharge? Report!" Teach was angry again, and it was clear that his yelling had flustered the reserved engineering tech.

"It's…uh…not possible to get an exact bearing without the computer tie-in, sir. General direction would place it in the Antoc system, almost directly astern. Magnitude looks to be less than a missile…maybe the size of a mine." Her voice rose as she finished, making the report sound more like a question.

There was a question in the look that Leung and Teach shared as well. Neither knew what to make of this development, but one thing they did not question was that William Brighton was at the heart of it.

CHAPTER 9
10 July

Ensign Monica Samuels strode toward the bridge purposefully, intent on appearing completely at ease. In the back of her mind she heard her voice of caution try to scream out that it wasn't time yet to take this risk, but she was confident that she had made herself trusted, or at least not overtly mistrusted by Teach or Leung. She pointedly ignored that voice. While they had been able to construct a new bridge computer/astrocomp, they were really no closer to controlling the ship. Her decision was made and she had to go forward with it if she was going to have any chance at stopping Teach. She was certain of the success of her worm as long as she was able to insert it unobtrusively into the new computer. Her smooth confidence didn't wane as she approached the bridge hatch.

A quick glance to the sides showed that no one was in the corridor. She took a moment before keying entry to the bridge to school her features and straighten her uniform. She glanced at her wrist chrono; almost a full five minutes early for her duty shift. She took a deep breath, keyed the passcode, and walked onto the bridge.

She moved toward her duty station without really looking at anyone, just like she had any number of times when reporting for duty. She did note out of her peripheral vision that Teach was in the captain's chair, and was reviewing something and not really watching anyone or anything on the bridge. She quietly nodded to Brooke Fields, who was finishing third watch on Helm. Fields was a warrant officer, a technical specialist with some officer authority, as many helm specialists were, and perhaps a dozen years older than Samuels. Her features; eyes, nose, lips, teeth; all seemed a bit too large for her face. She had very long blonde hair pulled into a ponytail, with the clasp over her tunic collar. Samuels preferred her clip at the back of her head, so the hair stayed off her neck altogether. She couldn't imagine trying to manage that much hair, either.

She was a few minutes early for her watch, and so she would wait while Fields finished and turned over to her. While she waited, she fixed her hair, pulling strays from the collar of her uniform and returning them to her short black ponytail. To any and all observers she was just an ensign waiting to come on duty, which was exactly the way she wanted them to perceive her.

She was good at computer code-work, she decided once again. She kept her calm, knowing that the success of her worm lay in getting it safely installed. It wouldn't help her at all to be nervous or appear out of sorts on the bridge. She had seemed to remain under the active radar of Teach, but acting awkwardly would still arouse his paranoid suspicions.

Samuels waited, at ease, as Fields keyed out of Helm. Brooke stood and said, "All yours, Ensign Samuels, such as it is." She thanked her and sat down, quickly keyed in her code and started her beginning of shift routine. It was still odd to her that the system allowed anyone to key into the Helm system, as if all were normal, but it would not accept a single command issued to it. The only way it would accept new directions was if the 'piracy protocols' were overruled by either the ship's captain (meaning Captain Brighton) or three senior bridge officers.

Ensigns were none of the above.

Captain Brighton had activated the Piracy Protocols and locked down the computers as soon as he had seen armed intruders on his Bridge. Although his lockouts had included many things not usually part of those protocols. The lifepods had launched on their own and the astrocomp had burned itself out. Those were not normal results and she wondered when Captain Brighton had added them to the protocol. She had watched him hit the single button. He had not had time to add them at the last minute.

After she had completed the process of logging into the helm, she took a moment to casually assess who was on the bridge and where they were.

Fields, who had just finished third watch on Helm, was headed off the bridge to use the head and grab a sandwich before she would return to relieve CPO Young at the Environment station, where she would then have to remain for the next eight-hour shift. The short staff had everyone pulling two shifts out of three on the bridge, except for Teach and Leung, who had some other shift arrangement where they alternated six hour intervals as Officer of the Deck. This kept Teach on most or part of all three watches, but seemed to leave him on first watch the longest.

Teach was where he always was whenever he was on the bridge, in the captain's chair. He was engrossed in his command panel and was not really paying any attention to the rest of the bridge crew.

Warrant Officer Fields was quick to return, and Young was turning over to her as swiftly as he could, and within minutes he was headed for the hatch. Danis had come to take over the Engineering station for first watch after finishing a work assignment on third watch. Ensign Omundson had transitioned from Cartography to Astrogation, and had made the same quick run to see to his physical comforts. They had only recently been able to staff Astrogation, as Leung had gotten the scabbed together medical system in place as a replacement, though the astrogation database was rebuilt with only local star systems and the software reload was only fourteen hours old, so as yet untested. Those few who were going off duty had already made their exit before both Fields and Omundson, who never rushed back, had returned.

Samuels returned her gaze to her duty station, and made the notations to again indicate that she had no control over the current course heading but that she was logging all sensor data that they had access to.

Monica had spent quite a bit of time developing her plan, and far more in actually developing her worm. Her computer programming skills were top of her class at the Academy, likely due to the extra emphasis her family placed on those skills, and two of her favorite course sequences had been viralware/antiviralware and code-scouring algorithmic design. She had taken every single course in those specialties that was offered. Again, the needs of her family had been at the root of those decisions. Most of her fellow classmates had focused on Command Theory or Engineering courses. Only her missing roommate, Jherri Roberts had shared her fascination with the cyber world and even she had split her time between Command and Cyber pretty evenly.

Samuels happened to know the astrogation system pretty well, having run bridge watches from Astro several times under Captain

Brighton. She knew the worm would selectively and systematically tear apart the new astrocomp that Leung had worked so hard on as well as spreading to the main computer and to every subsystem if it was given enough time.

There were several things that the worm would do to the new system. First, it would tear down several layers of security for her and change access code stamps on several key files. These files would show simultaneous and independent accesses by Leung and the missing Lamont. The strings were set such that to any observer it would appear the two had passed files back and forth, as well as co-edited some together. In short, it would appear as if the two were definitely in collusion, and had been in close contact (via the system at least) very recently. It would also show new timestamps going forward, in case anyone followed up, further propagating the evidence of working behind Teach's back.

The next thing it would do was to alter the view stamps on Leung's logs, showing that Teach had accessed them at least daily, and that he had clumsily tried to hide that fact. It would look as if he was checking up on her to any other observer. It would also continue to show that he would be checking her logs at least every day from here on out.

Those two plants were there to drive a schism between Leung and Teach. If they "discovered" that the other was not trustworthy or fully honest about what was going on, they would likely spend more time fighting or plotting against each other and less time figuring out who the real saboteur was. Namely, one Ensign Monica Samuels.

Those were both somewhat easy add-ons to the core of her worm. What she was really doing was to insert a full-fledged Trojan that would allow her to backdoor into the Astro system from off the bridge, and from there she could hop to the rest of the bridge controls if needed. The problem with planting any kind of control Trojans inside her worm was that they would be fairly easily detected by the bridge counter-viral systems. Trojan plants, or code that allowed for remote accesses and controls, were one of the most common forms of viralware and therefore one of the most vehemently pursued by antiviralware.

So her plan had been adapted for the best chance of success using not just code but also hardwire changes. Her worm would seek and destroy some normal routines within the astrogation primary and ancillary systems and sieze control of the power cycling inducer, which was not located on the bridge. Because there were not supposed to be any cross controls, that subsystem was unprotected by typical antiviral softcode and she knew how to exploit it. She couldn't impact the actual power system, but she could impact the control system in Astro that sent commands to the power system.

She was counting on being in the right place at the right time to put part B in place, and the actual hardwire tap that would allow her to enter via the power systems and gain access into the bridge systems. Once her worm was fully in motion, the Astro system would continuously have power up and power down issues, erratically responding to commands from the console. She needed this to become a serious enough issue while she was on the bridge that her help was enlisted at the console. That one piece was hard to plan for.

Once that happened, she could perform her hardwire cross tap, and then barring any disasters, such as getting caught doing that, she would have external access to the bridge systems from multiple locations on the ship.

She knew that she had prepared as much as possible, but there were many variables in the situation. It was impossible to mitigate them all, but she had done her best to put herself in the best position to pull this off. She had even selected the watch and timing of her opportunity to insert the worm into the system, and would have to live with the consequences now.

Her first watch was at Helm, and she would just have to wait it out. She knew that the next three hours would probably be excruciating for her as anxious as she was to get the plan in motion. At 1100 hours, Teach would turn over OOD duties to Samuels and leave the bridge to go on his "tour of the ship." She would have almost one full hour to find an opportunity to insert the worm, and get the hardwire tap at Astro before Leung arrived.

The next three hours felt like ten lifetimes. Far from the "organized chaos" of the bridge as it had been under Brighton, with voices and data flowing all over, the Teach bridge was almost silent to a fault. No one spoke unless Teach asked them a direct question. Generally, Helm and Astro would be calling or pushing data back and forth regularly. With the astrocomp in its infancy of reprogramming and Helm completely useless, stillness reigned.

As the bridge chrono ticked away, with occasional grunts from Teach, they all sat or stood in silence. They were just going through the motions, and they all knew it, but because of Teach and what his attitude was like, no one would ever voice that.

At precisely 1100, Teach stood up from his captain's chair.

"Samuels, I am going on my tour. You have the Conn," he called out to her as he stepped toward the door. Samuels, expecting this, was already beginning to move from Helm to the captain's chair. When Samuels served a bridge watch with Leung, the XO remained on the bridge and in control for the whole time but Teach had a different routine. That was why she had chosen this watch for her sabotage.

"Aye-aye, sir. I have the Conn," she replied with feigned indifference.

Teach had keyed out of the captain's systems when he left the bridge. Most would assume that an ensign's command codes wouldn't entitle one to too much access on the bridge. This was certainly true in most respects. One of the things often overlooked, though, was that at the captain's control console, any officer had extended access. It came with being "given the Conn," which meant being given control of the entire ship. This control was systemic as well as authoritative. The WSN felt that anyone acting as Officer of the Deck, or OOD, needed to be able to manage any system at any time.

Nine minutes after Teach left the bridge, her opening came. Omundson had gone back over to Cartography to check some readings there and left Astrogation completely unattended. Everyone else was focused elsewhere. She casually reached out her hand to adjust one of the displays and inserted her micro-drive in the data slot. Ten seconds later, her work was completely injected into the astrocomp from her console. She forced the system to burn off the micro drive, erasing any trace of what used to reside there to any scan and removing it just as smoothly while leaning in for a closer look at something on the display. Samuels spent a few minutes appearing to be interested in some readings on the screen there, while erasing any log or system entries corresponding to the data injection. Then she waited for her worm to get to work.

If all systems behaved as predicted, she should start seeing Astro having power issues within ten minutes. She passed her time at the console scanning routine reports that all showed the same thing that she already knew, the ship controls were crippled and they were on a "straight-line" trajectory headed out of system.

Seven and a half minutes after her worm had been injected into the system, the astrocomp shut down while Omundson was standing there. She noticed out of her peripheral vision, since she was making herself not stare at that duty station, that Omundson was befuddled, trying desperately to reinitiate the system. Everyone on the bridge turned toward him as he slapped a hand down on the console, his frustration evident.

"Ensign Omundson, is there a problem?" Samuels asked him, leaning forward and focusing on him and the astrocomp.

"The new astrocomp primary processing system just powered off, and is not responding to power up commands," he replied, continuing to attempt those same commands over and over while talking.

Samuels took a moment and said "Omundson, do you need a hand?" as he continued to enter the same commands with no effect.

"I am not sure what is going on here, Samuels. It should be powering up, but the system isn't responding," Omundson muttered just loud enough for almost everyone on the bridge to hear before dropping his voice to unintelligible sounds. Suddenly, the system came online in the middle of his startup attempts. "Aha! There, coming back online," he proclaimed to everyone on the bridge triumphantly.

Samuels eased back in her chair, thinking that perhaps she had either missed her opportunity, or that this might be a longer process than she had planned.

No sooner had the excitement at Astro settled down when Omundson once again yelled at the system.

"You've got to be kidding me," he shouted as the system did a complete power down, the screen going dark.

Monica took her opportunity and strode quickly to Astrogation. No one would fault the OOD for checking on the newly installed astrocomp displaying such perplexing and potentially catastrophic behavior. She observed Omundson repeating the command to initiate the system several times and then suggested, "I think we need to check the hardware, Stuart."

"Yeah, this has to be a component failure of some kind," he agreed, if only to point the blame squarely on something other than himself as to the system's issues.

Together, Samuels and Omundson got the casings open and began separately checking several of the command and power systems for any component shorts, wiring problems or any other general sign of distress. She maneuvered around the system, ostensibly following some wires, until she was in the area she needed to be to plant her taps. She made a grab for another tool and climbed under the station housing to get at something just out of reach otherwise, and slid the two taps from her pocket (innocuous looking spans) and clamped them into place.

She spent another couple of minutes under there to make it seem like she was checking connections and tightening them. "It's all secure under here," she said pulling herself back up and out of the housing.

"Yeah, I am still not finding anything out of place either," Omundson said flatly, clearly hoping they would have found some failed component to explain the bizarre behavior of the system.

Samuels knew that if all went as designed, within a minute of the taps being in place, her malware would recognize the connections had been established, and revert the power control system to its normal state. She made sure they kept checking the cabling, connections, light emitters, fuses and capacitors for at least another five minutes just to be thorough. Then she said, "Let's try it again, Stuart, and see if there is any change."

"It's worth a shot, I guess," he replied, moving back to the control panel. The second he input the startup the system powered up and all internal systems to the astrocomp came to life as if nothing was wrong at all. Just as planned. "Seems like it decided to come online, Samuels," he said, shaking his head.

"Maybe just tightening up those connections did it," she said hopefully.

"I hope you're right. If this thing stays up more than a few minutes, I'll put the housing back together and get back to work on it."

"Agreed," she replied, handing him the tools she had pulled from his kit, and walked back to the captain's station. "Keep me posted if you see anything else out of the ordinary there," she said as she sat in the center seat. Everyone else on the bridge began to get back to what work there was to do.

She had to fight down a desire to smile and let out a giddy laugh. Her plan had worked perfectly, and she still had 24 minutes before Leung would relieve her as OOD.

CHAPTER 10
14 July

Gunnery Sergeant Eric Aichele looked up from the wiring assembly he had just finished repairing and deactivated the plasma fuser. He reversed himself out of the small access hatch through which he had been working, inwardly smiling at all the time he had spent skulking in other access hatches and ducts, and turned back toward Lieutenant Commander Leung as he lifted the protective face shield and wiped his brow with a kerchief from his back pocket. She didn't even seem to notice what he was doing, apparently much more concerned with the poor work that had been done by Philip Beacham as she told him in no uncertain terms that it would not suffice, and it would have to be redone.

Crystal Giannini moved into Aichele's view and motioned him to slide out of the way so she could inspect the rewiring he had just finished. He did so, carefully stretching out the muscles in his legs and back cramped by the long immobility. He was still not accustomed to working under access panels and crawlspaces, but he was getting more practice at it every day, especially in the ducts that allowed him the unrestricted accesses to the ship. He had expected at first to be a major suspect, but as the week and a half had gone on, they seemed to be paying less and less attention to him. He wasn't about to relax, though.

"Wow, Gunny, I think you missed your calling," Giannini told him as she climbed back up from under the access panel. "That's good work. You spliced and patched that perfectly, which is a lot better than I would expect from a Marine Sergeant," she added as he helped her to her feet.

He let the incorrect rank pass this time, tired of the chore of constantly correcting it. "Doesn't matter what I'm asked to do, I always give it my best," Aichele said instead, smiling a very genuine smile. He had done good work on this, and every other job he had been given. He wanted to give no cause for extra suspicion to Leung, Teach or any of the other pirates. The fact that no one had figured out that he had sabotaged five different ship's components so far meant they likely never would. He had been extremely careful to leave no evidence behind, and so the principle danger had always been to be discovered in the act.

Leung looked over at Aichele and Giannini after completing the task of scolding Beacham. She got an affirmative nod from Giannini as a response to her raised eyebrow, an unspoken question the specialist was used to interpreting, and then nodded back before moving to the other side of the bay to check the third group in the team.

Leung was beginning to think that maybe her suspicions had been wrong about Aichele. She had been sure, at first, that he had something to do with the communications failures, but she had been watching him or having him watched, sometimes overtly and sometimes covertly, around the clock since then, but not one step had been out of line. She harrumphed to herself as she thought about the fact that she had assigned him to her tech crew to keep an eye on him, but was finding that he was surprisingly good at this. Go figure, a soldier who could do tech work. What would she come across next?

She checked over the work the others were doing, more to track the progress than to verify the quality. Most of her team didn't require quality hawking.

She wasn't sure what to think about the comms dying, but if it had been sabotage, and if it wasn't Aichele, then who was it? She wasn't convinced that he was really onboard for the reasons she would like, but she was growing more confident that he wasn't actively working against her. If he hadn't stepped out of line for a week and a half, especially when he didn't know he was being watched, he most likely wasn't going to.

Aichele smiled at her and gave her a small nod from across the bay and turned back to Giannini. Aichele was aware that Leung had initially suspected him of being opposed to the traitors. He was also aware, of course, that he was being watched. None of the engineering crewmen who had tried to watch him were skilled enough to escape his notice. They would never have made it out of Security School, even if they had somehow found a way to get through Marine training. Even with their ineptitude, he knew that he would still have to be careful. Leung would probably keep him under scrutiny for a while yet.

Good Marines knew that no matter how skillful you were at your job, getting cocky would probably get you killed.

For both of their sakes, Aichele had avoided visiting Burton again. He had heard that Leung had ordered her to be kept sedated, so her assistance was impossible anyway. She would likely make a full recovery, although it would take a long while. Much as he wanted to see her to make sure, he knew he shouldn't. Being constantly watched, he knew that visiting her would give them more evidence that he wasn't really working for them.

One of the ways to allay suspicion was to make friends among the core of the enemy. Giannini was one who had warmed up to him. He wasn't sure that she had really wanted to be among the pirates, but she had made her choice and was trusted by Leung, apparently. For that matter, he wasn't sure that she didn't want to be more than friends. He thought admitting to his real age would cool her off, but such did not appear to be the case. If he could turn that into an advantage, though, he would.

He knew that Leung's tech crew was the best place to start making friends among the enemy. Generally, people like the casual helper, so he turned to Beacham and asked if he could use a hand, motioning Giannini to come with him.

"It's times like this I don't know why I am even doing this," Beacham muttered as they came closer to his assigned work area.

"I think it has something to do with the money coming our way, most likely," Aichele responded, offering a smile. They all chuckled.

"Thanks, by the way, Aichele. I apparently can't get a closed fiber group in my splice," Beacham said shaking his head.

"Gunny can. He should have been teaching at tech school instead of running security rounds on a ship," Giannini supplied, smiling mischievously at Eric.

"I can still break heads better than I can splice, but I can help out here." Aichele replied, smirking.

He knew that everyone had always kept a little distance from the security group, even before Chowdhury took over, and he had probably always seemed a little aloof to these crewmen. He had to win them over without them thinking he was trying to win them over. He hated playing mind games, and he certainly had no desire to be a spy or saboteur, nor to play on a young woman's affections, but he had a job to do. And as he had already expressed, he did his job to the best of his ability, no matter what it was. Even so, breaking a few heads was still an appealing option to him.

If only his life could be that simple again.

* * * * *

Staff Sergeant Jill Burton came awake slowly. She began to be aware of sounds near her, which seemed very odd. Soon enough, though, she realized that they were the sounds of medical monitors. Her consciousness floated slowly to the surface, and then she abruptly remembered what had happened to her, and why she had medical monitors within her hearing.

She had been attacked.

She tried moving her extremities, and realized that her left wrist was bound to the rail of the bed she was in. She tried to flex to see how securely she was held, which only demonstrated how weak she really was. Burton was not used to feeling weak. No Marine would ever get used to such a condition.

The sound of an opening hatch behind her announced that she was not alone in the medbay. She wasn't sure who was coming in, and anything she might overhear could potentially help her, so she closed her eyes again and slowed her breathing to feign sleep. She discovered it really wasn't that hard to pretend. Indeed, she found herself fighting to remain conscious as sleep's welcoming arms tried to wrap her in its cottony embrace at once. Her fight did not last long.

Dr. Johnson was the one who Burton heard enter the medbay. She moved over to the monitoring equipment to double check the readings for the eight minutes she had been gone. The readings showed that her patient's heart rate had picked up briefly, and her EEG was indicating a return to safe brain level activity. Those were good signs. She looked over at the sergeant and admired her internal will. Many people would not have pulled through the surgery and massive transfusions that the doctor had been forced to perform. More than simply pull through the surgery, it appeared that the sergeant was likely to recover completely. Dr. Johnson knew full well that Burton would not have recovered, would not have lived, had the Marine been left aboard *Pathfinder* without the doctor remaining to operate. This wasn't to say that only Dr. Johnson could have saved her, but with Dr. Ward headed out on

Vanguard, the medical skills of those left aboard *Pathfinder* would not have been enough to have kept her alive without the Doctor's presence.

Burton's breathing was slightly on the shallow side of normal while she slept. The doctor watched her patient, and she began once again to think about what was happening around them. She was concerned for both of their welfares, frankly. Sergeant Burton was close to being out of the woods, yet obviously had a tougher physical challenge ahead of her. But Meghan had no less a challenge herself. With a sigh, she reached up and adjusted the sedative to a higher level and watched as the vital signs dipped and settled.

To Johnson's mind, there were not a lot of options open to her. She hated the thought that the crew of *Pathfinder* had mutinied, and that circumstances had forced her to stay aboard with them. She wished there were some way for her to have stopped it, or for there to be something she could do now to deprive these... pirates... of their theft. Her choices, however, were very limited. There were many of them, and only one of her. There might possibly be help from Burton in several weeks, if she recovered. Even so, there was little Johnson felt the injured Marine could do. The doctor had thought Aichele might be sympathetic, but he had fallen in with the others now. At any rate, there would be no way to stop them without the use of force that she could think of, and therein lay her problem.

She had taken upon herself the Hippocratic Oath many years ago. She took it very seriously, especially as it pertained to her patients. She would "keep them from harm," even if they were criminals. Every member aboard *Pathfinder* was in her medical charge as Chief Medical Officer. They were all her patients.

Meghan had been stewing over this issue since the day she had decided that her oath required her to stay in the operating room on a ship controlled by thieves. What they had done was wrong, and she wanted no part of it. Yet she was held by that same oath not to fight back. Doing no harm almost limited her to inaction, but she had realized only a day or two ago, that she had also sworn the next two words that followed those in the classic oath: "...keep them from harm *and injustice*." The loyal crew members who had departed on *Vanguard*, and Sergeant Burton were her patients too, and she had sworn an oath to keep them from harm and injustice.

It was not an easy path that lay ahead for her. She would, for now at least, be patient and care for the one who most relied upon her. Dr.

Johnson made a promise to herself, though, to watch for an opportunity to live up to that oath in its entirety.

Part of that oath, of course, included letting Sergeant Burton come out of her sedation when it was no longer beneficial to her recovery, regardless of who had ordered otherwise.

CHAPTER 11
15 July

Ensign Stuart Omundson hurried down the corridor to Lieutenant Commander Leung's berth. He began knocking before he even came to a full stop in front of the unadorned gray metal hatch knowing from past experience that she would ignore the soft door chime. He heard no immediate sounds in response, and so he knocked again more forcefully on the doorway.

Omundson was the junior ensign aboard *Pathfinder*, as a result of the fact that he had been outscored by Ensign Monica Samuels on nearly every competency exam given before, at, and during their current posting. Stuart was not an idiot, but Samuels grasped the examinations better than he had. He was not worried about this minor fact. He knew that his intelligence was vastly superior to most everyone around him but he had never felt the need to push himself to the limit. After all, he knew his place in the galaxy and it had nothing to do with tests.

He stood as calmly as he could, having been sent once again to awaken the executive officer during her only six hour sleep rotation, which had started only an hour ago at the beginning of first watch. Omundson again drew up his 1.75 meter, lightly-muscled frame, swept the unruly blond hair out of his face and raised his arm. Just as he began to pound on the hatch for the third time, he heard movement inside the berth.

"Whoever you are, this had better be an emergency! What is it?" Leung fired the words through the closed hatchway like a salvo.

Omundson did not particularly like to be the bearer of bad news, but he knew he had better get to the point. Leung had been losing her temper regularly of late. The unending list of problems aboard *Pathfinder* and the utter lack of sleep was not helping things for her.

"Ma'am, I am sorry to wake you up, but Captain Teach sent me to report to you that the sensor arrays are failing at random intervals. I was on duty on the bridge and they just started going crazy and falling off, then coming on randomly about ten minutes ago," he called back. "So far, ma'am, I have no idea what is happening or why, but we are losing sensors all over the external grid."

"That's just great, Ensign! I will add it to my thirteen page list of things to investigate aboard this cursed boat. Thanks for waking me up to inform me that you have no idea how to handle a problem! Duly noted, Ensign Omundson!"

The last sarcastic dig almost lost some of its bite as her pitch and volume seemed to be approaching hysteria. "Since we are headed in a straight line that we have plotted for several days now, the random loss of sensors in no way constitutes an emergency, no matter how bizarre. Now, be a good little ensign and get yourself away from my hatch before I find a blunt implement of some sort in here to come out and use on you," she called heatedly. Her tone and volume had come back down, but he could tell she was angrier than he liked. Stuart was sure she was serious about the beating she threatened. He knew she could never act on it, though, not for someone of his social level. He also knew that he had more news she was certain not to like.

"Ma'am, I would love to, but Captain Teach ordered me to inform you that you are to report immediately to the bridge to help investigate the problem with the sensors," he said as quickly and succinctly as he could manage through the still closed hatch, feeling no need to hide his slight grin.

Deathly quiet came in response to his statement. Omundson waited for a good thirty count before beginning to repeat himself.

"Ma'am, I was told--"

"I heard you, Ensign," again there was a long silence. Omundson waited as quietly as he could this time, deciding against the idea of attempting to prompt a response from her. "Tell the captain that I will be on the bridge momentarily," she finally seethed through the barrier.

"Yes, ma'am. I will let him know, ma'am," he said quickly as he headed back to the bridge.

Inside the berth, Leung swore under her breath. "What a blazing, bloody mess," she said a little louder. She looked at herself, unshod but still in a rumpled uniform. She knew she had better clean up a bit, even if it took her a few more minutes to present herself to the mighty Captain Teach.

She disrobed quickly and blearily headed into her private shower, one of the perks of being a senior officer, and quickly flicked the single lever over to full. A polar blast of ice water hit her at full strength in the face. She was too shocked to move for a moment, but then flailed at the controls to shut off the water. She could feel the anger which had been smoldering within her catch flame. She was wide awake now.

A few minutes later, she was fuming her way through the corridors of *Pathfinder* and heading directly to the bridge. She had clipped her damp hair back behind her head to get it out of her way, and donned a fresh service uniform, knowing that she would probably be in it for more than three standard shifts.

She reached the massive battle armor portal, keyed entry swiftly and almost walked right into the closed hatch that had not opened. Angrily, she reached over and keyed entry again. Nothing happened. She keyed her code a third time paying close attention that the system gave the "green-light" recognition, thus ensuring her code was still a valid one, but nothing happened. The system appeared to be granting her access, but the hatch was not opening. She seethed as she slapped the control unit and attempted a third time to open the bridge portal. When the doorway failed to open the fourth time she commed Omundson and asked him in deadly calm monotone if he was on the bridge, when he replied he was, she ordered him to get over to the hatch and see if he could open it.

A few seconds later the hatch slid open, a somewhat bewildered Omundson standing on the other side of it. She shouldered past him and moved onto the bridge.

"Lt. Commander Leung, reporting to the bridge as ordered, sir." She said it quickly enough that Teach may or may not have missed the fact the she did it through barely unclenched teeth.

"About time, Leung. Every sensor is now dead," Teach said from his position at the Cartography and Sensors station. Omundson had now recovered sufficiently that he was almost back at his duty station at Cartography. "What was that business with the hatch? Did you forget your code or something?" he continued in an almost sneer.

She bit back a flaming retort and moved over to see what they were looking at.

"The hatch has an issue, it apparently won't open to a code from the outside, or at least not to mine. I will take a look it after we resolve this issue," she finally said.

Leung checked the sensor system display, which showed every single external sensor dead. She motioned Omundson out of the way and input some basic queries. The diagnostic suite showed the sensors were actually out – completely offline. It wasn't possible for them to have all been damaged. The odds of something like that, even in the middle of an asteroid field, were incredibly unlikely. With the way *Pathfinder*'s sensors were arrayed, the ship would be structurally unsound and coming apart at the welds if every sensor had been damaged by external objects.

There had to be a glitch in the sensor collection system or software. That was what made the most sense. The problem was her system queries and tests proved her wrong.

"Captain, I need some more hands over here," she said almost absently as she shifted fully into her detached "Chief Engineer with a problem to solve" mode. She was still angry, but it was a distant anger now. This was a bigger issue than she had assumed it was.

"Omundson, get Goodwin and Sullivan up here right now!" Leung said as she turned to Teach and motioned him away from the station he was at. "Giannini, get over here – sign off of Engineering, I need you over here."

"This is that bad, isn't it, Leung?" Teach asked as he let her take the main sensor console from him.

"Yes it is," she said flatly.

"I'll be at my station. Keep me informed on the progress, Commander," he replied as he headed back to the captain's chair. He didn't know how or why, but he could feel that this was something deliberately perpetrated by someone. It was possible it was another of Brighton's plans within plans in the advanced protocols he had enabled to lock the ship away from them. He wasn't sure it wasn't someone else aboard, though.

Katherine Leung was a good engineer. You didn't get to be Chief Engineer on a Warner black project if you weren't. She knew every system aboard *Pathfinder* as if she personally had designed them. Unfortunately, that didn't help her figure out how to fix something that was theoretically impossible to break. Leung knew that there was no way for the system to allow her to power off every single external sensor on the ship even if she wanted to. Somehow the entire system had shut itself down. The problem with that situation was that since it was not supposed to be able to do what it had done, there was no easy way to undo it.

Leung spent the next several hours working with Goodwin, Giannini and Sullivan all over the ship, checking sensor wiring and power connections in various parts of *Pathfinder*. After nearly four hours of troubleshooting, she had taken OOD from Teach as he went on his tour of the ship. She had slaved all of CartSen to the command console and continued working from there. She had managed to nod politely to Omundson in response to his proffered, "Good luck with this one, ma'am. I wish I could be of some help," as he left, rather than delivering the backhand she wanted to.

When Samuels took over Astro from him, Leung realized that it must be 16:00, since second watch had now taken the bridge. Teach had relieved her as OOD at 06:00, and she had been back on the bridge by 08:05. That meant that she was now in the eighth hour of this process. At 16:20, Sullivan found something in one of the aft relay stations that got Leung's problem solving brain moving in a different direction.

Thirty minutes later, Leung called over the comm system for all three of them to close the relays they were finished reworking, and to stand by for power-up. She energized the sensor grid and, one by one, the sensors came back online and began sending the surviving buffered data and the live data as well.

Leung sat back in the captain's chair as she watched the system for any signs of problems now that all the sensors were functional again. After ten minutes of solid data coming in from the entire sensor suite, she commed the three who had been working with her.

"Good work, everybody. It looks like we have the sensors back online and they look to be staying stable," she said. "Please stand by for another ten minutes and then return to your duty station for this shift. Bridge out."

Leung waited a moment, then commed Captain Teach. She got the blip indicating the captain was out. She recorded, "Sensors are back online," and disconnected.

Katherine felt herself just barely beginning to relax from the tension of the last hours. She eased into a more comfortable position, just becoming aware that she had been on the forefront of the captain's chair the entire time.

She knew herself well enough to know that she was irritable and tired. She had not had anything but momentary glimpses of sleep for so many shifts in a row that it was something of a mystery to her how she was upright. As the minutes passed, she continued to gain confidence that her changes were going to hold and the suite would stay up and operational.

Reassured, Leung began to pay a little less attention to the sensor grid and started going over all of the other OOD reports and queries that had hit her queue while she had finessed the sensors back into submission.

Leung took the time to switch the main bridge screen back to sensor suite view, showing them the virtual re-creation of the space they were traveling through. The stars and blackness were calming after the last several days, and last ten hours especially.

She took a few moments to review her logs, preparing to make new entries regarding the issues of today, when she noticed something in a security flag on a simple privacy algorithm she used. Upon investigating, it appeared that Teach had been reviewing her logs, at least daily, and that he was rather clumsily trying to cover his tracks.

Why in the world would Teach be reviewing my personal logs? Leung thought to herself. The idea led her down a track that didn't end with a pleasant thought. Katherine realized that Teach distrusted her and was trying to find out things she was working on without talking to her. There were a lot of reasons why he might be doing it, but none of them made her very happy. If he didn't trust her, and was going behind her back, she couldn't trust him either. She supposed she should have come to that conclusion already.

She found herself staring at the main screen while she contemplated this in light of everything else going on. Leung knew that she had the Conn until 18:00, when Teach would retake the fourth of their six-hour OOD watches.

She was proud of herself for not screaming at people during the sensor work. However, regardless of the outward calm she was fighting to maintain, inside, Leung was a writhing flow of furious lava. If and when her calm broke, someone was going to pay a vicious price.

Just as she reclined into the captain's chair and closed her eyes to try to regain her center, she saw the lights flicker through her eyelids. She snapped her eyes open but was greeted by normal bridge lighting.

"What just happened?" she asked of the rest of the bridge staff.

Then she saw it reoccur, the entire main view screen flashed a bright yellowish light and went back to the virtual space view.

"What was that, ma'am?" Hilary Calvi asked from Helm.

Leung didn't respond. She was frantically digging into the sensor suite to make sure that the sensors were still passing clean data and not beginning a second meltdown. Fifteen minutes, and twenty-seven more colored flashings later, she was sure the sensor suite was fine. She had tried to toggle the main view away from the sensor grid display, but it had locked up and was unresponsive.

"Astro, can you toggle the main view to the astrocomp display, please," Leung called to Samuels.

"Aye, ma'am," Monica acknowledged the order while attempting to do just that. Several discordant bleeps followed her inputs as the system responded with a negative confirm. "Ma'am, it doesn't seem to be accepting my command to change the view. I can't push the astrocomp onto the display," Samuels called to her while urgently trying several more commands on her duty station.

"It appears to have me locked out as well, Ensign," Katherine said.

Leung had stopped trying to change the display, though Samuels was still trying, and instead the older officer began running diagnostics on the view connectivity system. The main view display on the bridge was interconnected to all of the bridge systems, so that it could be used to visually present information from any of them. If it were having problems, the root cause could be in any one of the bridge systems. Moreover, the problem could become systemic if it bridged through the misbehaving system.

Just as Leung was getting a real-time data stream on her console, the main view flashed again, only this time it started to strobe with ultra-bright white light, and then shifted into some sort of psychedelic color and a montage of swirling patterns and bright flashes.

The data feed from the connectivity system showed perfectly normal parameters and data flowing from the sensor suite to the display. Nothing was apparently wrong, according to the system.

It was all Leung could do to keep herself from screaming.

She launched herself out of the captain's seat and went straight to the Engineering station occupied by William De Saumserez, who was staring at the screen. Calvi appeared to be looking down at the floor to keep from either getting dizzy or going into a seizure.

The XO shouldered De Saumserez out of her way and popped two access panels open. She reached in and quickly identified and physically ripped out three separate cable couplings. The view display went dark and the room lighting changed back to normal as a result. Everyone on the bridge took a moment to re-adjust to the normal, consistent bridge lighting. Leung stood up and handed the shredded couplers to De Saumserez who took them without voicing the question evident on his face, "What am I supposed to do with these?"

Thankfully, he just held onto them and went back to his duty display while she moved back to the center chair.

Before Leung had seated herself, there was a noise on the other side of the bridge hatch, and Ensign Omundson commed them to please come and open it for him. Calvi moved to the doorway and opened it and Omundson came on deck.

"Ma'am, Captain Teach ordered me to report that the captain's direct comm line to the bridge is no longer functional. It stopped working about ten minutes ago. This news was delivered from his position about a meter onto the bridge, where Leung's glare had stopped him dead in his tracks.

"I cannot believe this!" Leung yelled at everyone and everything on the bridge, but was still looking directly at Ensign Omundson. "AAAAGGGHHH!" she belted out the sound as if a volcano was erupting inside her. "That is IT! Omundson, as XO of *Pathfinder,* I herby assign you as her Chief Engineer. You add Teach's comm line to your new list of everything on this bucket that has to be fixed, and you do it all!" she shouted at him.

The bridge was shocked into silence as much by the assignment as by her outrage. The silence lasted thirty seconds or so, until Omundson, still transfixed in Leung's baleful stare, spoke.

"Ma'am, may I assume that I am being promoted?" he asked, suddenly intent on her.

"What?" Leung shouted the question at him.

"Regulations specify that there shall be no department head named who shall not hold in full promotion and good standing at least the rank of Lieutenant Junior Grade," the Ensign pointed out in complete earnestness.

Leung bit her tongue. She wanted to slap him silly.

"No, Ensign, you cannot assume that. I hereby assign you as Assistant Chief Engineer, and withhold the staff position of Chief Engineer for myself. I further assign you to go see to the captain's comm line right now," she said to the cheeky bugger, knowing that he was supposed to be off duty this watch. "Now, get off my bridge and go get to it!"

"Aye-aye, ma'am," Omundson replied. To his credit, he came to full attention, executed an about face and marched off the bridge.

Leung looked around the bridge to make sure everyone was back on task. Calvi had moved back to her station completely unobserved during that exchange. Leung continued on her way to the captain's chair to figure out what in a thousand black holes had caused the display malfunction.

I swear I am going to kill somebody before the day is out. What a bloody, blazing, stinking mess!

CHAPTER 12
17 July

Ensign Monica Samuels toweled off and slipped into a clean shipsuit quickly. The simple, one-piece garment, this one a dull blue in color, was snug at the joints and loose in between, making it easy to move without restriction. They were originally designed for life on long-haul trading ships, where artificial gravity was an inconsistent luxury.

She probably shouldn't have any shipsuits in her possession, since it gave a clue to her real history, but they were far and away the most comfortable thing to wear while not on duty. Whenever she had been asked about them at the Academy, that was what she had said. A few had even been converted and had purchased their own. Fortunately, though they had originated as serviceable clothing for those who worked in space, they had caught on somewhat and now could be seen in all walks of life.

Great comfort, minimal risk, she had decided.

The gyrations necessary to get into her clothes brought Jherri Roberts' vacant bunk into her view, and the familiar guilt hit her. The bed was made with military precision, and looked the way it had when Samuels and Roberts had first arrived here. On the second day of life under the command of Captain Teach, Monica had carefully packed away all of Jherri's personal possessions into her foot locker, and stored the locker under the bed. She had immediately felt guilty about it.

That was exactly the procedure to follow if a shipmate died while on deployment, but Jherri was not dead. Monica prayed that Jherri was not dead, but packing away her friend's things made her feel like she had given up on ever seeing Ensign Roberts' smiling face again.

After two days of living with the guilt, she had unpacked everything and put it all back the way Jherri had it arranged. Then she felt guilty that her actions might betray her true feelings, and put it all back away again. So now she had avoided betraying what she was up to, but the guilt of betraying her friend was still there.

Arguing with herself that it was necessary, or that Jherri would understand and approve, didn't seem to matter.

She seated herself facing her terminal and reached into the small compartment she had hidden beneath the desk, pulling out a bundle of wires and components, all hooked together. Monica handled it gingerly and placed it carefully on the desk beside her terminal. Next, she attached the power and data leads to her system. She would need to provide a more durable casing for the unit eventually, but there was no sense covering it all up until she was sure it was working properly.

The signal she was getting in her room from the device hidden on the bridge was strong enough to serve its purpose, she thought, but now she needed to test whether or not the data port she had constructed at this end worked.

She tapped her feet impatiently while the unit warmed up and went through its initialization process. When it was done, she fired off a simple ping test to see if a stable connection was present. The two units were tuned to the same channel, so they should have linked as soon as the unit in her quarters was activated.

There was no response on her screen. If it had been up and running the ping would have come back in less than a second. She pulled out her portable signal monitor and rechecked her previous reading. It still showed a value that should have been large enough to connect. She didn't dare make it any more powerful either, for fear of it being detected. She was taking considerable risk as it was.

She couldn't imagine that even the minimal signal she was using now would have gone unnoticed if Major Chowdhury were still on the ship in charge of security. She didn't think that Teach or Leung were paying any attention to such things at the moment, but she couldn't be certain of that.

Samuels had designed her unit on the bridge to accept outside commands, and she could program it to only broadcast on a specific schedule. Unfortunately, that left her with the choice of either setting it to transmit all night and shutting it off after connecting, or setting it to send out a signal for a short time, and increasing that if she needed to after the system was connected. The second option was the less dangerous of the two, and so that was how she had set it up.

It looked like it was a wise precaution at this point. Without a connection, she wouldn't have been able to shut it down until her next bridge shift in five hours. Of course, on the flip side of that was the fact that she only had another thirty or so minutes to figure out what was wrong before wasting this evening's window.

Methodically, she spread the components of her receiver unit out on the desk in front of her and inspected them closely for loose connections. Seeing none, she grabbed a stylus-sized multimeter from her bag and began measuring the power levels at various points. While software was the area in which she excelled, she had spent too many years surrounded by both delicate and heavy machinery on which her life depended not to know her way around solving hardware problems as well. The internal power looked right, so what was…

Aha! The signal wasn't being picked up enough to cross the detection threshold. And since she didn't dare boost the output of the transmitter, she was going to have to increase the sensitivity of the receiver. Once she knew where the problem was, the solution was easily completed; she doubled the length of her antenna and added a small 5x amplifier where it joined the rest of the unit. When she tested again, the ping returned instantaneously.

A very pleased smile crossed her features. She carefully gathered the pieces into a smaller pile, careful not to allow any of the exposed wiring to short circuit, then connected the data port to the socket she had installed for that purpose at the rear of her terminal. A few keystrokes was all that was needed to show that she had access to all the same files and systems as if she were sitting at one of the stations on the bridge.

She would have said access to everything but unfortunately that wasn't true. The lockdown that Captain Brighton had implemented while he still held the bridge excluded her right along with the bad guys. She had been puzzling about that problem for days, trying to find some way around the barriers that kept her from doing what the captain wanted her to do. The irony of the situation was not lost on her, but it hadn't helped her find an answer.

She had found an answer, though.

At least, she thought she had. She would find out before too much longer.

The first step was to change the time for her illicit data link to shut down. She was going to need more time to accomplish what she had planned. Now that she had a viable connection in her room, she knew she was too excited by the challenge to sleep now, anyway.

Next, she launched a program she had written last week and sent it searching through the data core for locked and hidden files. It was less than a minute in reporting its results, and she piped these into a filter program to sift out the two or three files she most needed.

The solution Ensign Samuels had identified attacked the problem from the flanks rather than head on. She knew that in order to get into the system, she had to have three bridge officers' security codes. There were currently only two such officers on the ship, so getting those codes from the people who held them was impossible. Cyber warfare had been her focus area at the Academy, and everything she had learned there only emphasized that there was no way through the front door for her, but the back door was still open a crack.

There was someone else who had the information she needed to unlock the system; or, to be precise, some*thing*. Those codes had to be stored somewhere in the computer system's database, or it would have nothing against which to match a code that was entered. It would be encrypted, of course. It would also be hidden from normal view, to keep people from finding it unless they knew where to look.

As she worked, Monica was bemused by the greater irony that the knowledge Warner had happily stuffed into her mind was exactly what she needed to know to be able to attack and defeat Warner's defenses.

Of course, that was why she had enrolled in the Academy in the first place. Warner had the knowledge her family had needed, and they had gone to great lengths to make it available to her even if they didn't know why she wanted it.

The sifter blipped and told her that no files met the parameters she had given it, and she cursed aloud. So much for her back door approach. Unless…

She had another thought abruptly. The database had to contain a record of the codes she needed, and it *also* needed to know where those files were. She just needed to convince it to provide her with that little tidbit of information.

Quickly, she wrote a short script to log the name and location of all files accessed by the system and launched it. Then she attempted to access an area she knew was locked out. The system asked for her command ID, and she put Brighton's designator in. She had found a file with everyone's ID designators in it. The file was useless without the individual's access codes. The computer then asked her for the

Captain's access code, which she didn't know so she put in a random string. The system politely declined to have anything further to do with her.

She disengaged that thread and checked her log. There it was, the ninth one on the list was the only one for which she couldn't identify a purpose. That one had to be the file containing Brighton's command code, in an encrypted form. Monica fired up her decryption platform and turned it loose on the file. When it was done, however long that took, it would report back.

While it was working, she repeated the process for Commander Teach, Lt. Commander Leung, Lt. Johnson, and Lt. Lamont. Those five executables churning away, she was about to disconnect from the bridge. They would keep running whether she was watching or not. She stopped herself before she did so, remembering that she needed to double check that there would be no evidence of what she was doing that would point back to her if someone noticed it.

While she was checking that, an alert hit her screen that Brighton's code had been successfully decrypted, the twenty character alpha-numeric string attached to the notice.

That was days faster than she had expected! Someone should have a talk with the admiral in charge of Naval Security. Someone besides Monica Samuels, she supposed. The other four reported their results before she had finished testing Brighton's code on the system. It worked, and so did the other four.

The unanticipated good fortune caused her to alter her plans for the night, meaning that sleep was no longer on the list at all. Sending a coded command to her bridge unit, she set it to shut off ten minutes before she would have to be at her duty station. With her time constraints removed, she considered which of the items she wanted to work on was the highest priority. She wavered between three possible ways to hamper the escape of the ship, before finally landing on a fourth.

There was still a great unanswered question in the back of Monica's mind about what had prompted Captain Brighton to send her back onto *Pathfinder*. Was she here because Captain trusted her, or because he didn't? Did he think she could stop the theft? Or did he think that she could come rescue him and the others somehow?

There was probably not much chance of discovering what he was thinking at the time. But if he had reason not to trust her, there would probably be some record somewhere. She found that it was more of a burning riddle to her than she was previously aware. With no way of finding the answer, she had buried the question and left it alone. Now that she had access, she needed to do something about it; she needed to know that answer more than she could possibly need anything else.

She took a moment to pull her hair up into a ponytail before beginning. Her drying hair was starting to become more mobile and distracting. She considered going to the galley to grab some food; she had come straight to her quarters after her shift, anxious to test her data stream; but tossed the idea out. She ought to be asleep, and she didn't want anyone to start asking questions about why she wasn't.

Using Brighton's access code, she brought up a list of both his personal and official files. She used these as the target for a grep program and searched for any reference to her first or last name in all of them. It took quite a while to read all of the references. She was pleased to see that Captain Brighton was planning to provide marks well above average in several areas. There was even a copy of a letter to Admiral Cosina recommending her to COTS! That didn't mesh very well with her memories of critical rebukes she had received from him in the past. *He thought I was ready for Command Officer Training School?* That certainly wasn't a stop on her plotted course. She had other priorities. Still, it was nice to know that he had thought so highly of her.

In no document was there any mention of suspicions Brighton had held against Ensign Monica Samuels. That was a relief, but there was still one other place she needed to check. Brighton trusted absolutely in Major Chowdhury's judgment, and Chowdhury was suspicious of everyone. You couldn't pass her in the corridor without her scrutinizing you, looking for concealed weapons or something.

Although perhaps that paranoia kept her alive when the attack finally came. From what she had gathered since the takeover, Chowdhury had been considered the biggest threat, and six armed people had been assigned to take her out. They caught her and Burton just leaving the security suite and attacked with all the surprise and other tactical advantages on their side. Result: two dead conspirators, a broken arm, and a dislocated shoulder against a single blow to the head that knocked her out momentarily. Burton was seriously wounded in the first seconds and didn't participate in the fight. Word was that both of them would have been dead, except Chowdhury was not surprised at all.

Chowdhury was not the sort of person you wanted to underestimate, by any means.

The problem was, though, that the Marine computer system was almost entirely isolated from the rest of the ship. The command codes she already had would not do a thing to get her access to that system.

The good part, if you could look at it that way, was that Chowdhury had made her nervous as soon as Monica joined the crew. This was not the first time she had wanted to check up on what the Marines were doing, so some of what she needed she already had. She had found a datapath between the two systems, so she had a way in, and she had a way to mask her accesses so the Marines wouldn't see them. It probably didn't matter now. She wasn't sure if Aichele was allowed access to the Security computer network and Burton was unconscious in Medbay. There was no one left to find her fingerprints in the security system.

What she didn't have was a way to log into Chowdhury's account to be able to view her files.

Wait... There was one thing she now had access to that she hadn't had before – the major's personnel jacket, the file that contained her history in the Marine Corp, was stored with the naval crew's so that the captain and executive officer had access to it.

She pulled another tool out of her virtual bag of tricks. The personnel jacket went in one end, a list of possible passwords was generated in the middle, and then the possibilities were tried against the account log in. She set it running and waited.

It was a long wait. She had dozed off twice, and at the second time she was again considering going to the galley for something to eat. It was almost late enough in her off shift that she could probably do so without arousing suspicion, and the walk there and back would help wake her up.

Monica eventually decided that was the most efficient thing to do, she wasn't accomplishing anything as it was. She did take the time to dress in her uniform and do her hair before she went out. After eating a filling breakfast of wheatcakes and eggs, she was back in her quarters within twenty minutes.

The chime that announced success came ten minutes after that. It turned out that Chowdhury's password was a combination of her sister's name, the date she was admitted to Elite Corps, and the serial number of the rifle she had checked out the night of the coup on Humboldt; in reverse order.

Hardly a simple matter to guess; it was impossible but for the fact that she had unlimited access to the complete records of her life. With the way open for her now, she moved through the various levels of files looking for anything that looked like official logs or investigation files. Monica tagged any folders that looked remotely related, and then fired up her search tool to scan for her name again. Surprisingly, there was only one entry:

"Typical ensign," it read.

Samuels was not too pleased with the impression she had apparently failed to make with the Marine, but better that than if she had done something to cause the security officer to think twice about her.

She started backing out of the system, but stopped abruptly at a folder titled 'cyberwar.' She couldn't pass that up without taking a look, and the sheer volume of information, once she began looking, was almost overwhelming. There were folders with data mining software, viruses, antiviruses, worms, crowbars, pills, and crystal walls. She delved into them to see if she could pick up any tricks she hadn't already learned, and was shocked to learn that, compared with Major Chowdhury, she was little more than a babe in the woods.

Much of the coding she couldn't follow. Some appeared to be set to do things that were clearly impossible, or so she had believed. Her last thought, before her timer disconnected her was, *Oh, that's nasty.*

CHAPTER 13
18 July

Lieutenant Merissa Smiley woke up with a headache. She had done so every day since the takeover, but at least they seemed to be getting less debilitating. Smiley was not her real name, but it had become a comfortable default persona. Smiley had been the first cover she had adopted within the Warner Marines, and the combat and stealth skills she had self-programmed were always comforting to have close at hand.

Her real name was Stassia, but that was a persona she hadn't visited in so long, she wasn't sure it still existed. Out of curiosity, she peeked and found that Stassia was doing just fine. She always had been meek and patient. Merissa said a silent hello and put her back to bed.

If ever there was someone born to work under deep cover, it was Stassia/Merissa. Her superiors had always been pleased and impressed with her ability to maintain cover no matter how difficult the situation. If only they knew how natural it is to become someone else for one who had struggled with multiple personality syndrome since puberty. The hypnotic techniques she had learned to help control her condition turned out to be just as useful in creating entire personalities with hidden instructions. Such a person could endure torture, and had on three occasions, without revealing anything at all, because that person knew nothing about the mission. There was never a slip-up where she stepped out of character, because she *was* the character.

This one particular talent had led to a long and successful career for her. Never before had there been the slightest hiccup in carrying out her mission objectives. The string of successes had brought her notice, and increasingly difficult assignments. Until this one; the most difficult, and the first hiccup.

Hiccup didn't begin to cover the enormity of her predicament, actually; Grand Mal seizure would be a closer analogy. To make her predicament worse, she didn't even know how it had come about. Part of the limitation of her method of undercover work was that when the assignment was over, the hypnotically inserted instructions triggered, and she would cease to be her cover persona. She would return to being Merissa Smiley. As Smiley, she had no memory of any events that had transpired while she was someone else. She managed to avoid problems by leaving hypnotic compulsions to keep a copious journal, and sometimes her cover identities had to send in interim reports that they neither understood nor remembered.

Her assignment here on *Pathfinder* was far from complete, so she should not have awakened yet. She should still be someone else. Clearly, something had happened that caused the programming to fall apart, and that something had coincided with Teach taking over the ship. She had no idea what that trigger might have been.

Whatever it was, it was undoubtedly the source of the mind-jarring headaches she'd been suffering. They made it hard to think, hard to move, hard to do anything at all. Much as she wanted just to bury her head under her pillow until the pain relented, she knew that people back home were still counting on her to fulfill her primary mission and keep *Pathfinder* safe.

Merissa had tried to piece together what had gone wrong, replaying past events as far as she could to look for some subtle clue. For her, the assignment had started with an urgent summons to Colonel Valencia's office.

* * * * *

Colonel Stefan Valencia sat back down in his own chair and watched her for several moments. Merissa had known the Marine colonel for many years, dating back to when he was still a captain working in the field, rather than the head of Covert Intelligence.

"Thank you for coming in so quickly," he said finally. "I know that you had several more weeks of leave coming to you but we've had a bit of a situation come up."

"It is not a problem, sir."

"Be that as it may, I appreciate your rapid response."

She nodded slightly.

"Here is the documentation on Project Argo," he said as he slid a folio chip across the desk to her. She reached out and caught it as it came to a rest in front of her. "This is 'eyes only,' so you will need to read it in the outer office before you go. The folio is not to leave this office."

He waited for her to nod before continuing. "I'll let you get the details from the file, but the final crew transfer is tomorrow morning and I need you to be on the shuttle."

"Yes, sir. Any details that are not in the file?" she asked, holding up the chip.

"A few. First, and most important, you are to remain covert at all costs. Two officers are already dead and your primary function is to find out what is going on and report back. You will stay covert, no matter what else is going on around you. Major Chowdhury has been assigned as the head of the shipboard security detachment, but they are very understrength. She is replacing Lt. Sepulveda, who was killed with Captain Vanderjagt in a shuttle crash. I suspect it was not an accident. You will run a concurrent investigation, but you will not inform Security of your identity."

Her eyebrows went up slightly at this addition.

"What if I'm captured as a spy by Security?"

Valencia snorted. "In that unlikely event, you will stand court-martial in your cover identity and get sent back to Earth to serve your sentence. We'll get your report at that time."

"And get me released as well, I trust."

"We will make every attempt to do so, yes," he added with a barely suppressed smile.

"You will also find," he continued, all business once again, "when you read the details of the project, that successful completion will be of enormous benefit to Warner, but the opposite holds equally true. If the project fails, it will be a serious blow to the Family. If the technology we have been working on were to fall into the hands of another Family, they would be able to circumvent a major source of the Family's income, perhaps enough to destroy us.

"It is of paramount importance that you do not let that happen. Is that understood?"

"Yes, sir. Do not let the technology out of our control, and remain covert to everyone but you."

He nodded acceptance of her understanding. "Your cover ID is included in the folio. Memorize everything and be on that shuttle at 07:00."

"Yes, sir," she said, recognizing her dismissal.

After an hour or so intently studying the information given her, she had left the office, packed her things, slept, and reported as ordered at the appointed time. Smiley hoisted her duffle onto the stack being loaded onto the shuttle and joined the queue forming at the security barrier. Most of those already in the line were officers just barely younger than she appeared herself. Though she was actually older by at least a decade. The four huddled together near the front were clearly newly promoted ensigns, just out of the academy. A fifth ensign stood to one side as if he were not associated with the others, though he wore the same sparkling new rank pin as they did. Several enlisted crewmen were standing in a knot to one side and talking loudly to each other.

The tall Marine Gunnery Sergeant at the barrier asked for the ID packet from the first ensign in line. The young woman noticed that the electronic sign above the Marine's head was blank instead of showing the ship's name as was customary. The stunningly beautiful young officer handed over her packet and waited while it was examined.

"Everything is in order, Ensign Roberts. Standing orders are to report to the XO at 15:00 after you have settled in. Your berth is on Main Deck, A6," he said without consulting his datapad.

"Thank you Gunny," she replied in a clear firm contralto. She moved through the hatch and the next ensign stepped forward and handed over her packet.

"Everything is in order, Ensign Samuels," The NCO said after a moment. "Standing orders are to report to the XO at 15:00 after you have settled in. You are also in A6 on Main Deck. Welcome aboard."

She noted that even now, the grey haired non-com did not name the ship. Security was very tight and they were taking no chances here on dockside.

No major clues there. Fast-forward through the short transport flight as well. She had had several days to get to know all the officers and crew being assigned to Project Argo. The XO had briefed everyone at 15:00, and she had to act surprised to learn the name of the ship and purpose of the assignment.

The flight from Earth to Betre had taken almost six days. She had been very friendly to all of the new crew members. You never knew when one might be a potential source of information. Especially those young Ensigns.

And then, four hours before docking with *Pathfinder*, Smiley had submerged herself into her new role and went to sleep.

She didn't remember anything else.

* * * * *

Smiley sat up as her memories ended without giving a clue to her present state. She moved carefully and quietly, getting out of her bunk and into her clothes. There were two others still sleeping, and she hoped to leave them in that state. She had just met them since the take-over and she was still feeling her way through what her relationship was with the crew. Or what it had been under her cover identity. Besides the three of them, the room housed three others that were currently working on the repairs that dominated their lives. She slipped on the soft-soled shoes of her work uniform and moved out of the quarters without a sound.

This morning's task was aimed at figuring out what had happened; hopefully as it related to her constructed identity, but the clue she had left herself could lead almost anywhere. She'd find out soon now.

Her memories were not very sharply defined when she transitioned from one personality to another. She remembered programming the details into her portable unit, taking the correct drugs, and starting the automated process. Then fuzziness similar to falling asleep, and more fuzziness as she woke up in a locked room. Someone came for her not long after and ordered her to work. With no understanding of the situation, and more than a little disoriented with headaches, she did her best to keep her head down and just go along until she could figure things out.

Several people tried to talk to her, which was awkward. She had no memory of these people as anything but personnel summaries in her mission briefing. Should she be friendly, guarded, antagonistic? She didn't know, so she opted for withdrawn, hoping that recent events would be blamed for any perceived discrepancies with what would have been normal for her.

While she had been working, she discovered a video chip in her pocket, and she hoped it contained information that would help her. Unfortunately, in order to view it, she needed to find both a time and a location where she could do so without any chance of discovery. Her own quarters would not do. Even when empty, there was always the chance that someone would enter. That was the reason three weeks had already passed and she was still in the dark. People were always watching, and her primary mission was to stay covert.

She had, almost on impulse, disabled the engine coolant monitor a few weeks back. That had been a reckless act, and since then she had been more deliberate in her approach. There had been four other opportunities she had manufactured for disabling equipment, some large and some small, all aimed at keeping the ship out of enemy hands.

The corridors were all deserted at this time of night, as she expected. There was a faint odor of ozone in the air, a residue from the plasma torch used earlier in that area. The scrubbers would pull it out of the atmosphere soon.

Moving quickly but noiselessly, Smiley descended the midships ladder to lower deck. Near the end of the first hallway, she slipped into a room that was unlocked and unattended. The placard affixed to the door announced that it contained 'Weapons Control.' She breathed a sigh of relief as the computer recognized her crew id and opened the door. It had been randomly unreliable of late. She latched the door and sat at one of the stations away from the main controls. Normally, this station was used for running simulations and training new crew, but today she hoped it would help Merissa begin to understand why she was awake.

Smiley pushed the chip into the data slot and keyed the display to the correct mode for playback. The image that appeared on the screen was dark and unfamiliar at first, then resolved itself into her hand as it drew away from the pickup. She saw herself turn away, or at least her body did, revealing the interior of a lifeboat. As she got farther away, she revealed a young man tied up in one of the chairs, Lt. Lamont. She knew him from her briefing, though they had never met.

The interview was certainly for the camera's sake; Lamont's answers were given quickly enough that it was clear he was not revealing anything his interviewer did not already know. It was obvious that some type of drug was used to get at the truth. Equally obvious was that this recording was not meant to help Smiley figure things out, but as evidence to be presented in a military court.

For the most part, Lamont was allowed to tell his story as he wished, but occasional questions clarified or elaborated on certain points. Lamont was the third person involved in the plot to steal *Pathfinder*, the first two being Teach and Leung. Teach was the leader of the secret cabal, and Leung had made contact with the Forrest Family to find someone willing to buy the ship and her secrets. Teach and Leung had gathered a good portion of the crew to their side with promises of riches and a new life. Smiley's voice asked for their names, and they were rattled off methodically, by order of rank.

The takeover was set to happen in two more days. They would take Captain Brighton in his quarters and get him quietly off the ship. Major Chowdhury was the next greatest challenge, and the plan called for stunning her in her sleep, and then also taking her off the ship in one of the pods. From that point, they had three officers to transfer command to Teach, which the computer would duly recognize. The rest would simply be mopping up details.

Smiley heard her own voice asking Lamont why he had been inside one of the lifeboats, and Lamont responded that he had been disabling their communications in order to make good their escape with the ship before there was any pursuit. Something about the way his eyes moved set off alarm bells for her. That last answer was a lie, or at least not the full truth. She wished she'd been awake for this, because the interviewer accepted the answer given and moved on to something else. There was only so much programming you could put into hypnotic suggestions, after all.

The feed ended shortly thereafter. A second of black screen passed and then a new scene was shown, this one facing the hatch leading to an escape pod.

"Colonel Valencia," she watched herself saying, "I will forward a copy of the preceding confession to you at my first opportunity, as it relates to the other parts of your current investigation, and provides the names of agents within the Forrest Family that should be flagged by your office.

"In order to maintain my cover, I was forced to eject Lt. Lamont's pod from the ship. He will undoubtedly wind up on Antoc-A3 and can be collected there. My next steps will be to safeguard the ship by bringing this information to the attention of Major Chowdhury and—"

The speaker stopped abruptly and her face pinched up. Her hands flew to her temples and a low moan escaped past her slack jaw. A tear slipped down both cheeks and she looked around herself, confused about something. Then she saw her own hand approaching the video pickup, then blackness.

CHAPTER 14
18 July

"What the blazes?" Lieutenant Merissa Smiley swore under her breath. "What the deuce was that?"

She hit the upper left button on the control panel and accepted the vid chip as it slid out of the port. As with many investigations, the revelation she had just received carried with it more questions than answers. The playback did, as she had been hoping, record the events that triggered the collapse of her cover identity. Unfortunately, she had watched it happen, and she still didn't know what the cause was.

Smiley racked her brain trying to understand it. Was there something that happened outside the field of the recorder's view? Had she just done a poor job constructing the identity, and it happened to unravel just then?

She levered herself out of the seat and moved back into the corridor. There was no time to waste at the moment. The longer she was out of her bed, the greater the risk of discovery. The passageway was still deserted, as she had expected. There were just as many things to repair or bypass on the lower deck as the others, but they were of a much lower priority. Nothing down here contributed to either controlling the ship or to the jump engines.

Merissa was only a few meters from the midships ladder when she started moving, and her cautious, cat-like steps made no sound at all. She crept up to Main Deck and inched herself up to take a quick peek into the hallway beyond. No one in sight.

From here, she walked more normally; moving not to avoid detection, but to avoid notice. Another two minutes and she was once again in her room, quietly slipping back into bed. The vid chip went back into its makeshift concealment in her bed frame. She would need to keep that as evidence against the thieves when they went to trial. Definitely when, and not if.

So, the best plan for her was to go back to her normal routine, keep her head down, and slow the repairs whenever she could. Her normal routine would involve sleeping at the moment, and, tired as she was, that seemed very welcome.

But she couldn't let go of the mystery that easily. Merissa lay in her bed staring at the underside of the bunk above. What had gone wrong? And why just then? She replayed the recorded events in her mind one by one to trace the logic behind them.

The first event, even before the recording began, was that she had caught Lt. Lamont and drugged him for information. In order for her to have physically restrained him, he must have represented an immediate threat to the ship, right? Her shell personality must have seen or heard something that prompted action, otherwise she would have stayed hidden and gathered information to send back to Earth.

The recording didn't say what that specific trigger had been, but it must have involved the lifepods, since that's where he was when she acted. She must have discovered him disabling the communications in the pods, interpreted that as affecting the safety of the ship, and then taken action to stop him.

Okay, logical so far, she supposed. Would broken comms in the life pods be dangerous by itself? She didn't see how, but clearly Merissa didn't have all the facts. She had been coerced out of her normal pattern by one of the priority routines being triggered. And once there, determining the extent of the danger to the ship would have been the next step; thus using the drugs from her kit.

Following that, there was the matter of Lamont being aware of her undercover status. There was another embedded routine to cover that necessity, and once activated, it required her to jettison the pod as the best means of resecuring her hidden identity.

The string of decisions seemed pretty clear to Smiley, and she was nearly at the end of her available data.

So, last step, the "Secure the Ship" routine determines that the only way for her to keep the ship out of the hands of the pirates is to talk to Major Chowdhury, who, based on everything Smiley had heard since waking up, she very much regretted never meeting.

Still, that was the end of the line, but there was nothing in that sequence that should have unraveled the whole construct like it had. It did put her identity at risk, taking the story to Security. In fact, it was almost sure to blow her cover, because Chowdhury would have asked for proof, and the proof she had would demonstrate that she was not who and what she claimed to be.

Regrettable, but not unanticipated. When Smiley had received her orders, Valencia had indicated that she had two top priorities. He had assumed, of course, that if it were a choice between the two, a good agent would simply weigh the consequences of each and act in the best possible way. That was what people do all the time, evaluate and then act.

There isn't any way to program one's self to have two top priorities, though, and Smiley hadn't tried. She'd done the evaluation ahead of time, and put the safety of the ship ahead of staying covert, exactly as her doppelganger had proceeded. So why had something gone wrong? It was frustrating, not knowing the answer to that question.

Merissa turned her head to look at the wall chrono and sighed inwardly. It wasn't worth trying to sleep now, and she doubted she could stop worrying about this enigma until it was resolved.

Okay, back to square one. From external evidence, it was the last decision she'd made that caused the breakdown. What was different about that decision?

She had decided to act against an order to remain covert. That was certainly different. But, she had allowed for that by making the ship, and the technology it represented, of higher priority than her stealth.

Had she made some drastic error in creating the "Stay Hidden" routine? Possible, but unlikely. In fact, not possible. The routine functioned perfectly just a few moments before when her other self had ejected the lifeboat, so that was working fine. The other major routine was also working fine, clearly. Both of them were working—

Smiley sat bolt upright in bed. *Nine hells!*

That was her mistake. *Stupid, stupid girl!* she berated herself.

She hadn't actually created the program to give priority to the ship. She had written the decision tree so that, if faced with a choice between staying covert and saving the ship, she would activate the "Save the Ship" routine, but she had neglected to put in a safeguard to keep both routines from being active at the same time, which is what had happened with the way events had played out.

Her carefully constructed cover identity had not been able to handle the strain of the conflicting requirements and had simply turned itself off. The true irony was that it had happened immediately before Teach and Leung had launched their mutiny, so she had been incapacitated and unable to affect the outcome. If her programming had still been in place, or even if her true personality had reasserted itself more rapidly, she might have been able to stop the takeover before Brighton and the others were set adrift in *Vanguard*. Smiley would certainly have given Chowdhury a few hours warning of what was coming. That alone would likely have saved *Pathfinder*. Her mistake had led to this state of affairs. Merissa Smiley was going to see to it that things were put right.

CHAPTER 15
23 July

Lieutenant Commander Katherine Leung awoke with a start and realized she had dozed off. Again. She had the bridge watch, for what it was worth, and she was struggling to remain awake.

Nearly four weeks ago they had taken *Pathfinder* away from Brighton and his crew. Since then, they had been flying blind with the exception of a few days, and unable to change vector due to the crippling of *Pathfinder*'s systems. The only things they were currently able to do on the bridge were to monitor communication and keep tabs on the other systems.

She wasn't sure whether or not she had slept for more than a two hour stretch since the takeover. She was trying to read the display in front of her in the captain's chair, but her vision was still fuzzy from interrupted sleep. She just needed to close her eyes for a few moments and let them rest a bit to be able to refocus. The moments stretched.

Ensign Monica Samuels noticed that Leung was nodding off in the command chair. She understood, and took a little bit of vicious delight in the fact that it seemed neither Leung nor Teach were getting any sleep. Other than the worm she had implanted in the Astrogation system, which by now had infested several layers of the command systems, she had not had an opportunity to do anything to slow the ship's repairs. She knew that she would find another favorable situation eventually, and she had plans to take advantage of it. Monica also knew that she had to be careful, since Leung and Teach probably had her on their suspect list for any problems. She was glancing over the few system reports that were still accessible when she heard the comm chirp.

"Engineering to Bridge," Ensign Omundson's voice came over the circuit.

Leung jolted awake a second time in the command chair at the sound.

"Bridge here, Ensign. Go ahead," Leung answered in a quiet, flat tone.

"Ma'am, we are ready to proceed with testing the Astrogation circuits. Request permission to power up Astro and run the full circuit test," Stuart said, his voice equal parts anxiety and weariness.

Leung glanced over at the empty Astro station. Samuels would typically be at that duty station on this watch rotation, but because of the circuit restoration and testing it was unmanned. Samuels watched Leung hit a few keys and, as Monica knew she would, Leung pulled the Astro control slave off her terminal, leaving Astro completely offline.

"Omundson, proceed to bring the circuit online. Power up Astro remotely and start the test algorithm suite," Leung said into the comm.

"Yes, ma'am, remote power up and full test suite to begin in ten seconds," he called back.

Leung, Samuels, and Calvi were the only three on the bridge currently, and they all waited as the seconds ticked away.

"Test begins in four... three... two... one." As Omundson concluded, they all turned to watch Astrogation.

The sheer volume and power of the whooshing flames that shot out of the computer and duty station startled everyone on the bridge, including Ensign Samuels.

Before anyone could even get out of their seats, Leung screamed into the comm, "Omundson, cut the power! You idiot, you started the Astro station on fire!"

Leung was keying frantically into her terminal as Samuels realized the automated fire suppression had not kicked in immediately, as it should have. Sparks continued to shoot from within the roaring flames. She checked the command system from her terminal. "Astro still powered, ma'am!" Ensign Samuels almost shouted to make sure that Leung heard her.

"Omundson! Cut the power to Astro NOW!" the XO's shrill voice demanded.

No response came from Engineering. Samuels double checked connectivity on the bridge systems. What she saw shocked her. Engineering had totally dropped off the display.

Leung jumped up, completely frustrated in her attempts to force the automated fire suppression system to kick in and ran toward one of the manual fire suppression ignitions while she shouted to Calvi to get the other one.

Samuels tried to reinitialize the connection, and got no response.

"Ma'am, Engineering is offline. I have no communication or sensor readings on the display. No datalink connection at all. I tried a system restart, and still have nothing," Samuels reported to her above the pandemonium while the other two women raced across the bridge.

Leung glared at Samuels as the fire suppressors deployed, but gave no immediate response. By the time Leung stepped around the argon fog tower surrounding Astro, her face had changed to a fierce set. "Are you telling me that Omundson can't even hear me?" she called. Leung was hurrying back to the command station. Samuels decided the question was rhetorical and remained silent.

"Ensign Samuels, cut the power to Astro from your terminal," Leung yelled.

Samuels tried to follow the order, but was thwarted in every attempt. "Ma'am, I have no access to the command protocols. I can't connect to Astro at all," Samuels called loudly back to Leung, who was almost back to her command chair.

Leung about-faced, shouted an expletive, and pulled her tunic up over her face. She threw herself down onto the floor and sprawled just into the argon cone, reaching her arms into the fog to get hold of the manual power cutoff under the station. Samuels was actually a little surprised to see how quickly the engineer was able to cut power to the station. She realized Leung probably knew where every cable, conduit and circuit in the entire ship was by now.

Leung slowly stood up and pulled her uniform tunic back into place as she returned to the command station.

"Now, Ensign, what is going on with Engineering?" Leung said more quietly, but with obvious frustration.

"Ma'am, all data and voice connection to Engineering was severed, and I can't say why," Samuels answered as calmly as she could. After a few minutes of frustrated key punching and quietly muttered oaths, Leung once again left Command and moved over to the Engineering bridge station. She spent another five minutes attempting various commands and diagnostics before declaring, "Something has to have happened on their end, Samuels. This is too screwed up to be a glitch."

The fog cone finally disappeared from Astro, and Leung glanced over at it and consequently so did Samuels and Calvi. The station was still steaming and blackened. From its appearance, there was considerable damage done. In fact, there didn't look like there was anything salvageable in the whole mess.

"I would have to agree, ma'am," Samuels replied, looking away from Astro and intently back at Leung to see how the XO would respond to this. She didn't have to wait long. Leung shook her head at the whole situation and quietly cursed.

"This is just un-bloody-believable." Leung turned to face the ensign. "Samuels, you have the bridge. I am heading down to Engineering to find out just what in blazes is going on."

Samuels keyed a temporary lock on her duty station at Cart/Sen and stood to head to Command as Leung moved to the bridge hatch. Samuels had nearly reached the captain's chair when she heard a strangled noise from Leung. She turned to see her slapping the pad at the hatch.

"Ma'am?" Samuels queried.

"The hatch seems to be glitched!" Leung screamed. "The bloody thing won't open!" Samuels checked the console at Command which said the system was working normally. She tried to force an override, which failed to even initiate.

"Ma'am, the system shows no problems, but it won't reinitiate, or even link to the hatch," Samuels reported to Leung, who was now beating the door's control system repeatedly. Katherine Leung stopped as she processed what Samuels had said. She turned back to face the bridge crew.

"Calvi, grab the tools in the emergency locker and bring them to me," Leung ordered.

"Yes, ma'am," Hilary responded as she moved quickly to comply.

"Samuels, keep trying to get the system to engage the hatch controls," Leung ordered as Calvi arrived at the hatch. Leung took off the data panel cover and peered inside.

"Aye-aye, ma'am," Samuels acknowledged and turned back to the system. She was glad both of the bridge's other occupants were behind her, so she could let a smile escape. Pleased as she was that her worm had glitched the hatch, though, she wondered about the Astro fire. That had to have been deliberate damage, and it hadn't been her doing. Someone else on the ship must also be working to slow the repairs.

But who?

As the minutes turned into hours, Leung finally gave up trying to get through the hatch. They had determined that not only had they lost comm and data connectivity to Engineering, but they had lost power to several panels on the bridge. The hatch panel was completely unpowered from the inside. There was no way for them to open the door, and they had tried everything they could think of to force it open.

It took Omundson almost two hours working on the outside panel before he had a working comm connection into the bridge so that Leung could help him work through the process to get the hatch open.

Leung was aware her watch was winding down and Teach would be coming to take his bridge shift in another two hours or so. She was furious at the turn of events, and it was not lost on her that it was not just today's comedy of errors that had her fuming. She felt like her emotions had burst into flames along with the Astro station.

It took Leung, working through Omundson, a little over an hour to get the hatch open by completely disabling the locking mechanism. Leung littered the communication with invectives directed at the incompetence of those on the other side of the door. During that time,, Leung had ordered Samuels to investigate what condition Astro was in while Calvi watched all the bridge stations, slaved to her console at Helm.

Once the hatch opened, Leung turned to Samuels and with a weary and yet still angry look said, "Ensign Samuels, *now* you have the bridge. Prepare a full report on Astro's status to present when you are relieved." With that she stormed off the bridge, shoving Omundson out of her way when he appeared before her.

"Aye-aye, ma'am, I have the bridge," Samuels responded to Leung's back.

Calvi looked at Samuels and shook her head before passing control of the rest of the systems back to Command, where Samuels now sat.

Omundson stood there at the hatch for a brief moment and glanced at Samuels, completely befuddled, before turning and following Leung down the corridor. The newly-appointed assistant chief engineer looked like his duties were starting to take their toll on him already. His eyes were red-rimmed, and his haggard features hadn't met with a razor in at least two days.

"If this ship and its crew could cause me a little more grief…" Leung muttered as she moved aft on the main deck, intent on getting down to Engineering at the rear of the ship. Her temper had not cooled when she arrived to find Crystal Giannini staring blankly at a power monitor. "What in all the stars in the galaxy are you doing?" Leung shouted, "and what in bloody blazes is going on in Engineering?"

"I'm sorry, ma'am," Giannini managed to get out while trying to come to attention. Omundson managed to catch up to Leung at this point and fell under Leung's baleful glare, which shifted to him the second he came into view.

"So nothing was done in Engineering that could have caused this?" Leung asked, making it clear she expected the truth.

"No, ma'am. One second the comm and datalink systems were tied to the bridge, the next they weren't. It happened right after the Astrogation test was started. Nobody did anything other than starting the Astro test, and I was watching the terminal when it happened," Crystal answered for both of them.

"Nothing in the Astro test should have been able to interrupt the whole communication and data array, but it also should not have been able to induce a volcano out of the duty terminal, either," Leung said, taking another moment to rake them both with her blazing eyes, pausing on Omundson to let him know that she still felt he had done something to cause this mishap. "We verified all the command systems from the bridge end and everything checked out. Can I assume that you also verified the command systems in Engineering are in full working order?" Leung paused to look at them until they both nodded that it was so. "That means something interrupted communication between the bridge, forward main deck, and Engineering, aft lower deck. The data and comm cables all run through the main relay compartment between main and lower deck. Our problem has to be in there somewhere," Leung began interpreting the situation out loud, as she often did when starting in on troubleshooting.

"What could have interrupted it, ma'am? There shouldn't be a power conduit close enough to damage any of the data-comm links, even if there were serious spikes or shorts," Giannini said, starting to dread that this had been deliberate.

"No, there is nothing close to it. That can't be what happened. We need to get in there and check it out. Crystal, you go rouse Sullivan and tell her to meet us in the aft deck exchange ladder, starboard side. We can get into the relay run section from there. Ensign, you go gather Bezates and De Saumserez. Grab the test gear as well. Tell Biltcliffe she has Engineering until one of us relieves her. I will go and get the sensor gear. We all meet there in twenty minutes," Leung ordered, motioning for Giannini and Omundson to get to it at once.

Lieutenant Commander Leung was agreeably surprised to find the whole group waiting for her when she arrived after having changed into her work fatigues.

Obviously, Crystal and Stuart had used the threat of Leung's wrath to get them moving. As she climbed down the access ladder to the small landing, she saw his disheveled look and remembered that Bezates had been on a long double shift already. He had probably been tearing systems open in Engineering, checking and double checking everything to verify that the issue was not there. Sullivan looked as if she were still a little asleep, and scared at the same time. De Saumserez, who was just finishing one full watch in Engineering, was in his coveralls and appeared to be the only one not showing any outward sign of fatigue or anxiety. He was also the bulkiest of those in this group at 140 kilos. Perhaps not the best choice to crawl through the ship's innards, but Leungs options were limited. Omundson looked exhausted and slightly manic, and Leung, with vindictive glee, thought that he might have been on duty almost as many hours in the last week as she had. A small part of her tsked at herself for enjoying his exhaustion, but there it was. Giannini, who must have grabbed a set of coveralls on her way here, looked worried and worn.

Nobody spoke as they moved quickly behind the service ladder between main deck and lower deck. The landing between decks held one of the three entrances to the relay mini-deck. It was more than a crawlspace, a 1.3-meter-high access area to service power, data, communication, environmental and other systems that ran throughout the ship. The area was big, almost the entire breadth of the ship, with lots of semi-enclosed pathways for different systems. If you needed to, you could move between these different systems' run alleys at fairly regular intervals for the entire length of *Pathfinder*.

Leung had not wanted to speak for two reasons. First, she was exhausted and still very angry. So mad, in fact, that she knew her own decisions and speech were being impacted by it. It was clear to her that this was not the fault of Giannini, or of any of these crewmen who had been in Engineering, but if Leung kept talking, undoubtedly, Crystal, Stuart or one of the other Engineering crew would get the brunt of that anger.

Second, and more important, she was almost positive this was sabotage, which meant that the external communications going offline right after they took over the ship a few weeks back had probably been sabotage as well. She needed proof, however, before she could shift to that problem full force. She was not one to act without all the facts. Engineers who make decisions without their facts straight usually cause more problems than they solve.

Leung grabbed one of the portable lights from the access panel storage rack just outside the access way and handed it to Giannini. She distributed the minicomp sensors to Bezates and De Saumserez and gave another light to Sullivan. Omundson already had one of each. She handed Crystal and Amber both toolkits as well, keeping one for herself, along with the fourth sensor.

"Make sure those lights are on and working at all times, ladies," Leung said to them while moving to the hatch. There was no telling if all the ship's internal lighting would be working, and the last thing she wanted was to get in there and have it all go out.

"Bezates and Sullivan, I want you to head up the starboard chaseway. If you find anything, you comm us and let us know. Just in case it isn't clear, we are looking for the possible cause of the loss of communication between Bridge and Engineering," the commander said in her calmest voice, pausing to let it sink in, "De Saumserez will come with me to the central causeway, where we will check the main junction. Omundson and Giannini will head to the port chaseway and check there. If we don't find anything by the time we get to the necked portion where the chaseways converge, De Saumserez will join Omundson and Giannini and they will head toward the bridge, scanning the larger causeway, and I will head to the cross paths to check them out for anything that could be causing the interference." She had divided them so that no one would be alone. She didn't know if she could trust any of them, so she made sure that they were paired with people they didn't normally associate with. Leung unholstered the sidearm she carried and shifted it to her left hand. No one else in the group was armed.

"It's possible this could be sabotage, and the saboteur may still be in there. Be sharp, and if you see someone, be careful. Comm me and I will come to you," she concluded, looking to each of them in turn. She nodded to the group and opened the access panel.

Once in the mini-deck, she hunched down and moved slowly toward the center of the ship. Behind her, she heard Omundson and Giannini moving on to the port side. Leung could also hear muffled movement as Bezates and Sullivan headed forward in the starboard causeway. Leung silently hoped they would find a simple problem with a simple solution. She wasn't betting on it, though. Their luck had been cursed since this enterprise had begun.

As she and De Saumserez approached the needed pathway, Leung watched the center wall. She had an uneasy sensation that someone or something was there. The odd angles of the equipment and conduit, combined with the placement of the lighting, made for shadowed areas. Even though there were ample light sources here, they were not overly bright. *Reminds me of my Engineering staff sometimes.* She motioned De Saumserez to stop, and she held her pistol ahead of her as she moved toward the suspect area.

She was sure she had seen something move. As she approached, she could hear something too, a muffled rustling that could be anything or nothing. She jumped across the spine of the ship and aimed her pistol at the area she had pinpointed in her mind. There was nothing but the environmental shaft. The motion had to have been a small manufacturing printout secured to a vent in the shaft. It was flapping occasionally, and as she studied it, she realized the shadows had indeed amplified its motion to alarm her.

She shook her head and moved back over to the crewman, who relaxed a little. She was glad that Sullivan was in a different causeway. If she had been here for that little episode, she might not be worth anything the rest of the day.

"All right, Will, let's go up this central pathway slowly and see where our problem is," she told him as nonchalantly as she could manage. It came out far more calmly than she had feared it would.

They moved up the causeway, taking care not to disturb the cabling as they scanned it up to the junction box. She could hear both groups nearing the same intersection. As they approached, Will's sensors bleeped a signal tone steadily, indicating that the cable breakage was near.

Leung hurried to the box, and tested the main data feed cables going into it by pulling on them slightly. There was slack. Leung's breath caught as the cables slid free from the box just as the extra light from De Saumserez' lamp caught up to her.

"Oh, ma'am..." Will's incomplete statement said volumes. The lines she had tested had been eaten through by some sort of acid. Fibers were melted, and metal was splattered in a giant mess. Leung stared at the lines with bile coming up her throat. She immediately headed over to the backup data relay junction and found the same mess. She sat there staring at the burned off cables.

She was a startled by Cody Bezates saying something from the other side of the open area. Leung's shocked and exhausted mind had missed his arrival.

"Ma'am, it's worse over here. The whole backup junction is trashed, maybe even worse than the main one," Bezates said in dismay. Leung climbed around and confirmed that statement in one glance. It had to have been a powerful acid, sprayed everywhere. It had eaten through and destroyed everything inside both boxes.

"Omundson, Giannini, come to the main junction, we found the problem," she said flatly into the comm. Her voice seemed to hold none of the dread and rage that she felt.

"Ma'am, we found something over here too. We will be up there in a few minutes," Omundson replied.

Leung cursed again under her breath. Her hope for a quick fix was not going be a reality. She sent Will, Amber and Cody to retrieve additional supplies for neutralizing and leaching out the acid puddle from the main junction as Stuart and Crystal came into view from the port side.

"What else did you find, Omundson?" she said, once he was close enough to address without shouting.

"Ma'am, the Astrogation cabling had several of these inserted in the line," he said, holding out an object.

Once she had it in her hand she knew she was looking at a burned out power amplifier, one that would produce about a twenty times gain on a power signal.

"They were all 20X?" she asked incredulously.

"No, ma'am. Two were 100X. There were five amps in all, and whoever did it knew what they were doing. The positioning and wiring were perfect for a max power gain on the circuits, and they even removed the bleed backs, cut all the connections to the redundant side to isolate the power circuits and reintroduced the feedback loops to keep power in the circuit longer than should be possible, even with the amps themselves burning out," he responded with a touch of both amazement and hysteria in his voice.

Leung's engineer's brain did the math before she could even stop herself. If they were used perfectly in sabotage, those three 20X and two 100X amps positioned that way would have sent roughly 80 million times more voltage up the power cabling than should have been sent to do the remote power-up of Astro. While a ship was resilient by design, the Astro duty station never stood a chance.

She was furious. *Who was doing this to her ship?* The more she thought about it the more she wanted his or her head.

"Omundson, we have to find this saboteur," she said to him with anger boiling over in her voice.

"Ma'am, all due respect, but in looking at this damage over here, something comes to mind," Omundson said to her as he surveyed the acid damaged junctions.

"What is that Ensign?" she asked without even really looking at him, her eyes blazing towards the amp in her hand.

"Ma'am, why would someone take the careful precision planning and execution to plant the amplifiers down here on the port side line with absolutely perfect mathematical and engineering placement for maximum power gain to completely annihilate that system, and then just spray a full canister of the most potent acid onboard onto the datalink and comm junction boxes? It's as if we are dealing with a schizophrenic saboteur. It doesn't make sense," he said trying to keep the utter confusion at what he was seeing from his voice.

Leung froze where she was. Omundson was right, and she should have seen it. Her anger was clouding everything, including her ability to think and reason through the problems they faced.

"You're right. It doesn't make sense. It doesn't make sense at all," she said. She needed to think this through and figure out what this meant. Her anger was completely handicapping her, but it wasn't going to be easy to keep it in check enough with all these issues, a saboteur on the loose, and Teach being obtuse and trying to work whatever angle he was working in the background.

They would be lucky to repair this kind of damage in a hard-pressed week rather than the hours she had hoped for. They would have to check all the wiring from the point of the sabotage to the astro comp for overloaded and burned out sections.

"What a stinking pile of horse dung!" she seethed to Omundson as she practically threw the burned out amp back at him. *Just how am I going to explain this to Teach?* she wondered. *He's going to blow a seal.*

CHAPTER 16
23 July

Lt. Commander Katherine Leung was tired. Her body was aching all over in protest of the non-stop rigors to which it was being subjected and this morning's crawl through the conduit runs had not helped. Her face was lined and the circles under her eyes seemed to grow by the minute. She wanted sleep, but the prospect seemed unlikely. She leaned her head against the bulkhead and took a long, mind-clearing breath and let it out slowly. She had thought to find Teach on the bridge since their watch had changed while she investigated the cause of the astrocomp fire, but instead discovered he had returned to his quarters after turning over the remainder of his watch to one of the bridge personnel. It was just another example of Teach doing what he wanted regardless of his expectations of others. She stood, shaking her head and straightened her tunic, then knocked on the hatch in front of her. It bore the name "William J. Brighton, Captain" which someone had tried to scratch out with a sharp instrument, perhaps Teach himself.

"What!" came the muffled response from the opposite side of the portal.

"It's Leung. We have a situation," she said tersely. She did not want to have this conversation through the bulkhead.

The hatch slid open to reveal Captain Teach in a rumpled uniform. His bleary eyes looked at her accusingly and he snarled, "What's the problem? Can't you take care of anything?" He continued without waiting for a response to his rhetorical question, "I have just barely gone off watch and you refuse to allow me any sleep."

Join the club, she thought. Instead of answering, she tossed him the data cables that she held in her fist and strode past him into the room. *Was he about to shut the hatch in my face?* she wondered.

"We just found those in the main data junction. Someone has sprayed an acid on the leads and corroded the terminals. Every cable going through the main box looks the same. They're useless and we don't have enough replacements for these fiber optic connections after running new lines all over the ship. We also found a feedback loop that caused the surge to the Astrocomp. The wiring and power connections we should be able to rebuild, but it will take time. The rebuilt Astrocomp looks like a total loss. We will need to build another, from spares this time. It will take much longer that way." She watched his face very closely for any evidence that he knew more than he was sharing with her.

"Who did this? What are you doing about it? This is the third instance of sabotage in the last few days. Obviously, we didn't get all of Brighton's cronies off the ship with him," he said in a rush.

"That much is obvious," Leung said as she sat in the armchair in the far corner of the room, ignoring his dark look at her presumption of familiarity. "It could be any number of people, but we need to figure out who it is, fast. We also need to get out of this system."

"I know that!" Teach screamed at her. "If I weren't surrounded by incompetence we would already be on our way."

Leung stiffened slightly at his tirade but said nothing. He was getting more and more irrational every day. It was probably just lack of sleep. Well, not *just* lack of sleep. Her thoughts went back to her earlier decision to be rid of him but her face showed nothing as she responded. "The fact remains that we need to identify the saboteur and stop these attacks."

"It's Samuels. You saw the way she was cozying up to Brighton before she left the shuttle. He gave her a mission, and she is toying with us," Teach said in a matter of fact tone.

Leung shook her head as she stood and began to pace in the small confines of the cabin. "No, she is too young and inexperienced to hide that level of cunning. Besides, she was on watch on the bridge when this happened. She never left. I have had her and Aichele watched. They were the most obvious plants because they came off the launch at the last minute. Sullivan came off the launch at the same time, but she is a dishrag. You can barely get her to quit crying long enough to finish a simple job," she said with distaste. "I checked on Aichele. He was on duty in Engineering for the last two shifts. Chin says that he never moved from his assigned duties. Burton is still shackled in sickbay. That only leaves people that we thought we could trust."

Teach did not answer immediately. A pensive look crossed his face. *Does he know something that I don't?* she wondered.

"What about Lamont?" he asked watching her face intently.

"Lamont? Lamont is either dead or gone," she replied. "Why are you so fixated on him?"

He stood there without moving, breathing heavily. He finally moved to the intercom on the desk and flipped it to ship-wide announcement.

"Bezates and Danis to the captain's quarters," he said tersely and sat in the desk chair without another word.

They arrived together, as they often did. When they had been admitted to his cabin, Captain Teach described the situation and what he had in mind. "Danis, you are now in charge of Security, with Bezates as your second. I want this saboteur found. I don't care what it takes."

Ben Danis was a large man. Judging by the evident aging on his worn features and the fact that his hair had turned completely gray, he was well past his century mark in age. His face showed every thought that passed through his mind. He was straightforward, blunt and always took the brute force solution to any problem. This is why he still held the rank of Petty Officer First Class despite his many years in fleet. He was not the sort of person that Leung would have chosen for the complicated task of ship security, but perhaps he could be effective in the role of saboteur pursuit. Bezates, on the other hand, was small, wiry, young, and an exact copy of his friend in demeanor and thought.

"You have two days to show results, and I want no further incidents in the meantime. Is that clear?" Teach continued.

"Yes, sir," they replied in unison while looking at each other in slight confusion.

"Dismissed."

Leung waited until they had closed the hatch behind them before turning on the captain. "That was a ridiculous waste of time. Neither one of them has any experience in security. They would have to be lucky to find vacuum outside the hull."

"The most important factor is that I know they are loyal. Danis is bright and sneaky enough to trap the one responsible for this. I am the captain and I know what is best. The fact that you are not qualified for command makes it difficult for you to be able to evaluate the situation properly. Those are my orders. You are dismissed."

Leung stood from the seat that she had reclaimed while waiting for the crewmen and stared at the captain. She ground her teeth while regretting that she had ever made mention of her rejection letter. Finally, she got control of her rising rage and exited the cabin.

Something strange is going on here, she thought as the hatch slid shut behind her, *and I'm going to get to the bottom of it before I kill him.*

CHAPTER 17
23 July

Ben Danis strode down the passageway from Captain Teach's cabin toward the boatbay and its access to Engineering. His shoulders were arched forward and his stride was quick. He looked at his friend and finally shook his head. His sudden stop caught Bezates by surprise and he had to pull back as he overran his partner.

"We're way out of our depth here, you know that, right?" Danis asked.

"What do you mean; it's pretty obvious who it has to be," Bezates replied.

"How do you figure?"

"Well, it has to be Aichele," Bezates added in a tone that indicated that it should have been obvious as they started moving to Engineering once again.

"Hmmph. Why Aichele? He wasn't anywhere around Engineering today," Danis responded carefully.

"Come on, he used to work for Chowdhury. Do you think he's just going to throw in with us? Look what Chowdhury did to Carl and Glenn. Do you think she would keep anyone around who would turn on her?"

"You might have a point, but he was still nowhere around the last damage. Just because he might not be totally committed to our cause doesn't mean he's guilty."

"Who else is there? Sullivan? Samuels? Omundsen? Don't make me laugh. None of those three could stay hidden for long enough to pull off any one of the jobs, let alone all three. If it's not Aichele, then who is left?"

"It's funny that you should talk about staying hidden," Danis added. "What do you think of the rumors about Lamont?"

Cody Bezates stopped dead in his tracks and turned to look at his friend. Danis' blunt features showed a mixture of skepticism and patience. "You can't be serious," Bezates responded. "We've searched the ship four times. If he were here, we'd have found at least some evidence of him."

"Not if he were actively trying to hide from us."

"Oh, come on, Ben. There is absolutely no proof of that."

"I was talking to Terry last night and he said Leung had him looking for Lamont before we even took over the ship," Danis added warily. "Why would she do that? Maybe he was already in hiding from her. That's what Terry thinks, anyway. He heard Teach and Leung talking about finding his passcodes in the computer, logged in as entering offices at times when no one else was around."

"No one can get into the computers to access the logs," Bezates countered.

"Hmmph. So we are told. Do we know it for a fact?" Danis turned the corner and took the cross corridor to the starboard passageway instead of continuing into the boatbay.

"Where are we going?"

"To where we can find some answers." Danis responded cryptically. Bezates followed him past the galley and back forward to the end of the corridor. As they neared the spot Danis had in mind, the walls showed evidence of some sort of altercation. The paint was blistered and blackened on the wall next to the door labeled Security and there were brown stains smeared on the deck and walls, as if someone had tried to clean up a large amount of blood and hadn't done a very thorough job of it.

Danis reached up and pressed his thumb to the lock screen at the right side of the hatch. The lights cycled three times across the top of the screen and then flashed red.

"Blast, the captain didn't change the codes to allow us access."

"Ben, he only assigned us to security five minutes ago. Do you want me to go ask the captain about it?" Bezates offered with an overly serious expression on his face.

"Very funny. Hold on." He slid his thumb along the outer edge to activate the comm panel.

"Bridge, Ensign Samuels," came the response after a few moments.

"Ensign Samuels, this is PO First Danis. The captain has assigned me and PO Bezates to deal with security but we are locked out of the security office. Could you override from up there and let us in?"

"Hold on, I need to get authorization from the captain," came the response after a long pause.

"Okay, ma'am, we'll wait here. Could you make sure we have access to the security computers also?"

"If I get the captain's authorizations, then yes; but I don't know how much functionality they have."

"Understood, ma'am."

After almost twenty minutes the intercom chirped.

"Danis," the big man replied after standing from his temporary seat on the deck.

"Okay, Petty Officer, you should have access now, but the rebuilt command system is still unreliable. Could you try it and let me know for sure?"

"Yes, ma'am," he replied and pressed his thumb once again to the lock screen. This time it cycled through the light sequence only once and promptly the hatch slid open to let them in. He confirmed his access to the young bridge officer and then motioned Bezates into the suite in front of him.

The sight that confronted them stopped them in their tracks for a heartbeat. No one had been in the security office since the takeover. The outer door had been one of the casualties of Captain Brighton's lockdown. No one had been able to override it until the main computer had been rebuilt. So the interior still looked as pristine as it had on the morning of the takeover. The visual comparison to the rest of the ship was striking, especially when the compartment was entered from the site of the only bloodshed of that day.

Security was divided into several different areas. The common area nearest the door held six workstations, with a glassed-in office for the section head at the back. Inside the office, on the forward wall, was an access hatch that led to the armory. There was a second hatch in the corridor to the armory, but so far it had resisted all efforts to break the access codes. Not even the captain currently had access to that compartment. The Security Officer's quarters were located to starboard of the office, with a hatch leading to it in the center of that wall.

Opposite the armory was the brig. It was a small compartment, meant to hold prisoners, if such were ever necessary. Next to the brig entrance was a passageway that led around the brig to the Security NCO berthing, the aft-most of the rooms in the suite.

Danis moved to the nearest workstation and sat down in front of the console. They were more likely to find useful equipment in the section head's office, but neither of the new operatives even considered that option. Given the fact that Major Chowdhury had been the head of the security detachment, and that she was also the one responsible for the blood splashed across the corridor outside the hatch, neither crewman was anxious to try to enter her inner sanctum and find out what security measures she might have thought were necessary to protect her secrets.

"Go check those storage cabinets for anything that we can use while I see if I can get into the computer logs," Danis ordered as he sat at the empty desk.

His thumbprint and log-in were successful and the screen lit up. The icons on the screen were unfamiliar and not labeled in any way. Danis sat and stared at them for a few seconds trying to decipher their meaning. Finally, shaking his head, he hit one at random. The screen flickered briefly and lit with what appeared to be vid files of various locations on the ship. Each had a timestamp that was several months old. He exited that file and hit another icon at random. This one showed a list of encrypted files that failed to open to his password. He set those aside for later. He had no experience with encryptions, but maybe Bezates could make something of them. He always claimed he could scam any game.

"Ben, check this out. Are these what I think they are?" Bezates asked holding up several small disks. They were round, about two centimeters across, and not quite flat. Each had a slight blister-like dome in the middle.

"That depends, what do you think they are?"

"These look like the descriptions I've heard of surveillance spy-cams, but I've never seen one."

"I'm sure that is terribly exciting, but it doesn't help us right now. Put those away and come help me with these logs."

"You just got done telling me to search these storage cabinets. Make up your mind."

"Hmmph. Just get over here," Danis said, indicating the console next to his with a sigh of exasperation, "and see if you can break into these encryptions."

Bezates put the spycams back into their box with obvious reluctance and sat down at the console.

Danis stood in frustration and began pacing. Finally, he took up where Bezates had left off and started rummaging through storage cabinets. The spycams, he found, were labeled with the same icon that he had seen on the screen that he hadn't recognized. Could those hold security vid files from other spycams already in place around the ship?

Danis continued to search through the bins, but he did not find anything else that was immediately useful. As he searched, he could hear Bezates humming that mindless tune he always used when he was really concentrating. *I really hate that song,* Danis thought, not for the first time.

Danis stood and brushed off his hands and started to move to the last cabinet when he heard Bezates go quiet. He looked to his friend, who was sitting at the console and leaning back in his chair.

"What's up?" Danis asked

"Wha… Oh, I was just thinking, we ought to move into these rooms. They're a lot bigger than our spaces in crew quarters."

"I think, if we don't find something to take to Captain Teach, our new quarters are going to be on the outside of the airlock." Danis snapped, trying to put as much heat into his words as possible. *Blast you, Cody; can't you take anything seriously for more than a few minutes?*

"Oh that," Bezates responded with a negligent flip of his wrist, "I think I have plenty to keep him happy for a while. Look at this."

"What is it?" Danis snapped again.

"Well, this column shows all of the access coded entries to all spaces on the ship," he said, pointing to the first column as Danis moved around to a point where he could see the screen. "I couldn't get it to give me the actual codes themselves, those would have come in handy, don't you think? Imagine we could go …"

"What does this show?" Danis growled, really beginning to lose his patience.

"What? Oh yeah, this first column…"

"Yeah, you covered that. WHY DO WE CARE?!"

"Well, these entries represent access by Lt. Lamont, after the take-over," Bezates grinned, knowing he had pushed Danis over the edge yet again.

"Really?" Danis asked, his anger evaporating.

"Yes, but the best part is this line," he said indicating the second column. "These three are Commander Leung's codes. This puts her in the same room at the same time as Lamont."

Danis stood upright, stunned. *That little witch, she's in it with him. Whatever 'it' is*, he thought. All he said aloud was, "We've got to get these to Captain Teach."

CHAPTER 18
27 July

Captain Teach sat in the command chair on the bridge of *Pathfinder* and surveyed his crew moving about their duties.

He felt good.

There had been no further acts of sabotage in the last four days, showing he was right to put Danis in charge of security. The mood on the bridge was peaceful and quiet. All here were happy that there had been a change in command. Leung was still constantly challenging his authority and questioning his decisions, but he was always proven right in the end. Even thoughts of Leung cowering in the engine room plotting against him could not tarnish the contentment he was feeling.

He glanced around the bridge to where Goodwin and Young were working on rebuilding the Astrocomp for the second time. He frowned at that thought, but not even the engineering woes and the computer issues were enough to dampen his euphoric mood.

Brighton was stranded on the third planet of this system's main component. It was a fitting punishment for usurping the command that had rightfully belonged to Edward Teach. The fact that Brighton had not been fit for that responsibility was proven by the fact that he had not been able to hold it in the end. Leung still felt the need to challenge him, but she had not even been capable of organizing the action that led to the taking of the ship. She had dithered and wandered around looking for Lamont, while Teach had done all the work.

Command belonged to those who had the proper abilities and intelligence. Warner Space Navy would pay the price for snubbing him.

He leaned back in *his* chair and smiled.

After a time, Teach leaned forward and watched his crew carefully. They appeared to be busy, but they didn't seem to be accomplishing anything. That was not acceptable. *We have to work hard if we want to reap the rewards*, he thought.

"Omundson, what is the status of all weapons systems?" he called to the tall, perfectly dressed ensign who sat at the weapons console to his left. Weapons control had returned after the main computer was reinitialized several days ago, and the young ensign was still learning his duties there.

"Sir?" came the shocked squeak in return. The lanky ensign still seemed uncomfortable with his superiors and he tended to fluster easily. He was comfortable enough lording over his peers and underlings, however; at least those were the reports Teach had heard.

"Are you manning the weapons board or are you asleep?" Teach called.

"I have the weapons board, sir," the Ensign replied as he started to regain some of his composure.

"Then I require an update on the status of all weapons. That is not beyond your capabilities, is it?" *Best to keep him in his place*, the captain thought.

"No, sir, all weapons are online and standing by."

"When was the last system diagnostic performed?"

"Fifty-two hours ago, sir, according to the log."

"Then how do you know that the weapons are online? Run another full diagnostic." *That will keep him out of mischief.*

"Sir," he replied with desperation in his voice, "a full diagnostic will take the weapons down for…"

"I am aware of the task parameters, Ensign. Carry on." *The insolent pup, trying to lecture me.*

Annoyed by the response from the young officer, the captain decided to reinforce his authority with the rest of the bridge crew. *I can't afford to look weak even for a moment*, he thought. Teach turned his full attention to the others. They were studiously looking at their boards and avoiding his eyes. "Giannini, what is the status of the electronics refit of those other bridge consoles?"

"Sir, it is in progress. It should be completed in about twelve hours."

"That is not acceptable. I expect the job completed within six hours."

"Sir, there are parts that we need to manu--"

"I am not interested in excuses," he snapped. "The job will be completed on time or I will deal with you." He held eye contact with her until she nodded her compliance.

"Goodwin, what is the completion time for the AO console? We need it up and running by end of watch."

"I'll do my best, sir, but we have to rewire--"

"See to it, and no excuses."

"Calvi--"

"Sir!" cried Ensign Omundson, interrupting further assignments.

"What is it, Ensign?" Teach asked testily.

"Sir, I don't understand it... It's not possible but... You see that it's not my fault, sir?"

"What are you talking about, Omundson? Make sense," replied Teach, thinking that the ensign should be able to show a little more backbone.

"Sir, it's the weapons. Or rather, it's the control stations. They aren't working, sir."

"What?!"

"I was running the diagnostic and they just won't work. The computer still shows that it has control, but the local control stations won't accept input from the computer or manually."

"Omundson, you idiot, you've left us with no weapons. Are you incompetent or are you actively working against me?" he asked. "You are confined to quarters."

"But, sir--"

"*Dismissed, Ensign!*" he screamed. "Goodwin, fix his mess."

"Aye, aye, sir."

"You are all against me!" Teach screamed at the bridge crew and stomped out of the hatch and headed for Engineering, completely oblivious to the incredulous stares that were directed at his retreating back. He pushed Omundson out of his way as the ensign headed aft to comply with his superior's orders.

As he walked through the open hatch into main Engineering from the boatbay, Teach yelled for Leung. She slid out from under a console, and he began to berate her before she could even get upright.

"Are you completely incompetent?" he yelled as he closed the distance from the hatch to her position.

"What are you talking about?" she asked quietly as she motioned towards her office, trying to move this confrontation out of sight of the crew.

"The weapons," Teach began, ignoring her invitation to move the discussion. "They are out of computer control and won't accept manual direction. Someone has been tampering with the command codes."

"Why are you coming to me with this?" she asked as her temper started to rise. "You put Danis in charge of finding the saboteur, have him look into it."

"You can't evade your responsibilities that easily. I don't need him for this. Who has worked near the weapons controls?"

"As the captain is aware," she began icily, "the main console is in the weapons bay, the auxiliary controls are here in Engineering and, of course, the command console is on the bridge. I have had more than half my crew working near one or the other today."

"I want their names by the end of shift. You will also assign double shifts and extra work for each. In addition, they will go on half rations for the next seven days."

"That is completely unwarranted, sir. Everyone is working double shifts now. Half of these men are assigned to second shift with me but they are here now trying to get this ship operational. Punishment without proof goes against Fleet regs and is detrimental to morale."

"Are you questioning my orders?" he screamed at her, closing the already narrow gap between them.

"No," she replied, stepping back and trying to retrieve the situation before it was completely lost and trying even harder to rein in her anger, which was threatening to escape her control.

"No, what?"

"No, sir," she said through gritted teeth as he stomped out of the engineering bay.

She finally gave in to her anger and vowed that a day of reckoning would come for him soon. Fortunately, not aloud.

As that thought took root in her mind and began to grow, her grimace gave way to a steadily expanding grin aimed at his retreating back. *I couldn't have asked for a better show, Captain.*

* * * * *

The atmosphere inside the medical bay was much more relaxed. Lt. Meghan Johnson moved to the side of her only patient as the white clad form started to move and showed signs of regaining consciousness. Within several moments the brown eyes cleared and the mind behind them began to process the situation.

"What happened?" she asked.

"You are lucky to be alive. You received a blast from an energy pistol at close range. The damage was extensive but I managed to put you back together. You have been unconscious for about eighteen hours, this time. The attack came about four weeks ago. We have had this conversation several times before but you may not remember it as it was necessary to keep you heavily sedated. "

"That seems an excessive length of time even for these injuries."

"I had orders from the XO to keep you comatose."

The doctor watched her features again for some sign of the thoughts going on behind Burton's eyes. Seeing nothing, the doctor continued. "You will still be very weak for quite some time, but you will need to move around now in order to regain your strength. We have kept you isolated from the rest of the crew. There is some resentment over the deaths of their friends." Burton's head snapped over to focus intently on the doctor who simply continued her narrative while watching the guarded features.

"Carl Brandon and Glenn Morales were killed by you and Chowdhury in the incident in which you were injured, and it seems that they had friends among the crew. Major Chowdhury accompanied the Captain and the others when they were exiled aboard *Vanguard*. She was apparently unharmed. So you are the only target their friends have available."

The doctor again studied the face of her patient. The right side of her head was still heavily bandaged and there was a complete lack of expression on the visible portion of her face. There was a slight clenching of the jaw muscles which might have indicated determination or simply the painkillers wearing off. She was quiet for several moments as the doctor studied her then she let out a long, heavy breath. Still, she said nothing but merely shook her left wrist and rattled the handcuff that was attached there.

"Yes, I'm sorry about that. That's also part of the XO's orders," she replied with a slight shrug.

"No one can gain access to this section of the medbay without an officer present, and officers are currently in short supply. You are as safe here as I can make you." The doctor waited for some response from her charge, but the features became less animated rather than the reverse.

"Gunny Aichele was in on the first day," she continued. "He said to tell you 'Rio Bravo.' He said that you would understand."

Again, the doctor waited for some response from the security sergeant. When none was forthcoming, she took a deep breath and said, "I will not knowingly harm the crew. Keeping that in mind, what can I do to help?"

Burton didn't move and her facial features seemed locked in place.

"I know you don't think you can trust me but what do you have to lose?" the doctor asked with a wave towards the handcuffs. "I have been thinking about this for a long time. I stayed on this ship because I was in surgery on your arm when Captain Brighton was forced off. I have never been part of this conspiracy and I don't plan on ever being a part of it. While Teach and Leung feel they can trust whomever they made a deal with, the truth is I don't believe that any of us will be left alive to tell the ultimate location of this ship. Therefore, in order to protect this crew, I have to keep the officers from delivering *Pathfinder* to its intended destination. So, I ask again, … what can I do to help?"

* * * * *

Teach stepped through the bridge doors and resumed his seat in the command chair. *The nerve of that woman,* he thought, *trying to excuse and coddle the incompetent members of her staff and crew. She's obviously trying to curry favor with her people and turn the crew against me. What a sorry excuse for an officer.*

He studied those around him intently, as if trying to discern any traitorous intentions. All were studiously attentive to their duties.

There is the difference, he thought, *if you expect good work, the crew will always respond to a true leader.* He sat back in his command chair and savored this newest victory over Leung.

As he released his breath in a long sigh of relaxation, all the consoles went dark and the lighting inside the bridge flickered and went out.

"Leung, what have you done now?!" he shouted into the inky blackness.

CHAPTER 19
1 Aug

Leung surveyed her quarters as the hatch slid shut behind her. Her cabin was normal for a senior officer in that she was not required to share the space with anyone else. *Pathfinder,* having started her life as a destroyer, was a small enough ship that personal space was truly at a premium, but her small ship's complement and even smaller officer's cadre allowed Leung, as Chief Engineer, to have private quarters that were three meters by four and with enough room to leave her unmade bunk in the down position without making it impossible to move around. At least it would have been possible to move around if the floor were not covered with hastily discarded clothing and shoes. The desk against one wall held a jumble of data disks and hard copy schematics that she had not yet returned to her office. There simply had not been time to take care of any of these extraneous activities. Although she had more items on her job list now than when she'd begun the day, she had successfully completed seventeen tasks since she went on shift eighteen hours earlier. The length of her job list failed to shrink each day as she checked tasks off the master list; in fact, the work load seemed to be increasing daily. *At this rate,* she thought, *I'll never be done.*

With this thought, she grabbed a pile of dirty clothing from the seat of her desk chair and moved to the laundry receptacle on the port side of the cramped cabin. She tossed the whole collection inside and hit the cycle button with the flat of her left hand, sending the offending clothing on a journey to the laundry room in the bowels of the ship. She started to turn away, but then quickly stripped and sent her current, foul-smelling uniform and undergarments into the bin and cycled them away also. She suddenly wanted to be clean. She shook her head as she noticed a dirty uniform tunic that remained on the back of the chair that she had otherwise cleared. She ignored it as she went to the narrow drawers situated in the lower half of her closet and opened the top one to pull out a clean set of underwear.

An empty drawer stared back at her. *I couldn't have gone that long without doing laundry, could I?* she wondered. With a shake of her head she reached down and opened the third one from the top. There were no pajamas left either; or at least none that she could wear. The mass of pink ruffles and lace that her mother had sent her for her last birthday sat wadded up in the back corner. She had cringed when she had opened the package. Luckily, she'd had the foresight to open it in the solitude of her cabin. This wasn't her mother's first attempt to make her daughter into someone more 'ladylike.' It was only the latest salvo in a war that had been going on for nearly fifty years. She had steadfastly refused to wear the hideous abomination.

There was nothing else.

With an angry sigh, she looked around the room. In the far corner partly under her bunk was a pair of discarded work coveralls. She strode over and picked them up, shook them straight and decided they were better than the pink alternative in her drawer. She tucked them under her arm and retreated to the shower.

A few minutes later, she emerged in her semi-clean coveralls and a towel wrapped around her drying hair.

She looked longingly at her bunk but turned instead to her desk. She carefully slid schematics to the floor and switched on her computer console. Something that Teach had said today had made her think that he was looking at files that should have been locked out. If it had been even two weeks before, *everything* would have been locked out.

One of the many top priorities in the repair schedule had been to regain use of the central computer system. The shipwide lockout that Brighton had implemented had many facets to it. The data communication network, which relayed commands from the bridge throughout the ship, was the most straightforward in nature. The connections had all been physically interrupted, and they would remain incapable of doing anything at all until they received the reset signal from the main command system. And that system required the access code of the captain or three rated bridge officers.

The solution had been equally straightforward. The disabled fiber optic cables had been torn out and replaced with new sets; or, the crew was in the process of doing so, anyway. The command and control system, though, was an altogether different problem.

The lockout there was not a physical one; it was not a matter of replacing damaged cables. The problem was in the command software. The computer needed the proper codes in order to be functional again. So the solution was more complex in this instance. Part of the solution was still physical, though. In order to get enough access to begin working on the programming, Leung, along with Giannini and Samuels, had to wire in a completely new interface. Those two had also been primarily responsible for coding new command pathways that allowed them to restore, little by little, the access they'd previously enjoyed.

Samuels had been a quick study; she really was a bright girl. Leung or Giannini would have to show her how to do things at the beginning of the project, but never more than once. Full access still hadn't been restored, and probably wouldn't be until after the ship was handed over, but they had enough working that they were able to complete all basic functions.

Right now, though, Leung needed to make sure that Teach didn't have access to her private files, and she didn't need to be on the bridge to check on those. If he could get into them, he might be able to discover the name of her Forrest contact.

That name was Kate's insurance. Without it, Teach would not be able to complete the deal to sell *Pathfinder*. Teach had to keep her alive if he wanted to get paid. The opposite was not true, however. Leung smiled as she hurried through the logs of monitors and security blocks she had put in place to keep snoopers out of her files. Everything looked to be intact but there was much more activity than normal. As she scrolled through the data she stopped suddenly. There were three unsuccessful attempts to access her encrypted files. As she suspected, Teach had made two of the attempts, but the third caused her to inhale sharply. The tracing tag attached to the attempt belonged to Lt. Neil Lamont, and it had been attempted since the takeover.

Lamont was still alive and hiding on the ship. And it looked as if he was working with Teach.

* * * * *

After two fruitless hours trying to track Lamont through his cyber-signature, Kate finally surrendered to her exhaustion and laid her damp head gently on her pillow. She might have better success from a bridge terminal, but she didn't dare be caught at it, where word might get back to Teach. She forced down any thoughts of Teach, Lamont, schematics, or component replacements and closed her eyes to the clutter that threatened to overtake her cabin. She took a deep breath and instantly began to snore.

Leung had been living in her present quarters for twenty-four months. In all of that time, she had never forgotten that her overhead storage cabinet lay a mere 80 cm above her head. It had become an ingrained habit for her to swing her torso out as she sat up and thereby avoid the very solid metal cabinet. But when the evacuation alarm began its strident blaring, she lost track of that previously ingrained habit. "Blast!" She yelled as she recognized the alarm and sat up in her bed, and "Argghh," as she collapsed back down, holding both hands to her injured forehead. She rolled onto the floor and made her way to the door, grabbing the dirty tunic from the back of her chair as she went by, still holding her other hand to the growing lump at her hairline.

She exited her cabin and shrugged her arms into the sleeves of her uniform jacket as she ran. Her assigned lifeboat was number six, which was just inside the boatbay on the starboard side of the ship. She moved on auto-pilot until she found herself in a rapidly growing crowd in front of the hatch.

"Clear the way," she called. "What's the holdup?"

The milling of the crew ceased as they turned to look at her.

"The lifeboats are gone," Biltcliffe said in a childlike voice. "There is no way off the ship. We're going to die!"

A momentary panic clutched at Leung as the words hit her. After all the careful planning and work to gain possession of *Pathfinder*, it wasn't fair for it to end like this. The constant stress, the abuse from Teach, the endless days and now it turned out to be for nothing. She fought down the surging panic. After a calming breath she reasserted command of the situation.

"There are no operating sensors forward to trigger a collision warning; this has to be a false alarm. Everyone calm down and move away from the hatches."

As she started to disperse the crowd, the alarm went silent, leaving a slight echo in the voluminous boat bay.

"Everyone get back to your duties, if you are on watch. Get back to your quarters if you are off shift. Let's clear this area," she called loudly to cut through the discussions that were beginning.

The crowd finally began to dissipate and she moved to the Engineering hatch at the aft bulkhead, rubbing her still throbbing head.

"Report, Ensign," she called as she stepped through the hatch into Engineering. The crewmen were milling around the four lifepods in the engineering spaces and Ensign Omundson had made no efforts to get them back to their tasks. They were taking their time and treating the disruption as a break from their normal duties.

Omundson turned with a look of surprise that quickly took on a slight smirk.

Leung stepped across the room and looked up at the bemused ensign. She hated it when she got that superior attitude from this little snot.

"Is there something funny, Ensign? I asked you for a report and you don't even seem capable of performing that simple task," she began in an attempt to erase the look. "Get your crew back to work and I expect you to complete repairs on the drive console and the water reclamation units by 0500. Is that understood?" she demanded in a steadily rising voice.

"Yes, ma'am," he managed to push out between clenched jaws.

"What in Hades is going on here?" she heard from behind her as Teach made his vocal entrance. "I didn't order any alarm drills!"

"Sir--" she began as she turned to face him.

"And what are you wearing, Commander? Those are not regulation pants. How can you expect to lead if you cannot even wear your uniform properly?"

She looked down, to see that she had instinctive thrown on her uniform tunic but underneath she still wore the work coveralls.

She was saved the need to reply by the sound of the evacuation alarm beginning its strident warning anew.

CHAPTER 20
3 August

Katherine Leung finally began to see the light at the end of her personal tunnel. Her engineering crew was done with the ridiculous punishment Teach had handed out following the damage to the engineering control panel and morale was finally starting to improve.

Just in time, too, she thought. Even with the extra shifts, progress on ship repairs had been decreasing. The crew was resentful of the punishment and they had begun a general slow-down in their work. It had been nearly five weeks since they had captured *Pathfinder* and they had not been able to regain more than partial control of the ship. Small acts of negligence or sabotage had constantly crept up and slowed progress to a crawl. No saboteurs had yet been caught, so he or they were being very clever. Either that or Danis and Bezates were idiots.

Maybe both, she thought.

She had started putting her plans into action to eliminate Teach. She simply couldn't trust him anymore. Further investigations into her computer had revealed many attempted intrusions, but so far she had found no evidence that any had succeeded. Most were tagged with Teach's codes but two had been attempted by Lamont and one that she still hadn't been able to attach a name to. Each attempt looked to be getting closer to gaining access. Kate assumed that Teach and Lamont were working together. Lamont would have needed some ally in order to stay as covert as he had during the searches. Teach had always been close to Lamont; that was why she had used him to pull Neil into the takeover in the first place.

She needed to be very careful in taking out Teach, however. If the two of them were working together, she would become the obvious target if Teach died under suspicious circumstances. If the captain died, she had to be categorically absolved from any possible blame, or, she had to find and take out Lamont first.

Steps to aid the former were already underway, and if the opportunity for the latter presented itself, things would be resolved even more quickly.

These thoughts spun in her head and she found herself right back where she started. She was too tired to make any decisions. Maybe a good night's sleep would reveal options she hadn't thought of.

Consciously putting one foot in front of the other to keep from stumbling, she made her way to the starboard hatch at the front of the boatbay. Despite her efforts, she still caught her foot on the lower seal of the hatch as she exited and was forced to catch herself on the edge. She held on until she regained her balance and her head stopped swimming, a process that took too long for her comfort. *I have got to get some uninterrupted sleep soon, or I won't be any good to anyone, including myself,* she thought. *Any inattention might be fatal.*

She continued down the corridor toward her quarters. Finally, she came around the corner in front of her hatch. She went in and tossed her uniform tunic across the back of the swivel chair in front of her desk. Seeing two other tunics there, she remembered that she was wearing her last clean uniform and when she got up tomorrow she needed to throw the rest into the cleaning unit or she would have nothing left and she certainly never wanted to go through that indignity again.

The effort to take care of it tonight was currently beyond her capacity. Her desk was still cluttered with the data chips and schematics she was using to rebuild the jump engine controls again. She looked away from the mess before she could convince herself that she really needed to take one more look at the specs for that system.

Sleep was her greatest need at the moment. Taking two more steps she collapsed into her bunk without taking off the rest of her uniform.

Normally very fastidious in her personal habits, she closed her eyes so that she would not have to see the ruin her cabin had become. For weeks on end, she had had time only to throw herself down for a few hours of fitful sleep at a time and all nonessential duties kept being put off. If she concentrated on relaxing each muscle group, she could block out the mess in her room... and the cybernetic relay that was spread all over the boatbay in front of hold four... and the ...

"Attention all hands," came the blaring call from the intercom, "this is the Captain." She consciously screwed her eyes shut and refused to open them. *What now?* she thought. "Effective immediately, all personnel are confined to quarters while not on duty. Please cooperate with Security by keeping the corridors clear. Offenders will be dealt with harshly. Any personnel leaving their assigned duty area during work hours will require a pass to transit the corridors."

Leung began to shoot up to a sitting position but at the last moment remembered her overhead cabinet and veered slightly to the right to avoid another impact on her still tender forehead. She threw off her blanket and headed for the door, grabbing her uniform tunic as she went by her desk chair.

She worked her arms into her jacket as she maneuvered blindly down the length of the corridor and across to the central corridor at the bridge entrance. By the time she stepped onto the bridge, she had regained enough control of herself to ask to talk to Teach outside, away from the ears of the bridge crew.

"I have the conn. I can't leave the bridge," he replied, with an air of boredom, never looking up from his monitor. The three technicians on the bridge with him studiously ignored the exchange.

"Are you crazy? There is no conn. We have no control of this ship and you are making it harder to get our work done. Hall passes? What do you think this is, high school?"

"Commander, I will overlook your insubordination this once," he said mildly, finally looking up at her. "Get yourself under control and we can discuss this rationally."

"There is nothing rational about this situation," she said into the silence of the bridge as all work stopped. No one wished to draw attention to him- or herself by the slightest noise. "We are still no closer to finding the saboteur and you are making it more difficult with every 'pronouncement' you make."

"This will make it easier to catch the saboteur. Please let Security do their job." The condescending patience dripping from his words set her teeth on edge.

"This will severely afflict the morale of the crew," she said, amazed that she had to point this out.

"This is one of those command decisions that are difficult to make, but necessary in the long run. You would not understand," Teach added with a haughty look on his bearded face.

She took a deep breath and tried to rein in her surging emotions. The lack of sleep and long, stressful hours of work on the computer system had taken a massive toll on her emotional stability. She knew that, intellectually, but no matter how hard she tried, she couldn't stop the flow of words from her mouth. Admittedly, she didn't try *that* hard.

"I understand that dictators and martinets breed more discontent and trouble than they have ever been able to solve," she said with all of the built up venom of five frustrating weeks.

"For the last time, I will warn you," Teach grated, anger finally overcoming his superciliousness, "cease your insubordination and follow orders. You are not required to try to wrap your feeble intellect around the meaning or substance of those orders, merely to follow them. Is that understood?"

"Yes, sir, *Captain Brighton*, sir," she said with a mocking salute before storming off the bridge. Her only regret was that sliding hatches are impossible to slam.

CHAPTER 21
7 August

Carefully, Ben Danis poked his head just far enough around the corner to watch Crewman Aichele enter his quarters. Not his original quarters, of course. Those were located in the security suite and bordered the main weapons armory for the ship. Having been in security before the takeover, the ex-Marine was under a cloud of suspicion. Therefore, certain precautions had been taken, including moving him to different quarters and assigning him new duties. The captain was unsure of Aichele's loyalties, and so Danis and Cody Bezates had been assigned to keep a wary eye on him, among other suspects.

Once Aichele was safely out of sight, Danis motioned to Bezates to begin. While going through the equipment in the security offices, their new home, they had come across some very sophisticated surveillance gear. Both of them were eager to see how well it worked. A good test run might mean that they didn't have to be everywhere at once, and maybe they could get back to a normal amount of sleep.

Aichele was a good choice, in their minds, for this trial run. He had been one of their first suspects when ordered to find the saboteur, for many obvious reasons. Since that time, one or both of them had watched him almost continuously. He certainly could not have arranged the complex miswiring of the weapons control system, so he could not be the saboteur they were looking for. Still, the captain expected a thorough investigation, so they continued to watch him. If they could let these new gadgets do the watching for them, however, then they could concentrate on finding the real guilty party.

Possibilities as to who that could be were limited. Those who had joined the conspiracy before the takeover could be assumed to be loyal. If any were not, word would have gotten to Brighton and Chowdhury and the attempt to steal the ship would have surely failed. That removed twenty from suspicion, leaving twelve. Dr. Johnson hardly ever left medbay; eleven. Burton was handcuffed to her bed; ten. Pressure was mounting from above to determine which of the ten it was.

The Aichele was no longer a likely suspect; his movements, attitude, behavior, everything about him seemed to be just fine.

Topping Danis' list was Ensign Omundson. Bezates argued that he was saying that just because he didn't like the man. That much was true, but it still seemed unlikely to Danis that the grandnephew of the Warner CEO would trade sides against his own family. He certainly wasn't doing it for financial reasons, and not understanding the ensign's motives made him a questionable ally.

Bezates' money was on Ensign Samuels. Danis had to admit Bezate's reasons were perhaps just as valid,. Samuels had at first stayed with the group in the boatbay that was willing to join up for a share of the cash. Then she changed her mind and went with Brighton into the launch, dragging a blubbering Sullivan with her like a rag doll. Before *Vanguard* departed, however, she had changed her mind yet again. With someone that wishy-washy, who could say that she hadn't changed her mind a third time? Still, Danis argued that "wishy-washy" people didn't generally go around trying to destroy the ship they were in.

Sullivan was at the bottom of their suspect list, of course. That girl had about as much backbone as a wet noodle. Danis and Bezates had both shared watches with her nearly every day in Engineering, and both agreed that you could generally trust her to do what she was told but not to think outside of the immediate task or take even the slightest initiative. She had always been a fairly quiet girl, but since the takeover, it seemed like she would burst into tears if you looked at her cross-eyed.

There was mounting evidence to suggest that their elusive quarry might be none other than the missing Lieutenant Lamont. Security logs were showing him using his officer's code to access a number of restricted areas. Even before his disappearance, his code was used to get into the weapons locker in Engineering.

The idea that Lamont was armed, hadn't been seen in weeks, and had unlimited access to the ship was not a very pleasant one to consider.

Surreptitiously, Danis and Bezates moved about the immediate task of mounting the electronic spies to inconspicuous locations on the ceiling and walls. The tiny bugs adhered easily to the smooth surfaces and altered, as the newly-minted security force watched with amazement, to match the coloring and texture of the metallic sheeting exactly. From a few feet away, they could hardly be spotted, even when they knew where to look for them. Close up, they simply looked like a minor imperfection in the material of the wall, as if a small blister had been missed when the sheet was rolled out of the foundry.

Their trap set, Bezates nodded silently to Danis and the two of them made their way back to Security, congratulating themselves on finding a way to outthink their target. They saw no possible incongruity in using surveillance equipment to monitor Aichele, a man who had been using the same electronics for many years.

The monitors did indeed perform as advertised, communicating a live feed through the air to be seen and recorded at the central component of the system, located in the main security area.

Being engineers at heart, the two of them were pleased as could be with a new toy to play with, and they quickly put the system through its paces to see what it would do. The two were certain then that they would only need to review the records once or twice a day in order to be able to track everyone's movements. Much as they wanted to sit and play with the surveillance gear, they both agreed that they really had nothing left to test, and so they gathered more of the electronic devices and headed to the engineering section.

Impatient as they were to complete the placement, they weren't prepared for the difficulties involved. Thanks to Teach's orders that everyone was to remain in their quarters when not on duty, the corridors of the ship were largely unpopulated. Engineering, as a work area, was exactly the opposite. The two of them went through the section pretending to be looking at various things, waiting for opportunities to deposit the bugs without being seen.

The imposed delay strained their patience. Still, if they were discovered placing the devices even once, the cat would be out of the bag and the saboteur would know what to look for. This idea would only be effective so long as it was unknown to the ship's populace.

"Danis!" Beacham's call from across the bay made the engineer jump, and he quickly put away the bug he was about to plant. Beacham crossed the engineering section before speaking again.

"Captain wants to see you and Bezates in his quarters, double quick."

"More sabotage?" Bezates asked nervously.

"Captain didn't say, just to find you and tell you to come 'immediately, if not sooner'." Beacham could do a passable impersonation of the captain's deep bass voice.

The interrupted job momentarily forgotten, the two of them hurried to comply with the summons. Chances were that being called to the captain's quarters did not represent anything good for the pair, but making the captain wait was sure to make it even worse.

When they arrived at the captain's door, they took a quick second to make sure their uniforms were as presentable as they could make them before giving two sharp raps on the frame.

"Come in," Captain Teach said pleasantly. *Maybe this won't be so bad after all*, Danis thought. He had a momentary hope before reality returned.

Anger flared in the captain's eyes as soon as he saw who was at the door. "Are the two of you blind, or just incompetent? You'd better have a flaming good explanation for this!"

Bezates and Danis exchanged a confused look. Neither had the slightest idea what their superior was referring to, but neither wanted to be the one to ask.

"Well?" Teach demanded hotly.

Bezates was the one to cave in to the pressure first. "Excuse me, sir, but could you tell us exactly what it is you need us to explain?"

"Don't crack wise with me, boy, or I'll have you scrubbing the heads for the next month! You know exactly what I mean, now out with it!" the captain said as he slammed his fist on his desk for emphasis and began to pace in front of his newest victims.

Fear of punishment that they could not avoid held their tongues. Any answer they gave was sure to be the wrong one. Unfortunately, the lengthening silence only added fuel to Teach's rage.

"I gave you an order!" he bellowed. Danis flinched but rigidly stood at attention, maintaining the only proper way to receive a tongue lashing in the navy. Bezates had beads of sweat forming on his face, but he, too, remained motionless and silent. "Clearly the two of you are blind, incompetent, and insubordinate! Now answer my question! How did the data in the new astrocomp become corrupted when it was only loaded into the databanks three days ago?"

"Sir," Danis offered hesitantly, "this is the first we've heard of this problem, but we'll begin investigating it immediately."

"Idiots! I ordered you to find the saboteur, and you have not! That's disobeying a direct order. I could put you away for five years for that offense, you know. Perhaps I should do exactly that."

"No, sir. I mean, as the captain wishes, sir, but Danis and I have just found a way to track and record everyone's movements on the ship. If the captain would allow us to continue, we will find the guilty person, sir." The sweat was running in rivulets down Bezates' face, but he dared not move to wipe it away.

"Very well, Bezates," Teach said in a moderate tone. "I will allow you to continue your new duties. But to make it clear to you that I am expecting results soon, you and Danis will be on half rations until the saboteur is caught and punished. Dismissed!"

They spun on their heels and escaped as quickly as decorum would allow. Almost without thinking about what he was doing, or what the consequences might be, Danis thumbed a bug onto the doorframe as he left.

Harsh as the punishment was, it had not been as severe as some of the other punishments they had heard of in the last few weeks; most equally undeserved. Teach seemed to revel in exercising his power to control everyone on the ship. It was no wonder that having a saboteur aboard, someone who blatantly disregarded his authority, had the captain in a frenzy. Relief flooded into them that they had managed to leave with their skins intact, and that the captain trusted them to complete their assignment.

* * * * *

Trust was not something Captain Teach had been feeling of much lately. As soon as the new security team was out the door, a sudden idea hit him that heightened his unease. Both Danis and Bezates were from Leung's engineering group, and they had been recruited by her. His eyes narrowed suspiciously. Perhaps he should be more careful in dealing with them.

If Leung was working against him, and it seemed more and more certain that she was, it was most likely that she would have brought Danis and Bezates in on her plan. Clearly, their loyalty would be to her and not to him, their rightful commanding officer.

In fact, if Leung was behind the sabotage in order to delay them until she could make her move, she would have to have their support. What other explanation was there? She could even have assigned them to perform the sabotage themselves. This new strategy of recording everyone's movements could just as easily provide them with times and places where they would be sure to be unobserved.

With new resolve, he straightened and strode to his desk. He needed to act quickly to guard against their plot.

Guardians were needed to guard against the guardians. He must have others, from outside engineering, to watch Bezates and Danis.

He crossed to his workstation and tabbed the direct link to the bridge.

"Bridge, Ensign Omundson. How can I help you, Captain?" There could be no one else on that circuit, for it connected nowhere else but the captain's quarters.

"Is Commander Leung there?"

"No, Captain. Shall I send someone to fetch her?"

"No, that's all right. Instead, send someone to have Young and Kasdorf meet me in my quarters, double quick."

"Aye-aye, sir," the Ensign acknowledged, then killed the circuit.

It was less than five minutes before the sharp rap on the door brought him back out of his unpleasant thoughts. "Come in," he said.

The two entered and braced to attention. Their appearance left much to be desired, in Teach's opinion. CPO Young had his work tunic sleeves rolled up and his arms were covered in grease to above his elbows. The receding wave of brown hair needed to be cut back to a regulation length. He was a tall man, and muscular, not quite into his middle years.

Brian Kasdorf's wrinkled uniform and red-rimmed eyes indicated that he had been wakened in order to report, and hadn't found it necessary to dress first. Kasdorf was also tall, a couple centimeters short of Young's height, dark skinned, and also athletically built. His black hair was perfectly in order. The tight curls were kept trimmed short, but this was not because he had taken any care in order to be presentable.

Hardly the respect one's captain deserves, Teach thought, *but I suppose the quick response will excuse some slovenliness... this time.*

Young came to attention and saluted, not quite touching his forehead with his fingers so as not to add another smudge of grease. Kasdorf quickly followed suit, though judging from his delay, he may not have thought of it if left to himself. "Chief Petty Officer Young and Crewman Second Class Kasdorf, reporting as ordered, sir," Young announced for both.

"At ease," Teach ordered, after returning the salute. "I have an assignment for the two of you to complete, and I do not want it discussed with anyone else, is that clear?"

"Yes, sir," both responded together.

"I want the two of you to follow Danis and Bezates, and bring me evidence that they are either concealing the identity of the saboteur, or enacting the sabotage themselves."

"Sir?" Kasdorf asked, looking at his commanding officer as if he didn't understand the order. *Perhaps he was not the right choice for this assignment,* the captain thought. *Doesn't appear too bright. Too late now, though. I can't exclude him now that he knows what I'm doing.*

"You *are* aware that there is a saboteur on my ship, are you not?" Teach began, pacing back and forth as he spoke.

"Yes, sir," Kasdorf answered, much more sure of himself.

"And you are aware that I have assigned Petty Officers Danis and Bezates to find and apprehend that saboteur, correct?"

"Yes, sir."

"And you are aware that they have yet to find the saboteur, despite fifteen days that they have been looking?"

"Yes, sir."

"Very well. I believe the reason they have not found the guilty party is that one of them *is* the saboteur, or in league with him… or her. My suspicion is that Lt. Commander Leung may be behind all this. I want the two of you to find me proof of that. Do you follow me?"

"Yes, sir." Both men exchanged a look of surprise. Leung? Sabotaging *Pathfinder*? As likely as finding architects knocking down their own buildings! Fortunately, Teach happened to be pacing away from them at the time, so he missed their dubious expressions.

"Can you do that?"

"Yes, sir."

"Excellent. Dismissed."

Obediently, the two turned and walked out. Young made a comment that he would keep the captain apprised as he closed the hatch behind him. Neither was very happy that additional work had been given them, but Young had other worries as well.

"You know what this means, don't you?" he said to the crewman.

"Sure. Same old story; more work, less sleep."

"No, I don't mean that. I mean the way the captain has been acting lately. Everyone has been walking on eggshells around him, trying to avoid being punished for things that aren't their fault."

"Yeah, so?" Kasdorf rejoined.

"Look, he assigns Danis and Bezates to find the bad guy in the ship. They do everything they can for two weeks and when they can't produce, what does the captain think? That it must mean they are guilty, too."

"Like I said, so?"

"So what do you suppose the captain will think if *we* can't produce?"

"Oh."

"Yeah, oh! I have a bad feeling about this. This is not going to end well," the chief predicted.

Teach, conversely, was extremely pleased at the way his sly plan had outmaneuvered Leung. *That blazing backstabber is not going to succeed,* he thought contentedly, almost gloating to think of his brilliant foresight. *Young will get me proof, and then I will try her for treason! She thought she was better than me, that she should have been in command. I see it in her eyes every time we meet; she envies my position.*

Well, command is more than a position. It's planning and leading and doing what has to be done. I'll show her why I was meant to command. I am the born leader, and if she can't see that, then she's going to get exactly what's coming to her.

153

CHAPTER 22
7 August

"So what do we do about it, then?" Cody Bezates demanded. He and Ben Danis had come straight back to the security office upon leaving the captain's quarters. That had given them a front row seat to the conversation Teach had conducted with their replacements.

"Blazes if I know, Cody," Danis said while pacing back and forth in the small office. "None of this makes any sense. When I left, I was grateful my skin was still intact. Now I can't see why it was. If he was going to replace us, or even if he didn't trust us, then why did he let us just walk out with no punishment? If he thinks Leung is behind things, why doesn't he relieve her of duty and put her in the brig? If he thinks we're helping her, why didn't he do the same to us?"

Cody Bezates didn't answer immediately. He stared at the cabinets next to the armory hatch and sighed. The security suite had become more familiar over the last few days, but even though they had moved into the compartments that had formerly housed the security detail, the place still didn't feel like home in the way the engineering crew berthing had. They each had their own room instead of being in a common berthing area but that still didn't make enough difference to be worth it to Cody. The ambiguity of their situation with the captain just reinforced in his mind how far out of their depth they were getting.

"I don't know, Ben. Maybe he thinks he has to have some evidence before he acts," Bezates offered finally.

Danis scoffed at that. "Huh, lack of evidence clearly hasn't kept him from convicting us already."

"No, I suppose it hasn't," he agreed with another sigh. "That still doesn't answer my original question, however. What should we do?"

"Well," Danis said levelly, "it looks to me like we've got three options here." He seated himself next to Bezates, facing the incriminating monitors. "First, we could find Lamont before Young and Kasdorf do. In that case, we will restore Captain Teach's trust in us, and our current dilemma should disappear.

"Second, we could find evidence that implicated Leung in causing the sabotage. Again, if we bring it to the captain before Young and Kasdorf, it should restore us to his good graces.

"Or third, we could sit back, do nothing, and place bets on who destroys the ship first, Captain Teach or Lamont."

Bezates frowned. "You think it's Lamont doing all the sabotage, then?"

Ben Danis chuckled, without any mirth. "I guess it's too early to say, but it makes more sense than any of the other people we've suspected. All of them have alibis for most of the destruction. The only one who doesn't is Lamont."

"Yeah, but no one's actually seen him," Cody countered. Danis made no verbal response, simply shrugging it off. After a moment, Bezates continued, "About your options, I can't say I like the odds either way. Option three seems to be a no-win scenario. Option two is impossible, since I don't think that any such evidence exists. And option one is what we have unsuccessfully been attempting for the last two weeks."

"There is a fourth choice," Danis said quietly. Bezates looked at him closely. Something in the tone of his voice had set off all kinds of warning bells. "We could arrange an accident for the captain and let someone sane take over."

Bezates saw not the slightest humor behind Danis' eyes, and fear closed his throat for a moment. The most frightening aspect to the statement was that Cody found himself more than a little tempted to agree.

Almost certainly, morale would improve on the ship if Teach were no longer breathing. Bezates, personally, would feel their chances improved with Leung at the helm. It would not solve all of their problems, of course; there would still be a saboteur to catch and a ship to repair. Still, it might make those efforts easier without the constant need to be looking over your shoulder.

Bezates' eyes were drawn to the armory hatch once again. He wished that he had access to the armor and weapons that were stored within that compartment. The hand weapons Teach had been able to access from the small weapons locker near the bridge were scant comfort to the growing unease within his chest. If he could wrap himself inside a suit of Marine armor, Teach could do his worst. As things stood, however, Teach was a lingering sword of Damocles hanging over all of them.

Bezates was abruptly ashamed of himself for even considering such a prospect. Stealing a ship and selling it off was one thing, but murder was quite another. There was no way he could live with that kind of crime weighing on him.

"No," he finally pronounced; not harshly or condemningly, but firmly enough to show that he meant it.

"All right then," Ben said, and he looked more relieved than angry at being contradicted, "which of the other three?"

"I guess I'll take the first one. Slim our chances might be, but at least there's *some* chance of finding Lamont."

"Agreed. I was thinking, now that we've started using these surveillance bugs, that maybe we'll only have to crawl through the interstitial decks one more time. Much as I hate walking around hunched over for a couple of hours, that thought ought to make the task bearable."

"Where do you want to start?" Cody asked, rising to his feet.

"Engineering. That's going to be the main target for Lamont, or whoever is doing this," Ben amended quickly when he saw Bezates' reaction to the name.

"Makes sense," was all he said out loud.

As they exited the security office and moved down the port corridor, Danis had a sudden thought as they passed the mess. He pulled Bezates into the room with him and pulled a tray from the stack. He started loading up his tray and after a moment Bezates caught on and did the same. Both Green and Trendle were on duty, but neither of them so much as glanced at the new security team. Danis was happy to see the former was free of his arm sling at last.

As Ben had thought, word of their half ration status had yet to arrive. This was going to be their last full meal for quite a while, and it was fortunate for them that Danis had thought of it before they had missed their opportunity.

Being the middle of second watch, the galley was practically deserted. Giannini had come in and had taken a tray of sandwiches and coffee up to the bridge, but she was the only other customer.

When they had eaten as much as they conceivably could, they resumed their trek aft to Engineering. Beacham nodded to them as they went past and Leung pulled a stray bit of hair out of her eyes and looked at them curiously. Otherwise, they were ignored.

They passed through the engineering work area and took the port ladder up to the landing midway between main and upper levels. Bezates mounted a bug to the opposite wall while Danis opened the abbreviated door that led into the ship's bowels. Each man pulled out a flechette pistol as they entered.

It was a rare location in the interstitial level to find no pipes, conduits, beams, or framing to keep one from standing erect. This affected Danis more than Bezates, who was almost 20 cm shorter than his senior, and yet there were places where it was necessary for both to get down on all fours to continue forward. This area, like the rest of the ship, was compartmentalized to avoid the complete loss of atmosphere should *Pathfinder*'s skin be punctured. Each frame line and transept was walled off and had a narrow opening with automated air-tight doors. At about every fourth or fifth one of these, one of the two would place one of their remote sensors. They had found quite a stockpile of the little things while they were going through their new inventory, but they still needed to be conservative with their placement. They might have hundreds of the devices to use, but the central system could only monitor a maximum of 32 of them at once.

The two men moved slowly and cautiously, alert for any sound or motion that might indicate they were not alone. This was not as straightforward a prospect as might be expected. There were not many moving parts in this area, although there were a few. The sounds of the engines, power lines, and operating equipment, though, was more than enough to mask any incidental noises an intruder might make. Had the engines been fully operational, they would have needed ear protectors.

"Great place for an ambush, don't you think?" Bezates said as they approached another of the small apertures. He had neared each of these with some trepidation, but this was the first time he had voiced any reservations.

"Hmmph. Keep it down, Cody. If there *is* anyone out there, I don't want him to hear us coming."

Bezates snorted. "That's not likely, with all this going on," he retorted, though more quietly.

"All right, in you go," Danis directed.

Bezates leaned forward to poke his head through, supporting his weight with one hand on the door frame. He looked every direction quickly and, seeing nothing out of place, hurried through. Danis followed, and they moved through the area rapidly, checking behind pipes and shafts of various sizes and purposes.

As they went along, Bezates grew a bit more relaxed, though still alert. They completed their exploration, arriving at the exit to the starboard stairwell after placing four monitors. Danis positioned another that included the access door in its pickup field, then spent more than a minute stretching his spine back into usable shape. Bezates, meanwhile, sealed and locked the door behind him. Acting on a sudden thought, he used his security oversight code to bring up the lock's usage log. He scrolled through the information, but did not see anything that was out of place.

Once Danis could again walk upright, they headed down the steps to the other interstitial space between main and lower decks. They proceeded as they had before, slowly and carefully. At the next opening, it was again Bezates' turn to go first, and he repeated his habitual procedure, leaning forward to peer at what was on the other side first. As soon as his hand contacted the doorframe, there was a crackle of energy and Cody flew backward nearly a meter. He lost consciousness at once, and had no control of the pistol in his opposite hand, which flew back and hit Danis solidly in the middle of his forehead. Both men went down and lay insensate for some time.

Danis was the first to come to, and the pain in his head made him immediately wish he hadn't. He sat up, regretted the hasty action, and lay back down. Seeing Bezates next to him, though, he overrode the pain to crawl over to him and check on his status. His pulse and breathing were normal, thankfully, but his left hand was badly burned.

"Bezates! Bezates, wake up!" Danis attempted to rouse him, but got no response. Cautiously, he crawled over to the gap and inspected the perimeter of the opening closely. There were black marks where Cody had placed his hand. The air smelled like burned meat mixed with the ozone scent of a welder. He couldn't see anything else until he carefully leaned through without touching anything.

A power feed was laid down in the angle of the wall and floor. One of the wires had come loose from the junction box there. The arc from the high-voltage line to the neutral door frame had melted the metal and welded it in place.

Ben pulled himself back and away and found that Cody was beginning to wake up as well. Danis was glad that he wouldn't have to drag and carry him all the way back to medbay.

"Bezates, you with me?"

"Hmmmmoohhhh. What happened?"

"You suddenly became the path of least resistance for a few thousand volts. How do you feel?"

"My hand is throbbing, my head is pounding, and every muscle in my body aches. Thanks for asking."

"I see that your sense of humor is still intact. Come on, let's get you to the doctor."

Bezates moved awkwardly, and Danis had to support him much of the way; this was extremely problematic in the cramped space between decks. Danis answered the other's questions about what had caused the problem, which prompted Bezates to suggest that they should report it to the captain as another piece of sabotage.

"I don't think that's a good idea, Cody," Ben said in a flat voice.

"Why not? You don't think that wire got there by itself, do you?"

"Well, it could have, sure. And maybe it didn't. But if it was a trap, whoever set it could have permanently removed us while we were out," Danis offered.

"The saboteur could have just left it for whoever was the next to come along, without actually waiting to pounce on them."

"I suppose that's true, but I still don't think it's a good idea."

Bezates looked at him quizzically. "Why?"

Danis sighed. "How do you suppose the captain will react if we tell him that we encountered a trap laid by Lamont, or our saboteur, whoever, and that it took both of us out of action?"

"Oh," Bezates said glumly, "I hadn't thought of that. But we should at least tell Commander Leung so she can see that it gets fixed before someone else comes across it."

"Well, we can't just log a work request in the system, since they are limiting access to the main computer, so we'll have to go and talk to her. Given what we know of Captain Teach's thoughts lately, what will he think when Young and Kasdorf report that the two of us had some information that we had to convey to the Commander?"

Bezates swore. "Ben, this situation stinks, no two ways about it. There is no way we can do our job while we're busy covering our own posteriors, and it's the same for everybody else, too."

"I know it. Generally, I'm strictly opposed to the "watch your back" mentality. However, I find I have changed my opinion now that it's my back that needs watching."

"What if we tell Leung in front of witnesses? Maybe in front of Young?" Bezates offered.

"And word gets straight back to Teach, and we're convicted of insubordinate incompetence," Danis pointed out.

Bezates swore again. Danis had to agree.

Danis led Bezates down the right hall to the general duty room once they reached medbay, automatically looking into the recovery room and noting that its lone occupant was still both handcuffed and unconscious. That reminded Bezates that they needed to set up a regular schedule to check on Burton. Even though the former security Marine was handcuffed in medbay instead of residing in the cells off the security room, she was just as much their prisoner and their responsibility.

Dr. Johnson saw to both of them as soon as they came in. She treated Bezates' burns first, and Danis' goose egg after.

The doctor asked both of them what had happened, and neither knew what to tell her. Nor what to tell anyone else who was bound to ask.

CHAPTER 23
8 August

Monica Samuels took up her accustomed seat before the workstation in her quarters. She was again dressed in a shipsuit, this one a deep purple with white and gold accents. This was the riskiest of her off-duty clothing, since it was the color scheme of her family's business, and so she wore it only when alone, just to be on the safe side. She washed it herself, too, not trusting it to the ship's automated system.

She had developed a routine for coming off duty that included eating, showering, and changing clothes before spending at least two hours on her "other" projects. The line in the mess was shorter than normal, and part of the meal was always portable, allowing her to finish while walking back to her room. As a result, she had a few minutes before her surreptitious transmitter would switch itself on.

Samuels popped the catch open on her hidden compartment without looking under her desk and extracted her receiver unit. As she had promised herself, it was now more compact and protected. She had accomplished this by emptying the contents of a radiation monitor and stuffed her circuitry into the case. Now it was a quick and easy connection, and the telltale lit at once, indicating a good signal.

Wait. That wasn't right. She checked the chronometer on her wrist, and then confirmed the time with the unit on the wall. It was still too early. Her heart froze and she couldn't find her breath. Someone was looking for her.

Immediately, her finger found the panic switch, disabling the unit from transmitting; handshake signals, remote commands, anything at all. If anyone had been watching for her to connect, though, it was already too late. Someone would come through the door and point a weapon at her, order her to stand, and march her down to the brig. There was nothing she could do to escape at this point. There was nowhere she could run.

There was still a chance she had disconnected before they had noticed, or at least before they had isolated her location. If so, she had to act fast.

Monica watched the seconds tick by on the wall unit, feeling the sweat form into drops that rolled down her face and neck. Her door might open at any moment and that would be the end. She held stubbornly to the idea that her fate wasn't sealed yet. That quick action might yet save her.

When the proper second arrived in which the bridge unit activated, she unlocked her device and sent the instant shutdown signal to power it down. It didn't respond. She sent it again, but no acknowledgment came back. Now what? The other signal she had picked up must be interfering.

With no better option, she tried it a third time and finally received a hang-up signal in response. It was a great relief, but not a total one. The transmitter had been active long enough that it could have been tracked to its source.

Monica put her ersatz rad meter back in its slot and latched it closed, toweled off her face and lay down on her bunk. She turned away from the door and tried hard to slow her breathing, as if she were already asleep. It wasn't likely that she would fool anyone.

It wasn't likely to matter.

She wasn't going to complete the assignment Captain Brighton had given her. She wasn't going to finish the mission her father had given her. It broke her heart to let Dad down, but she would not allow herself to cry. It wouldn't fit if someone walked in, so she wouldn't allow it. Oddly, she found that she felt almost as badly about disappointing Captain.

Thoughts of her father brought her back to the reason she was where she was, the convoluted path that had led her here, and now would lead to her capture, and most probably to her death.

Her father, Victor Bybee, was not a common figure around the family house in Christchurch, New Zealand on old Earth where she grew up. When you were operations manager for a shipping line, as her father was; most of your time was spent off Earth. She grew up with her two older sisters and younger brother, mostly supervised by Mom.

When she turned 10, though, she was allowed to follow the family tradition and travel with Dad on one of his six-month rounds. Unlike Tessa and Hadley, though, when she returned, she asked if she could go again. And again.

In fact, from that time on, she lived the ship-board life of a regular worker; well, perhaps she had avoided a few of the least-liked tasks by being related to the owners, but there were many of those she hadn't been able to avoid as well. On a cargo ship, mass was cost, and they couldn't make ends meet carrying around dead weight.

What she wouldn't give to be back aboard the *Lady Marie* or the *Constance True* again, instead of lying in her bunk, waiting to be arrested.

Hightower Interglobal Transport had been the reason for her change in career path. Monica remembered that it was a month or so after her 17th birthday when she had her first clue that something was amiss. She'd come to the vessel's control deck to report some problem or other, she couldn't remember what it was now, and overheard her father arguing with the ship's captain. She understood at once the nature of the problem, having spent as much time learning the ins and outs of the business as a whole as she had learning the details of operating a spacecraft.

They were in the Tammerlane system, still a couple days from orbit, but they'd gotten word from their local agent that there was no cargo waiting for the next section of their rounds. Dad hadn't been able to believe it. They usually had work lined up months in advance. The agent had been at a loss to explain it. He had gone so far as to reduce their normal bids by a significant margin, but still they had been underbid.

The captain had given the crew a week's liberty while they waited for something to turn up, but eventually they'd had to go on with their holds less than full. They were under contract to get what consignments they still had to their intended destinations by a specific date.

But then at Morgan, the story was repeated, albeit without the liberty, because they'd already used up any slack time they could afford. Then the same again at Pollex. The Bybee agent for that system, though, had a message from Uncle Hugo recalling Dad to Earth, by the fastest available means.

She tried to pull her mind back from long-past history to focus on the here and now. She needed to appear to be asleep, and her racing thoughts made it harder to calm her body. Still, she had more success with the latter than the former, though her train of thought had switched lines to the present dilemma. How had they gotten onto her? What mistake had she made? If they knew what frequency to watch, they had to have picked up one of her previous sessions.

But that made no sense. If they had picked her up before, why hadn't they come for her earlier? Maybe they needed another opportunity to triangulate her location. So they were monitoring the right frequency.

Why would they be broadcasting on that frequency? She sat up in bed and put her feet on the floor. That didn't make sense either. It had been the signal she picked up that alerted her to the fact that something was off. They wouldn't have wanted to let her know they were watching that channel until they had scooped her up.

Might it be that the signal she picked up was *not* intended for her? Was it possible that she wasn't in any danger?

Possible, but not certain. She rolled herself back under the covers and feigned sleep.

Once prone again, her thoughts strayed back to that winter day almost five years before. She and her father were back on Earth three days after receiving the recall, and Dad had gone straight from the spaceport to the board room. He was the only board member whose responsibilities took him off-world regularly.

Monica did not have direct knowledge of the meeting, of course, but her father had summed it up for her. Bybee Transstellar was the fifth largest shipping line, and the largest independent shipper, but not being part of one the major Family corporations meant not having the internal resources to do everything for yourself. That was why computer security had been outsourced to another independent business.

And that security had been compromised, either by hack, extortion, or bribery, by Hightower Interglobal Transport. By breaking into all of Bybee's systems, Hightower had been able to undercut all of Bybee's bids, effectively stealing their opportunity to work.

Uncle Hugo had not waited for the full board to convene before he acted, demanding from the security firm that they repair the breaches and compensate their loss, and moving to change all of Bybee's codes. It had taken months before everything was once again secure, however, and it might take years of legal wrangling before they recouped their losses, if they ever would. It had been six years of court battles so far with no result.

The meeting that Monica's father had attended had included only himself, Uncle Hugo, Aunt Cecily, and Grandpa Chuck. They were looking for long-term answers; how to make sure that this sort of thing never happened again. The loss of income for so long a period had pushed the company to the very brink of ruin.

It was sixteen hours before Dad returned home, and he asked Monica and her mother to come into his office as soon as he crossed the threshold. She remembered being shocked that he included her in the conference. Dad crossed the room, sat at his desk, and waved for the others to sit opposite him. No sooner had they sat down than her father popped back up and began pacing.

Monica remembered how nervous she had been at the unusual behavior. She and her father had become quite close in the preceding years, and had had any number of open and frank discussions. That he had something important to talk over was clear, but that he was nervous himself about it, and that he couldn't bring himself to start was unnerving.

Eventually, he explained what the executive council had come up with, and asked if Monica would be willing to go along. Bybee needed their own computer security expert, who would be loyal to the family, and not to the highest paycheck. After looking at the potential candidates, they believed that Monica was the best candidate to go out and acquire the needed training.

The plan would require her to assume a new identity as well, because the IT Guild held their secrets very closely, and bound their journeymen and masters very tightly to them. If they knew that someone would be taking their secrets outside their control, there would be severe consequences. Her father had concluded that since there were many serious risks involved, no one would blame her if she declined, and the next most suitable candidate would be approached. When she'd asked who that might be, he had answered that her cousin Mick's name had been mentioned.

Looking back, Monica was sure the name was used to goad her into accepting. There was no way Mick's name had come up in the discussion, unless it had been preceded by, "There's no way we can use that idiot," and followed by, "for anything more complex than mopping floors."

The thought made her laugh to herself, and she began to feel that the danger had passed. If all they needed was to know was where she was, they would have been here already to pick her up.

Samuels went back to her desk and reconnected her equipment. She was about to link into the bridge systems, but didn't. The unexplained new signal had her suddenly curious.

Her receiver picked the signal up easily, and she captured a portion of the data to analyze. At first pass, it was gibberish. There was a pattern that repeated every 5 microseconds, though; that was something to work on. The signal was isochronous, so if the pattern was just a basic "start of frame" marker, that would allow her to calculate the encryption algorithm.

After a few more key taps, the data morphed into a series of images; a video stream. It was an unchanging image from one of the aft ladders; she couldn't tell which one.

Hmm. She expected it would have been more difficult to break a security encryption than that. Another item to bring up with Naval Security. Eventually. Or maybe the people using them didn't know what they were doing. Yes, that was more likely. From everything she had picked up from Major Chowdhury's files, she knew for a fact that the security under the Marines would not have made anything that easy.

Well, where there was one such video source, there were sure to be others, and now that she knew how to co-opt them, they might prove to be a valuable font of information. Extremely valuable.

It took less than an hour, working with her signal monitor to identify all the channels being used, and to remotely program her backdoor port on the bridge to use a frequency far removed from the others, so there would be no chance of cross-communicating.

That was good, but not perfect.

Back to that in a minute.

First, she wanted a way to collect and record the video streams, and to do that Monica would have to make her receiver able to handle multiple channels at once. That would require getting into the stored equipment in the holds, retrieving what she needed without being seen, and building a larger receiver in her room, one that would be a lot harder to conceal. All of those things increased her risk. Was it worth it?

Next, she needed to find a way to record the video streams in order to review them each day. That meant using a lot of memory, more than her unit could store locally. Which would involve less risk, stealing components to augment her machine's capacity, or storing the files in the ship's databanks?

Ugh. Idiot, she berated herself.

The files had to be being stored already for review somewhere, almost certainly in the computer system belonging to the new security team. This was, after all, a system she had already managed to get into without leaving a trace. No changes to the status quo meant no increased risk, except for Danis and Bezates who were clearly doing something to find her, and something productive at that. There were bugs all over Engineering, all over the ship. There was not much chance of her movements going unnoticed from now on.

Also, with them broadcasting signals throughout *Pathfinder,* they might stumble across her link to the bridge at some point. She needed to make sure that didn't happen. Her heart couldn't take another shock like the one it had just felt.

So, back to Cyberwarfare 101; if you wanted something to go unnoticed, make a bigger fuss somewhere else that needed immediate attention. The same tactic could be applied here. It was just a matter of identifying what fuss to make. It had to be some distraction that would take all their focus away from the effort to find her.

She had provided one other target for their search with her trick of faking Lamont's codes in the logs, but that wasn't helping enough. They were still looking for him, so any slip she made they were probably going to find anyway, even if they originally thought they were after Lamont. She needed something else, something bigger.

Samuels sat and stewed over that problem for ten minutes, with no ideas coming to her. What could she do? It had to be big, yes. It had to distract both of them at the same time. It had to keep them distracted for a long time. She had to stay hidden while she did whatever it was; any direct attack would tip her hand. It would have to be something that was a higher priority to them than looking for the saboteur. What would be more important to them than that?

She let her mind percolate on that while she remembered the end of the informal interview with Mom and Dad. She'd accepted, of course; she never could turn down a challenge or an adventure. She'd had one improvement to the plan to offer, however. The Compman's Guild was paranoid about keeping their secrets, and keeping them from discovering her identity would be tricky.

They were not the only ones who could teach her what the business needed her to know, however. Most of the Major Families had internal computer security divisions, many attached to their military. If they thought they could fake an ID with Warner citizenship, their naval academy would be second only to the guildhall, but with much less scrutiny. Warner ran half of the inhabited worlds out there, many with backward or limited records; faking a set of records from somewhere away from Earth turned out not to be too difficult after all. They'd had to pay quite a bit to get the work done, but Monica Samantha Bybee had become Monica Samuels after years worth of false records were inserted into Warner's mountain of data.

Suddenly, she had it: inserting false records! The one thing more important to Danis and Bezates than finding the saboteur would be protecting themselves. What she needed was some way to threaten them indirectly…or anonymously. What if there were some evidence that implicated them and it came to the attention of Captain Teach? That would do it, wouldn't it? Then they would be much more interested in proving their innocence than finding her.

It was a good idea, but it still lacked refinement. What "evidence" could she manufacture that would implicate those two? How could she be sure it was seen by Teach or Leung? No, seen by Teach; Leung didn't have the authority to worry them if Teach was in their corner.

Maybe with her newfound access to the video recorders, she could dummy up both an access log along with video showing the two of them entering a room right after Lamont. Maybe include Leung in the clandestine group. A little more dissent in the ranks couldn't hurt, and it was clear that none of them really trusted the others, already.

No, that wouldn't work. She was not supposed to have access to video or security logs, so she couldn't just hand one over to Teach with no explanation as to how it had come her way. Even if she sent it anonymously, it would alert Security that she had access she shouldn't have, which was bound to lead to increased scrutiny, and that was what she was trying to avoid. She had already inserted false information in the logs that had them chasing after Lt. Lamont. If she gave them something that implicated someone, at least those people would know it was wrong, and that would get them looking harder in areas she didn't want them looking.

And even then, Teach would know that nobody but Ben and Cody should have access to those records, so he would start looking into the situation as well.

No, that was clearly a bad idea.

What else was there? And how could she present it in a way that wouldn't put the source in doubt? What source would Teach even trust? He didn't seem to trust anyone anymore. Even if he did trust the source, he would still want to verify it.

She checked the chrono on the wall again. She had gone well past the two hours she wanted to spend and was burning into her four hours of sleep that she *needed* to spend, sleeping.

She wasn't ready to sleep yet anyway. Too much excitement and too many questions floating around. There had to be some source she could use that... She had it.

Captain Brighton.

Teach would not only accept Brighton's judgment and truthfulness without a second thought, but he was a source that was no longer available to cross-examine. *And* Teach was living in Brighton's quarters. That should make it possible for her to plant something for Teach to find. Maybe she could put something in Brighton's personal logs, and change the code to something easier to break.

That would do for the how, now for the what. A nasty thought crossed her mind, perhaps from so much time reading through Chowdhury's tactics. If Teach was feeling a little paranoid, then why not give him some proof that *everyone* was out to get him.

Let's have Brighton notice several meetings between Danis, Bezates, Leung, and Lamont and comment on them in his logs. Maybe that was the reason he put in extra fail-safes in the system, the reason the command computers were locked out. That would seem plausible.

Samuels was still too excited to sleep, but now she had somewhere productive to channel her nervous energy.

CHAPTER 24
11 August

Bone-deep weariness assailed Katherine Leung, but she refused to allow it to keep her from doing what needed doing. *Especially not today,* she thought. *Today we start moving forward again.*

She and Teach had set up a six-hour rotation for standing bridge watch, which meant that her watch changes did not align with the rest of the crew. It would have been easier to put everyone on a four watch rotation, but there simply weren't enough people available to accommodate that. Everyone was working two shifts out of every three as it was. That level could not be maintained forever, but certainly longer than assigning three watches on to everyone off.

There were still two hours remaining in first watch when she took over as officer of the deck, and she had waited until second watch began in order to have the crew she wanted in position to run tests on the astrogation system. Ensign Samuels was already at the helm station for first watch, and Leung had altered her schedule today to man the Astro console for second watch.

The XO felt that Samuels had really been the cream of their crop of junior officers assigned to *Pathfinder*, with Roberts an easy second. Of the other three, Mitchell and Hayes needed more seasoning; well, just to grow up, she chuckled to herself, and Omundson was, for lack of a better phrase, a pain to work with. Perhaps her impressions were flavored more by the fact that he always seemed to be the one to wake her in the middle of whatever sleep she could manage, though the fault had never been his. Still, it gave her a great deal of satisfaction to assign him to handle the Engineering end of today's tests during second shift, when he would otherwise be off duty, and likely sleeping.

Leung was impatient to begin the final system tests, to finally have this major item removed from her work list, so she had to clamp down on her desire to call Engineering to find out what was taking so long.

It was fifteen minutes after watch change when Omundson finally called. She felt the urge to snap at him when he did, but managed to restrain herself when she realized it probably took that long to receive a passdown and status report from Young, who had nominal command there for the last two hours of first watch.

Young, too, had expressed a great deal of satisfaction at the unexpected extra shift off. He had definitely earned it, in Leung's mind, by taking over many of her mundane duties to allow her to focus on the ever-increasing problems all over the rest of the ship.

"Engineering to Bridge."

Leung tabbed the communication channel open. "Bridge, Leung."

"We're ready to begin testing down here, ma'am," Omundson said, sounding more competent to handle this task than Leung knew him to be. He had only been out of the Naval Academy for a little more than two months, after all. This was his first deployment, and putting him in charge of an area without supervision normally wouldn't happen for another year, at a minimum. Even then, the normal progression would have been a minor responsibility, not an entire shift lead in Engineering. Normal, though, the current situation most definitely was not.

"Very well, Ensign. We'll begin with calculation number twelve. Stand by to receive data."

"Engineering standing by to receive data results from equation twelve, Standard Test Pattern, aye," came the formal, and again competent sounding, response.

"All right, Monica. Pattern twelve, please," Leung asked pleasantly.

"Pattern twelve, aye, ma'am," the junior officer reported, pausing between each sentence while she worked. "Entering data. Data entry complete. Calculation complete. Transmitting data to Engineering Main Control Board."

"Bridge, Engineering, Omundson. Received data matches expected data."

"Acknowledged, Engineering," she answered. The pleasure and relief in her voice were evident. "Stand by for equation number thirty-eight."

"Standing by for pattern three-eight."

Leung's happiness spread quickly around the bridge as the first bit of major progress toward getting themselves out of the predicament they were in materialized. The first smile anyone had seen from her in two or three weeks lit her face as she continued. "Go ahead, Monica."

Samuels allowed herself to grin in return, since it would have been perfectly natural to do so. Hers, though, had more to do with the shock she knew was coming for everyone else than for the transitory success. She turned quickly back to her station and prepared herself to feign surprise credibly when the tests failed. That they would fail was almost mathematically certain. Regulations specified twenty-five consecutive correct solutions before the equipment could be logged back into service, and her embedded worm reduced the chances of receiving the correct answer by ten percent each time the system was utilized. The odds were asymptotically small that a bad result would fail to appear.

"Pattern thirty-eight, aye, ma'am." Monica's voice was again all business, but this caused no special notice in the others. "Entering data. Data entry complete. Calculation complete. Transmitting data."

"Bridge, Engineering. Did you say calculation three-eight?"

"Yes, Ensign. Three. Eight." Leung confirmed. *Idiot.*

"Ma'am, received data does not, repeat, does not match expected data."

"What!" exploded from both officers on the bridge at once.

Improbably, the event happened after only a single iteration, while Samuels was still trying to figure out what to do to make it look like she was surprised. Her shock at not having the time to do so made a perfect cover for not being surprised that it happened at all.

"Are you sure?" Leung followed. She was certain that Omundson must have made some sort of error. "Are you looking at the right line?"

"Ma'am," he said confidently. "I am certain that the data does not match. I am reading a course of 17.2156 by -14.7071. Pattern thirty-eight should result in a course of 12.44 by 64.0." By the end of his statement, it was clear that he felt affronted by the lack of belief shown by his department head. As always, his display of superciliousness made Leung want to reach through the comm link and throttle him.

"Monica, what do you show?"

"Ma'am, when the calculation completed, and I forwarded it to engineering, it read 12.44 by 64.0, as expected. Those values are still displayed on my board." She waved at the offending instrument as an invitation for Leung to verify the reported information. The commander did just that, the engineer in her needing to see for herself.

"Run it again," Leung ordered. The optimism she had possessed only a few moments ago was gone now, dashed against the rocks of another problem to be found and corrected, she feared. Her head suddenly started hurting, as if her temples were being squeezed together in a vise, and she returned to the command chair and sat down hurriedly.

"Aye-aye, ma'am. Inputting data. Processing. Course calculation complete. Correct results confirmed. Transmitting data to Engineering."

"Engineering, Bridge, how do you read?"

"Ma'am, results now read 12.44 by 64.0, as expected."

Leung let out a long breath she wasn't aware she'd been holding. "Very well, Ensign. Stand by for test pattern nineteen. Monica, if you would?"

"Pattern nineteen, aye. Entering data. Data entry complete. Calculation complete. Results confirmed. Transmitting to Engineering."

There was silence from Omundson for long enough that Leung was worried that the comms had failed again. She was about to ask for his status when he finally responded with a sigh. "Ma'am, received data does not match the expected output. I checked the—"

"Unidentified contact!" The unexpected shout from Hilary Calvi, who was covering Scan from her seat at Helm, had all heads turning her way, the astrogation problems forgotten. "Bearing is 2-1-2 point 4 by 0-5-1 point 8. Distance: 2-5-2 million kilometers. Closure at 4-1 kps. IFF ping outbound."

A chunk of ice congealed in Leung's guts, but her ingrained responses took immediate control. She didn't need to wait for the Identification, Friend or Foe system to know that anyone coming toward them way out in the back of beyond was most likely an enemy. Forrest knew where they were, of course, but they would not risk trapping themselves in a closed system without hearing from Leung first. "Terry, sound general quarters. Samuels, take Tactical. Calvi, make your " She had forgotten that there was still no direct link from Helm to Engineering. Nor was there any way to drive the ship locally from Engineering.

Thanks to the repairs to the scanners, they could see the pursuing ship, but they were powerless to evade. *What else can I do?* she thought frantically.

Her contemplation was cut short by the bridge hatch unsealing and Captain Teach striding angrily in. "What the devil's going on?" Leung stood quickly and moved away from the center seat to avoid the likely result of being shouldered aside should she not move swiftly enough.

"Unidentified contact at seven o'clock high," she reported. She wanted to add more, but there really wasn't anything else to recount. Her only action, really, was to sound the alarm, which he already knew about or he wouldn't be out of bed.

He looked at her askance but offered no criticism, thankfully. "Who is it?" he asked instead. "Is it our Forrest contact?"

"No response yet to our IFF," Calvi supplied, "but minimum turnaround won't be for another half minute."

"Very well, Ms. Calvi. Move us away at half speed until we know for sure who it is."

"Uh, Captain," the helmswoman started to explain, but words failed her. Leung came to her rescue.

"Captain, the engines are currently powered down until repairs are made and control restored," the executive officer said, nervously. The captain's behavior had been odd lately. *Abnormal might be a better word for it*, she thought, *or pathological*. Still, this was different than what she had already noted. He had never before failed to be aware of the current status of the ship.

"Oh, yes," the captain responded affably. "Best speed, then, Ms. Calvi."

Delusional, Leung judged. Then she wondered what in the universe she was going to do about it. Hilary took the decision out of her hands for the moment, by responding herself.

"Best speed, aye, Captain," Calvi said, and the normality of her tone and inflection made Leung turn to see if she were indeed surrounded by madhouse escapees, as her world was rapidly making less and less sense to her. The look that Calvi gave her in return made it clear that she was quite sane, but also terrified at the captain's slipping grasp on reality. Her eyes pled with Leung to fix things.

This behavior was not what Leung was expecting from Teach. Some lack of focus, perhaps, was understandable, but not this disconnection from reality. The XO didn't know how to respond, nor did she how to repair whatever damage Teach's mind had suffered. She was an engineer, and a good one, but a human intelligence was not the well-ordered logical thing that she had the capacity to analyze and understand. She'd have to keep a much closer eye on him, to make sure he didn't go too far off the deep end.

The look Calvi had given her was just the sort of thing she had been hoping for, the crew looking to her for answers rather than Teach, but she definitely did not want it at the cost of all their lives. Something had to be done about Teach, but only after she had answered the question of what Lamont was up to, or at least if the lost lieutenant was going to protect Teach.

That was long-term, though, and the present situation needed immediate action. But what should she do? Indecision held her fast, the more so since she was so unaccustomed to its presence. Normally, she had her responses mapped out in advance for whatever might arise. This was not an eventuality she had foreseen and so was totally unprepared to deal with it.

Calvi's next words again made her ponderings moot.

"Contact lost! Scan shows clean board!"

"What?" Teach exclaimed. "Where did they go? How could a whole ship disappear like that?"

"I don't know, Captain. One second the ship was right there, and the next it was gone."

"Preposterous! It must be somewhere. Did it jump?"

"No, sir," Hilary defended herself. "If it had jumped, the energy discharge would have shown up on our scanners."

"They would have if you'd been paying attention instead of looking to Leung to see if you should obey me or not! I'll have you up before a court martial if I see that sort of insubordination again!" Teach's voice became louder and more strident as he went along. "I am the captain of this ship! No one's authority supersedes mine! Now review your data feed and tell me what happened to that ship!"

"Aye-aye, sir," said a mouse's voice from the Helm station.

"Captain, if I may," Leung began.

"No, you may not! I've had just about enough of your plotting and backstabbing, Kate! I relieve you as officer of the deck. Why don't you sit at the Engineering station where I can keep an eye on you."

A million retorts and counter-accusations flooded her mind and she clamped her jaws shut on all of them. When she had control of herself, she said, "Aye-aye, sir," and crossed to the indicated seat. Teach glared at her for a moment, but she ignored him, staring at the disabled main viewer instead.

Samuels, now at the Tactical post, was seated next to Leung. She purposefully kept her face averted and pretended to be intent on the tactical displays. She put on her best poker face and ignored Leung. She hoped that the others on the bridge would simply assume that she was trying not to be noticed by Teach. That would certainly be reason enough, she was sure.

Leung herself was too preoccupied with her own thoughts to notice what Monica did or didn't do.

Samuels was pleased at the results of her worm, and yet she wasn't. It was doing a beautiful job of making the ship's equipment unusable, which was its primary task. Repairs on the ship would slow down now that there was an entirely new problem to fix. It was even aiding in her efforts by adding to the growing division between Teach and Leung, which slowed things even further.

Yet she felt ashamed of herself for taking pleasure in destroying Navy equipment, and even more ashamed that her work seemed to be driving the captain right off the cliffs of insanity. Irrational, she knew, and indeed told herself several times a day. That didn't help to minimize her feelings, though.

Neither did it keep her from doing what she had to.

"New contact! 3-5-1 point 0 by 0-0-4 point 2 at 1-4 million kilometers," Calvi sang out unexpectedly.

"How did they get all the way over there?" Teach wanted to know.

"There is no ship," Leung stated flatly.

Teach spun his seat around to face her and narrowed his eyes. "What is that supposed to mean? The ship is right there," he said pointing just to port of *Pathfinder*'s centerline.

"I don't think it is, Captain. I think it is a sensor ghost. It's the most logical explanation based on the evidence."

Teach shot to his feet. "What have you done to my ship?!"

"Me?! I haven't done anything except try to fix everything that goes wrong! Why don't you ask your friend, Brighton, just what he did to 'your' ship before he left?" Leung had almost said Lamont, and only at the last instant substituted Brighton. If the two of them were working together, there was no need to let Teach know she suspected anything.

Teach sat back down and mumbled something that sounded like, "plans within plans."

"Contact lost," Calvi said into the resounding silence.

CHAPTER 25
14 August

Impatiently, Commander Leung sighed and dragged herself back out of the datarun where it passed through the pressure partition. "I said 'data probe', not 'power probe'." She felt like yelling at Jenkins, who certainly knew better, but she didn't have the energy. She wasn't sure it would do any good, anyway, either to improve Jenkins' performance or to make her feel better.

The crewman accepted the incorrect tool and looked at it blankly for a moment. Finally, the light went on, as if it had taken several moments for Leung's words to have any meaning for him. He retrieved the correct instrument and handed it over silently. Leung sighed again, lay back down, and wiggled herself back into her former position.

Six weeks had gone by since Brighton and the others had been removed from the ship, and progress toward regaining control of *Pathfinder* had stalled.

Despite working an exhausting schedule, they were not nearly as far along as Leung had expected them to be. By her initial estimates, in fact, they should have completed the last item needed the previous week. Yet the ship stubbornly held to the same course and speed she had when Brighton cut the engines during the takeover.

Many of the main ship's computer systems were restored, the notable exception being astrogation. There, the computer was up and running, but had not passed the diagnostic tests they had run. She still had no idea what the problem was, as other items had pushed up to the top of her list of things to fix. It was of limited priority at this point anyway. What good was it to accurately calculate the path to some destination, when you had no central engine control to drive yourself along the path?

Local control of the engines had been restored and tested just the day before, but not yet used. What was the point of trying to go anywhere? It didn't matter where they were once the jump engines were working. At that point, they could simply take themselves directly to the rendezvous point, regardless of where they happened to be. So *Pathfinder* had been allowed to continue her aimless journey, and no one seemed to care.

That was the real problem. People had quit caring.

When this had all started, and the crew had learned that Brighton had crippled the ship before being booted off, everyone had rolled up their sleeves and pitched in to get the job done. The entire crew had worked sixteen, eighteen, some even twenty or more hours a day to put *Pathfinder* back together. Trendle and Green had kept hot food available around the clock, even taking meals out to the work areas to keep the crew happy and fed.

In the intervening weeks, a deep lassitude had taken hold of the crew. No one worked more than they had to. No one worked as hard as they should. No one cared about much of anything, except avoiding punishment.

The most frustrating part was that she couldn't blame them. Teach seemed to have gone out of his way to destroy the crew's morale. Reprimanding everyone to make sure the guilty party was punished was his answer for everything. Where was the motivation to pitch in and help the guy next to you if you were going to be chastised for anything he or she did wrong? Or, why work harder if you were bound to be penalized no matter what you did?

Slow work was now the norm because everyone was wary of who might be watching them do their jobs. Someone was always taking notes on who was working where. If some glitch developed there later, they would immediately be suspected of deliberately causing the problem. Most were also being cautious about approaching work areas in case the saboteur had left booby traps behind. Word of what happened to Danis and Bezates had gotten around, much as they had worked to avoid that embarrassment.

The result was that no one wanted to do more than the minimum, because the fewer things you worked on, the fewer things you could be blamed for if someone else broke them.

Add to that Teach's edict against being found anywhere but at work, in the mess, or in your quarters and it was easy to see how morale had slid so low. The crew was increasingly pressured, but they had nowhere to let off that steam.

What a filthy, stinking mess! she thought. *One almost entirely of Teach's making.*

Well, she did have to take some of the responsibility for that, she supposed. She had taken steps to make Teach look bad to the rest of the crew, but this state was certainly not what she had imagined. Regardless of her outside influence, it shouldn't have made him *this* irrational and suspicious. They should still have been able to get the ship moving without too much lost time.

Delay was the worst thing for them right now. If they waited long enough, something else was sure to go wrong. The faster they got to their destination, the fewer the opportunities Lamont would have to cause problems.

What kind of a leader was he if he could not see that? *If I were in command, things would certainly be different, that was for sure.*

Failure to keep to their original schedule may have already cost them too much. Forrest had made contact with them just before the takeover to make sure they were still on time. The appointment to hand over *Pathfinder* to them was five weeks past, and Leung was worried that option might be lost to them for good now. There had been no way at all to contact them with the long range communications out. The rendezvous was to take place in the Worth system, which was Warner territory. It was not likely that they would hang around this long waiting for them to arrive. Warner authorities were apt to have gotten suspicious long before now.

Leung inchwormed backward to exit the restrictive conduit and handed the probe back to Jenkins, who accepted it with a bland expression.

"Well, this section checks out," she said brightly, hoping to have some positive effect on her team. "Giannini and Sullivan did good work. Now let's go check on how Aichele, Semrad, and Beacham managed the next one."

She may as well have kept silent. Jenkins rose like an automaton and followed her, eyes on his shuffling feet. A thought occurred to Leung and she stopped and turned around. "Let's take a break first, Jenkins. I have some business to see to on the bridge, why don't you go to the galley and get some dinner. I'll see you back here in a half hour."

"Yes, ma'am. Thank you, ma'am," he responded leadenly. He said nothing else while they climbed the ladder from the interstitial space below the main level back to Engineering. They separated in the boatbay, where he took the port corridor toward the mess while she headed for "Broadway," the central hallway.

She didn't make it. She stopped when she heard running footsteps behind her. Ensign Omundson's shouted, "Commander Leung!" She turned and waited for him to catch up, not wanting to expend the energy necessary to retrace her steps.

"What is it, Ensign?"

"Power's out on the lower level, ma'am. The entire port corridor went into lock down, and then the power died. I went down with De Saumserez and Biltcliffe, but nothing seems to work, including wiring in external power. I can't get any of the doors to open."

Leung had grudgingly started to be impressed with the young officer's ability to handle a number of things on his own. All of the status he had gained in her esteem was undone at once when she heard the whine in his voice. *Spoiled, arrogant brat.*

She could see that he viewed the new problem as a personal affront. *'It's not fair.' 'Why me?' Baby.*

With some difficulty, she drew her focus off the snot-nosed kid and back to the problem he had come to report. The port corridor on lower deck contained, let's see…two missile storage rooms on the starboard side, one missile launch bay, one laser battery, three storage rooms, the ventilation pump room, automated laundry room, and the water reclamation room. None of the duty stations there should have been manned, and she couldn't think of any work she had assigned there. Still.

"Is anyone locked into any of those rooms?"

"No, ma'am."

"So what do you recommend?"

Rather than catching him flatfooted, as she had expected, Omundson had actually thought about the problem. "Ma'am, I'd like to call Young, Aichele, and Giannini off of their assignments to work with us on this. Young and Giannini know the electrical system inside and out, and De Saumserez and Aichele are our best welders. We're going to have to cut into the walls to get at the power locks."

"And what will you and Biltcliffe be doing?"

"She and I will track down why the power is out and get that back online." He grinned at her. *If he knew how infuriating that was he wouldn't do it,* she thought. *Or maybe he is too arrogant to care what anyone else thinks.*

"Very well, Ensign. See to it."

She dismissed him and started back down Broadway, remembering her delayed errand to talk to Teach about lightening up on the punishments. She didn't know if it would do any good, but she had to try.

She was resolved to keep the discussion calm. No positive action was going to result if she and Teach could not find some common ground, so she had to do her best to make him see reason.

Calm, Leung thought to herself. *Just stay calm and maybe we can have a pleasant conversation for once.* The thought seemed reasonable to her at the moment, but Teach seemed to know exactly the thing that would make her explode, and never failed to bring it up. As captain he should be extracting the best from everyone, not finding ways to bring out the worst.

At least Samuels had the bridge watch this shift, so she would have an opportunity to speak to Teach in private. He occasionally left Samuels or Omundson as OOD for an entire watch while he performed other duties. Of course, it was out of the question to let Leung have that same luxury.

Calm, she reminded herself.

Her stride slowed as she reached the hatch to the captain's quarters, and she took a moment to breathe deeply and make sure she could check her temper at the door. She looked down briefly to be sure her hands were reasonably clean before running them through her black hair. She knew she was stalling and made herself stop by knocking on the frame twice. *Can't put it off now.*

"A word with you, Captain?" she asked after being admitted.

"What is it?" he asked gruffly. He looked as tired as he sounded, and he sounded as tired as she felt. Besides simple fatigue, she had been having stomach problems the last few days as well. Pushing those feelings aside, she spoke as calmly and easily as she could.

"Request permission to speak freely, sir." Teach's eyes narrowed under his bushy black eyebrows, but he nodded his approval.

"Sir, I think that it would be in the best interests of the ship for you to relax the restrictions that have been placed upon the crew. I agree that we need to continue to seek out the saboteur and apprehend him. I feel it is equally important for us to make repairs to the ship as quickly as possible. The sooner the ship is back under control, the sooner we can reach our Forrest contact. At that point the saboteur won't have any room left to hide. We need the restrictions lifted so that we can quit looking over our shoulder all the time to get the job done."

"You'd like that, wouldn't you?" the captain fired back with considerably less calm than Leung had displayed.

"Yes, sir, I would like to see the job done," she responded, deliberately misunderstanding in hopes of avoiding the confrontation this looked to be headed for.

"That is not what I meant, and you flaming well know it!" His words were not a shout, but they were not far short of it. "What you would *like* is for me to countermand my own orders so that I look wishy-washy to the rest of the crew, isn't that it?" He hurried on, not waiting for her to respond. It was just as well, for she was trying to hold back an angry retort that would only make things worse.

"You have been spreading rumors about me among the crew to weaken discipline. You have been deliberately slowing down the work in order to justify exactly this type of request. In fact, I have reason to suspect that you are conspiring with others to sabotage the ship! You want my command, but there is no way in this universe that I will allow you to have it!"

Tight as a drum, her stomach pulled into itself with a reaction that had nothing to do with any illness. Edward Teach was losing touch with reality. The signs had been appearing for some time, but she had hoped that it was a temporary problem. Evidence would suggest that it was not. He thought that she was out to get him, and even though there was truth in that, it was up to her to keep him from doing anything irretrievable until they could sell the ship off to Forrest and go their separate ways. At that point, she hoped never to see the man again, but until then, he was in charge. She couldn't get rid of him yet, so she needed to hold him together, if only for just a little longer. Long enough to find Lamont and neutralize that threat, or long enough to fix the ship; either would do.

After that, her solution to the irritating captain might be more lethal.

She took a deep breath and aimed at a measured, relaxing tone. "No, Captain, I would never do any of those things. I certainly do not want to take command away from you, Edward." She hoped the increased familiarity was a good move; too late to call the name back if it was not. "I have headaches enough as it is. I have not done anything to work against you, and I don't have any reason to do so. I only want the same thing you want: to sell the ship to the Forresters and move on with my life."

"I no longer believe that, Commander, if I ever did." The stress on her rank indicated that using his first name had indeed been a bad move. His voice held less heat but more condescension now.

Leung wished she were confused by his reactions. She certainly had made no overt moves in the directions he seemed to fear, but there was no one to blame more than Leung herself. Hopefully, it was not too late to reassure him.

"Captain, I swear to you--"

"Stow it! It doesn't matter what you say now. I'll have proof of your lies soon enough. Now, get out before I throw you out. The sight of you disgusts me!"

"Captain," she tried once again, pleadingly. Teach reached out and snatched a handful of her tunic front and walked forward, leaving her backpedaling on tiptoes, never quite able to catch up to her balance. When he reached the hatch, he tabbed it open and flung her out into the corridor to land painfully on her backside.

Any opportunity to reason with Teach ended with the resealing of the hatch.

CHAPTER 26
14 August

Commander Leung sprang to her feet as if the deck plating were a hot griddle. All of the internal barriers she had constructed to hold back her anger melted in the nova of her blazing triphammer heart. She felt like chewing her way back through the hatch and spitting shrapnel at that infuriatingly obtuse man!

She briefly considered pounding on the door to be admitted, but just as quickly discarded the notion. What good would it do? The man was blind to the needs of the ship, and blind to what was needed to finish this mad undertaking. This was not the way it was supposed to happen. A little paranoia on his part would play into her plans, but this was, was, a mess! A putrid, flaming, stinking, vomitus, monstrous, ghastly, abysmal, unmanageable, ruinous, rancid, appalling, decomposing, reeking mess!

Finding no immediate outlet for her boiling anger, she let out a fierce yell.

The lack of decorum immediately brought her up short. She still felt angry, but embarrassment at losing control overshadowed her rage for the moment.

After a time, she started back to her unfinished work, checking on the repairs her teams had completed that day. There was nothing to be gained here. Fury still held sway, but she hoped to get a handle on it during the walk aft.

Teach could not have done more to slow the repair work down to a snail's pace if he had deliberately set out with that goal in mind! The random thought entered into her mind with such force that she stumbled, almost forgetting to complete the next step.

What if it was intentional? What if his sudden irrationality was just a ruse, a cover to explain bad orders? She expected some erratic behavior from him, but this was more than her interference could account for.

If that really was what he was doing, and she had to admit it would allow some logical explanations for the directives he had dropped on the crew. Was he then responsible for the sabotage? She had been considering potential culprits off and on while she worked. Some repairs required you to focus on what you were doing, but some were mostly rote action that left the mind free to consider other problems. Up until this point, she had not even considered any of those who had signed on before the actual takeover. One word from any of them to Chowdhury, and the plot would have been over within a few minutes. Their success, incomplete as it was, had been entirely due to their ability to keep it a secret until they acted.

No, none of them had any reason to be trying to stop the show now. They all wanted what Leung herself wanted, to be paid. But what about Teach? For that matter, what about Lamont? Could they be working together for some reason? Could they have other motivating factors?

The possibility existed, but why would Teach want to slow the ship down? Why would he want to postpone the payoff now that he controlled the most advanced ship in the explored galaxy? Her engineer's mind opted to sort through all of the available data in search of an answer that made sense. She quickly found herself retracing well-worn facts that she had previously established. To these, she tried to fit the idea of Teach acting intentionally contrary to her previous assumptions.

He certainly had plenty of reasons to be bending over backward to get the ship, and especially the jump engines, running again. When *Pathfinder* finally met up with the Forrest contacts, he would be paid a share almost equal to hers. Of course, he didn't know he was to be getting less. She had told him that all bridge officers were to receive the same compensation. Then again, she had told him that she hadn't made contact with Forrest when she already had most of the deal worked out with them previously.

Could he have found out somehow that I brought him in after the fact? Or that I will be getting a bigger chunk of the pie?

She didn't know, but she doubted it. No one else on the ship had that information, and they currently could not contact Forrest, due to sabotage. But, wait. Teach had been trying to contact Forrest when the sabotage had been discovered. What had he been trying to contact them about? Had he already been in contact with them without informing her? It had seemed innocuous enough at the time, but now she wondered.

Well, no way to know for sure, but it was doubtful that he had gotten any information incriminating her from Forrest. It would not be in their best interest to foment discord on the ship before they had it in their possession.

Besides, his share actually went up with the disappearance of Lamont. The bridge officer's portion would now be split only two ways instead of three.

A dark suspicion sent a chill down her spine. Could Teach have killed Lamont for greed? People had killed for less. It would be enough motive for Leung to do it, she knew. The amount she had quoted him was a small fortune, but why settle for one fortune when you could have two? It would not be the first time that such a person cracked up mentally from the guilt, either.

If true, though, Leung would almost certainly be a target, as well. Why settle for two fortunes when you could have three? *Now there's a cheery thought.* She was going to have to not only expedite repairs, but watch her back while she was about it. She could see the ultimate result of that plan. She would be working as slowly as everyone else had been, and for much the same reason, covering her rear.

That didn't really fit the pattern, though. If he were looking to increase his share, he would still need a working ship, and for that he needed a breathing chief engineer. He would have needed Lamont's bridge codes also, so he wouldn't have tried to cut him out, at least not at that point. Except.

Except that at that point, before the takeover, Teach didn't know that Lamont's bridge codes would be needed. There had been no advanced warning that Brighton would lock down the command and control systems before Teach and the others were able to pry him out of the ship, so it was certainly possible that he had done in Lamont, and it was equally possible that he had been driven around the bend by the guilt associated with that act. Popular media may make it seem like people kill other people all the time with hardly a thought after the fact, but Leung knew from personal experience that once you had taken away someone else's life, you would carry the weight of the act around with you wherever you went thereafter. Of course, a pile of money did make that guilt much easier to live with.

That would explain two of the pieces to this bizarre puzzle, but it did not explain the sabotage. Breaking parts of the ship, slowing down the repairs, those actions would seem to be the exact opposite actions one would take if money alone were the motivating factor. He wouldn't be behind both the sabotage and Lamont's disappearance, but he could have been behind either. Unless Lamont's disappearance did not mean that he was dead, but instead that he had gone into hiding.

What would be Lamont's motive for that?

She was drawing a blank on that score, so she moved on to something else. Could there be anything that would motivate him to try keeping them from jumping clear of the system?

Supposing he had nothing to do with Lamont's disappearance, and that the irrationality was simply a blind so that he could cause the crew to be always looking over their shoulders, sabotage would fit in with the other pieces, as a means of slowing or stopping their departure from the Antoc system. Still, there must be some explanation for his odd behavior. Either he really was a few bricks shy these days, or he was deliberately pretending to be. No one would go around making random declarations and handing out arbitrary punishments just to exercise their own authority. Such a person would be not simply mad, but power mad.

Her foot again had trouble remembering to complete its trip to the decking. Power mad.

That described Teach to a tee.

She had thought it only a moment ago. Teach was in command of the most advanced ship known to man. Someone who felt slighted to lose that command before would guard it twice as jealously once he had it back. Such a man would go to almost any length to hold onto that power. Turning the ship over to Forrest would remove the source of that authority.

She should have seen this coming. She should have known this was the fire burning in Teach's soul, and avoided throwing more fuel on it. Teach had been approachable because he had painted himself as the victim, but once a person is comfortable viewing themselves as an injured party, they find it hard to let go of their status as the target of someone else's misguided attack. "Often, we will do almost anything to hang onto our victimhood, even if it means destroying something we treasure," she had read somewhere.

If Teach were trying to remain the righteous sufferer, there had to be someone out there attacking him unjustly. Teach had assigned that role to Leung. In his eyes now, rather than Brighton taking away his command, it was Leung who was working to take it away. *What a screwed up mess.*

So there are two possible explanations for Teach's behavior, based on completely different motivators. Either would only explain half of what is going on, she thought. If he was after a bigger share of the payment from Forrest, he might be behind the disappearance of Lamont and he could be going mad from the guilt, but then he was not responsible for damaging the ship. If he wanted the power and privileges of command, then he would not be too anxious to turn the ship over. That meant he might be behind the sabotage, and the erratic behavior was probably not a symptom of some mental malady, but rather feigned to contribute to the delays. He might or might not have been responsible for Lamont in that case, but she could not see any reason that he would have been. Of course, Lamont may have presented some challenge to his authority that Leung knew nothing about. The two had certainly had heated words the last time she had seen the absent lieutenant.

What a flaming, insane, convoluted mess!

At least it was if any of her suppositions were true, and not just speculation. Leung needed to find proof of what Teach really was up to. But how to obtain it? Judging from how the last interview had ended, she wasn't going to be able to get anything from direct observation.

Danis and Bezates were in the best position to monitor him. It would fit right in with their new duties. She considered it at some length, and finally decided not to risk asking them to spy on him. Teach had appointed the two of them to their current duties. If he were behind the sabotage, he would not have done so without gaining their complicity first.

Samuels, maybe? She had turned out to be fairly reliable in performing assigned tasks. Certainly the most dependable person she had on the ship now. Not too imaginative, though. Asking her to be stealthy might be beyond her capabilities. Omundson was probably sneaky enough, but Leung didn't trust him for exactly that reason. Besides, Teach would have his guard up around officers, even ensigns.

There must be someone, but she would do some observing before approaching anyone. Best to be sure of them first.

Another problem was going to be staying off Teach's radar screen. Instances of him keeping tabs on her whereabouts came to mind; startling her in medbay, tracking her down after the last search for Lamont, as well as a few others. All were times that she should have been able to count on him being occupied on the bridge. Had she been up to something before, he likely would have caught her at it, which did not bode well for her starting something now, especially now that it was clear he did not trust her.

Why was he so anxious for a report on the searches for Lamont? She had been too tired to think about it at the time, but *four* complete searches of the ship? That lent credence to the theory that he did not have anything to do with Lamont's disappearance.

Did he intend to give that impression to throw others off the true trail? Could Lamont still be out there working with Teach to keep him in command forever? *Pathfinder,* the eternally lost ship, haunted by the mad Flying Dutchman captain?

She was driving herself mad with all these byzantine possibilities. All of them could not be true, but they all seemed equally plausible to her. She really needed someone to discuss them with to get a fresh viewpoint. Danis and Bezates were out. The ensigns were out. *What a mess!*

She had stopped walking some minutes before, but was only now aware of that fact. Her mind was too preoccupied to even keep her autopilot going. Her anger, simmering away just under the surface, made the thinking even harder.

Hell! she concluded. *It's too much to sort through, and I have had enough! Maybe Lamont is out there working with Teach, but I don't care anymore! The time has come to push Teach the rest of the way over the edge, and damn the consequences!*

Later, though. She needed to get back to checking those datapaths. *Jenkins should be done eating by now.*

* * *

Dr. Meghan Johnson looked into her mirror as she sat and brushed her short hair. It was something that she did by habit and the soothing routine allowed her mind to pursue the thoughts that were circling within.

Behind her, the cabin seemed empty without her exiled roommate, Dr. Ward. She glanced at the bare mattress on the bed against the far wall and was caught again by a growing feeling of desperation. Her irrepressible colleague had been gone on *Vanguard* for nearly six weeks, but she was still occasionally caught off-guard by the emptiness. She still turned in the medbay to ask him a question only to be reminded of his ordeal. *Was he even still alive?* she wondered.

She looked at the lithograph on the wall over his bed. He had been so proud of that piece. An original Kerstain. He had brought it out from Earth using all of his personal space rations for that alone. Now, it looked as abandoned as she felt.

Everything in the room reminded her of his fate.

Leonard Ward was like the son that she had lost thirty years before. Ken had also possessed the same easy-going amiability that allowed him to be friends with anyone. He lightened any room he walked into.

Now she had lost Leonard to another senseless accident.

But it wasn't really an accident this time, was it? It was a calculated event that left a third of the crew marooned on an undeveloped planet with little chance of survival.

She had worked diligently to maintain her neutrality in this conflict. As a doctor, her duty was to the sick and injured regardless of their standing with the law. She now saw that her presence could be construed to mean she was supporting the criminals who were doing their best to kill Leonard and the Captain.

Finally, she tossed her brush onto the dressing table in front of her, grabbed her pillow and blanket and walked out of the room.

It was a short walk down the corridor to the medbay. She tossed her belongings onto the small cot in her office and walked to the examination room with a new resolve.

Sgt. Burton sat up a little straighter in her bed as if she could sense that something was about to happen.

"How are you feeling?" Johnson asked as she went to the sergeant's side and began to check the readings on the bed's monitors. With no computer left in the medbay, the doctor only had the monitor record for the last three hours. Normally, they would be automatically uploaded to the computer's permanent storage.

"Fine," was Burton's clipped response.

"I have come to a decision," Johnson said as she reached down and unlocked the handcuff from Burton's wrist. "You are still too weak to stand, let alone do much else, but I will only lock this cuff when Danis comes to check on you. I will be sleeping here in my office, so you won't be disturbed, but you are not safe among the remaining crew. Be very careful."

With that pronouncement, she turned and left the room before the stunned security sergeant could say a word.

CHAPTER 27
16 August

Captain Edward Teach preferred, when he needed to speak to someone, to call the bridge and have the OOD send someone to fetch them to his office or quarters. Failing that, he would opt to have them paged over the intercom to report to him. It seemed most fitting. He was the captain, after all; they should come to him.

Neither of those options was viable when you didn't want anyone to know to whom you had been talking. Still, having to go yourself to find the people you wanted to see was distasteful to the self-promoted officer.

That partly explained the scowl on Teach's face as he fumed down the corridors of the ship. But only partly. The majority of the responsibility for his expression, and the mood that caused it, was the reason he had come out to look for two men. He saw the first of them ahead, just coming out of the mess room along with three others, one of whom was Ben Danis.

So much for keeping our meeting a secret, he thought.

"Kasdorf! Report to my quarters at once!"

The crewman turned quickly, his ebony face showing his immediate distress. "Yes, sir," he responded, bracing to attention and saluting, the other three a moment behind him. "At once, Captain."

As soon as Teach's return salute dismissed him, he was running forward to await whatever punishment seemed about to fall on him.

A quick look inside the mess told Teach that the second person he needed was not in one of the three allowed locations. He hoped to find him in the second, his quarters. The third area would be his assigned work area, which he did not know and had forgotten to look up on the computer system. That meant that in order to find Young he would have to ask the officer in charge of work assignments where to find him. That officer was Leung, and there was no one else on this ship he was less likely to let know whom he had been interviewing. So, he was required to go and check the computer system himself.

Rick Young was in his quarters and was, in fact, sound asleep. At least until the captain's booming bass voice snapped him awake and to his feet. The order he had given to Kasdorf was repeated, with similar results, and Teach stormed out.

When he arrived at his quarters he found Brian Kasdorf at attention to the right of his sealed hatch waiting for him. Teach entered and the nervous crewman followed after him. The captain sat at his desk and stared at Kasdorf. For his part, the athletically-built sailor straightened to attention once again, pulling up to his full height, more than 30 cm taller than his captain, even before the officer had sat down.

Brian stood exactly the required one pace from the table edge and locked his gaze on the far wall at precisely eye level. And he waited.

No command came from Teach to "stand easy," so he remained tensely erect. He could feel beads of sweat on his face from the tension, and muscles beginning to complain before there was a knock on the door and Young joined him. Kasdorf could not turn to the side to see the newcomer, but he felt some relief at no longer facing whatever was to come alone.

"Mr. Young," Captain Teach began in a deceptively moderate tone, even though his eyes still flashed angrily, "What was the nature of my last assignment to the two of you?"

"Sir, Crewman Kasdorf and I were to observe the activities of PO First Class Danis and PO Second Class Bezates. We were to report directly to the captain with any evidence which suggested that they were colluding with Lt. Commander Leung, or that they were in any way responsible for the sabotage which has been occurring on this ship, Sir." The chief petty officer replied without inflection, never dropping his gaze to look directly at his superior.

"I see. And can you now tell me why this is the first time I have seen the two of you reporting to me?"

"Sir, we have not found any evidence supporting the assertions you made, and therefore have not had anything to report."

Teach's face reddened. He was not used to a junior telling him he was wrong, and he was not about to start.

"Then explain to me how every single pressure suit was taken from every airlock storage room in the ship, and yet there is no evidence that the saboteur did it!" he demanded in a voice that was no longer moderate in the least.

Kasdorf gulped. Fortunately for him, Young was less amenable to groveling and was in control of himself enough to respond for both of them. Young had known two weeks ago that a day like this was coming. He had decided then that when it came, he would not try to make excuses for not doing the impossible. He would stand his ground and defend himself and his actions. In the end, he knew it would make little or no difference. The captain was sure to punish them regardless of the facts. His only concern was being able to tell himself that he had done everything that could be done.

"Captain, I did not know anything about any of the EVA suits being missing, nor, I'm sure, did Kasdorf. However, our assignment was not to guard the suits, nor any other part of the ship, only to watch Danis and Bezates to see if they were doing anything to work against the ship. If you would like, sir, I will endeavor to find out as much as possible about the situation. To do so, though, will probably bring our activities to the attention of Danis and Bezates, who *have* been assigned to guard the whole ship."

"So you are telling me that there is no way that this theft could have been accomplished by Danis or Bezates, or even by Leung herself?" Teach asked suspiciously. Teach's paranoia had already selected the culprit to blame.

"As far as we have been able to determine, Danis and Bezates have not been anywhere near those suits," Young looked to Kasdorf for support, and he nodded agreement. "but we were limited in what we were able to observe. We could not go about wandering through the ship during our off duty hours without being hauled into the security office to talk it over with Danis or Bezates. If that were to happen, we couldn't very well tell them we were on a special assignment for the captain without also telling them what the assignment was, or even refusing to say anything, which would make them suspicious of us.

"So we have tried to blend in and keep our eyes open instead, sir. Our first and foremost priority was to keep the two of them from realizing that they were being watched, or else they would be even more careful and we might never find anything."

The explanation seemed very reasonable to Young. It was not anything of the kind to Teach. It was simply an excuse to justify failing to do as they were told.

"Unlawful dereliction of duty," were the next severe words escaping from the black shag surrounding the captain's mouth. "One month in the brig and forfeiture of your shares of the bounty for taking this ship."

Young had expected some form of punishment to be meted out to them, but *this*!

"But, sir! You can't do that to us after all we've done! We've been doing as much as we could to--"

"Silence!" Captain Teach roared. "I have given you a simple task, and all you bring me back are excuses! Well, I didn't just fall off the turnip truck. I know that there is only one reason that you did not fulfill your assignment. You're working with *them*!"

Young's jaw dropped open. Kasdorf's eyes went wide, but he remained tautly at attention, the shock of the captain's pronouncement freezing him in place.

Teach selected the "shipwide" position on the table's comm unit and said, "Security to the captain's quarters, double quick."

"Disloyalty will not be rewarded so long as I am captain of this ship!" Teach continued. He rose from his seat and began pacing about the room. "Conspiring to oust me from my rightful place to replace me with that incompetent, Leung! You must be imbeciles to fall for whatever sweet words she used to lead you down the garden path! But you're going to get yours now, and she'll get hers too. You mark my words!"

"Captain, I've never done anything to work against you," Young denied frantically. "On the contrary, I have faithfully carried out all your orders to the best of my ability, sir. I have never conspired with Bezates or Danis." He wanted to add more, but decided against it. When Leung had visited him and asked him to keep an eye on Danis and Bezates, he had had a tough time keeping a straight face, but had accepted the assignment. What else could he do? Technically, though, that meant that he had conspired with her, and saying he hadn't would not be true. He had never been a very good at telling lies, and now was not the time to be caught at it. His effort was utterly wasted.

"*Liar*!" Teach raged. He seemed ready to launch himself at the pair, and both shied away instinctively. He might have followed through with the perceived threat, but a firm knock on the door gave him another focus.

"Come," the captain said calmly. The sudden change in temperament was more disturbing to Young and Kasdorf than the temper had been; it was less immediately threatening, but more…unsettling.

196

Ben Danis and Cody Bezates filed into the room. Danis carried a flechette in a hip holster, but Bezates was not armed. In fact, Bezates had clearly just been awakened by Danis; his hair was flat on one side and his eyes were bleary. "Danis and Bezates, reporting as ordered, Captain," Ben reported for both.

"I want these two thrown in the brig," Teach declared venomously.

Danis looked at Young and Kasdorf, then back to the captain. "Aye, Captain. Under what charges should we hold them?"

Teach looked intently at Danis to see if he was being his usual cynical self. The older man's face seemed impassive and earnest, but Teach suspected he was still laughing up his sleeve. "Are you questioning my orders?"

"No, Captain. Certainly not. I ask only for the sake of the record once we log them in as confined personnel."

"Very well then, for the record, they are both charged with willful disobedience to orders, dereliction of duty, and...and...and failure to report for duty."

Young was pale and his jaw hung slack, but he made no effort to defend himself any further. Kasdorf eyed the two security men warily, perhaps judging his ability to fight it out. Both he and Young were larger than either of the security men, which made it a reasonable supposition. When his eyes fell on the drawn weapon in Danis' hand, though, his shoulders relaxed and he followed Young out of the cabin meekly.

The walk from the captain's quarters to the security suite was not a long one, and the trip was made in silence. Bezates went in front and opened the doors, the two prisoners shuffled in behind him, and Danis stayed out of easy reach at the rear of the procession. Bezates had to spend a moment unlocking the door to the brig, and then opening a cell.

Young and Kasdorf walked in, head down and flopped onto a bunk. Not a word was spoken at all, but as the cell door closed, Young gave Bezates a look that told him that he understood, and didn't hold any animosity for his captors.

It didn't make Bezates feel any better at all.

CHAPTER 28
16 August

"This doesn't change anything, you know," Ben Danis said as soon as the airtight and soundproof brig door had sealed behind Cody Bezates.

"Of course this changes things," Cody said, "just not for the better."

"Hmmph," Ben agreed. "You know what they say, 'The more things change, the worse they get.'"

"Hmmph," Cody agreed, taking a seat facing his partner. "I do agree that arresting the pair of bird dogs that Captain Teach put on our trail does not get us out of the woods."

"What I meant was that this doesn't really change the three options we had before."

"So either we find Lamont, prove Leung is a saboteur, or watch the ship fall apart around us," Bezates scoffed. "There has to be another option, Ben. Or else we've got to think of a better way to catch Lamont."

"I think I'm leaning more toward option three, Cody. Fatalistic, I know, but if there is another choice, I haven't been able to think of it."

"Maybe if we got Young and Kasdorf to help us search, we could—"

"And how are you going to convince Teach to allow that?" Danis fired back heatedly. "Any choice there is that would make any sense is blocked! So I ask you, why should we bother? What could we do that would leave us anywhere but in the cell next to the two we just locked up?"

"If we could just find Lamont…" the younger man began, but his heart wasn't in it. He couldn't muster any positive energy to counter what was looking more and more like a foregone conclusion; that there was no way out for them.

An uneasy silence held the room for more than a minute. Finally, Bezates said, "Well, I'm going to get supper and go back to bed, then. I'll see you at watch change." He turned at the door, and made as if to offer another suggestion. Whatever it was, he thought better of it and made his way out of the room. Danis just watched him go.

Cody wasn't in the mood for company, so he had simply planned to grab a couple sandwiches and take them with him. When he walked into the commissary, he found he didn't have to; the dining area was unoccupied. Since going back to his quarters meant back to the security suite, he opted to eat in the galley instead.

He told himself that it was not because he was trying to avoid Ben Danis, but because he wanted some time away from the constant threat hanging over them if they didn't produce results. Bezates sat for several minutes after his meal was finished, idly thinking about nothing, or trying very hard to do so, at least. Finally, he decided that he needed the sleep he was skipping more than he needed to unwind.

He gathered up his used dishes and passed them into the waiting receptacle on his way out. He felt a little more relaxed, anyway. Maybe it would be easier to fall asleep than it had been of late. He certainly hoped so.

Thoughts of sleep evaporated when the door to Security slid open and Danis sprinted out, heading his way with a blast rifle over his shoulder. In all the time Bezates had served with him on *Pathfinder*, he had never seen Danis move at anything faster than a moderate walk. Bezates paled at the thought of something dire enough make the older man run like this.

"Come on, Cody," Danis shouted as soon as he caught sight of Bezates. "Emergency situation in Engineering."

"What's going on?" he asked, easily matching speed as Danis reached him. "Did someone spot Lamont? More sabotage?"

"Don't know, but the call I got ended with the sound of a blaster discharge."

A blaster? Who could have pulled a blaster from one of the weapons lockers? Those had been locked out by Brighton, and Teach had thought it best to leave them that way. There were several checked out during the takeover, but Teach and Leung had made sure they were all accounted for when it was clear that someone on the ship was a saboteur. They were all locked up in Security. Except…

Except that both Teach and Leung still had their weapons, both of which were blasters. The bottom abruptly fell out of Cody's stomach and he really wished he could turn around and head back the other way.

Bezates pulled his flechette pistol from its holster as he ran. Danis pulled his carbine from his shoulder to carry it in both hands, making it more ready to use if it were needed.

Though the Armory was still inaccessible, they had bypassed the lock on the small arms locker in Security by means of an hour and a half of careful work with a plasma torch and then adding a new lock. There was no way anyone could have used those means on any of the other lockers without everyone knowing about it, so either one of the top officers on the ship was discharging a weapon in Engineering, or someone had taken one of the weapons away from its owner.

They slowed to go through the hatch into the boatbay single file, then raced across the open area beyond. When they reached the center door into Engineering, Danis held his partner up.

"Cody, we don't know what the situation is in there, so let's be cautious. The call came from environment station 4, in the main area, so that's where I'm headed. I want you to take the rifle," he handed it to him, "and go up to the next level's catwalk to cover me. I'll give you a couple minutes to get into position before I go in."

Cody accepted both the rifle and the orders without comment, handed over his pistol, and sprinted for the port ladder. It had seemed like good tactics to Danis at the time, but now he was having second thoughts. If someone were loose with a gun in there, how could he justify waiting out here when going in now might save someone's life?

It might also get him killed. He stayed put until he was reasonably sure Bezates was in place.

The air-tight hatch that led into the engineering section always made a soft chuffing sound when it opened, and Danis was worried about that giving him away when he entered. He took a deep breath, readied his pistol, and pushed the admittance tab.

The worry was wasted effort. As soon as he was on the other side of the barrier, he could hear Captain Teach shouting at the top of his voice.

Danis moved cautiously, staying close to the machinery, and what little cover it offered.

"One minute left!" Teach's bass voice boomed out.

Danis inched forward to where he could take a peek around the cooling tower. He saw Teach pacing toward him with a blaster in one hand and he ducked back behind the metal sheathing. Not fast enough, though.

"Show yourself, whoever you are!" the captain ordered.

Danis took a moment before stepping out, tucking his weapon into the back of his belt and wishing desperately that there were any other choice. He cursed his luck that he had been spotted at all. Once he was in the open area, he could see the catwalk if he turned that way. He fought the urge to check on Bezates, to see if he had any cover at all yet.

"Danis!" Teach boomed. The blast pistol snapped up and Ben found himself faced with the emitter end. "I should have known you were working against me, just like all the others. Now where is Leung hiding?"

Danis wanted to speak calmly, to try to reassure the captain that there was no need for any of this, but it was simply more than he could manage. "I don't know where the commander is, Captain. Would you like me to locate her for you?" Running an errand that took him well out of Teach's sights seemed like a great idea to Danis at the moment.

The blaster stubbornly maintained its focus on Ben's forehead while Teach advanced on him. "No," the officer screamed, "you're not going anywhere. I can't trust you, either. Get over there with the others."

Danis made to comply, facing Teach to conceal his gun and skirting to his left to give as much space between himself and the primed weapon as decorum and the press of equipment would allow. "The others" included Beacham, whose right arm now ended in a charred ruin ten cm above where his wrist used to be, lying prone on the deck beneath what used to be and intercom receiver; Giannini, who had Beacham's head in her lap and was trying to keep him from slipping into shock; Aichele, who appeared unnaturally calm; and Sullivan, crumpled to the floor and bawling her eyes out.

"Stop," Teach ordered abruptly. "Your flechette gun, throw it over here."

Danis hesitated. Teach was insane, it was clear, and Ben didn't want to be without a weapon. There was nothing he could do, though. Teach already had the drop on him.

"I gave you an order, Crewman!" the captain bellowed, frenzied at the delay. "Either obey it or I will execute you as a traitor!"

"Yes, sir," Danis responded meekly, trying to swallow his fear. He carefully reached into his waistband and, removing the pistol, bent down and laid the weapon on the floor.

"I said throw it over here." Teach's voice was again calm and moderate, but his eyes still looked wide and wild. They darted back and forth like those of a cornered animal.

"Yes, sir," Danis repeated. He bent back down slowly, keeping his eyes on Teach. The different angle allowed him to take in the catwalk without making it noticeable. Bezates was up there in the shadows and the rifle was aimed at Teach's center of mass. A little of the tightness went out of Danis' chest.

"Are you sure that's what you want me to do, Captain?" Teach squeezed the blaster with both hands, but Danis hurried on before the madman could speak. "I mean, you also ordered me to secure the ship and catch the saboteur. I can't do that unarmed, and I don't want to disobey an order you've given me, sir."

Teach loosened his grip and his head tilted to one side as he considered. An instant later he shifted back into a full rage.

"Traitor!" he screamed, firing the blaster. Danis had only an instant's warning and he dropped flat on the floor. He couldn't escape completely and the blistering heat from the edges of the blast flailed at his back. Ignoring the agony, he wrapped his pistol in his grip and rolled toward Teach, extending his arms and lining up to take his shot.

Looking over the gun's sights, he saw that it was already over. Teach's corpse had just begun dropping to the deck, enveloped in the blue glow of high-energy plasma.

Danis decided he didn't like lying on his scalded back and rolled onto his stomach. That important item accomplished, he promptly passed out.

CHAPTER 29
16 August

Danis was still on his belly when he came to, but instead of the metal decking, he was on a soft bed in medbay. The pain was mostly gone, but the skin of his back didn't move quite right when he shifted positions; it was stiff and inelastic. He carefully sat up, but decided not to try for more than that. He held his head with both hands and waited for the ship to stop spinning on a crazy axis.

Dr. Johnson came in at once, obviously called by some telltale she had set to notify her when he awoke. "How are you feeling?" she asked.

"Half-baked," he quipped.

She smiled in response. "I see your sense of humor wasn't damaged. What about the rest of you?"

"Well, ma'am, my back isn't hurting much, but I can't say I feel great."

"Understandable. Some of the chemicals floating around inside of you are great for what they do, but the side effects can be…uncomfortable."

"Like this headache?"

"No, you come by that naturally enough. That's leftover from the shock and trauma. It should dwindle away in the next day or so. If it's too much, I can give you something for it, but that will slow down the rest of your recovery."

Danis considered a moment and finally announced, "It's not that bad. I've felt worse after a three day liberty. How long will I be stuck here, then, ma'am?"

"You're free to go. Don't overstretch your synthetic skin for the next two days, until it's fully bonded, sleep on your stomach until then, and come see me every day until Wednesday."

Danis nodded at each instruction, but the last one made him frown. "What day is this?"

"It's Sunday," she answered, leaning in to look a little more closely at his pupils. Satisfied with what she saw, the smile returned. "You only lost consciousness for a few hours."

"Thank you, ma'am. Do you mind if I ask you a few questions in a professional capacity?"

The smile disappeared and a somber countenance replied, "Not at all."

"Teach is dead?"

"Yes. I've already prepared the death certificate."

"Leung is in charge?"

"Yes. She's been in twice since Captain Teach was killed."

"Beacham? How was he injured, and how is he now?"

"Beacham was trying to call for help when Teach shot the comm. It seems he didn't care that it was still in Beacham's hand at the time.

"I've got Beacham still sedated in the operating room right now. You and Burton are taking up all the available spots in the recovery room. That's one of the reasons I'm kicking you out." Danis looked behind him at the placid face of Jill Burton, whom he had completely forgotten about.

Johnson continued, "The operation itself was pretty straightforward. I removed the dead and damaged tissue, treated the area to accept regen roots, and sealed it off. With the amount of tissue lost, it should only be six weeks before I can unseal it and he can start training the new hand. Probably nine weeks to be fit for duty again."

"Teach's body?"

"Placed in the freezer, right next to the bodies of Morales and Brandon."

Danis nodded, thought a moment, then said, "Thank you, ma'am. I can't think of anything else right now."

He slid off the bunk, but his knees were slow to take his weight. Johnson reached out to support him, but his legs came back under control and he stood on his own before she could do much to assist.

"Are you all right?"

"Getting there. I think I'll be fine after I get some rest."

"Let me walk with you back to your quarters. Just to be sure."

"Don't you have patients that need you?"

"Just you, at the moment."

"Hmmph," Danis said. "Let's go, then."

They walked down the corridor slowly at first, picking up the pace as they went. By the time they reached the security suite, Danis was shooing the doctor back the other way. He didn't wait for a cordial goodbye before racing to the head to take care of one of the side effects he'd been warned about. Bezates looked up as he entered and was getting up to welcome his partner back, but Danis shouldered him aside unceremoniously.

Several minutes passed before Danis emerged, wiping his face with a towel.

"You okay?" Cody asked cautiously.

"Peachy," Danis fired back.

"Well, since you're in such a good mood already, why don't you sit down and let me show you something that will *really* brighten your day."

"Can it wait? I feel like someone's using my eyeballs as tympanis, and I want to go sleep it off."

"I wish I could say yes, Ben, but this is bad, and I don't know what to do with it."

"Hmmph," Danis said. He started to cross to Bezates' desk in the main area, then stopped abruptly. Noting the open hatch next to him, he went through it to the holding area and reappeared momentarily.

"Where are Young and Kasdorf?" Danis asked.

"I released them on their own recognizance, pending Leung's okay to return to duty. After all, we both know they didn't do anything wrong."

"Hmmph," Danis said and set himself gingerly into the open seat at the terminal Bezates was using, carefully avoiding contact with the backrest. "So show me what's so important."

"When I had to kill Teach," Bezates stopped abruptly and worked his jaw. Ben knew what he was feeling and reached out to squeeze his shoulder. Several moments passed this way until he again had control of his voice. He cleared his throat and continued, "Anyway, you weren't here to talk to, so I started going through the backlog of work to stay busy, give my mind something to focus on.

"Before today, the bug in Teach's quarters was pretty low priority for us, so we hadn't looked at the feed for quite a while. After today, I thought maybe I could figure out what was going on in his head, so I started catching up on that."

Cody restored power to the terminal on the desk, which had the feed from Teach's office frozen on the screen. When he started it again, the former captain's deep bass filled the room.

"Look, Neil. I'm telling you it's all of them together. They're all against me."

There was a significant pause, during which Teach appeared to be listening to someone.

"No. I *do* have proof. I finally broke the encryption on Brighton's files. He was becoming suspicious at the end, but not about *us*. He made detailed notes about who had been meeting with whom and when. Leung, Omundson, Green, Danis, Young, Sullivan, Bezates, Kasdorf, Beacham, Giannini, all of them were working together way back then."

Danis' heart froze, and his other discomforts were forgotten as he leaned in closer to the monitor. Another pause, which was followed by the Teach's response. "Yes, I know. That had to have been what tipped him off, and led to him setting the command and control systems to lock down. Blast their double-crossing hearts! If they hadn't been so clumsy, we might have gotten away scot-free!"

Ben reached out and paused the replay once again. "It's obvious he's communicating with Lamont, but why can't we hear his side of the conversation?"

"I don't know for sure, but if I had to guess I'd say that he was either using a subdural implant, or some kind of ear bug," Bezates opined.

"Maybe we can zero in on the frequency they were using and find Lamont that way."

"Maybe," Bezates said, without enthusiasm. "It's worth trying, I guess, but if Lamont is aware that I shot Teach today, he won't have any reason to turn his equipment on."

"Unless there are others working with them," Ben ventured. "Not everyone was on that list he just detailed."

"Yeah, well," Cody drawled, "If you listen to all of his conversations, he doesn't leave anyone out, except Lamont."

"Hmmph. I still don't understand why Lamont went into hiding in the first place. If the lieutenant was working with Teach, and Teach had taken control of the ship, what was the benefit to Lamont of disappearing?"

"What if Teach ordered him to do it?" Bezates countered.

"I still don't see a motive. Whatever he's been doing, he could have been doing while still sleeping in a bed every night like the rest of us."

"Unless..."

"Unless what?"

"Well, let's say that Teach had doubts about the rest of us, or he feared a double-cross when we would turn the ship over. What if he ordered Lamont to disappear and start the sabotage to slow us down until Teach could identify those he could really trust?"

"Hmmph. That would fit with the log record of Lamont taking explosives from the small arms locker *before* the takeover had started. It should have been a couple of days before then, if the plan hadn't had to be moved up at the last minute."

Danis sat pensively for several moments. Finally, Bezates interrupted, "Do you want to see the rest of this conversation?"

"Is there anything else to learn from it?"

"Not really. At least, I don't think so. I might have missed something helpful, I guess."

"I'll go through the rest of it later, then. First we need to make a copy to give to Command— I mean, Captain Leung so she—"

"No!" Cody interjected forcefully.

The shout was so out of character for Cody that Ben recoiled in his seat. The pain that spiked immediately in his back from the increased pressure made him rebound forward just as quickly. "Blazes!" he swore from between clenched teeth. "Why not?!"

"Sorry," Bezates winced. "It's because... Well, watch the second thing, and it will be clearer."

Danis was about to ask another question, but decided against it, trusting that Cody had some reason for his outburst. The younger man worked the controls and jumped to a preset bookmark; the image on the screen altered slightly. The desk and wall remained the same, but Teach disappeared and the objects on the desk jerked to new positions or disappeared. The timestamp in one corner showed that the feed was more than three days older than the first one, which had been logged on the eleventh.

The timer rolled by for a few seconds with nothing changing in the scene, then a figure came into the room, passing right next to the bug on the doorframe. It took a few more seconds for the figure to be far enough away to be identified, but then it was easy to see the rank stripes on the cuff of the uniform, the streaked dark hair, and modest stature that could belong to no one other than Katherine Leung.

The engineer walked quickly into the room, heading straight for the captain's desk. From her tunic pocket she pulled a set of medical gloves and put them on before extracting a jar from the opposite pocket. She opened the jar carefully, used a swab to soak up its contents, and applied them generously to the terminal's keypads and controls. Once done, the swab was placed in a bag and sealed there, the jar was carefully closed and pocketed, the gloves went into yet another bag, and both bags went into the opposite tunic pocket. The most chilling sight of all was the wicked smile on the woman's face as she moved again toward the bug and out the hatch.

Danis stood up angrily, but once up he didn't know what to do with himself. He turned to his partner and demanded, "What was that?"

"Blazes if I know!" Bezates fired right back. "It sure looks incriminating as all get out to me, though. More importantly, what do we do about it?"

Ben figured out what to do with himself and he began pacing up and down the small guardroom. "Okay, it certainly doesn't look good, but we don't know for sure what she was doing."

"All right, I understand the need to give everyone the benefit of the doubt, but can you think of one single thing she might have been doing that would be considered innocent?"

Danis made a dozen more laps of the room before answering dejectedly, "No, I can't."

"And thus we get to my dilemma—*our* dilemma: this is certainly bad, but what do we do with it?"

Danis' energy finally wound down and he seated himself carefully on the edge of his seat. "Okay, you were right about not sharing any of our footage with Leung. If she knew we had a bug in Teach's quarters, she'd know we knew…whatever it is we know."

He paused for a few more moments before continuing, "We don't actually *know* much of anything, do we? I mean, we suspect she's somehow doing something wrong, but we don't know what it is."

"How do we find out, then?" Bezates asked.

"We gather evidence," Danis said. "We figure out what she was doing, and what else she's been doing."

"All right, that sounds like a plan of action, but what's the goal?"

"What do you mean, 'what's the goal?' We're ship's security now. If a crime was committed, isn't it our job to investigate it?"

Bezates took a deep breath and thought idly of just leaving it at that, but he needed to clarify exactly what they were after. "Right. Investigating is our job. Again, we're discussing what we should *do*, but ignoring what we're *after*. If we investigate, gather evidence, build a case, whatever, who do we turn the evidence over to? Who do we make a case to? The only authority left on the ship is Leung. So how do we investigate her when the only one we can report to is Leung?"

"Hmmph," Ben summed up eloquently, belatedly recognizing the difficulty they were headed for. "We could take it to Samuels or Omundson. They are the next highest in rank, as the only other officers on the ship."

"Can we trust either of them? We may have ruled them out as saboteurs, but they might be working with Leung in whatever she's doing." Bezates was sounding somewhat plaintive now. It was clear that this was ground he had already covered in his head without finding a solution.

"All right, take it easy, kid." Danis sat and thought for a few moments before saying, "Look, we have to find out what's going on, if for nothing else than self-preservation. While we're at it, we can't let Leung know what we're up to, either directly or indirectly. That means no one can know that might report it to her. Let's focus on that for now, and maybe when we know better what's what, we'll be able to decide what to do with the information."

"Okay," Bezates said, brightening. "At least it gives us something to aim toward. So, where do we start?"

"Teach's desk," Ben said, rising. He moved to the rear of the compartment and opened a large drawer with nine printed labels on its front, one of which read, "Chemical Evidence Kit." Retrieving that piece of equipment, he made for the door.

"So you know how to run the chromatograph to figure out what the purple goop was that Leung put on the keypad?" Bezates asked.

Danis stopped short. "No."

The younger man sighed. "So…"

Danis recovered quickly. "So we entrust it to Dr. Johnson, and we tell her nothing about where it came from or why we need to know what it is. I think she may be the only one on the ship that we can reasonably expect to be a neutral party."

"I hope you're right, Ben," Bezates said, standing up and joining his partner at the door. "I really do."

CHAPTER 30
16 August

Katherine Leung sat in her quarters and rolled her new title off her tongue.

"Captain Leung," she tried. "Captain Katherine Leung." The syllables caused no change in her demeanor, no thrill of pleasure, no sudden desire to jump for joy. *Oh, well,* she thought, *I won't be holding onto the title any longer than I have to, anyway.*

It was odd, when she thought about it. The desire for promotion, to keep her career advancing, had been one of the foremost reasons she had started this plan to steal a ship and hand it over to Forrest. Not that that had been the original plan, either. Three times she had applied for a command slot that came open, and three times she had been denied. So she had decided that perhaps there were other means of assuring a pay raise.

She had been the chief engineer of the biggest secret research project in more than a century. If the information in her head wasn't worth a fortune, she didn't know what would be. That had been the extent of what she'd wanted out of the situation; to trade the information she had for money and then retire to some quiet corner of the non-Warner galaxy and enjoy life.

At first, all was going smoothly. She made a few contacts, got her idea in front of the right people, and found a wealthy buyer who would meet her asking price. She had even sent a few samples of the technology along as teasers, and had received a down payment from them.

Once she was committed, though, the terms of the agreement were changed out from under her. Forrest wanted more than just the plans, they wanted the prototype. It wasn't enough for them to have the same advantage as Warner, they had to be the only ones with the information.

That introduced some serious turbulence to her smooth sailing. She had thought about just calling the whole thing off, but that wouldn't work in the long term. She had been very careful in hiding her financial dealings, but they couldn't be kept hidden forever. That would be all the corroboration needed if Forrest carried out their threat to expose her arrangement with them if she didn't deliver. And disappearing into retirement was not an option, either. The down payment wasn't *that* big.

So her small little scheme had turned into a major undertaking. First, she had to recruit enough people to make it work; enough of the *right* people. She wanted three bridge officers in case the computer got locked down, as it had. *Yet another thing that had gone off the rails from the start,* she noted internally. But that large a recruitment was difficult to arrange without giving yourself away. It required patience in massive amounts, along with the ability to make the other person feel that they were doing the right thing.

Maybe that was why she had lost her patience working with Teach; she had used up all of her remaining stock just organizing this flaming mess.

Thoughts of Teach brought no sadness with them, no twinge of regret, any more than the .thought of being *Pathfinder*'s captain brought elation. His death was her fault, she was fairly certain, though, again, that hadn't been her original intent. She would have been just as happy to leave him alive if he hadn't made himself so… irritating to work with. The drug she had administered was only supposed to make his thinking a little more fuzzy. The plan had been to make him more indecisive, perhaps even a bit wishy-washy, less of a leader that the crew would follow. The paranoia and lashing out had not been at all what she desired, and for quite a while she hadn't thought herself responsible at all. She *had* seen him literally looking over his shoulder *before* she had drugged him, so she knew the tendency was there already. But the more things fell apart between them, the more she wondered. Finally, she had looked into Dr. Johnson's medical reference while the doctor was sleeping and found that both paranoia and violence were possible side effects of the drug she had used. She had stopped re-administering the solution, which had to be done every week or so, at once, but by then it was too late.

That Teach's death might have been avoided was regrettable, in an abstract sort of way, but now that he was gone, things would certainly run much more smoothly. Within the week, everything should be back on track again. The work would be done, the ship would be delivered, and one Lt. Commander Katherine Tyler Leung, Captain of *Pathfinder*, would find a remote and isolated engineering workshop in which to putter whenever the mood struck her and settle down, with the finer things in life at her beck and call.

* * * * *

"Ensign Samuels, Ensign Omundson, report to Captain Leung's quarters," the ship's commanding officer's voice squawked over the annunciator. Samuels heard the summons on the bridge, where she was standing the now deceased Captain Teach's watch. She was about to call back for clarification as to which of her current duties took precedence in this case, then decided against it. Captain Leung knew very well where she was at the moment, since her assignment had come from Leung in the immediate aftermath of the situation in Engineering.

It seemed so sterile to call it a "situation" in her mind, but she supposed that was an automatic defense mechanism everyone had. It insulated her from dwelling on the violence of the brief exchange that left one dead and two injured.

Samuels stood from the command seat and tersely announced, "You have the bridge, Fields." She crossed to the hatch and entered her code to open it. She was about to step into the corridor beyond when an alarm in her subconscious, pounded into her brain through all the months of repetition at the academy, brought her up short.

She turned around to look at the back of the warrant officer at the helm station and said, "Brooke, did you hear me?"

Fields started as if she were sitting on a suddenly live wire. She turned her seat to face Samuels, cheeks reddened with embarrassment. "Uh, no, ma'am. I'm afraid I was thinking of something else."

I still felt odd to Samuels to have a woman ten years her senior deferring to her, but she let none of that show on her face. "I said, you have the bridge, Fields. I need to report to the captain."

Fields stood to attention, though such was not required of her while manning the helm. "Aye, ma'am. I have the bridge."

"Very well, Warrant," Samuels said gently. She completely understood how easy it was to be wrapped up in your own thoughts with the events of this day fresh in everyone's mind, and so she presented a compassionate air. Leadership was as much about knowing how to deal with each personality as anything else. Coming down hard on the woman for inattention to duty at such a time would not have helped anything, and would have been remembered and resented by everyone in the room.

Samuels walked out then, reaching back to tab the controls outside. The armored hatch dutifully resealed itself with a soft chuffing sound. The two petty officers assigned to Security were just coming out of Captain Teach's quarters, visible from the bridge hatch, undoubtedly charged with the duty to seal the dead man's personal effects in his foot locker. Danis seemed to remain stiff while he watched her pass, but she remembered that he had caught a partial blaster charge on his back. It was a wonder that he was standing at all, stiffly or otherwise. She greeted them detachedly and continued on, knocking on the new captain's hatch for admittance once she arrived.

"Come," the clear alto voice on the other side directed at once.

Samuels tabbed the door open and entered. Her new captain was in the process of gathering up various pieces of the ship which Samuels could not immediately identify and sorting them into some sort of order against the far wall. When Leung directed her to sit down, she saw the desk and chairs on the opposite side had been mostly cleared.

"Do you need help with this, ma'am?" Samuels asked earnestly.

"No thanks, Monica." The engineer chuckled. "If I don't move everything with my own hands, I won't be able to remember where something is when I need it."

"All right, Captain," she said, taking the previously indicated seat. Leung looked up suddenly at the honorific, not expecting it, but went back to her work with no more than a moment's pause. It was less than a minute later when Ensign Omundson rapped on the door and was admitted. Captain Leung took the last bit of equipment, part of a data switching node, Samuels was happy to recognize, off the other chair to accommodate him.

Leung took her own seat then and fixed each of them with a serious look. "I'll skip the social niceties and get right to business. Both of you are perfectly aware of what happened in Engineering this morning, and you are equally aware that leaves me in charge now. I'm sure it has also occurred to you that the three of us are now the only line officers left on *Pathfinder*."

Monica glanced sideways at Omundson, unsure of where the conversation was headed. For his part, Stuart was grinning and seemed quite at ease. When she turned back to Leung, it was clear that she had noted the grin as well. A sour look briefly visited her features before she smoothed them back to their normal cast.

"Since that is the case, I am reassigning you both in order to divide up the workload. Omundson," an edge of ice crept into Leung's voice, "you are hereby assigned the position of Chief Engineer. You will oversee the Engineering department and keep it running, but I will still manage the work schedule."

"Yes, ma'am," Stuart said, clearly pleased at his new title.

"Monica," Leung continued, "I am making you the ship's executive officer and I am promoting you to the rank of lieutenant, junior grade."

Samuels was thunderstruck at this turn of events. Finally, she got out, "Yes, ma'am. Thank you, ma'am."

A bitter laugh came from the older woman. "Don't thank me, Lieutenant; at least not until you know how much extra work I'm about to dump onto you. You, XO, are pretty much going to take over responsibility for the whole ship, while the Chief Engineer and I get it running again."

"Yes, ma'am," Samuels said, feigning anxiety while her mind raced with the possibilities that had suddenly opened up to her.

Stuart wasn't quite as pleased as he had been a moment earlier. "Wait a minute," he said plaintively now. "If I am going to be in charge of a ship's department, then by regulations, I would also have to be promoted to at least lieutenant (jg), too."

Leung turned her stern eyes to consider him. A look of distaste that she didn't try to disguise colored her next words. "What regulations would those be, Ensign?"

"Well," he reached into his memory for a moment, then found what he needed and continued, "it says so in section 23 of the Warner Naval Code, right after the section on chain of command."

"Indeed it does," she said pleasantly. Omundson smiled, sensing that he was getting what he wanted. In an instant, though, Leung became the embodiment of pure malevolence, leaning forward and causing both junior officers to recoil. "But we are no longer bound by Warner's rules, in case that fact has failed to penetrate your pea brain.

"You work for me now. Don't forget it again."

CHAPTER 31
16 August

Lieutenant Monica Samuels, newly promoted to that rank, closed the hatch to her personal quarters and thumbed the toggle to lock it from her side. As she did so she let out a breath that she hadn't realized she had been holding. She took the few steps to her bunk and threw herself down on its cushioning surface. Her mind was racing as she tried to calm her body with limited success. Her pulse had been pounding and her thoughts were an ever-circling jumble since meeting with Commander Leung after Captain Teach's death and her own subsequent promotion.

She had not had a moment to herself since being summoned to Leung's quarters. Her head still spinning from the unexpected promotion, she had gone directly to the bridge to finish her watch. She had seen the confusion and speculation in the eyes of the rest of the bridge crew as Captain Leung had used the ship's intercom to inform the rest of the crew of her change in status.

With the supervision of the work crews and the routine of the watch, she had not been able to sort through her thoughts properly at that time.

Now, as she tried to focus her thoughts, she still could not concentrate. No matter what topic she examined, her thoughts kept going back to the shooting of Captain Teach. He had been getting more and more erratic with the crew, but to lose control totally and attack the engineering crew was beyond the pale. How had he gotten that bad that quickly? It didn't make sense. Was the stress of command with all of the sabotage added in simply too much for him to handle?

Was this merely an extension of the persecution that he felt from Captain Brighton that led to the mutiny? Was there some sort of triggering event? How could she know?

She realized the circular nature of her thoughts would get her nowhere, so she forced herself back to her personal routine. She got up and showered quickly, dressed in a comfortable cream colored shipsuit and sat down at her console.

While she was showering, she realized that with the vid files from the spycams, she had a database full of images she could mine for information.

For some unknown reason, security bugs had been placed in a completely random fashion throughout the ship. Some areas had duplicate coverage while others were not covered at all. Of course, the sheer volume of information meant that she had only viewed a small percentage of the total take so far. In order to find what she was after, she needed to view all of Teach's interactions with the crew. She set up a search program to pull out any footage of Teach and set it to work. While that ran, she opened the next file in her queue and viewed it. It was from the aft cross corridor, just in front of the boatbay access on the port side of *Pathfinder*. She set the controls for 3x viewing and scrolled through the images. She saw nothing out of the ordinary. No one was traveling the corridors alone. There were large groups turning the corner and heading forward to the galley. Nothing else. She hit the key to advance to the next file. This one showed the upper area of Engineering, on the catwalks above the engine chamber. Again, she saw nothing out of the ordinary. As she prepared to move on to the next file, her search program let out a soft beep to let her know that it had completed its task.

She hit the series of keystrokes to bring up the search log. She was shocked to see over 15,000 hits for files with Teach. She hadn't thought he was out of his cabin enough to be picked up that many times around the ship, even considering the multiple views. She brought up the first file and sat back in her chair stunned. *Who had the nerve to plant a spybug in the captain's cabin?* she wondered.

Could Brighton have done it himself? No, she decided, the view was too clumsy. Brighton was very precise in everything he did.

With a few more keystrokes she set up a second search to look for similar files of Brighton from his cabin before he was forced from the ship. She left that to run in the background and turned back to the file of Teach. The Brighton footage was strictly to satisfy her own curiosity.

If there was no similar footage, then someone had put the bug in to spy on Teach; if there was, then someone had originally been spying on Brighton and had caught Teach only by accident after the former XO had promoted himself to Captain and taken over Brighton's quarters.

She moved back to the file she had started reviewing and double-checked the timestamp. The date indicated was shortly after Teach had moved into the Captain's quarters. The file showed Captain Teach as he crossed to his workstation and activated the direct link to the bridge.

"Bridge, Ensign Omundson. How can I help you, Captain?"

"Is Commander Leung there?"

"No, Captain. Shall I send someone to fetch her?"

"No, that's all right. Instead, send someone to have Young and Kasdorf meet me in my quarters, double quick."

"Aye-aye, sir," the Ensign acknowledged, then killed the circuit.

He stood in the center of his cabin rubbing his hands together for nearly five minutes before the sharp rap on the hatch made him jump.

"Come in," he said.

Young and Kasdorf entered single file and lined up at attention. CPO Young was dressed in a work uniform liberally spotted with grease, especially on his bare arms. Brian Kasdorf looked like he had just rolled out of his bunk. His work uniform looked to have been slept in and his face probably hadn't seen a razor in days.

Young saluted and Kasdorf quickly followed suit. "Chief Petty Officer Young and Crewman Second Class Kasdorf, reporting as ordered, sir," Young said precisely.

"At ease," Teach ordered, after returning the salute. "I have an assignment for the two of you to complete, and I do not want it discussed with anyone else, is that clear?"

"Yes, sir," both said.

"I want the two of you to follow Danis and Bezates, and bring me evidence that they are either concealing the identity of the saboteur, or enacting the sabotage themselves."

Lt. Samuels watched the file until the two crewmen left and Teach paced the length of the cabin mumbling to himself with his chin cupped in his right hand, until finally he turned off the light and lay down to sleep in his uniform. She advanced the speed and thought about what she had seen. He was obviously starting down the paranoia track already at that point. To suspect Leung of sabotaging her own ship, as he had suggested to the pair as part of their assignment, was very unlikely; but to set a pair of spies to watch his own spies was ridiculous.

On the screen in front of her the captain tossed and turned in high speed on his bunk. She hit the key to pause the footage. *What was that?* Some sort of movement by the computer console. She backed up to where the figure first entered the view and advanced the images slowly. Whoever it was came from the left side into view as the figure moved toward the desk. The face was hidden; only the back was visible. As they rounded the desk and turned toward the bug, their face was still in shadow and it was impossible to make a positive identification, but the slight figure was wearing an officer's tunic and had a long ponytail. As the Captain had just pointed out, there were only three officers left on the ship. Only two of them wore ponytails and she knew she had never snuck into the Captain's quarters in the dead of night.

Monica knew she was looking at Commander-- Captain Leung. The Engineering Officer was putting some kind of substance on the computer keyboard interface and other items on the desk. She packed up her bottle and left back into the shadows.

Samuels sat there stunned for several seconds.

She quickly queued up the next file. She sorted through several files at high speed but nothing resembled that first file.

She saw several examples of Teach giving contradictory orders to various crewmen. It was almost as if he were trying to stall the completion of repairs. *Why would he want to do that?*

Finally after filtering out all files that were not in the cabin she found what she was looking for. A second file that showed nearly the same as the first. This file, however, showed clearly the face that she knew had to be there. This time the cabin was lighted and the officer entered from the hatch and passed right by the bug. As she turned, the face of her new commanding officer was clearly visible. The vicious smile on her face as she cleaned up her supplies and exited the cabin was so reminiscent of her expression with Ensign Omundson when they received their new assignments that Samuels' spine stiffened with a chill all over again.

Two things were very clear to Lieutenant Monica Samuels. The first was that her new captain had had a hand in the destruction of her previous captain and the second was that she was a very dangerous person to cross.

"Now what do I do?" she said to the chill emptiness around her.

CHAPTER 32
17 August

Dr. Meghan Johnson looked up as the outer hatch to the medbay slid open and Petty Officers Danis and Bezates stepped through. They had no sign of their previous strut or swagger. There were dark circles under their eyes and if she had to choose one word to describe them, it would be harried.

"Do you have any results yet, ma'am?" Danis asked in a voice heavy with weariness.

"Yes I do, Petty Officer. Would you mind telling me what this is about?" she asked as she handed over a data disk.

"I'm sorry, ma'am, but this is a security matter and it could be dangerous to members of the crew if the information got out."

"I understand, but I could be more helpful if I understood what was going on."

"I am truly sorry, ma'am, but for the moment at least, I need to keep it completely confidential," he replied as the two security men backed out of the hatch without turning away from the doctor.

"That was pretty slick," Bezates said once the door had closed behind them. I thought she was going to insist that we tell her what was going on."

The pair began moving back to their security suite and Danis looked completely around to ensure that no one could overhear before he responded.

"Hmmph. Well, I didn't lie. I just didn't tell her that the lives in danger were ours. If word ever got back to *her* that we even suspected what was going on, our lives wouldn't be worth spit," he added, consciously not using Leung's name even though he was sure they could not be overheard.

As they came around the corner in front of the security suite they abruptly broke off their conversation. Crewmen Morrison was down on his knees next to Sheila Semrad. Both had scrub brushes in their hands and a bucket of mop water between them. They were busily attacking the smooth surfaces of the corridor walls and deck. The fact that those surfaces were cleaned each day by automated equipment made it clear what was going on.

"I told you to keep your mouth shut," Semrad said to Morrison as the two security men came around the corner. "She was in no mood to talk about shares--"

The conversation dropped off as Bezates and Danis came fully into view and the workers redoubled their efforts in silence until the security door closed behind the pair.

"What was that about, do you think?" Bezates asked.

"Hmmph, you know Clint. He's always whining about something. It looks like someone was in a bad mood and he opened his mouth at the wrong time. Too bad Sheila got caught in the middle of whatever it was."

Bezates immediately sat at the console he had claimed as his own. He reached up for the data disk and inserted it after Danis passed it over. The screen lit up immediately with a spectrographic analysis of the compound. Cody tapped the screen to advance it as neither of them understood what they were looking at. The next screen was just as useless to them, showing a group of connected lines and circles representing the molecular arrangement of their sample. Cody tapped again and the screen advanced to the next page of the report. Still useless.

Eventually they had scrolled to the first appendix. In it they found a description of the compound and its effects on human nervous systems.

"Wow," said Bezates after a long whistle. "This stuff is nasty. It reminds me of a girl I knew on Gateway."

"Paranoia, hallucinations, headaches," Danis recited as he scrolled his finger through the list on the screen. "Hmmph. No wonder Captain Teach was on edge; or over it. It looks like the effects wear off after a few weeks, though. I wonder how long she was dosing him?"

"That isn't as important as what we do about it."

"Well, we can't go to her, that's for sure," Danis replied as he took a seat and turned to face his partner.

"What about one of the other officers? They could at least detain her."

"No," Danis replied after tipping his head back in thought. "The doctor is outside the chain of command and the other two are so new, they squeak. Neither will go against her. Either from fear or greed, she has them tied to her apron strings."

"You dessicated old goat, where do you get these sayings? My grandmother used to use that one. Apron strings!"

"Never mind, where do we go from here?" Danis asked, trying to keep Bezates from another descent into trivialities.

"Well, I think you're right. The two newbies are out. They'd probably only see a way to increase their shares by getting rid of the last officer in their way."

"I don't even think they're *that* smart."

"Well," Bezates began, "that only leaves Lamont."

"No, I was thinking more along the lines of NCOs instead of officers. Besides, if Lamont were willing to be found, he would have been by now. No, he's playing some game of his own. I don't know what it is, but it was more important to him than trying to save Teach while he was still alive. We couldn't trust him even if we could find him."

"Non-commissioned officers? Are you talking about Burton?"

"No, actually, I was thinking of Aichele."

"Aichele! Are you nuts?! He's been working alongside us, and we've just about cleared him of any complicity in the sabotage, but that doesn't mean he's trustworthy. I'd almost rather look for Lamont one more time."

"Hmmph. Maybe this time he'll succeed in electrocuting you."

"That *could* have been accidental."

"Yeah, and Teach *could* have been a master tactician, but you know he wasn't; just like you know that was no accident."

Cody Bezates stood suddenly and paced in the space between the consoles. His arms twitched as he tried to control his rising anger, the frustration of the last several days catching up to him and erupting through his body.

Danis leaned gingerly back in his chair, sat silently and watched him as he moved. Finally, Bezates seemed to run down and threw himself back into his chair.

"Okay," Bezates said after several moments, "but that still doesn't mean I want to trust Aichele."

"There is no one else." Danis said quietly, holding his hands apart in a gesture of resignation. "We either trust him or we do it ourselves. I don't see any other option."

"Okay, but let's cover our backsides with the Old Lady. We can give her a copy of the recording of Teach's conversation with Lamont and we can let it get around that Teach was working with him."

"That's not such a good idea, Cody, and we already discussed why. If she knows there's a bug in the Captain's cabin, she'll know we have proof of what she's done."

"Right, and I thought about that after our last talk. So I scrubbed the record to make it audio only," Bezates grinned like a school boy. Danis was impressed at the initiative.

"Hmmph. Good thinking. I'll forward the file to her now," Danis said. "That will allow us to show some progress and keep her off our backs for a while.

"Check Aichele's duty schedule so we can catch him in his quarters. As we go out, make some casual mention of Teach's conversation with Lamont. Morrison will make sure it gets around to the crew."

"Oh   yeah,"   Bezates   chuckled.   "No   doubt."

CHAPTER 33
19 August

True to her word, Captain Leung had dumped the entire load of running the ship onto Lieutenant Monica Samuels. The newly minted lieutenant entered her quarters and threw herself on her bunk with a loud exhalation. She couldn't remember ever being so exhausted.

She lay face down on her bunk for a few moments, exulting in the luxury of doing nothing. After a moment, she let out a sigh and forced herself up before she no longer had the energy or will to do so.

She had been putting off doing anything about Leung and Teach for more than a day because she wasn't sure she knew what she needed to do, if anything. Also, the promotion and assignment she had initially seen as a boon had turned out to be much more of a hindrance than she had thought possible. Instead of freeing her of supervision, she was now the focus of the whole crew, who were constantly looking to her for decisions, assignments or simply to report completion of some task. With all the extra work, she hadn't had a spare moment to puzzle out the proper response.

Samuels wearily pushed herself up from the bed. After stepping to the hatch to double-check the lock, she moved to her console, retrieved her transceiver and activated it. It connected to the bridge tap instantly and she downloaded the day's take without reviewing any of it. She considered disabling the device as she had solo watches on the bridge as often as not, now that Leung was in charge and focusing the crew on repairs, and she could access most of the files directly from there. Instead, she shut down the device and stowed it back into its holder. Best not to take any chances, she thought. Even though she was alone on the bridge, someone could walk in at any time, and if she disallowed access to the already locked hatch, it would look suspicious.

With that task completed, Monica opened her personal folder from the console and double-checked her list. At some point two days ago, she discovered that items she had been planning to do were being dropped off her plate, undone. She finally decided she had to create a personal task list. She had always hated such lists. It had been a matter of pride to her that she had always been able to keep such things in her head with perfect accuracy. Her father had taught her many tricks to aid her memory, but she rarely needed them. She just didn't forget *anything.*

Lately though, she had begun to find herself letting things slip through the cracks. It really bothered her that she had needed to start recording her list to make sure she didn't forget anything. However, at this point, every step was too critical to the ship, and to her personally, to allow any chance of failure. It had taken her a half day to create another, completely separate encryption exclusively for her list. As she scrolled down, she was pleased to note that she had not forgotten a single item on it.

Having completed her required tasks, the worn out lieutenant sat back and thought about what to do next.

She had spent a considerable amount of time thinking about Captain Leung's visits to Teach's quarters. It was obvious from the way Leung avoided any possible contact with the liquid that it must be something she wanted to avoid. Still, it could have been just about anything, from some kind of poison to something as innocuous as a sedative. Teach had seemed to spend a lot of his off duty time sleeping, but that was hardly unusual among the overworked crew.

Samuels sat upright and tossed her stylus on the desk in front of her, knowing what needed to happen, as she subconsciously had known since viewing the recorded video feed. She put her head in her hands and gently massaged her temples. She was done wasting time trying to debate with herself. What she needed was more information.

Her decision made, she opened her link to the vid files and set it to loop the recordings of the corridors between her quarters and Teach's door. She then did the same with the spybug feed from inside Teach's cabin. Finally, she hid her tracks into and backed out of the vid logs. The two new security guys hadn't proven able to encrypt their files or track intrusions into the system, but there was no guarantee that they were the only ones looking. She had seen enough evidence to prove that Leung was a highly capable hacker. Samuels had vowed she would take absolutely no risks with Captain Leung.

When Monica was satisfied with her efforts, she stood and went to the head. She pulled a pair of surgical gloves from the dispenser inside the medicine cabinet. After putting them on, she went back out and reached under her roommate's bunk, slid out the footlocker that was stowed there and removed the evidence kit she had dug out of stores last night. With that tucked casually under her arm she exited her quarters and strolled to Teach's door. She scanned the corridor as she approached the hatch. Turning quickly, she input Lamont's override code and the hatch slid quietly open. She stepped through and immediately locked the hatch behind her.

Without wasting any further time, she moved to the desk. She pulled out several of the sample collecting pads and wiped one on the keyboard, then a second on the screen, and finally a third on the desk surface, sealing each pad into its individual sterile pouch as she used it.

When Monica was done, she checked to make sure she had left no trace of her visit and then moved to the hatch. Using her datapad, she accessed the vid feed from the corridor outside. She double-checked to ensure it was the real feed and not her dummy loop and then moved out into the corridor and quickly back to her own quarters. Once there she again locked the hatch and re-hid the evidence kit. She took the three samples and put them into a pouch and then into her tunic pocket.

That done, she returned to her console and set the vid monitors back to their proper function before heading to the med-bay.

Dr. Johnson looked up curiously when the new executive officer entered the medical suite. The doctor was just exiting the recovery room where Sgt. Burton was restrained and the older woman firmly closed the hatch to forestall any inquisitiveness by the new lieutenant.

For some reason this annoyed Samuels. As XO, she was responsible for anything that took place on the ship and she shouldn't be denied access to the recovery room.

She immediately caught herself before she could complain. This request to the doctor needed to stay as casual and low-key as possible.

"Dr. Johnson, I have a request to make," she began, hoping that no trace of her annoyance showed on her face. "I have three chemical trace patches that I need to have analyzed."

Dr. Johnson looked up sharply at the request and her eyes narrowed slightly.

"What kind of samples?"

"I am not at liberty to discuss the details."

The doctor stood and looked at the young officer for several moments. Finally, she pushed her hair back over her ears and folded her arms across her chest.

"Look, Ensign…"

"Lieutenant," Samuels interrupted forcefully. Her fury erupted suddenly and all of the frustration and fear of the last several weeks came flowing out. She knew she needed to back down, that she was being irrational, but she was powerless to stop the flow of venomous lava.

"What?"

"I was promoted to Lieutenant, by order of the Commanding Officer, two days ago. I was also appointed to be the Executive Officer of this vessel. As such, I am second-in-command and barring orders to the contrary from the Captain, I do not answer to you. Now I repeat, I have three chemical trace patches that I need to have analyzed. Can you do this for me without questions or interference?"

The doctor stood rigidly upright. Her face was turning red and she paused for several seconds, anger suffusing her features, before replying.

"Yes, Lieutenant, I can test them for you. Please return tomorrow for the results." She took the proffered patches and strode into her office without waiting for a dismissal or any further comments from the young officer.

Samuels watched the hatch slide shut behind the doctor and headed back to her own quarters. The fury had ebbed as quickly as it had overcome her restraint, and now she realized the danger she had skirted. Above all, she had to keep control of her tongue, regardless of how overworked she became. She had secrets that needed to remain locked away from everyone. Outbursts like that would only get people talking—and asking questions.

So much for doing it quietly, she thought.

CHAPTER 34
19 August

Eric Aichele checked his telltales as he came into his quarters before he peeled out of his work tunic and pants. Both of those last items went directly into the laundry hopper for cleaning, while he continued straight to the shower to give his own body the same treatment.

He knew it would happen eventually, but hadn't thought it would be this way. His first act of sabotage, to disable a field generator unit, had finally been discovered. Ironically, he and Giannini had spent all of last shift trying to fix it. They still weren't done, and Giannini was still working on it.

Giannini's flirting had become more direct of late, and Eric had played along, somewhat noncommittally. So far, he'd been able to keep things from progressing very far by the fact that their off shifts did not overlap. No telling where things might go in the future, though; she was a very beautiful girl.

She was also a thief, of course; hence the distance Eric strove to maintain.

Seven minutes later, he was back in his sleeping area, dressed in his Marine class Cs, ready to head directly out on another escapade.

Before heading out, he retrieved his carryall from its spot buried at the bottom of his footlocker. He unzipped the top to check the contents, then rezipped it, pulled the strap over his head to run diagonally across his chest, and jumped up to the top bunk to unlock the vent cover. Once inside, he realized he had forgotten the small dimensions of the air system here. He had to pull back out, take the bag off and push it in ahead of him before re-entering.

At the first junction point, he dropped down a level this time, moving with a specific destination in mind; two destinations, in fact. He stopped first at the small maintenance closet, which was located on the starboard-side corridor on lower deck.

The room was empty and dark when he arrived, as he had expected. Aichele dropped easily to the floor, though he had to be careful not to twist an ankle on the parts, packing material, and general refuse that had been left strewn about. Kneeling down, he pulled a large toolbox from behind the storage locker that housed the plasma torch, and opened it. He set down his rucksack next to it and quickly began transferring his collection of food and water into the box. Returning it to its hiding spot, he checked his chrono. Only six minutes short of his original plan.

The rucksack was infinitely lighter now with only a single item remaining, a fact Eric very much appreciated when he leapt up to grab the edge of the opening and muscled his way up and back into the ductwork beyond. Moving silently, an ingrained habit, he made the short transit across the center section to the auxiliary bridge.

The Marine Sergeant was still kicking himself over not thinking about this room sooner. Part of the reason was that the main bridge ventilation system was self-contained. There was no way to use the ducts to get to the bridge. When battle stations sounded, the back-up command center would be the same, running its own air filtration system, and isolated from the rest of the ship. Because of those two facts, he had assumed he couldn't get to the bridge, and had started looking for other targets at once.

Eric may have been slow to realize it, but now he knew there was an open path he could utilize. Had he been more methodical in his planning, he would have been farther ahead in attaining his goals.

Major Chowdhury's voice came back to haunt him again. "Think things through when you have the time to do it. Think it through once, twice, ten times if you can. That way, all your planning is already done when seconds count, when you no longer have time to think."

Chowdhury had taught him a lot in the short time she'd been his commanding officer, but he guessed it was true what they said, some guys did have to learn it the hard way.

Eric carefully worked his unitool through the grate and unsecured the fastenings, collecting the screws, and then popped the grate out of the way. The opening was narrow, and he almost didn't get his shoulders through. Finally, he wriggled his way in and dropped to the deck of the secondary bridge.

The lights were out, and Aichele thought it best to leave it that way. Most likely, no one would spot the power draw on a monitor board, and most likely no one was going to walk by and notice anything, either. But he didn't want to count on "most likely."

He retrieved a light from his thigh pocket and the portable power supply from his carry bag, leaving it empty now. He sat at the nearest station, Tactical/Weapons. The corresponding station on the main bridge had been reworked into a combination Cartography and Tactical center during *Pathfinder*'s rebirth as a survey ship, but the same step had not been taken here. This bridge also had an astrogation system, of a sort. It was capable of charting a course from point A to point B within a system, but it was not designed to calculate jumps. The original destroyer had depended on jump gate control stations to get her from one system to another.

The refit had left the secondary bridge untouched. Aichele assumed that was because if something happened which necessitated transferring command to the backup systems, chances were the ship would not be worrying about completing its primary mission. If the ship was wounded that badly, fight or flight were going to be the new primary concerns.

Working quickly and easily, Eric connected the power source to the unit using the built-in port, and bootstrapped the work station to life. Once it blinked at him, it wanted him to enter three bridge officers' access keys. Aichele had been expecting that, and he fervently hoped that Major Chowdhury's back door would get him in, even with the system locked down. Otherwise, that would be that, and he would just have to turn around and head back.

In the field for 'Officer Name,' he carefully typed, 'Security Override Alpha' and then put in the 18 character code Sheli had made him memorize. He repeated the same pair two more times, crossed his fingers for luck, and hit the enter key.

He fought down the urge to whoop when the screen cleared and displayed an initial menu. He didn't bother suppressing the smile, though. That wasn't going to give him away to anyone.

He saw at once that most of the options shown on the menu were disabled. This was also expected. The back door the Elite Marine had set up was not a substitute for the full access a bridge officer had, and the system was still not unlocked. Major Chowdhury had described it as "a guest account with authority to snoop." Right now, he would take it. That privilege, combined with the uninhibited access allowed on bridge terminals, should answer a lot of questions for him.

He selected the file retrieval system and went looking for personal files belonging to Teach or Leung. Digging into personal files was not normally allowed, even from the bridge, but Chowdhury's hack made it workable somehow. Aichele had had some training in the area of electronic counter-espionage and data mining. He considered himself to be proficient with those skills. But compared to Sheli Chowdhury, he felt like a babe in the woods.

Leung's files held little of use, unless the reader happened to have a thing for robust maintenance and repair schedules. All the files Aichele could find were work-related, and none had been updated since the takeover.

Teach's files were a different matter altogether. The dead traitor had made notes on everything; his first meeting with Leung to start organizing the theft, bringing Lamont carefully into their confidence, assigning Leung to find a Family to sell the ship to, even the reasons for moving earlier than planned to take the ship. "A true leader will move into action when that is what the situation calls for. Destiny spoke my name, and I knew it was time to act!" What did Teach think he was doing, writing an epic history?

Maybe he had. He hadn't exactly had both oars in the water.

The abundance of details made Aichele's job easier. The first bit of helpful information he found was the identity of the Family who had agreed to buy *Pathfinder*: Forrest. The next was the location for the rendezvous to turn the ship over, which was the Worth System. That made little sense, when Eric considered it. Why would you want to meet to transact highly illegal business in a system that was controlled by the Family you were stealing from?

Maybe Forrest thought that the Warner registry for a military ship would keep the system authorities from asking too many pointed questions. Still, if it had been Eric planning the buy, and knowing that *Pathfinder* could go anywhere she was pointed to, he would have chosen somewhere far away from Warner-controlled space to make the exchange.

Maybe Teach had insisted on it. Possible, but again, if it had been Aichele in Teach's shoes, that wouldn't have been his first, or second, choice. Eric knew there was little chance of figuring out the reasons without a lot more data, so he put the puzzle on hold and moved back into his search.

Eric was making copies of the files containing the condemning evidence, and he was going to need to find a secure place to hide the datacube. *Another problem to think about later*, he reminded himself.

Once he had finished going through Teach's records, he tried to figure out what had been bothering him for the last hour or so. Something he had seen was off somehow, but he couldn't clarify in his mind what it was. The feeling came just after he'd looked at Leung's logs, and before he'd started in on Teach's.

He brought up the list of Leung's files again, but nothing caught his eye. He tried doing an expanded listing, which added more file details but again, nothing he was looking at gave him that a-ha feeling. Just for thoroughness' sake, he tried showing the hidden file characteristics that Chowdhury always used. Again, nothing.

He was about to move on, when he realized what it had been. Leung had not updated any of her records after 28 June. Had she stopped keeping logs, or had she started keeping them somewhere else? He initiated a data sort for all files updated since that date, using the hidden time tags rather than the normal ones, and then excluded standard ship's logs.

The terminal dutifully displayed several screens worth of information. He was about to add another filter to whittle it down when the last couple of files listed caught his attention. The file owner showed as Captain Brighton.

Clearly the captain had not accessed those files from Antoc A-3, so who had? The file details that should have told him had been erased. The most he could glean was that whoever had altered the files had used a clearance level reserved for bridge officers. There was only one of those left on the ship, though there had been two at the time the alteration had been made. Still, what could either of them gain by altering the captain's log after he was gone? Their plan had been to jump to Worth, sell the ship, then go their separate ways.

Something else had to have been going on, and it bothered Eric that he couldn't see even a possible explanation. Taking Chowdhury's advice this time, he closed his eyes and tried to expand his analysis outside of what he would normally consider. His chrono chirped at him to let him know he needed to leave if he wanted to be back to his quarters in time.

Eric logged out, collected his things, and climbed back into the vent. Rather than replacing the screws, he attached the same clips he was using in his own room. They made it much quicker and easier to open and close the covers, and it would take a very minute inspection to see the difference. Once he was on his way, he returned to the latest puzzle he had stumbled upon.

What reason could either Teach or Leung have for altering Captain Brighton's logs? Could it have been a way to cover up evidence in case *Pathfinder* were to be retaken by Warner? That would be a logical reason, but dubious as well. If the ship were retaken, how much more evidence would they need than that she was in the possession of Teach instead of Brighton? Could Leung be trying to throw all the blame onto Teach? That wouldn't work now, with no Teach around, but it might have then. No, that wouldn't make sense, either. Well, casting blame elsewhere might, but what could you put in Brighton's logs that would have that effect? If Warner caught up to them, it would only be *after* they had come to investigate and rescued Brighton from his imposed exile on A3. With Brighton in company with the pursuing force, anything in Brighton's logs could be easily verified by the source.

Unless one or both of them assumed Brighton would be dead. Perhaps they had done something to ensure that result?

Aichele paused when he reached his quarters, waiting to be sure the room was still unoccupied before popping the cover plate out and climbing onto the top bunk. He slid down to the floor and quickly removed his Marine uniform, stowing it back in its concealed location. That done, he checked his chrono and decided that he had enough time for a REM cycle before he had to get ready for his next shift.

Eric really wanted to understand what the changes to Brighton's logs were all about, but recognized that he was just circling around and around the same track in his mind. Chowdhury's advice about considering every possible angle of a problem was all well and good, but it didn't tell him how to push new possibilities into his head when they weren't coming of their own accord.

He dropped into his rack, suddenly tired, and began reciting ancient poetry to himself. At the third line, though, a stray thought finally came to him. There were five people who had bridge officers' codes before the takeover. Two had left on *Vanguard*, and two had remained behind in command. But that fifth officer had disappeared with no adequate explanation ever offered as to why or how. What if it had been Lamont messing with Brighton's logs?

Well, that was certainly a new angle to consider, but it didn't help explain the why. What could Lamont have been hoping to gain? Without the original logs to compare, Eric had no way of knowing what had been changed, so—

Aichele cursed himself as an idiot once again. He couldn't compare, but he should have at least made a copy of the changed file so that he could read it. Maybe whatever was in it that incriminated someone would stand out and point to who had done the changing and how it would profit them.

Tomorrow, he promised himself, then began the poem once again:

It is an ancient Mariner,
And he stoppeth one of three.
'By thy long beard and glittering eye,
Now wherefore stopp'st thou me?'

CHAPTER 35
20 August

Gunnery Sergeant Eric Aichele wearily approached his quarters at the end of another exhausting shift in Engineering. He was grateful that he still had his quarters to himself. It made his nightly jaunts so much easier to arrange. With these thoughts running through his mind, he was wary when he saw Danis and Bezates standing outside his hatch. There were few enough reasons why they would be standing there, and none of them he could think of were positive.

Aichele was sure that he had made no mistakes and left no record of any of his visits to Engineering and was equally sure that none of the sabotage could be directly linked to him. He had meticulously reviewed all of the vid files in the Security database. There was nothing to implicate him in any of those visual records although he had been shocked to find that they had not even locked out his passwords.

Overall, Aichele's impression of the new security operatives was that they were in over their heads. Security required a mindset that bordered on paranoia. It was something that you acquired over time and these two had been on the job for only a few weeks. Their background was in engineering and they hadn't had the opportunity to become devious enough. That did not change the fact that even amateurs could get lucky if you left them anything to work with. Aichele was sure he had not left any such evidence.

As sure as he could be. It was always the mistake you didn't know about that was bound to come back to get you; thus his current state of wariness.

Danis took a step forward as Aichele approached. "Could we talk to you for a few minutes?" he asked tentatively.

"Certainly," Aichele said and came to a stop in front of the non-com.

"Not here," Danis responded nervously, glancing furtively from side to side. "Let's go inside."

What in the heck is going on here, Aichele thought to himself. *The last people I want in my quarters are these two, but they've got me curious now.* He motioned to his hatch as he thumbed it open and managed to keep any sign of his thoughts from his face.

Twenty minutes later, it was even more of a struggle to keep his features impassive.

"Are you seriously suggesting that Commander Leung purposely set Captain Teach up to die?" Aichele asked. "I thought you pulled the trigger on him yourself, Bezates."

"I did, but that's not the issue. We think Leung was dosing him with something to make him erratic. I'm not sure whether she intended for him to die or not, but that was the result."

"We have proof in the vid files. At first we thought it was Lamont, but we saw her in Teach's cabin with the drugs."

"Lamont is dead," Aichele said flatly. "We'd have found him if he were around."

"No, he was working with Teach. We have files of them talking together," Bezates said.

"You saw him?" Aichele asked, not suspiciously, but wanting to be sure of the facts.

"Well, no," Bezates admitted. "We heard the captain—Teach, that is—talking with Lamont on one of our video records."

"Then you heard his voice?"

"Well, no. I guess not."

"Hmm," Eric said. "You may be right, but I don't think you have enough evidence to *prove* that Lamont is still alive. Didn't you say that one of the effects of the drug was hallucinations? Even if he were alive then, it is just as likely that Leung was using Lamont to set up Teach and she disposed of him after his usefulness ended," Aichele answered.

"I don't think so," Bezates countered. "I think Teach was an accident. I don't think Leung really wanted him dead, just...oh, I don't know." Danis shook his head as if this was a long-standing argument, but he said nothing.

"You know, of course, that she could be responsible for up to four deaths, if Lamont really is dead. Consider the fact that it was the deaths of Captain Vanderjagt and Lieutenant Sepulveda that brought Brighton and Chowdhury to *Pathfinder* in the first place."

"But that was a shuttle accident," Bezates protested.

Danis cut him off with a stern look and Bezates settled back and did not continue.

"Okay, you could be right," Danis conceded. "I hadn't connected those deaths to our current issues because they happened so long ago. But that doesn't change the fact that we need help. In actuality, it underscores that fact. You think like *they* do and the farther we get into this, the more I feel like I'm drowning."

"What about the money? If you cross Leung, at a minimum you are going to lose your share of the ship. You could lose much more than that," the Marine asked.

"We are aware of that," Danis said as he looked over his shoulder at his partner. "At this point, we just want to make it out of this with our skins intact."

"You know, if Lamont is still alive, he could have been working with Leung to help set up Teach, or working with Teach against Leung as you believe. We actually have no proof either way."

"That is exactly our problem. We need you to help us gather evidence."

"Okay. Let's be very clear, so we all understand each other. What, precisely, are you asking me to do for you?"

It was clear to Aichele that the two men had not thought things through enough to have an itemized list prepared. Their discussion lasted another hour before Aichele finally rousted them out with the excuse that he needed sleep. He still wasn't sure he could trust them. The paranoid side of his personality saw too many ways that this could be a set-up.

In the end, he committed to nothing more than to gather evidence and then to sit down again and reevaluate the situation.

CHAPTER 36
3 September

Samuels sat back in her chair at the helm of *Pathfinder* and looked around the bridge as she stretched her back slowly, feeling every pop in her spine. The bridge was quiet as a midnight churchyard. *What a contrast to the noise and excitement that it had as we came through the jump point into the Antoc system,* she thought. It was hard to think that a mere ten weeks had passed since that monumental event.

Samuels ran through her personal list of items that needed to be accomplished in an effort to stay awake. She was nearing the finish of her second duty shift and was having a difficult time focusing her thoughts. She couldn't allow herself any mistakes at this point. She especially couldn't slip up here on watch with Captain Leung sitting behind her. She had evidence of what happened to those who got in the way of the captain's plans.

Giannini and Sullivan were talking in low tones to each other at the Engineering and Environmental controls on the port side of the bridge, but their conversation was not audible to Samuels at Helm, let alone to Leung in the Captain's chair.

Samuels was pleased to see that Sullivan had found someone else to spend time with. It was obvious that Sullivan was gradually recovering from the stress that had torn her apart so badly during the take-over. Samuels felt extremely conflicted about abandoning their friendship, especially after she had dragged Amber back into this situation, which she could have escaped, but she just didn't dare allow Amber any chance to guess what she had been up to. Monica was at least partially mollified by the thought that the environmental specialist was healing better than she probably would have while dealing with the struggles Captain Brighton and his group must be facing.

She wondered absently if there might be some way to get word to Brighton about events here, and perhaps hear back on his status. She added it to the bottom of her mental list to check on.

There was an air of anticipation throughout the bridge. No one was sure why the captain had changed procedures for this bridge watch.

The astrogation console was currently unmanned, which had been the normal state of affairs for *all* of the bridge stations up until this watch. Samuels had been OOD during third watch, which she had been standing in solitude. She had been shocked when Captain Leung had entered with all the others and had directed them to their stations.

There hadn't been enough crewmen or officers to man every station all of the time; consequently the bridge had usually been empty, with the exception of the Officer of the Deck.

In her manning of the bridge watch, Leung had not assigned anyone to astrogation. While they had finally regained engineering control of their in-system engines on the bridge after two weeks without any further sabotage, they had no computer to calculate their jumps for the jump engines, and only an idiot would make a jump without a computer to calculate the vectors and specifics, so Astro was empty.

Things had been very quiet throughout the ship in the two weeks since Teach had died.

Monica couldn't help feeling a certain level of responsibility for Captain Teach's death. While it was obvious that Leung had been the major mover in the events that had culminated with the death of Teach in Engineering, and that Bezates had pulled the trigger, Samuels had taken every opportunity to insert wedges into the relationship between the two senior officers. Her sabotage alone raised the tension among all the leadership of the mutiny. She put aside the guilty feelings as best she could and moved down her list to the next item. That one was a real stickler. She didn't know what to do with the information implicating Leung. Doctor Johnson had delivered the identity of the compound, and it had been all she could do not to explain herself to the older woman, with all the questions she had asked Monica. The doctor definitely knew that something was going on. Hopefully, not too much.

Samuels sighed inwardly. There was nothing she could do about Leung's further guilt, and it made no difference, in the end, to what she had to do. Yet the feeling that she ought to do *something* about it still nagged at her. Maybe, if she found a way to get a message to Captain Brighton, she should include that tidbit. If she knew anything at all, she was sure that Brighton would be able to hold on long enough for a rescue from Warner to reach him. It would be a good idea to give him as much information as she could before he reported back to Earth.

The automated tone signaled the end of first watch and everyone stood to give way to their replacements.

Omundson was there beside Leung, "I have the watch," he said as he took over second watch as Officer of the Deck. Samuels knew that he was just finishing his watch in the engine room where he had taken over as Acting Chief Engineer. He had already been assigned as Assistant Chief Engineer, so the promotion had seemed inevitable. With the death of Teach, there were only three officers left aboard the ship. As such, each of the three was responsible for one of the three bridge watches and nearly everyone was working double shifts. Samuels stood and turned over the helm controls to Hilary Calvi.

Leung stopped at the access hatch as she was exiting the bridge and called back, "XO, if you would meet me in my quarters in fifteen minutes, please."

"Yes, ma'am," Samuels responded immediately. It no longer startled her to be called by her new title. She had hoped to get some uninterrupted sleep before she was due back on the bridge as OOD for third watch, but that possibility was starting to look less likely. After a quick trip to her cabin to freshen up and an equally quick trip to the galley for a cup of coffee, she presented herself at Brighton's cabin, which Leung had appropriated for her own.

"Enter," Leung called at her firm knock.

Samuels straightened her tunic and went through the hatch. "You asked for me, ma'am?"

"Yes, Lieutenant," she said. "We are ready to begin testing on the jump engines. Please set up a schedule of tests that will enable us to jump as soon as it is safely possible. We are already several weeks overdue, but I don't relish the thought of jumping before we are prepared." The new captain paused with a deep breath and then looked squarely into Samuels' eyes. "However, having said that, I expect us to be ready within the next four days. Is that clear?"

"Yes, ma'am," Samuels began while she desperately tried to think of some way to delay. "Do you think that is wise, ma'am? The astrogation computer is still under repair and I wouldn't want to risk a jump without checking our calculations."

"The computer will be ready before we jump, but I want all testing completed and the engines ready."

"Yes, ma'am. Anything else?"

"No, dismissed."

Samuels walked out of the cabin still trying to figure out how to fulfill her orders and still be able to delay the jump. Things had been very quiet for the last two weeks. The security on the engines and vital systems had been increased and because of that there had been no further acts of sabotage from Samuels or from the other that she had yet to identify. Samuels had been working very hard to ingratiate herself with Leung. Apparently, it had worked, since Leung had seen fit to name her as second-in-command. But she had been so busy with her act she had forgotten her primary goal. Getting close to Leung had been done only to make it easier to derail attempts to jump out of the system, but so far the only potential target she had access to was the communications room. While this would not directly affect the jump, *Pathfinder* needed that room to be able to communicate on the other side, so it might cause Leung to postpone. It was a very thin possibility to hang all her hope onto. It also looked very risky to attempt. She would not be able to hide her participation as well as she had up to this point.

Either the ship was falling apart on its own, which she didn't believe, or else there was at least one other saboteur operating on the ship. Samuels had not been able to determine who it was. The rumors pointed to Lamont, but that was her doing. She knew it wasn't Lamont. He had to have left with Brighton or else one of the other conspirators killed him. The only usages of his codes since the takeover were those she had planted.

She had initially suspected Aichele, but he had an alibi for three of the known attacks, other than her own, and his conduct had been what you would expect from one who had joined with the mutineers. Whoever the other saboteur was, they were better at it than she was most of the time, and Samuels had no way to contact them or to let them know that the timetable had been moved up. She would have to act on her own, regardless of how risky it was to her personally. She had been putting off this next round of sabotage because she had run out of easy, safe targets. All her other targets left some risk of injury or death to personnel. Samuels wasn't sure she was ready to take that step, but she could see no alternative. She only had two targets that were accessible to hcr, really. She had seen Danis and Bezates setting spybugs in the corridors and there were only two targets not covered by the bugs that she had been able to locate. She thought that she had located all of them, but there was no absolute guarantee of that either, even though she had identified each feed and the spybug it came from. Judging by the level of sophistication, or lack thereof, that Danis and Beztes had demonstrated, she was reasonably certain they hadn't been able to hide any from her.

She could always create loops in the video feed, but seeing no one near an area that was later damaged would tell Danis and Bezates, and Leung, that someone had access to their video bugs, which she wanted to avoid. Better to target an area left unmonitored.

The pieces were all in place to disable the communications room beyond repair, but she wasn't sure she could guarantee that no one would get hurt. The only other option was the environmental room. If that room were destroyed, it would likely result in the deaths of all personnel aboard *Pathfinder*. That would definitely be a target of last resort.

She looked at her chrono. *So much for sleep,* she thought.

She moved quickly from the captain's quarters to her own. There she got into the spybug program and again looped a feed to the camera from the forward cross corridor. Then she grabbed the emergency bag that she had assembled earlier and exited her cabin. She went starboard along the forward cross-corridor and around the corner to the communications room. The communications officer's quarters were unoccupied, just aft of the comm room, and the communications section office to the forward side of the comm room hadn't been used since the take-over. She knew she would have privacy, but she keyed the hatch closed and secured it using Lamont's access code anyway. She moved quickly to the back wall and opened the storage locker that contained the remote comm buoys. There were twenty-three buoys in a rack designed to hold twenty-eight. She pulled out the first one she could reach. The buoy was nothing more than a cylinder roughly thirty centimeters long and fifteen centimeters in diameter that had an incredibly powerful transmitter mounted in front of a small gravitic drive.

She needed to make some small adjustments to the programming before she could launch it, so she laid it on the worktable and hooked up a few data probes with deft movements. First she disabled the locator beacon, then she reset the destination to allow it to home on the communications gate back to Betre, after passing within comm range of A3. The next part was the trickiest. She had to get the buoy to transmit a directional signal to A3 as long as it was in range, then power down until after it transited the gate, whereupon it would reactivate the beacon to make sure it only went to Warner Command. Once that was complete, she composed her message.

She wasn't sure how many there were in the rack when they left Betre, but she had to assume someone would have that info and that her theft would be noticed.

She quickly planted the charges around the beacons and wired all of it to detonate at 24:00, when the compartment would be empty and she would have an alibi, then she set up a trip switch to activate the bomb early if anyone tried to force the access hatch.

Once she was done, she grabbed an extra comm buoy in case of emergency. This was also a big risk. If she was found with that in her possession there would be no doubt of her guilt. She tucked everything back into her emergency bag and carefully closed the hatch behind her. Using the remote in her bag, she activated the device and moved quickly back to her quarters.

It looked like she would get twenty-five minutes of sleep after all.

CHAPTER 37
3 September

Monica got to her quarters a few moments later and realized immediately that any thoughts of sleep were chimerical.

She could lie down for the half hour or so she had calculated, but then she would have to leave her incriminating comm buoy out in plain sight. As it was, she didn't have enough time to find a permanent hiding spot for it at that moment. Where could she hide it in the little time she had remaining to her? What had she been thinking of, grabbing it in the first place?

Insurance, she supposed. She didn't want all her hope of success dependent on one message making it back to a source of help. It was a great big, nasty universe out there, and no one was guaranteeing her anything. Her father had always told her that she was born with a clean balance sheet, meaning that life owed her nothing at all. "The only path that leads to success heads uphill," was his favorite dictum. Victor Bybee had been born with that same balance sheet, yet he was now head of operations for the fifth largest transstellar shipping line, due entirely to his own unflagging physical and mental exertions.

Thinking of her father unleashed a cascade of intertwined possibilities, and she didn't have time to untangle them at the moment. On the one hand, he would be the perfect ace in the hole because no one knew of any connection between him and the Warner Family, except on a professional level. On the other, if she sent a copy of her data files to him, it might lead to embarrassing revelations if they were intercepted before they reached him. More than embarrassing, criminal. The most likely outcome would be Warner blocking Bybee ships from using any of its jump gates. That would cause the family business to dry up overnight.

No, the risk was simply too great to broach. He would be perfect to hold the secrets safe for her, but there was no perfect way to ensure that he got them and no one else did.

Come to think of it, sending a record of what had happened on *Pathfinder* was less perfect than Monica had been thinking. It would have been perfect if Warner held her sole loyalty, and she realized abruptly that was exactly how she herself had been viewing the situation. She was so immersed in the problem Brighton was depending on her to solve, she had forgotten that it wasn't her only, or even her first, obligation.

Suddenly angry at herself, Samuels checked the time. She was down to twenty minutes before she had to relieve Omundson on the bridge. First things first: find a spot to store the buoy. Later, after she had time to carefully study her options, she would find an optimal solution. She would take the time to be sure of herself, identify to whom to send the records, whom she could trust, and then she would launch the second arrow from her bow--

Idiot! she railed at herself. *Unthinking, moronic, simpleton!*

She couldn't launch the buoy once the comm room was destroyed. Then, there would be no way to permanently get rid of the evidence of what she'd done.

She would have to hide the communications missile somewhere that it couldn't be found, and hope that no one would spot her doing it.

That was going to be tricky now. It was too close to watch change, and people were going to be moving about the ship to get to their next duty station soon. She had to move quickly if she wanted to get it out of her quarters. She would take it now and go…where?

Her brain flashed ideas one after another, sped onward by her mounting panic. The thoughts began making less and less sense, more desperate than anything else. She knew it was getting her nowhere, and she fought to seize mental control again.

She sat down on her bunk, comm buoy behind her, and rocked forward and back, taking deep breaths. A few seconds of this was sufficient to calm her racing mind once again.

Okay, let's take this one step at a time, Miss Monica Samantha Bybee, she told herself. First of all, she needed to give up the notion that she could send a duplicate message to another destination. It wouldn't work, so she should just drop it and move on.

Right?

Well, the data was already organized. It would only take a minute or less to upload it to the buoy's storage unit. There was programming the course, though. Unless she already knew the precise coordinates to send it to, it would take too long to look them up or to figure them out.

So drop it, already.

Except, there was one set of coordinates that she wouldn't have to calculate, and that was the family home in New Zealand. She *could* send it there in the time she had left. And she could encrypt it with the family keys without effort. That wasn't the same as making it totally secure, as Hightower Interglobal had proven, but it was better than nothing. Less risky, but still very dicey indeed.

She didn't have time to dither about this. It was now or never, and either way, she had to move in the next few seconds. Ignoring her swimming head, she tried to identify instead what *felt* right, and then it was a simple decision.

Monica hopped up at once, pulling the buoy up behind her. She removed her pad from her thigh pocket and brought up the view of the corridor outside. All clear at the moment. She kicked off the script to loop the video feed, then stepped out and moved quickly back to the communications room. She used the pad again to disable the explosives and slipped back inside.

She wasted no time in connecting the data ports and beginning the file transfer. While that was running, she tabbed the record button on the vid as she took a seat.

"Hi, Dad. I don't have any time to explain, but I'm in the middle of a mess. Big surprise, I know." Her face lit up with a smile for a brief instant before returning to its former solemnity. "This is the biggest yet, though, and it's possible that by the time you see this I might be dead. I hope not, but there it is. This message contains a copy of everything I've managed to gather about what happened. I say copy because I already sent this information to Warner's Naval Center. There are no guarantees that either of these will get through, but if you see this and it doesn't hit the news soon after, make sure it gets to those who need to know.

"Do what you can to protect the family. I know you will. But at the same time, Dad, it's not *right* to let these filthy parasites get away with the biggest theft in a hundred years or more. Any more that it would be right to let Hightower get away with what they pulled. I've made several plans along *those* lines, and I hope to implement them myself."

Tears came to her eyes, unbidden and unwanted. "It's worth it, Dad. The fake identity and citizenship, the four years without contacting you or anyone in the family, all of it, if we can make the guilty pay."

A beep interrupted her, and she wiped the tears away. "Times up, Dad. I've got to go. My love to all."

She punched the terminate key, uploaded the message, and then disconnected the data leads. Once the buoy was free of wires and the flight vectors programmed, she dropped it in the tube and pushed the launch button.

She checked her chrono. Blast, she was going to be late anyway. Stuart wasn't likely to be forgiving. She checked for traffic, left the room, reset the bomb, and, after making it back to her quarters, disabled the video loop.

Her door hadn't even sealed shut before she had turned and gone back out, sprinting for the bridge.

CHAPTER 38
5 September

Gunnery Sergeant Eric Aichele was not happy as he walked back to his quarters after his shift in Engineering. He would have less than eight hours to eat, perform any personal duties, try to get some sleep and then return to the bridge for his next shift. His Fleet fatigue uniform was stained and worn and his face carried an equally worn quality. He was working two shifts out of every three; he had been reassigned to electronics repair, an area where he had no previous experience; and he was being watched constantly. As disturbing as those things were to him personally, they were not the reason that he was upset. The reason was that he felt like a failure.

This was a new experience for him. In his nearly six decades in the WSMC, he had succeeded at everything that he had ever attempted. He had never had a teammate or commander who could best him at any form of armed or unarmed combat. At least that had been true until Major Chowdhury joined the team, he was forced to admit. He had been complacent in his duties on occasion, but he considered himself to be a competent, even exemplary, NCO. So it was distasteful to him to admit that he had failed to carry out an order that he had been given. Worse, he had failed to complete a mission that had been entrusted to him. In the weeks since the mutiny, he had only managed a half dozen items of sabotage. True, one had been to disable the comm system and isolate the mutineers from their supporters within the system and without, but in the two months since, it had become increasingly difficult to break free of his surveillance for a long enough period of time to do further damage now that the ventilation shafts into Engineering were monitored. He realized, now that he had access to the security vid files, he didn't need to use the ventilation shafts, but he couldn't guarantee that he wouldn't meet another crew member who would be able to remember him being where he didn't belong. With Bezates and Danis apparently trusting him, that might not be too hard to overcome, but their approach to him might be nothing more than a simplistic attempt to entrap him.

There were also many things that he didn't understand about the sabotage attempts other than his own. His goal had been to make as much of his sabotage as possible look like it could have been the result of natural causes, but someone else had stepped in and apparently did not care whether it was suspicious or not. Many of the attempts had been clumsy and not all had been effective. While it had taken attention off him, he wished they had left it to the professionals.

As he arrived at his quarters, he hit the door pad and entered with half of his concentration on his problem. His instincts froze him in his tracks as the door slid shut behind him. His knife appeared in his right hand as he touched the light control with his left.

"Stand easy, Gunny," he heard as the lights came on.

"Burton! Are you all right?" he asked, eyeing her scars and bandages and relaxing slightly when he noticed the security scanner by her hand. She had already swept the room for bugs, it seemed. "Should you be up and around yet?"

"Dr. Johnson finally admitted that I won't do any further damage. I'm being very careful not to exceed my strength. She also passed on your orders. I haven't been able to find an opportunity to check in with you but I've been active for the last couple of weeks."

"Report," he ordered as he took a seat in the desk chair opposite her position on his bed.

She leaned back and rested against the bulkhead behind her as she began. Regardless of her brave claims to the contrary, it looked as if her strength was almost coming to an end.

"I have access into and out of the sickbay through the ventilation system. Dr. Johnson has been covering for me. Danis always comes to check on me at exactly the same time every day. So far, I have two hidey holes set up. One in the main crawlway at pillar E26 and the other in the outer section of hold seven. I had another one set at pillar G16, but one of the searches picked up on it. I set up booby traps at pillars E25 and F26, so the first should be fairly secure and I took all of the EVA suits quite some time ago, so there is no access to hold seven except by way of my personal suit. I broke two of the external communications antennae and they won't be able to fix them without EVA suits. I stole a comm buoy out of the comm room, so we can still communicate if we can figure out their ultimate goals."

"They don't even know that the antennae are broken," he interrupted. "I've disabled the comm system from inside the ship, so they won't discover that problem until they fix their existing issues. How many suits did you save and how many did you space?"

"I saved fifteen suits. I didn't have enough strength to carry the rest to the hold, so I just jettisoned them."

"Do they know that the hidey hole they found belongs to you?"

"There was nothing there that could incriminate me personally, but they will know that someone was operating from there. They set off one of the minor booby traps and I didn't reset it. Luckily, it warned me to clear out in time. What is your status?"

"I assume that you have received general updates from Johnson," he said as he looked at her questioningly. At her nod he continued, "I'm watched constantly. After the comm room, I haven't been able to get to anything else. I did manage to get into Engineering and foul the jump engines and the main engine field generator, but I wound up assigned to fix the latter myself. Being watched at the time, the main engines are now back online. What about the engineering cable runs, was that you?"

"No, I've been busy with the hidey holes and EVA suits," she said with a sour look on her face. "I've managed to disable the firing circuits in the missiles, but that is the extent of my damage so far. Besides, the cable runs were way too sloppy for any Marine," she added with a touch of exasperation.

He held up a hand in apology. "Granted," he said. "That means that we have at least one other saboteur aboard. Someone sprayed acid on the data leads between Bridge and Engineering, they also corrupted data in the astrocomp and put a bug in the weapons targeting system that broke the control link to the bridge, but still showed up on the monitors as an active link. The corrupted data could be happenstance, but I doubt it. The data was just recovered and verified twelve hours previous. The acid spray is an anomaly. The other two are fairly sophisticated programming. The acid seems almost desperate. So far, there are about twelve acts of sabotage unaccounted for."

"Any ideas?"

"Whoever it is, they are playing it very close to the vest. Everyone appears to be on board with the new regime, but then, I've done my best to give the same impression, so who knows. There aren't many aboard who'd have the computer skills to manipulate the system the way they have. Based on access and opportunity I would have to guess that either it is one of the ensigns or else Giannini. Leung would have the access, but with control of the vessel, why would she need to break things?"

Jill countered, "But from what Johnson has told me, all of those incidents happened while Teach was still in command."

Eric's eyes widened. "You're right. I hadn't noticed that."

"Is there anything else that I need to know?" she asked as she looked at her chrono.

"Yes. It seems that Worth is the system they are trying to get to. They plan to meet a Forrest ship there, which I've confirmed from Teach's personal files. You need to get the comm buoy programmed and sent out with that information. Also, Danis and Bezates visited me yesterday. They say they have evidence that Leung is responsible for Teach's breakdown and death and they also say they have proof that Lamont is still alive."

"Do you believe them?"

'I don't know that I trust them at all, but they sounded believable. I'm sifting through the security files to find out what they have, but I haven't gotten very far into them yet."

"You still have access?" she asked incredulously.

"Shocking, isn't it," he said with a laugh. "But seriously, you need to get that comm buoy out as quickly as you can."

"Okay, I'll have to set it for some sort of delay or disable the scans on *Pathfinder* so they don't pick it up, but that should be do-able. It won't do any good until someone starts looking, but at least it gives them a starting point. I've given it quite a bit of thought and I can't come up with a better idea, can you?"

"No, I don't see any better option short of taking back the ship - and that doesn't seem very feasible right now."

"All right. I'll start looking into setting up something to start holding prisoners in hold seven just in case we need to move in that direction eventually." She glanced at her chrono again and sighed. "I'd better head back."

"OK. A couple of things first. Danis and Bezates have put spybugs into the engineering ducts, so avoid those, but they are pretty inexperienced with them. They never bothered to encrypt the stream, so you can tap into their feeds if you use this," he said as he slid a comm pad out of his desk drawer and tossed it to her.

"Also, let's not meet here again. We don't want to be as predictable as Danis. I'll mark the hatch to the electronic spares room with a vertical stripe if I need to meet with you, you can see that from the corridor ventilation shaft without coming out into the open, then we'll meet at the crawlway hidey hole at 0100. If you need to meet, put a mark on the wall next to the grate by enlisted berth 2."

"Roger," she said as she began the climb into the service shaft above the bed. As she jumped in head first, she was thrown back out onto the bed. The whole ship shook while the sound of a nearby explosion hammered at their ears.

CHAPTER 39
5 September

Petty Officer 2nd Class Cody Bezates was the second to arrive on the scene of the explosion, only seconds after his partner, Ben Danis. This wasn't really surprising because, even though the restrictions had been lifted regarding movement outside of work and meals, no one wanted to take the chance of being caught somewhere other than their cabin. *Even so*, he thought, *we still haven't caught anyone* doing *anything*.

The smoke was still flowing from the hatch of the communications room and Ensign Omundson was lying on his side at the base of the opposite wall. His uniform was scorched and torn across his chest. Blood was flowing down the side of his head and he wasn't moving. Danis was headed over to check on him, so Bezates moved cautiously to the door. He was well aware of the booby traps that the saboteur left for the unwary and had no desire to electrocute himself. The hatch had torn partly open and choking black plumes billowed from the opening, filling the corridor with the smell of charred plastic and rubber. As Bezates leaned over the torn edge of the hatch without touching any of its surface, he could see that the equipment inside was a shambles and debris littered the floor immediately in front of the hatch. When he could see no bodies within visual range inside the room, he started to turn his attention to the injured officer. Before he could turn, he heard his partner yell.

"Semrad!" Danis yelled at the face peering around the corner.

"Yes?" she responded tentatively.

"What are you doing?"

"I was supposed to be working repairs in the comm room, but we couldn't get in. Giannini went to Engineering after some tools and Ensign Omundson and I were trying to get the hatch to open," she responded as she moved slowly down the corridor toward them. Her long black curls were in disarray, her ponytail having come loose, and she had dark circles under her brown eyes. She walked slowly, as if she was not sure how to make her feet work and she had to concentrate on every action. Her eyes kept moving to the still smoking hatch as if it might do a repeat performance at any instant.

"So why was the Ensign hit by the blast and you weren't?" Danis asked suspiciously.

"We were trying to force the door. Omundson was prying on the mechanism and he assigned me to check the voltage at the junction box," she replied with rising anger, motioning to the open electronics panel and ladder at the corner.

"Convenient," he said

"Don't be an idiot, Ben," she snapped, finally coming fully to life. "If I had set a bomb, I wouldn't be stupid enough to be standing three meters away when it went off. I'd be hiding down in Engineering or the rear laser turret. I'd get as far away from here as possible."

"Like Giannini," Danis said quietly, ignoring the insubordination.

He stood quickly, coming to a decision. "Sheila, wait here with the Ensign until he is ready to move and then get him down to sickbay. Cody, you go find Commander Leung and report what's happened. I'll start trying to figure out where everyone was last shift."

Bezates cut his eyes to Semrad and asked, "Are you sure we should report it to Leung?" he asked softly enough to keep her from overhearing.

"We have to or she will guess that we know more than we should," Danis replied equally quietly

"How about if I check whereabouts and you report to Leung?" Bezates replied eagerly and loudly enough for Semrad to overhear. "I'll 'rock, paper, scissors' with you for it."

"My extra stripe beats your rock, paper, and scissors. Get moving."

"Come on, best two out of three?"

"GO!" Danis yelled in frustration and Bezates took off at a trot with a grin on his face.

Danis moved off to start checking locations. He could verify people's stories against the spybug records later, but first he needed to get their answers and he knew just where to start. The perfect place to start was far away from Leung.

He moved up to the corridor junction, turned to the right, moved to the starboard corridor and turned down it toward medbay. According to the last report, Burton had been being kept unconscious because Leung didn't want to have to deal with her. It wasn't very likely that she had been capable of the bomb blast but he still needed to eliminate her as a suspect.

When he entered the medical suite, he saw Dr. Johnson standing in the doorway of her office making notes on an old fashioned data pad. She looked up expectantly at his entrance and waited until the door closed behind him.

"What was that noise?" she asked without any trace of apprehension.

"We had an explosion," Danis replied.

"Do we have many injured?" she asked as she began to move in the direction of the large exam room.

"Just one, ma'am, Ensign Omundson, and he didn't appear to be too bad off. Head injury. He'll be down as soon as his vision clears." Danis replied. "How is our prisoner, ma'am?"

"Still being kept under. I just woke up when that blast went off and I was heading in to check on her. I wanted to make sure everything was ready for any casualties first, though."

"Well, if it wouldn't be too much trouble, could we check now, ma'am?" he said, motioning for her to precede him into the recovery room where the prisoner was kept.

At her sudden stop and sharp intake of breath he knew what he would find even before he forced his way past her.

The room was empty.

He turned quickly to confront the doctor and saw a look of horror on her face.

"What is it?" he asked, knowing instinctively that the simple fact that Burton was missing was not what was causing her distress.

"She was completely sedated. She could not have left here under her own power."

"What do you mean? Where is she?" Danis continued, forgetting military courtesy in his agitation.

"I don't know," she said, moving fully into the room. "She was right there in the bed were she always is."

"Well, she is not there now, ma'am. Where is she?" Danis yelled.

"I told you before, I don't know. She was unconscious and being kept in a medical coma. She was not able to move on her own. More importantly, she was handcuffed to the bed when I left and I still have the key," she said as she held up the object in question for him to see. "I left here and went to bed for the first time in twenty-seven hours. I was asleep until the explosion. For all I know, the explosion was a diversion so someone could come in here and dispose of her," she fired back, her voice rising in intensity to match his.

"What? Who would want to do that?" he yelled, but he went cold inside as he realized that he already knew of someone who was cold-blooded enough to have done it.

"Who?" she repeated incredulously, interrupting his thoughts. "Half the crew wants her head. Why do you think I started sleeping down here instead of in my comfortable bed?"

"How did she get loose?"

"You're the expert, you tell me. Now, if you don't have any further questions, I have wounded to take care of."

Having said that, she turned and walked out of the small recovery room and back into the main exam room, leaving Danis staring at the empty bed, and fortunately not at her trembling hands.

Before leaving the room, he searched the bedding and found a needle stuck into the handcuff locking mechanism. Someone had picked the lock and released Burton; unless she had done it herself. However, the doctor insisted that she was unconscious and not able to wake, and he had seen no evidence that the doctor was lying, so Burton didn't escape on her own. *Why would Leung have to pick the lock? She has a key. Would she do that just to throw us off?* Not knowing about our arrangement with Aichele, maybe she was trying to make it look like he was responsible. After all, who else would she go with willingly? He'd check with the doctor before he left to find out if releasing her would have awakened her. If so, there were only three options, either she trusted whoever had released her, she was sedated with a heavier dose before being released or she was no longer alive when she left the medbay.

He left the recovery room and asked his question of the agitated doctor. The sedative level would definitely have been high enough to keep her unconscious.

Why does this crap always happen to me? he asked himself as he walked out the hatch and into the corridor. Of course, he had no answer for himself, so he kept quiet.

He pulled his security headset out of a side trouser pocket and fitted it to his head. They hadn't tried to use them much because they were annoying and hard to get used to."Bezates," he said into the microphone that attached to his jaw. As he waited for a response, he rummaged through the tangle of electronics that he had pulled out with the headset. Security had all kinds of cool gadgets and one of these days, he was going to have time to figure out what some of these were for. He stuffed the pile back into his pocket as he heard the banging and rustling that meant Bezates was pulling his set out and attaching it.

"Bezates," came the response after an agonizing period of noise.

"Cody, are you still with the Captain?"

"Yeah, we are just getting back to the comm room."

"Let her know that Burton is missing."

"What!?" he yelled. "How the blazes did she get loose?"

"The doctor thinks someone took her."

"What? Who would do that?"

"I haven't got time to play guessing games. Just inform Captain Leung and let her know I'll be up to report when I have a better understanding of who was where."

"OK."

Now to review the monitor logs.

Two hours later he was more baffled than ever. The logs showed Aichele working in Engineering until the end of his shift and then going straight to his quarters, where he stayed until after the explosion. While they didn't have monitors inside individual quarters, Danis had positioned one that directly faced Aichele's door. It was clear he never left after returning from his shift. And at no time in the last week did he go near either the comm room or sickbay except to walk past. There was also no evidence of anyone else entering the comm room for anything other than repairs or their work shift.

Cursing mildly under his breath, Danis stood, straightened his dirty coverall and went to report to Leung.

He found her, still at the comm room, surveying the damage and assigning work to begin the repairs. Danis had spent forty-one years in the WSN and most of that in Engineering. He knew that the repairs being described were Depot-level work and that most would not be possible with the limited resources they currently had available. Nevertheless, they had to have some sort of functioning communications system or they would never be able to make contact with Forrest and, more importantly, they would never get paid. He waited patiently until she had finished and she turned her attention to him. The look that she turned on him was equal parts haggardness, accusation, and anticipation of yet more bad news. He looked closely for any sign that she knew more about this than she was letting on but could discern nothing.

"So, who did this?" she began without any preamble.

"I'm still checking alibis," he responded, not willing to admit he had no suspects other than her.

"I want him."

"Him?"

She made a throwaway gesture with her hand and said, "Him, her, it, them. I don't care who it was, I WANT THEM!" she said as she turned her full attention to the security NCO. "It was sheer luck that no one was killed. They have crossed the line, this time. Delaying actions are one thing; this is attempted murder."

Danis had his doubts about that. It looked to him as if the bomb was set to go off if someone tried to access the room, not after personnel were inside; but he said nothing.

"I want another search of all of the interstitial spaces," she continued. "I want them found. I want all alibis checked. If they are working among us then we are all in danger every moment. All work parties are to include at least three people so that everyone is watched."

"Yes, ma'am," he mumbled, thinking of all of the work they had just been handed. "We have been through every square inch on our searches for Lamont. We have never found anything."

"And you never found Lamont, either," she said caustically. "Start with the crawl spaces and then work through the holds and Engineering."

He hung his head in frustration. "It is possible that the explosion was a diversion to kill or remove Burton," he added hesitantly.

"Why would Lamont want Burton dead?"

"I don't know. Why is he doing any of this?" he asked in aggravation. "If it is him," he added under his breath.

"Get busy with those searches and report back to me as soon as you find him."

He and Bezates would have to perform all the searches, because no one else could be trusted. He absently rubbed the slowly fading goose egg on his forehead. He wasn't anxious to reenter those confined spaces. There were too many possibilities for fatal traps. *What if Leung and Lamont were working together? She could be sending us directly into a trap,* he thought. Regardless of his opinion about the nature of the bomb here, he wasn't anxious to test his theory with his life on the line. A quick glance at Bezates showed the same reluctance.

Not seeing any way out except direct disobedience, he motioned to Bezates, and replied, "Yes, ma'am. I'll let you know when I have something concrete."

After they had moved aft to the starboard stairwell and started down they stopped at the small access hatch on the forward bulkhead. Danis tapped the security code into the keypad and opened the hatch to the crawlway. Cody finally ended his silence.

"This is crazy, you know that, right?"

"It may not be totally out of line. I don't think anyone has been down here since the last time we came down. It would be a great place to hide and Lamont has to be somewhere."

"But, we've never seen anything on our spybugs."

"If you remember, we didn't put out that many. There are still lots of areas that are uncovered."

Bezates was silent for a few moments as he remembered the reason for their interrupted foray. He looked at his hand, but there was no evidence left there. The burns had all healed.

"We'll continue along this bulkhead, moving forward until we reach the weapons room, then we'll turn and come back along the E pillars. If we haven't found anything by dinnertime, we'll take a break and go through the port side between the A and B pillars after dinner."

"We could go get dinner now and tell Commander Leung we didn't find anything. It'll save us a lot of work."

Danis grunted in agreement but pointed into the crawlspace. "Let's go. And keep your hands in your pockets. I don't need any more souvenirs," he said tapping his goose egg.

* * * * *

Moving through the interstitial spaces was much easier than crawling along the ventilation shafts so an hour and a half later, they had covered two thirds of their search. They were working their way back along the E pillars and were almost halfway back to the access hatch.

They were dirty and tired and very grouchy.

"Watch it!" Danis called as Bezates slid over the horizontal ventilation shaft and landed on the backs of Danis' knees. Danis had, in reaction, fallen backwards on top of the younger petty officer.

"You watch it," Bezates snapped. "I was just laying here minding my own business and you sit on me. Jeez, find your own spot, will ya."

"Be quiet. You don't know who's down here."

"Oh, fer crying out loud, THERE IS NO ONE HERE," Bezates yelled back.

"Are you willing to bet your life on that?!"

Bezates sat back, rested his head on the conduits that ran under the ventilation ducting and glared back at Danis, but he didn't open his mouth again.

"Look, Cody, we are tied up six ways from Sunday with Leung. We can't go back to Warner now, even if we wanted to. We need to do whatever it takes to get out of this system and get our money. Once we do that, we can relax and cuss officers all we want to, but until then, I'm not going to do anything that will give any of them an excuse to throw me out an airlock. I want to live long enough to get paid. You saw what Leung did to Teach. Do you really want to get on her bad side?"

Bezates just stared back, but his glare didn't have the heat in it that it had moments before.

"OK, we're almost done with this row," Danis continued. "We'll finish it and go to chow. After that... we'll see."

Bezates grunted and they moved ahead into an area that was nearly unlit.

"Careful here, no telling what's out there in the dark," Danis said, still trying to get some response from his friend. All he got was another grunt.

They moved cautiously. The ceiling was only 160 cm high in this section, so both were hunched over and Danis noticed that Bezates was careful to move without touching anything unless it couldn't be avoided. They passed a light receptacle that was empty and skirted left around a framework that jutted into their path. After he had moved clear of the obstruction, Bezates moved back to his right and froze. "What's that?" he whispered.

"What?" Danis asked as he moved up next to his partner. Bezates had his pistol out and was sweeping his gaze back and forth trying to discern details in the darkness.

"There's something over there," he said, motioning with the barrel of his pistol.

Danis moved slowly and carefully toward the piles of debris. "These are uniforms," he called back to Cody, as he picked one up and looked at the nametag.

LAMONT, it read.

"Blast," he yelled. "DAMN, DAMN, DAMN. The prig *is* still alive."

"What is it?" Bezates called and moved over to join his partner. In his haste to move, he knocked over a box of ration bars that had been stacked precariously on top of its fellows. It toppled to the deck with a bang. The two security ratings swung their guns around at the sound and watched with horror as a grenade followed it down.

"Grenade!" they both yelled and threw themselves down to avoid the blast.

The grenade went off and flooded the crawlspace with what Marines lovingly referred to as "Vomit Gas."

Crap, Danis thought. *It's still two hundred meters to the hatch.*

I'll get Lamont for this.

CHAPTER 40
5 September

Blast, blast, blast, Burton silently cursed to herself, ignoring the sharp pains in her right shoulder as she pulled herself along the ventilation shaft.

Her guards were very predictable in their rounds to check on her in the sickbay. Normally, you could set your watch by their visits, but the explosion would surely break them out of their routine to check on her. In their defense, they had no reason to think she was conscious, so there was really no reason to vary their routine. Still, her security training cringed at the oversight.

She struggled to pull herself with her elbows as fast as possible without making any noise. Normally, if she needed to make a cross-ship journey such as this, she would climb up into the interstitial crawlway between Upper and Main decks then take the larger shafts that cross-ventilated the ship before dropping down into the smaller vents inside the main deck ceiling for the last section of the trek back into medbay, but today she just did not dare take the time. It was going to be hard enough to get out of her dirty uniform, into her med-gown and back into bed before someone got there to check on her.

She slowed and finally stopped as she heard voices coming down the corridor below her.

"...don't know what they used but it was powerful, ma'am," said the first voice. *Bezates,* she thought, holding perfectly still to avoid any betraying noise.

"Who was in there in the last six hours?" Burton heard Commander Leung ask in return.

Bezates continued, "We are still checking, ma'am, but we know for sure that Semrad, Omundson, and Giannini were just arriving to work on the comm unit. Giannini left to go to Engineering to get some tools to force the door. Omundson was standing in the doorway when the device went off. He was blown out into the corridor and has a cut on his head and probably a concussion from hitting the wall, but nothing seems to be broken. Semrad was working on the junction box down the corridor."

"And what about the Vocom room itself? What about the equipment?"

He shook his head. "We may be able to salvage something, but not much."

"Listen, Petty Officer, I want you and Danis to take this on as your only priority for right now. Pick two people that you are absolutely sure of to help you, maybe Young and Kasdorf, but I want you to get to the bottom of this. Giannini stays under guard until we can clear her. Find out where Aichele was for the last six hours - and I want every minute accounted for. Then start checking everyone else who might have had access."

"Yes, ma'am," he said with no trace of his earlier lightness. "That's going to be a big list, you know. Everyone is working double shifts and they are not segregated by their normal work areas."

"I know; but they have crossed a line. We are all in danger until they are found."

"What about Semrad?" he asked warily.

However, Leung's response was lost to Burton as the two moved down the corridor beyond her hearing.

She started moving again, disregarding the agony in her shoulder. *Dr. Johnson is going to kill me for this*, she thought.

Several pain-filled minutes later, she had arrived at the vent cover in the small examination area of the sickbay. She picked up her med-gown and listened to make sure that she was alone before opening the screen.

"She was completely sedated. She could not have left here under her own power," came an incredulous voice, as Burton noticed two people in the room that she was just about to drop into.

"What do you mean? Where is she?" asked Ben Danis, the new head of security.

"I don't know," Dr. Johnson said while entering the room. "She was right there in the bed where she always is."

Jill Burton held rigidly still inside the ventilation shaft. She was too close to the screen and could possibly be seen, but she didn't dare move away.

"Well, she is not there now, ma'am. Where is she?" yelled Danis, oblivious to the Marine two yards in front of and above him.

"I told you before, I don't know. She was unconscious and being kept in a medical coma. She was not able to move on her own. More importantly, she was handcuffed to the bed when I left and I still have the key," she said, pulling the item out of her pocket and waving it in front of him.

As Burton watched the scene play out in the room, she tried to think what to do from here. It was obvious that she was not going to be able to return to the medbay, which meant she was going to have to disappear. That was the tricky part. Where could she go? The explosion and her disappearance were going to trigger a shipwide search; with her as the designated target.

She listened with wonder as the doctor spun a tale indicating her death. Burton decided she never wanted to play poker with Dr. Johnson. Her story of Burton's demise was told with a completely straight face and was a very believable performance; and she had made it up on the spot.

Burton had seen enough. While the information gathering was a plus, even Danis would soon realize that the only way out of the sickbay without being seen was through the service shafts.

Burton had been careful to leave an IV needle in the handcuffs and pick marks on the doors so that they would never suspect Johnson had quit locking her cuffs several days ago. The only time that the cuffs were locked was when they came to check on her. The pick had been to protect Johnson. It looked like it had worked, but now it was time to get herself to safety for a while. She thought about warning Aichele that she was going to have to disappear, but he was probably safer if she stayed away, and she really didn't have any extra time to spare. She decided to take Johnson's hint and become dead for a while. The ship was probably going to be too hot for her until this blew over, anyway.

She pulled herself along the overhead ducting slowly and carefully. She had very little strength built up and no reserves. Burton had always kept herself in top physical form, but being shot with a blaster followed by weeks of lying in a coma had reduced her stamina to almost none. She had begun a limited workout regimen, but it would be a long time before she was back in fighting trim.

She decided to use the larger crossing vents after all. Her shoulder was on fire and the burns on her face were agonizing now that the pain medication had started to wear off. At the first vertical shaft, she made the complicated turn, heading up until she could get her feet under her, and then putting her back against the far end and slowly walking her way up. Her right shoulder was throbbing and she welcomed the relief of not having to use it for a while. When she reached the top of the shaft, she wormed her way into the cross-ventilation shaft on her back and used her feet to push herself along. It was slow going, but she had a long way to go and she didn't have enough strength left in her arms to get herself there.

Her ultimate goal was the dorsal air lock. Most of the crew only thought about the three airlocks in the main section of the ship because those were the only ones used for normal operations. The dorsal lock was situated within the upper ductwork and piping above Upper Main and was used only during refits.

After crossing the forward section of the ship in the relative safety of the larger shaft, Burton made her way into the small airlock where she had hidden her EV suit. It took her long, excruciating minutes to don the suit. She sat there, depleted, with her helmet in her lap for several minutes before she rose, snapped on the helmet and cycled out of the ship.

She was beyond exhaustion by the time she finally made it to what was now going to be her primary base of operations in hold seven. She had chosen this location because it was one of the few holds that were only accessible from outside the hull. She knew she was safe here because she had taken the precaution of bringing all the pressure suits and storing them inside the hold with her.

Burton struggled to enter the large outer doors of the hold and staggered across to one of the large storage containers. She entered the outer door of the container and pulled the hatch closed behind her, latching it securely. She leaned against the wall as the airlock cycled and the pressure began to come up. Her legs and arms were trembling from the strain of the slow trek across the circumference of the ship on the outside of the hull. The remote location of the hatch meant that it was not likely to be checked, but it was not very close to sickbay or to her final destination.

The indicator light finally turned green and she was able to open the inner airlock and stumble inside her bolthole. She stripped off the helmet and gauntlets and collapsed into her makeshift bed. She was glad that she had already been planning to use this as her home base in the future and had started to move as much as possible out here whenever she got the chance. With the blast and her being caught out of sickbay, she had been forced to move much earlier than planned.

Who am I kidding? she thought. *Nothing is going as planned.* She was still trying to formulate some sort of strategy when her exhaustion overtook her and she fell asleep.

CHAPTER 41
6 September

Belatedly, Clint Morrison, crewman second class, realized he had made a mistake. Not an insurmountable one, to be sure. Still, he was perturbed at himself as he dropped the heavy welding unit next to the corridor's wall. The quite public corridor's wall, where anyone might happen along and take note of his activities. Or lack thereof.

The changes to the situation aboard *Pathfinder* were not as uniformly detested as one might assume. Clint had started out like everyone else, pushing himself to do as much as possible to get the ship repaired in order to deliver it and collect on the big score they had been promised. When things started being broken, and blame seemed to be distributed randomly, rather than by merit, Clint had stopped doing any more than the bare minimum.

He had expected to get an earful from Teach, Leung, Omundson, and the various supervisors, and was surprised at how rare, and mild, such scoldings had turned out to be. *So what's the point?* Clint had asked himself. *The work will get done eventually anyway. Why work myself sick?* Since then, even after Teach's spectacular death, when random punishments had completely vanished, Morrison did his best to avoid undue effort without catching anyone's notice.

This was not always easy, and sometimes not possible at all. When his aims could not be met, Clint would inwardly shrug and put in the full shift's work. Most times, though, it was shockingly easy to put in no more than an hour or two of effort in each eight-hour watch. His foremost rule was never to volunteer for the jobs that required more than one person be assigned. You couldn't slack off in front of witnesses, after all. This had gotten especially difficult after Leung had ordered that everyone was required to work in pairs, which was supposed to protect people from being attacked by Lamont. That requirement hadn't lasted long. There simply weren't enough people to get everything done that way. His second rule was only to take assignments in low traffic areas for the same reason – no one around to spy on you.

Not that crewmen always got to pick out their jobs. That would be contrary to "The Navy Way." Lowly crewmen had to be told what to do at every turn. The trick was to prompt your supervisor into giving you the assignment you wanted. "Hey, Young, I see the data runs at frame nineteen are done. You need me to weld up those mounting brackets?' And there you go, down to the bowels of the ship to catch a nap.

Rule two was the one he hadn't abided by this time, and it was because he hadn't paid enough attention to the location printed on Omundson's jobs list. Rather than frame thirty, middeck two, his assignment for today, for which he had happily prompted the ensign to give him, he was welding closed the power and data runs at frame thirty, deck two; on the main deck, not in the more concealed space above the ceiling.

Well, so be it, Morrison thought, and began breaking the welder down into its operating configuration. If he pushed himself a little, he might be able to finish this section in five or six hours and still have the opportunity to knock off early. Once the plasma torch was set, he initiated the reactor, which took several minutes to heat up, while he started preparing the conduits. The metal boxes that housed the long stretches of power and data cables did not come in equally long sets. Such would be too unwieldy, since you couldn't coil them up the way you could the cables. Replacement housings came in 80 cm lengths, with separate three-sided and one-sided components, and had to be welded together in place. Fortunately for him, the runs had already been put together when the ship was built, so most of the work was done. The top sections had all been removed in order to allow the now useless feeds to be removed and replaced. Clint's task now was to weld the lids back on.

He bent down to retrieve the tops from the stack the repair team had left them in and started clamping them into place. He had enough clamps to set up four of them at once. That completed, he grabbed the torch and welded three spots on the top side and three more on the bottom side of each lid to hold them in place. Then he stepped back and powered down the plasma emitter while he pulled the clamps out of his way.

The clamps went into their own pile, and he repowered the emitter, running it carefully along the top edge, bottom edge, and then the four seams between the sections.

He powered down again, and checked his chrono. Twenty-two minutes. He was sure he could speed that up a little bit, but even so, at that rate, he could finish his assigned area in under four hours. Then he could find some convenient excuse to be somewhere else out of sight of anyone who might ask him what he was supposed to be doing.

Morrison hurriedly picked up the next set of metal lids and set about clamping them into place. Power up. Spot welds. Power down. Take off the clamps and toss them to the side. Power up. Top edge. He increased power to get the metal puddling faster and moved all the way to the edge of the last section. At that point, unfortunately, he stumbled against one of his hastily discarded clamps. He released the discharge trigger as soon as he started to tip, but it wasn't soon enough to avoid cutting through some of the data lines within.

Before he could even move his foot to catch himself from tumbling, a loud, strident alarm sounded and pressure doors at either end of the corridor slammed downward and locked into place with a *pff-snikt*.

"Ah, crap," Clint noted.

* * * * *

Leung physically jumped in the command seat on the bridge when the alarm sounded. She couldn't tell if she had been asleep or just distracted, but she was wide awake now. "Report!" she demanded of the air, hoping that the one who had the information she needed would respond.

"Decompression on main deck, amidships. Possible hull breach," Aichele announced from the Environmental/Engineering station.

"What! How?"

"I don't know, ma'am. There was no enemy action, and we would have felt a blast that powerful, anyway," Eric added.

Leung simply grunted, which Aichele correctly interpreted to mean that she had already figured that much out but her brain was currently too busy trying to work out what was going on to bother acknowledging the report.

Leung angrily punched a switch on her comm board. "Engineering, Bridge. This is Leung. What's going on amidships?"

There was no response. "Omundson, report!" Still nothing.

"Samuels, you have the bridge. I'm going to go see what's going on." The new XO acknowledged receipt and rose to take the command station.

Leung had already evacuated that spot and crossed to the bridge door, tabbed the unlock key, and then tabbed it again when it failed to open the door. The lack of response on the second attempt brought an involuntary shudder as she recalled the last time she had been stuck on the bridge for hours. She popped the locking mechanism open and read out the diagnostic board. It showed zero atmospheric pressure in the hallway beyond the fifteen centimeters of hardened steel.

Her ire at another delay suddenly turned to a lump of ice in her guts at the thought that some of her crew may not have been able to reach pressure suits in time, and were laying dead where they fell. When it occurred to her that there *were* no p-suits on the ship anymore, she immediately vomited on the floor.

"Ma'am?" Samuels said in a genuinely concerned voice, rising from the center seat. "What is it?"

"They're dead. They're all dead," Leung pronounced flatly. Her face was white and her eyes were unfocussed. "What a filthy, stinking mess." She crossed back to the center seat shakily and braced herself against it. Samuels was sure she was not simply referring to the pile of undigested lunch on the floor.

"Who's dead, ma'am?" Samuels asked, quitting her seat and lending an arm to help Leung into it.

"Everyone outside of the bridge, I think. The door is showing null pressure on the other side, and Omundson never answered from Engineering." She leaned forward and held her head in her hands, then abruptly straightened, a glimmer of hope in her eyes. "Aichele, where are you reading the hull breach?"

Aichele turned away and pulled it up on his screen. "The whole ship, ma'am," Aichele replied. Leung's head drooped and a low moan escaped her. "...including the bridge," Aichele completed.

Leung's head snapped up and seemed to draw her whole body erect after it. "How can that..." she began, but trailed off as her quick mind provided an answer to her own question. "It's a sensor glitch, not a pressure loss!"

She shouted this last as she was already moving back to the bridge door. After her last confinement, waiting for someone outside to come to her rescue, she had thought it bad planning that there was no way to access the door's controls from this side. She hadn't added a new access panel; she hadn't had time for nonessential projects. What she had done instead was to leave a cutting torch on the bridge, and she grabbed it to give her the access she needed, now that she was sure there was breathable air beyond the barrier.

Breathable air to be found on this side of the barrier was another matter altogether. Her gorge was rising just to come within a meter or two of the door again.

"Aichele, get over here and clean up this mess," Leung ordered nodding toward the puddle of her own making. Aichele hesitated not at all, but jumped to the assigned task at once.

While he was seeing to that problem, she pulled a grease pencil from her sleeve pocket and carefully marked lines from memory on the wall where the torch would not damage circuitry or power lines routed beneath. Aichele actually finished first, and offered to do the cutting for her. "I've got this, Aichele. You go back to Scan."

"Aye-aye, ma'am."

The process of opening the wall was slow and tedious, since she couldn't afford to use more than the minimum power output on the torch. Any more than that would destroy the control lines that she needed to work with. She had to pause twice to rest her arms from the strain of holding them up and steady. Sweat ran down both her face and back before she was finished and the metal of the wall section clanked onto the decking. With that completed it took no more than a minute to wire in an overriding signal on the sensor line and free the lock to respond again.

The door opened easily once the code was entered. Leung unfolded herself carefully as she stood, stretching out her knees slowly, thinking fondly of an increasingly distant time when she would no longer have to subject her body to long hours and hard work. "Monica, you've got the bridge. Aichele, you come with me."

"I have the conn, aye, ma'am," Samuels acknowledged. Eric rose from his station without expression and joined the captain at the bridge hatch.

"How fast can you move, crewman?" the captain asked him.

Aichele's non-expression turned to puzzlement. "Ma'am?"

"Nevermind. This one's going to be the only difficult one, and we still have warm bodies. Crystal, front and center," she called to Giannini at the engineering/environmental station, now back on duty after being cleared of any wrongdoing in the explosion. Aichele was not enlightened at all by this partial explanation.

"Ma'am, you need me to hold the signal?" Clearly, Giannini knew what was needed.

"Yes, just 'til we're through," Leung directed.

"Do you have another source pack?"

Leung's eyes widened. "No."

"Then how will you…" Crystal's contralto voice trailed off as she saw that her commander was trying to puzzle out an answer already.

"Close time for this door in the case of pressure loss is, what, eight tenths?"

She already knew the answer, Giannini was sure. She answered anyway, in case it turned out to be a non-rhetorical question. "Yes, ma'am."

"Blazes. That's not enough time to disconnect our override and toss the unit through the door while it's still open. We're going to have to rig something temporary."

Leung again knelt in front of the opening in the wall and used her data probe to find a line with an active signal. A simple cross connection did not do the trick for her. The increased load dropped the voltage under the valid threshold. Plan B was only slightly more difficult to enact, wiring a 10 kiloohm resistor to ground and then connecting the sensor to the hot wire. Solder threads held each junction in place, and that was that. Giannini removed the portable circuit probe and the door remained in its open position.

Leung collected the probe and Aichele and moved off down the corridor. "All right, here's the plan. You watch me override the signal on the pressure sensor circuit at this door, so you'll know what to do. I'll hold the door open while you go through and open the panel on the other side. When you're ready, I'll pull the probe out and throw it to you. You do the same to that circuit, and hold it while I come through. Then we do it all over again at every door between here and Engineering. Got it?"

"Yes, ma'am. Ready when you are."

She got to work, opening the access cover easily, wishing that there was a convenient acces on each side of the hatch. That there wasn't an access cover over the control lines for the bridge door was certainly a case of Security trumping Engineering; exactly the wrong precedence in her mind. Startled, she realized that thoughts of Security were taking priority over Engineering needs in her own mind.

Logically, Giannini should be helping her with this work. She would not have had to be told what Leung was thinking or shown how to countermand each door's lockdown. However, her mind had become too accustomed to her self-imposed directive always to have someone on the bridge that was part of the takeover from the beginning.

Not that Aichele, and especially Samuels, hadn't proven themselves trustworthy. She had even left Samuels alone on the bridge for entire watches recently. Had she thought about it, she probably would have taken Giannini instead. That was part of what bothered her. She wasn't thinking like an engineer anymore.

She shelved those thoughts for study some other time as the door slid out of the way and into its holding slot. Aichele moved wordlessly through the opening into the start of Broadway, the wide passageway that ran along the ship's centerline, and used his own multitool to open the cover. He held both hands open in front of him to indicate he was ready. Leung held the probe's lines in contact with the wiring while she shifted position and then tossed the small unit with its connections toward him in one quick, fluid motion.

The door shut more quickly than she had expected and the leading edge hit the probe, altering its trajectory. Not enough to keep Aichele from catching it anyway, and a brief examination showed it had suffered no damage.

It was about five minutes before the door reopened and Leung was able to join the ex-Marine. She complimented him on his work before moving to the next panel, but made no greater effort to start a conversation. Aichele seemed content with that.

The next repetition was smoother in execution. The captain managed to toss the unit through without it being hit by the closing aperture, and Aichele took only four minutes to have it open again.

When the following airtight door opened, however, Omundson's and Morrison's voices made a marked contrast to the amiable silence of the last quarter hour. Both men cut themselves off at the sight of the hatch retracting, and the three others inside turned to face her as well. The cessation was short-lived as both recovered from the shock concurrently and rounded on Leung to explain their side of things. Aichele took over the probe to free his superior officer to deal with the situation.

"Captain, I've arrested our saboteur," Omundson said gravely. He looked more tired than any human ought to be able to manage and stay standing.

"No, Captain, it's not true. Let me explain," Morrison pled over the top of the ensign's voice. His eyes were bloodshot and the surrounding skin was puffy and red as well.

"One at a time," Leung growled. "You first, Omundson."

"Ma'am, when the alarms sounded and Engineering was cut off from the rest of the ship, I was able to determine that the hull breach was false, and that the sensor system had been intentionally disabled at this location. I took Young, Chin, and Semrad with me and we disabled the pressure overrides at each door until we reached the scene of the crime. Here we found that Morrison had not thought ahead about the consequences of his actions, and his own treason trapped him here." Omundson gloated, not able to keep a smile from his face.

Leung's face was not smiling. It was feral and menacing as a wolf's. "Is that so, Morrison?" she nearly spat.

"No, ma'am. Honest." His voice quavered and it appeared he was likely to resume crying. "It was an accident, I swear it. I tripped over one of the clamps while I was welding and cut right through the data lines."

"That's not very likely, Captain," Omundson supplied. "The cut was made only ten centimeters from the main junction node. It is the only place on the whole ship where he could have destroyed both the pressure sensors and shipwide communications. And he specifically asked me to assign him here."

"No," Morrison protested. "I mean, I did ask for this job, but I never intended to damage anything. It was an accident!" His pleas crescendoed into a shriek and the tears finally broke over the dam and spilled down his cheeks. "Please, Captain, you've got to believe me."

It was the tears that gave Leung pause. Maybe it was an act, but she didn't think so. The man was terrified of what was going to happen to him if Leung judged him guilty. Not what she would have expected from a cold, calculating destroyer. Remembering her earlier thoughts, she tried to look at this situation logically, as an engineer should.

She stepped around Morrison and Chin to inspect the damage. He hadn't quite burned completely through the bundle of optics, but close enough. Had he been intending to sever the lines, he would have done the job completely. Although, if he had been trying to make it look like an accident, perhaps he wouldn't have. Objectively, it could have been either explanation. The damage could have been unintentional, or merely staged to look like it was. He could be truly petrified with fear, or acting as if he were. *He's a better actor than anyone I know, if that's the case,* she thought.

Her final thought, the one that convinced her, was that if he were the saboteur, he wouldn't have made such an obvious mistake to get himself captured. *Maybe he was duped into it by Lamont,* the paranoid Security voice countered, but she was able to ignore it for now.

"Morrison, you're an idiot," she said at last, "and I'm sure our saboteur is not."

Morrison sagged in relief. "Thank you, Captain—"

"Don't thank me yet, idiot. You are going to splice every single one of these lines back together right now. You are not relieved of duty until the job is done. Do you read me? No mess, no sleep, not even a head break until it is done."

Morrison wilted under her indictment, though he knew it was justified. "Aye-aye, ma'am," he said in a small, snively voice.

"Omundson, leave your repair kit here, and head back to Engineering. Find a way to restore communications first thing."

"Aye-aye, ma'am," the ensign acknowledged, all trace of his smug smile now missing from his features.

"Come on, Eric. Let's get back to the bridge."

As he nodded to indicate receipt of an order, Captain Leung realized that was the first time she had addressed him by his first name. She must have been harboring doubts about him, she realized, but now that her logical, engineering instincts were reasserting, she had moved beyond them.

It certainly is good to have people you can count on, she thought.

CHAPTER 42
8 September

Once again, Staff Sergeant Jill Burton collapsed onto the debris-strewn deck of her refuge in hold seven. It looked like all her hiding spots inside the ship had been compromised, which left her with the arduous EVA walk to the external hold. It had taken her nearly two full days of running back and forth into the ship to get all her supplies moved, but she had managed it all without anyone catching sight of her, and the communications buoy was now launched.

It would still take at least four weeks for the buoy to maneuver back to the jump gate, where it would be able to make transit back to the Betre system, but at least it was on its way. Once the alert was out, it would take another six to ten days for Fleet to respond, probably. Burton put her suit gauntlets into her helmet and pushed her sweat-soaked hair, the part that hadn't been shaved or burned off, out of her eyes as she contemplated the situation that would probably exist when Fleet arrived. By then, *Pathfinder* could be out of the system and infinitely harder to track. She knew from Aichele's foray into Teach's personal files that the ship was going to jump to the Worth system as soon as they could get control of the astrocomp.

She had a responsibility to slow down the ship and give Fleet a chance to catch up. She had looked for ways to disable the ship from the outside, but nothing was immediately obvious. She was the only one who could get outside, so it would be ideal to commit her acts of sabotage there, where there was no threat to her. The problem was that, apart from the communication aerials, there wasn't anything out there to break. It wouldn't do to have a warship that could be disabled by one soldier hanging onto the outside, obviously. She could rig up a mine, but with all the remaining suits in the hold with her, that would mean death on a larger scale than she was ready to contemplate at this point.

Suddenly, the enormity of everything hit her. She leaned her head back and began to strip off the remainder of the suit. EV suits were bulky and difficult to deal with under the best of circumstances, but alone, in a confined space, with no rack to hold the suit upright while the wearer got herself loose was as far from ideal as it was possible to get. While she mindlessly went through the process of shedding her encumbrances, she let her thoughts travel down other paths. Her right arm and shoulder were aching with the unaccustomed exertion and the still healing injuries, but she was able to do things on her own schedule now. Her face was still a mass of burns and scars on the right side, but she felt as if she had gotten off much more lightly than she'd had any right to. Much of what had happened on the day of the mutiny was still fuzzy to Burton. Part of that was the effect of the drugs the doctor had given her to keep her under, but a part was her own mind shying away from realities that it was not yet ready to accept. She could remember stopping at Major Chowdhury's quarters and asking for some help in calibrating a piece of equipment. Strangely, she couldn't remember what equipment. They had just come out the door from the security suite when Morales and others had jumped them. She remembered knocking the gun out of someone's hand - *Chandler?*- and making a dive for it on the deck when a knife flew over her shoulder and hit Morales in the throat just as he was about to shoot her. He still hit her, but the knife must have changed his aim enough to save her life. *Knives in the throat can do that, I guess.* The rest was a blank. There were three other crewmen there to disable them, but according to Gunny Aichele, Chowdhury had not only survived, but had been relatively unmarked. *Not me, though,* she thought as she reached up with her good hand and lightly traced the burn scars on her cheek.

According to Dr. Johnson, she had very nearly died. That brought her thoughts sharply into focus. At thirty-eight years of age, she had never really had to face her own mortality before. Her husband, Diego, had just retired in January after putting in his thirty-five years in the Marines. They had bought into the Warner Complex at Quito and she was just trying to finish out the last nine months of enlistment before retiring with her own twenty years completed. She had been torn by the assignment which she knew would take her far from her husband and family, and she felt even farther from him at that moment than she had believed was possible. She felt the odds of ever living to see any of her family again were decreasing with every passing hour. There would be no Chowdhury to protect her this time. It was up to her and Gunny.

There must be something they could do to further slow the ship's progress. She ran through her mental list of potential actions again. It had taken her two days to steal the comm buoy and get everything the way she wanted it before launching it. She had needed to steal the IFF signature file from the Captain's computer in order to make the sensors ignore *Pathfinder* until it could get out of range. Luckily, Leung was rarely in the captain's quarters. The buoy reprogramming had consumed all her thoughts and energy to that point, so now she needed to make further plans. There must be more she could do.

Leung had assigned guards to cover the engineering areas and they were starting to make regular patrols through the crawlways and access areas. Bezates and Danis were also using spybugs to monitor the engineering spaces, the interstitial spaces and some of the ventilation shafts. This had caused her to move through the edges of the crawlspace and not take the most direct route most of the time. She had almost been trapped by Goesch and McGough as they had made a sweep to check the crawlspace yesterday, when she had gone in to retrieve the comm buoy from her hiding place. She had been forced to lay down in the shadows and hope. They had walked within two meters of her hiding spot, but they were too busy complaining to each other to notice. If she had possessed a weapon, Burton could have killed them easily. She could tell by their conversation that both of them had been in on the conspiracy from the beginning, so they weren't just going along with Leung out of fear. It made sense to give the guns to those that you were sure of. She looked at the pile of pistols that she had been able to steal and smiled. *At least I won't have the same problem the next time that we meet.*

The lack of real security was turning into a great benefit. No one had done anything to change security override codes on system files, surveillance equipment, or even the small arms lockers.

She was drawing a blank, though, on what target to strike next. It was too hard to do any deep thinking just then. Finally divested of her suit, she slid under the covers of her makeshift bed and dreamed of home.

CHAPTER 43
10 September

Crewman 3rd Class Alex Green entered the mess once again at 0800. As one of the two cooks left aboard *Pathfinder*, he essentially lived in the galley. Usually, he and Trendle were both on duty for first watch. Today however, they were running their modified rotation since, with some extra work that had to get done in the mess, Green had worked four of the last five watches, so Trendle had stayed and worked third watch. Green appreciated Rod letting him get some sleep.

Trendle nodded to Green as he came through the cooks' doors into the kitchen. One look at him and Green could see indications that Trendle felt just like Alex had when he left the mess a short eight hours ago. Most days, they got enough to eat, but neither got very much sleep. The last few days they were pulling extra hours as they tried to handle random groups' requirements.

Alex Green was only two years younger than Trendle, and they had become friends in their posting aboard *Pathfinder*. Green was taller at 1.85 meters, but was still slender, weighing less than 80 kg. He had a shock of reddish-blond hair that he had not cut since a month prior to the "event." His hair was longer than regulation, but there had been no time to cut it, and since Smith and Alcaraz, ship's barbers, had both gone with Brighton, he honestly wasn't sure there was anyone to do it even if he found the time. He doubted anyone had noticed, or cared.

Trendle tossed a dirty towel to Green, then put his hands down on the countertop and rolled his head around to loosen up the tension in his neck and shoulders.

"All yours, man," Trendle said as Green caught the towel. Trendle looked up and stood up straight again. "I am going to go get some sleep, Green. Have a good one," he remarked as he headed for the doors that Green had just come through.

"Thanks for letting me catch some sleep, Rod. I appreciate it," Green called to him as the departing cook made his way through the exit.

"No problem, Green. See you in about eight hours, man," he answered without looking back.

Green looked around the kitchen to survey what was left of the breakfast chores that Trendle had not yet completed. Most of the kitchen was already in good order, but the cooking pans and pots were all sitting in the steaming water of the deep soaker. There were also two parts of the prep station that needed some cleanup.

"Well, Alex, it isn't going to clean itself up and you only have a short window before you have to start lunch," he said aloud as he started in on the prep stations first, deciding to let the pans soak a while longer in the hopes that they would come clean more easily.

Once he had finished in the kitchen area, he went out into the main part of the mess where the dining tables, chairs, and condiment stations were. He noticed that the mess was a bit cooler than normal. Maybe it was just the fact that it was empty, but usually it seemed warmer in there. The galley aboard *Pathfinder* was not really a large room, but it was sufficiently sized for the crew. Having served in one other posting, aboard a newer class destroyer, Green knew that the mess onboard *Pathfinder* was smaller than on most ships her size. That made sense, since she had been redesigned as a survey vessel and would never again host the same officer, crew and Marine contingent she had under her initial name and designation.

Still, the mess was probably the only open space where crew normally tended to congregate. A few crew members had come in shortly after he had arrived, looking for a quick bite before hitting their berth for some sleep. Green could sympathize with them on that score, and had handed out the last few sandwiches and fruit trays that Trendle had left ready for the stragglers. Other than those few visitors, though, nobody had been in the mess with him. With the constant double or triple shifts that everyone aboard was undertaking, most didn't even want to linger in the mess longer than it took either to grab something to eat in their berth or to eat as rapidly as possible in silence there in the mess.

Green spent a few minutes cleaning out the last of the breakfast condiments before heading back with the small service cart to the mess kitchen to stow them in storage. The mess kitchen had a dry storage area, where he stowed most of the packaged items, along with a refrigerated storage, kept at a cool 5° C, where those needing refrigeration were stowed. There were also two freezer rooms, the main freezer, where all the day to day items were kept, and the deep freeze, farther along in the back, where long-term storage was kept.

About weekly, someone would need to go to the deep freeze to get more supplies to move into the main freezer for the coming week's consumption. After reviewing stock and finding that there were none of the meats and a few other items in the main freezer, Green knew that today was such a day.

Alex was not ashamed to admit, at least to himself, that it had bothered him to go to the deep freeze ever since the takeover because of the dead bodies of the crew who had not survived that day, which lay in black plastic bags under a draped cloth. Green wasn't even sure who was in there, or even how many. He just knew that there were bodies in there and it was deeply uncomfortable to enter.

There was nothing to be gained from trying to wait for the next shift though, since undoubtedly Trendle would just ask him to go get the items while he tended to something closer. So, steeling his own resolve, Green set off for the deep freeze. When he got to the door, he paused, took a deep breath, gathered his nerve again, then opened the sealed door.

He was immediately assaulted by cool flowing water running out all over his lower trouser legs and shoes. The water continued to pour out of the deep freeze as the cook stood in mute shock. Then, the unthinkable happened.

Three airtight black body bags floated toward him on the outgoing tide. His heart leaped into his throat and made its intent to escape his body plain. Escape seemed an eminently sound plan to Green as well, and he scampered all the way to the far end of the kitchen, where he climbed up onto a prep table and hunkered down, knees pulled up to his chin.

It was more than five minute before Green got his wits back enough to think straight. The bodies, and the water that carried them, came no farther than the large drain in the center of the floor, and that alone had saved Alex' sanity. It was several more minutes before he could bring himself to look inside the deep freeze and see that things were thawing, and a lot of ice had melted. The interior thermostat read 21°. He double checked the external setting and confirmed it was still set for -20°. In fact, the cool room, as the exterior area to the deep freeze was called, was cooler than the deep freeze. Knowing that they were in jeopardy of losing significant portions of their supplies, Green ran back to the main room to get to the wall-mounted comm unit there.

When Green reached it, he keyed Engineering. The comm toned, but he got no response. Several attempts brought him the same result. He tried to comm the bridge, even though he had never done that before. The bridge too toned back with no answer. *Crap*, he thought. There was no way this could wait.

Green threw his gloves on one of the counters on his way out, leaving his apron and cook cap on. He headed straight to Engineering, hoping to catch Captain Leung there.

When Green arrived in Engineering, he realized that Leung was not there. Ensign Omundson was talking to Crewman Louie McIntire heatedly about temperatures. Apparently, other crew members were complaining about the ship temperatures dropping in other areas. Green placed himself next to the officer duty station to wait for Omundson, who was fuming at McIntire. McIntire continued his report that no matter what the system was set at, the average shipboard temperature was now about 10°, and dropping, even though the thermostats were set to 21°.

Omundson, finally appearing to realize that Green was there after about the third throat clearing, turned to him, bloodshot eyes staring him down and asked, "What do you want, Green?"

"Sir, the deep freeze is almost completely thawed out. There is water everywhere, and the inside temp showed 21°. The majority of our food supplies will be ruined if we don't get it regulated quickly," Green told Omundson as fast as he could.

"What?" Omundson shouted incredulously. "I can't believe this. Is this whole ship falling apart around us?"

"I am not sure, sir, but the mess definitely needs some help if we are going to salvage anything in the deep freeze," Green responded, taken aback by Omundson's response.

Omundson looked around Engineering and then at something on his display at the duty station before giving an exasperated eye roll and saying, "Well, Green, there is nobody else I can pull off anything, so I guess I am going with you. Come on." With that, the officer grabbed a tool kit and headed out.

Alex followed Omundson out of Engineering and back to the mess, and straight to the deep freeze. The new Assistant Chief Engineer was muttering to himself the entire way, so Green kept silent and stayed on his heels. When they arrived, Omundson checked the freezer inside, and then went to work on the control panel. He continued to talk to himself under his breath, and though Green was tempted to respond to a few of the comments, he realized they were not directed to him.

Omundson kept at the panel for far longer than Green would have thought necessary, jacking in and running some programs against it. Green decided that either Omundson was way too overworked, or he was partially crazy, the way he was arguing with himself under his breath. Perhaps both. Omundson checked several relay panels for issues and took several readings.

Green, while watching Omundson, happened to notice that the 'cooler room' was now about 8°C. He commented on that to the ensign, and was rewarded with a withering glare before Omundson went back to his readings.

"Well, obviously there is a problem in the thermo control system somewhere, but it isn't here in the mess. I am going to have to check the main environmental systems in the access areas," Omundson said finally. Green assumed that this time Omundson was talking to him, since he seemed to pause after speaking to look up. "And Green, get those bodies back in the deep freeze."

"Sir, with the temperatures cooler out here, don't you think…" Green was unable to finish that comment as Omundson cut him off.

"That's an order, crewman. Get them back in the deep freeze," he shouted.

"Aye, sir," Green replied quietly.

Omundson quickly gathered his tools and made his way out of the mess. The ensign spent the next two hours moving from one enviro control to the sensors, and back to another control system, moving all around the access areas trying to isolate the issue. Just as he was homing in on the problem area, Captain Leung came into the corridor he had just entered.

"Ensign, what in nine hells is going on with the temperature?" Leung yelled as she rounded on him.

"I am working on it, ma'am," he replied, showing his own ire.

"Do you realize that much of the ship is below freezing, Ensign?" she grated out at him, her own breath visible as she spoke, and she quickly closed the distance to invade his personal space.

His breath steamed out of his mouth as he responded. "I hadn't noticed. I have been too busy trying to find and fix the problem, ma'am," he said with obvious irritation.

"Well, maybe if you noticed a few things around you it wouldn't take you three hours to figure out that there is clearly a malfunction in the environmental control system," Leung derided him.

"Ma'am, I am--" Omundson started angrily, but didn't get a chance to finish as Leung cut him off.

"--skating on thin ice, Ensign," she finished for him. "It should not take this long to isolate the problem. It's probably an inversion in the master enviro controls. I want the issue resolved in 30 minutes or I will have your hide." She glared at him.

"I checked that system first, Captain, but everything looked fine to me then. I know it has to be there now though, since every other subsystem and all the sensors are working fine, but the response data coming back from the main enviro system is completely backwards of what it should be, so I am heading back," he replied.

"What do you mean everything looked fine?" she asked him.

"I mean I ran all the diagnostics there and nothing flagged red. The system showed no access other than the routine checks performed by Engineering and the usual input data from the sensors and sub-controls throughout the ship," Omundson said defensively.

"Well then, someone was far more clever than you in their system manipulation, or this is the most colossal failure of routine Engineering check work we have seen," she retorted.

"Ma'am, how good a programmer was Lamont? Whoever did this knows their way around the enviro system better than most everyone in Engineering, and is a more devious programmer than I thought we had on board," he managed to say without trying to bite her head off.

She stood there looking at him for a minute as what he was saying registered deep enough to penetrate her anger and irritation.

"Actually, Ensign," she said without nearly as much bite as she usually included with the word *Ensign*, "he was one of the best programmers I've known, and he definitely knew his way around most of the ship's systems."

This revelation caught Leung off guard; she had forgotten that she and Teach had Lamont scrubbing the communications traffic and the logs on the system, since he was something of a burgeoning genius at manipulating systems.

"So you think this could be him, ma'am?" Omundson asked.

"It might be, Ensign. Watch your back, but get the main enviro system back under control ASAP. I also want you to post vid monitoring on the system controls and have it added back into the random patrol and system status checks so that someone is at that station watching it as much as possible," she said trailing off and turning to head back towards the bridge.

He stalked back in the direction his most recent readings had confirmed the source of the problem lie, the master environmental control system suite.

He got to the master system console again and keyed into it. After digging through subroutine after subroutine, he finally found the rogue code that appeared to be confusing the system. Someone had it set to reverse all of its main programming on the heating and cooling systems, cooling where heat was required and heating where cooling was required. The way this was hidden, there was no way to see it without digging through millions of lines of code, or isolating enough sensor data and system response data, as he had, to see the inverse commands being issued by the core subroutine section of the main enviro suite. It was inserted elegantly, with no trace of it not being part of the normal code base of the system. There was nothing in the log to indicate who had inserted it, and no time or other discrepancies to indicate when it had been injected.

The problem was actually quite simple to repair, now that he had identified the problem area. In a matter of ten minutes, he had the inserted code scrubbed out of the system and made a system backup of the main control suite so that if something happened again, all he would have to do is drop the clean version of programming back onto the system. He locked the console out so that only bridge officer codes could get back in, and flagged it to alert him if anyone logged into it. He changed the vid monitoring of the room to be 100% capture and set it to record to multiple security system storages so that no one could erase the footage, then left the suite. He worked his way back to the main corridor muttering to himself about the situation and headed back to the mess to see if things were returning to normal.

He didn't say a word to Green, who was at the far end of the mess, as he went straight to the deep freeze. The cook followed him, though. The ship was cold, and Omundson did notice that Green had on his cold gloves as he came through the kitchen area.

When Omundson yanked the deep freeze door open, he saw immediately that there was very cold air pumping into the unit. He watched the thermostat drop a degree while he stood there. A small smile of vindication came to his lips. He turned his attention to the freezer now, though, and with Green they began to quickly take stock of what was not going to be salvageable. The unit was sitting at close to 33°. From the looks of the first few shelves, the odds were not good for a lot of the foodstuffs in here.

The ducting that fed super cold air to the unit under normal conditions also had heat ducting next to it to keep a balance of the temperature. The grid over the heat duct was very hot, and apparently had been dumping hot exhaust into the deep freeze, probably coming in at close to 50-60°. It was then that Omundson realized that another one of those feeds was right above where the bodies had been restacked in the deep freeze by Green, at Omundson's own orders. He froze in mid-motion, and changed direction.

He went back to check on them and, as he came around the shelving, half gagged on the smell.

"Oh, blast it," was all he got out of his mouth before turning back toward Green and the door and emptying his stomach contents on the floor between them.

CHAPTER 44
10 September

"Kasdorf, take Chin and get rid of these bodies," Ensign Stuart Omundson said to the petty officer who had just walked into the galley. "Then help Green decide what can be salvaged out of this mess." He motioned to the food that had been pulled from the refrigerator. He rose shakily to his feet and wiped his mouth with a rag he was still clutching in his hand. The pun clearly wasn't intentional.

"Sir, what do you want me to do with them?" Kasdorf asked the shaken ensign.

"Take them to airlock one in the boatbay and cycle them out."

"Sir," Kasdorf protested, as if shocked by the suggestion, "we need to have an officer to say something over them. We can't just space them as if they were trash, sir."

"Kasdorf," Omundson replied with exasperation, "does it look like we've got time or people to spare for niceties? Don't try to turn the crew against me. Get this taken care of immediately; that's an order." The harried young officer turned on his heel and stomped off before he could hear any further protests.

"Yes, sir," the crewman said quietly to the retreating back.

Omundson never heard the acknowledgement as he hurried around the corner toward the boatbay access. He nodded to Lenore Chandler, who was standing at the boatbay hatch with a flechette pistol. She looked bored and she had the same haggard look that was visible on the faces of most of the crew. Her arms were folded across her chest and she was visibly fighting the urge to sit down and sleep. She didn't even acknowledge his presence as he passed.

Once he was through the hatch, he picked up his pace. He glanced without interest or recognition at the work going on around him. There was simply too much in progress for him to keep track of all the projects. Most of the work here in the boatbay was being done by third watch, under the direction of CPO Young. As such, he ignored them. If he wasn't directly responsible, he wasn't interested. His head started throbbing at the quicker pace, so he slowed before reaching the aft hatch into the engineering section. He pressed his palms into his temples, the site of his still recovering injury, in an attempt to contain the pain. When the ache began to moderate, he reached out and opened the hatch. Workers straightened and one even came to attention when he entered.

"As you were," he called absently, as he walked to the toolbox and unloaded tools and data analyzers from his carry bag back into their proper places. Bending over caused his headache to amplify and he felt the need to retch returning, so he dropped the half-emptied bag onto the deck and leaned back against the workbench. "Beacham, take care of that for me."

The named crewman, who should still have been on inactive status while his hand regenerated, moved to the task. Ensign Omundson turned his attention to Giannini, who had taken over in Engineering during his absence. It was good to have her back out of the brig, even if it had taken much longer to convince Leung of her innocence in the bombing than it should have. Was there a reason besides security that Leung was trying to keep Giannini out of Engineering? he wondered. Other than creating more work for him, he couldn't think of any.

"Report," he said quietly, closing his eyes and trying to make the pain subside.

"Morrison is down in the crawlspace rerunning the Astrogation data leads. That should be the last of the cable runs. I sent Semrad and McIntire to check all the forward sensors..."

Her report was interrupted by a loud sizzling noise from the access panel, behind the tool box, that housed the main electrical wiring runs for the whole section.

Omundson had just started to turn toward the noise when he felt his body being forced to the deck by an unexpected pressure. He grunted and started to fall as his suddenly increased weight overburdened his body, which was poised on one leg during his turn. He closed his eyes with hopeless frustration as his already abused body was slammed to the deck.

He struggled to breathe as the weight pushed him into the cold metal of the deck. A crash and scream from the rear catwalk told him that someone had been unlucky enough to be working high above the walkway and had fallen. He decided to try to force his way to his feet and pushed with all of his might against the simulated weight pressing him to the floor. After several seconds, when his strength was just about to give out, he was released by the invisible hand and his push resulted in his being thrown upward and rotating backward.

Stuart Omundson had never liked zero gee maneuvers, even when they had been required in the academy to qualify for shipboard duty. He liked them even less now. Coming as a surprise, with no time to mentally prepare himself, the motion caused his stomach to rebel and he was on the verge of heaving his already emptied stomach when the pressure again seized him and threw him down to the deck on his back. His already battered head slammed into the plating and his vision was obscured by flashing lights. There were further screams from around the engineering bay, but Stuart had no time for others' injuries.

His head felt like lightning was dancing on his nerve endings! The pain was unbearable, and the pressure pinning him to the floor kept him from doing anything to relieve it. *What was happening? Who was doing this to him? Why were they out to get him?*

As his vision cleared, he felt the weight again leave his chest and he held perfectly still. Any movement would cause him to lift from the deck which was certain to be painful when the gravity reversed itself again, which it seemed to be doing on a cycle of every four or five seconds. As he began to relax, he saw Giannini fly over his face, just barely clearing his prostrate form before the gravity reversed itself again and she grunted with the impact as she was slammed into the deck and slid a short distance before coming to a complete stop.

What an idiot, he thought. *If she'd just hold still, she could ride out the surges without killing herself.*

Omundson endured three more cycles before the nightmare finally stopped, leaving everyone floating with whatever momentum they had acquired from the buffeting. Stuart remained motionless, even though he could hear others cautiously attempting to get to their feet in the microgravity.

"All clear," he heard Giannini yell from the other end of the bay. "I've shut down the grav generator."

When he cautiously sat up and looked, he could see her floating in front of an open control panel with several wrenches and tools floating around her like oblong metallic satellites. When he continued to rise and rotate forward slowly, he realized that his movements had not been as cautious as he had intended. He injudiciously reached out to grab the leg of the workbench to his right but simply added another dimension to his rotation. Finally, he managed to grab a handhold and stop his aimless gyrations.

"Report," he yelled, using his volume to vent his frustration. "Any injuries?"

"De Saumserez fell from the overhead, sir," Katrina Biltcliffe called from the catwalk. "He's not moving."

"I think I broke my arm," wailed Beacham from just behind him. "The tool bag landed on top of it." The junior rating was pale and there was a large bruise already visible on his left arm, but he was clenching and unclenching his left fist, the one he still had, which made broken bones unlikely.

"Secure all those loose tools," Omundson directed at Giannini, waving his arm and almost losing his grip with his other hand. He grabbed hold with both hands and continued. "Biltcliffe, you get De Saumserez and Beacham to sickbay."

When they started to move, he turned his attention to Giannini. "What caused this mess?" he asked.

She was busily snagging tools out of the air while holding herself in place with a single foot tucked under the edge of the workbench. "It sounded like the wiring at least partially melted," she said, pointing to the panel by his head. "I think that was limiting the power to the grav generator and it wasn't getting enough for it to function properly, so the breaker tripped. I don't know why it kept resetting and tripping; it shouldn't do that."

"ENGINEERING, BRIDGE," Leung's voice blasted from the intercom on the bulkhead behind his right ear. "What's going on down there?"

Omundson shook his head to clear it and instantly regretted his action as the pain of the continued abuse caused another wave of dizziness.

"Omundson here," he said, after toggling the intercom. "The grav generator failed. We have it shut down and are beginning repairs. I'll let you know when we have an estimate of the repair time."

"Get it done," Leung yelled. "We can't do our jobs while floating."

"Yes, ma'am," he began, before realizing that she had cut the connection.

He surveyed those still looking at him. "OK," he called. "Giannini, collect Morrison, McIntire and Semrad. Make sure there are no other injuries and get that thing fixed. Pull in everyone. That is your highest priority."

"Yes, sir."

Blast, here we go again, he thought.

"Sir, if I might make a suggestion?" Giannini began.

"What is it now? Can't I leave you to do anything?" he shouted.

"Yes sir, but I think it might be a good idea if you went to the medbay as well. You're looking a little off, sir."

"Are you trying to get me out of here so you can take over?"

"Good one, sir," she laughed. As she turned to go, he tried to figure out why she thought he was joking.

CHAPTER 45
10 September

Dr. Meghan Johnson surveyed the swarm of people who had descended on her domain. The random gravity cycling was sufficient to cause dozens of injuries, some obviously severe enough for them to wind up here in medbay.

There were a couple of minor injuries as well. Kasdorf had dislocated his shoulder, but didn't appear to have done any lasting tendon or ligament damage, thankfully. Trendle had a broken nose and a severely sprained wrist where he and his berth floor had commenced a disagreement and Beacham had a deep bone bruise where some tools had landed on him during the episode. This was a case of adding insult to injury as he had only been released that morning to return to light duty after losing his right hand to Captain Teach.

De Saumerez would be unconscious, fortunately for him, for a while. She had been forced to perform surgery in two separate locations to staunch internal bleeding and had pinned his shattered hips back together, but none of his damage looked to be life-threatening. He would hurt like blazes when he came to, so she had him on a narcotic drip for now.

Two others had concussions, Hilary Calvi and Lenore Chandler. Chandler had a lump on the back of the head that looked like it might just turn into a baseball. She had logged that both would have to be removed from active duty for four days.

When Omundson had presented himself a short while ago, his symptoms had her checking him for a concussion as well, but it didn't appear that the scans agreed with her. Despite the lump on his head from his previous injury during the bomb blast, there was no trauma to the brain, and no internal swelling, but he had massive headaches, blurry vision and was behaving slightly erratically.

"Ensign, please stay here while I check my system to compare the latest test," she said to him as she walked past De Saumerez' sleeping form on the next berth and went to her small, inadequate backup system that she had to make do with as her medical computer.

"Okay," was all he said.

He seemed to be going from staring at the wall in front of him, to furtively checking behind him and looking at all the corners of the room, quickly swiveling to look at the hatch again, only to groan and grab his head. He was almost constantly muttering something under his breath as well.

She had tried to engage him in conversation while she ran the tests earlier, but had found he was only half listening to her or not hearing some of what she was saying to him. He had seemed to switch from calm to paranoid to disconnected, then back to calm in the space of a five minute conversation.

"So Ensign, do we know what happened that caused the gravity mishap?" she asked as she pulled his brain scans from his routine physical to compare with his current one.

"They did it on purpose, Dr. Johnson," was his response, while checking the doorway.

"Who did it, Ensign?" she asked him, looking up more intently now.

"It had to be him, ma'am. He thought I was getting close, or that I might, with the enviro issue I found and fixed, so he sabotaged the grav system to take me out," he said, finally looking at her.

His eyes looked manic to her. This wasn't good. She watched him while she asked him a slew of follow up questions and gauged his responses. He didn't seem to shift into disconnection, like she had originally thought, but rather he seemed to have just a deeper paranoia he was working with. From the way he spoke and the looks he gave her, she was certain that he had a solid start on a persecution complex, or perhaps even persecutory delusions.

"How are you sleeping, Ensign," she asked him again, since he had only muttered under his breath the first time she asked it earlier.

"I am hardly allowed to, Doctor," he said quickly. "Leung has me running everywhere and manning two-thirds of the projects, so I barely have any time to get food and stimulants. And then every time I actually get to lie down something else seems to break and I am needed and I can't get to sleep and they won't leave me alone. It's like they want me to keep from sleeping so I won't do a good job and I will fail and then…" he just trailed off looking back at the hatch. He continued speaking, seemingly unaware that he had stopped for over ten seconds, "I don't know, ma'am. I am not getting enough rest, for sure."

"Are you waiting for someone, Omundson?" she asked, trying to gauge how aware he was that he was watching the hatch.

"No, why, did someone tell you they were coming?" he asked her, a trace of furtiveness in his voice.

"No, Ensign, I was just wondering," she replied. "You need to get some rest, you seem to have taken a nice buffeting in Engineering and your body and mind need to recuperate."

"Do I have a concussion too? Am I going to be pulled off duty? If you do, Leung is going to come unglued, and she will blame me." He said all in a single breath.

"All the scans show negative for any concussion, but I want you to try and take it as easy as you can for a couple of days nonetheless. Please try to get some rest in your bunk for a while," she said, helping him over to the hatch.

If Omundson really was developing a persecution complex as she suspected, or worse, persecutory or paranoid delusions, Leung needed to know about it. She already owed the Commander a visit to let her know that they had to pull two more crew off active duty due to the concussions, so she might as well bring along the data she had, as well as the recommendations on treating his condition. As she closed the hatch she turned and grabbed a couple of data chips off her desk, double checked the readings on De Saumerez and before heading out to the corridor to go find Leung.

* * * * *

Stuart Omundson had headed out of medbay with the intention of following Dr. Johnson's recommendation to get some rest in his bunk. He had started down the corridor from medbay toward his berth, when he began replaying certain parts of the exchange with her in his head. Without warning, he halted and checked behind him. There was no one there.

Omundson realized that Dr. Johnson had specifically told him to return to his bunk. She wanted him to be at his bunk, resting. He began to wonder why she had been so adamant that he should go straight there, and he had a sudden disturbing feeling that she was somehow trying to make sure he could be easily found. His stomach sank. If she was somehow in on it, then whoever was trying to hurt him had a broad reach.

He ducked into a cross corridor, as he thought this through. Dr. Johnson had asked if he was expecting someone, and she had asked him all sorts of questions about the last few days. She had been probing him and he hadn't even realized it at the time.

He was exhausted, and his head was throbbing so badly that his vision blurred occasionally. He was in the process of clearing his vision again when he heard someone passing by in the main corridor.

He returned to where he could view who had passed by and saw that it was Dr. Johnson. Now he was truly alarmed. She had left the medbay and De Saumerez in wretched condition and was headed somewhere in a hurry. He wondered if he should follow her, but there wasn't really any way to do so without being noticed.

He tried to pace behind her, watching to see if he could see where she was going. He knew he wasn't the stealthiest, but he had to know what she was up to.

He stayed far enough back that he twice had to check a couple of intersections to make sure which way she had gone. When she stopped at Lt. Commander Leung's hatch, and was admitted shortly thereafter, Ensign Omundson knew for sure that Leung and the doctor were conspiring against him.

His stomach lurched again, threatening to empty itself of what little he had been able to get into it today. Leung had to be the one to mess with the gravity generators. There was no way that Lamont could have. She must still be working with him; it was the only thing that made sense. He managed to get his convulsive stomach under control, as he headed back toward the other side of the vessel. He still couldn't believe that Dr. Johnson was in on it too.

He didn't know where he was headed for sure, but one place he would not be was in his bunk sleeping. There was no way he was going to make this easy on them. If they were coming after him he wouldn't be where they would look.

He needed to make a plan, but right now his head hurt so badly he couldn't think straight. He was still so tired, but there wasn't time to sleep now. Not with them thinking they could close in on him.

CHAPTER 46
15 September

Silent as the void outside, Burton opened the inner door of the ship's dorsal airlock. Cautiously, she checked the two spots hidden from her view through the window of the hatch. No one. She lowered her pistol and replaced it in its holster with a twinge.

Her shoulder still ached all the time, but moving about added painful jolts at unexpected moments. It didn't help that she couldn't stand erect in this forgotten crawlspace, either. She needed to use her arms as well as her legs to maneuver, and the added strain took its inevitable toll.

Expending various grunts and groans, along with twice the time it should have taken, she wriggled out of the vacuum suit and stored it in her hiding place.

Difficult as it was, she was starting to get the hang of changing in and out of the tight-fitting suit in the cramped space, and using her right arm as little as possible. Some things were impossible to do left-handed, though, and she was getting equally adept at gritting her teeth against the pain. The interstitial space above the top deck was mostly ignored, but she didn't want to tempt fate by allowing a yelp of pain to escape her.

These crawlways full of conduits and ventilation ductwork were both a blessing and a curse to her. A blessing, because they allowed her to move unobserved about the ship, and a curse because of the pain and effort it took to do so.

Security was paramount in her mind, so she stayed on the same level and relocated to her first fake hidey hole. Unlike the places she had managed to stash things of value, her dummies actually looked like what search parties would expect to find. They were much less hidden, to start with, and they also had been rigged with their own booby traps.

This one still was, so no booby had happened upon it yet. She left it undisturbed and made her slow, painful way ten meters downward along the outer skin of the ship on the starboard side to the next interstitial space. It was a snug fit among the power leads, but the cramped area helped her make the descent without putting any extra strain on her bad shoulder. Coming back up would be another matter.

Once she was between main deck and upper deck, it was a short slither to the access to Aichele's quarters. Fortunately, the fact that Leung was shorthanded meant that few had to share quarters, and Aichele wasn't one of those few.

She took a quick minute to remotely loop the surveillance equipment someone had left, against regulations and normal respect for privacy, in the room before sliding the vent cover out of the way. Aichele was not there. According to the last information he had given her, he should have been off shift at that point. Things change. She would adapt. She closed the vent, reset the bugs, and made her way through the ventilation shaft to the bulkhead they had agreed on to leave messages for each other. She would stay cautious, though. Just because no one had tripped her snare, didn't mean they weren't still out looking for her.

When she got to the appointed place, she patiently watched the area for fifteen minutes before finding a moment without anyone near. Engineering was a busy section around the clock, especially now, with all the repair work going on, but the portion near the holds was less so. She slowly stuck her hand out far enough to wipe grease on the wall and drew it back. Quick motions draw the eye, she knew from having it drilled into her repeatedly in training. No alarms were raised, and she retreated farther into the shadows, undetected.

When she had made it as far as one of her real boltholes, the only one Eric knew about that he could get to, she laid down to get some sack time. If Aichele did not arrive at the appointed time, she would check back in his quarters after watch change, when he would hopefully be coming off duty.

She was wide awake and straining to hear the slightest sound at 01:00, though no one approached.

He was just arriving when she checked back at his room at 08:20, so she flipped her way into the room to lie on the conveniently placed upper bunk after disabling the spybugs again. Eric was relieved to see her looking and moving as well as she was. Her color was definitely improved, and her blonde hair had started growing in. At some point, she had cut off the rest to match the right side of her head where a near miss from an ambusher's blaster had burned it away. Two millimeters all over was better than shoulder length on half and none on the other. There was also some tightness on the right side of her face. The involuntary grimace and the shorn hair gave her a dangerous appearance that fit well with her current role.

"You're looking better, Jill," Aichele commented as she hopped down to the deck. "How are you feeling?"

She glared for a moment, until she realized that he was in earnest. "I feel old and weak, thanks for asking."

He grinned for a moment, until he realized that she was in earnest. Soberly, he said, "I've liberated a short case of arbars, in case you need some."

"Thank you," she answered sincerely. Food and water were things you could never have in overabundance. It was a long-standing tradition in all martial services that the three things you never passed up when offered were chow, drinks, and sleep. Of course, she hadn't waited for Aichele to find a source of food and water, but she wouldn't turn down the extra, either.

"All right," Eric's voice deepened to a down-to-business tone, "let's have your report."

"Yes, Gunny. Since my last report, I have made two locations appear to be hiding spots, and left booby traps in them. The first is tucked into the corner of frame twelve and partition B above upper deck and the second is just to port of support G70 between main and lower decks.

"Once I'm outside the ship, I am safe from pursuit. My system of leaving the external holds in vacuum and staying in a pressurized container is working, but the containers' available oxygen is limited. I have already depleted two of them. With eight more that have the locks accessible, it isn't an immediate concern, but I will need to recharge them eventually. Recharge packs are not located in hold seven, and I have not tried extending a search to other holds yet.

"The message buoy was completed and launched four days ago. It is set to broadcast to any Warner ship it sees, but only in a Marine code. I thought it prudent to add one more level of security, in case there are other Warner ships which have been co-opted. If the ship is in the clear, the Marine security will be able to decipher it. I programmed it to keep *Pathfinder* from being able to see it. It's still two and a half weeks from reaching the jump point. Probably four before a rescue can be mobilized.

"By then, we'll be four months out from the jump point, if we haven't jumped into the Worth System already," she concluded a bit morosely. She sat down on his bed and leaned against the wall, too exhausted to be willing to stay upright when she didn't have to. Aichele relaxed as well, recognizing that this was more of an informal interview, and took one of the two chairs in the room.

"Any further sabotage?" the gunnery sergeant prompted.

"No. I've had opportunities for minor breakage to any of the systems running through the crawlways. I could even do some serious harm, but any damage there is sure to bring additional security to those areas, and I depend on being able to move freely through there. With the additional guards, I can't really get at anything worth the risk of action. If push comes to shove, though, I could do a lot of damage all at once and then go hide for a while."

"Let's keep that idea in reserve for now. That would probably work once, but I'm starting to get the feeling that we need to change tactics if we're going to get ahead of the other side."

"What do you mean?"

Aichele leaned back in his seat, took a deep breath and let it out, running his hand over the stubble on his head. It was as short as ever, and the gray at the temples had been there before, but it seemed more pronounced now. "I've been doing a lot of thinking about this, especially whenever I'm stuck on the bridge with not much to do."

"And?" Jill prompted when he remained silent too long.

"Okay, it's like this. I don't really know what we *should* do, but I can see that what we *are* doing is not going to work in the long term. Look," Aichele leaned forward and started punctuating his points with one forefinger stabbing the opposite palm, "when we started out, targets were easy to come by, but they've adapted and made it harder to take equipment offline. The longer we keep up the same approach, the shorter the odds we'll get away with it.

"Then there's the visit from Danis and Bezates the other day. I don't trust them to work in our interest knowingly, but maybe they could be nudged into furthering our cause. Perhaps sowing discord among the crew is another tactic we should work at.

"At the same time, it's certain that there is at least one other person who is deliberately slowing the ship down. My guess is two people."

"Why do you think it's more than one?" Burton interrupted.

"Originally, I thought we were looking for just one person, but I should have seen it sooner. I had already placed the unclaimed sabotage in two classes: sophisticated and blunt. The three that the sophisticated saboteur was responsible for were the astrocomp data, the weapons control relays, and the controlled explosion in the comm room. Probably the weird software problems we've seen should be grouped there too. The other set are the blunt ones: acid on the data cables, power feedback in the astrocomp lines, and yanking out handfuls of wires in Engineering. I don't have a name to go with either of them, but I am narrowing down the list on the sophisticated one.

"Logically, I should have had an easier time finding the straightforward saboteur. But as blunt as the actions are, whoever he is has been devilishly clever at leaving no trail to follow back to him. The attacks happen in areas that anyone and everyone could have gotten to. The materials used were accessible to everyone. Every time I try to narrow it down, I'm forced to admit that it could have been literally anyone."

"I think it was Young," she commented, "or maybe Giannini."

Aichele looked at her sidelong. "How sure are you? Do you want to go ask them?"

Burton's snort of derision was the only response he got.

"That does lead to an interesting question, though," she said after a while. "How exactly can we identify an ally, when we can't expose ourselves until we know for sure? If we can't identify allies, then we can't be certain of our enemies, either."

"I don't know," he admitted. "It's one of those things I've thought a lot about without finding an answer. The only thing I can think of to stop those responsible is taking *Pathfinder* outright."

"You mean take control of the ship back from them?" she asked disbelievingly. "Are you insane? There are only the two of us against..." She paused, trying to count those left. The ship's complement had been fifty-four. Jhonsruud was arrested; Morales, Brandon and Teach dead; Lamont was unaccounted for (best to include him until they knew for sure); eighteen went with the captain;

Dr. Johnson neutral or on her side. "…twenty-eight," she finished eventually.

"Twenty-six," Aichele corrected. "There are still the two other saboteurs on our side."

"Oh, yes," she rejoined, "four on twenty-six is ever so much better odds."

"Chin up, Jill," he said with a genuine smile. "We're the Marines. That makes us the majority."

"I hate repeating myself, but *are* you insane?" She couldn't help smiling at his professed confidence, though. Just a little. "But even to make those odds work for us, we need to coordinate, and we can't do that until we know who they are."

"You're right," he conceded. "I've thought the same thing a time or two, but I haven't been able to come up with any solution. For now, we can't trust anyone but the two of us."

"There's Dr. Johnson," Burton countered. "She can be trusted, though maybe not to take an active hand against the others. I'm not sure she'd be much help in a fight anyway."

"Okay, I'll accept that addition. I agree with your assessment of her usefulness. I don't really want to ask her to get involved, no matter how stacked against us the odds are."

"Agreed," Burton said easily. She already owed the doctor a great deal. If she could protect her from the coming conflict, she would. She might ask her for help in small things, but definitely not for combat.

Thoughts of the doctor who had saved her life led her mind to wander afield for a moment, and there was silence in the room while both percolated possible strategies. Perhaps there *was* something she could ask the doctor to help her with.

"I may have an idea," she said, breaking Aichele out of his mental exercises.

"What is it?"

"I think we need better odds."

"I do too, but that's not a plan, that's wishful thinking."

"That's not the idea, that's the short-term goal. *This* is the idea." And she explained what she was thinking, glossing over details she hadn't worked out yet. Before she finished, the aging gunnery sergeant was grinning like a little boy.

"I like it," he confessed. "I like it a lot; most especially because I think it has a good chance of succeeding, if the good doctor is able to give us what we need. We use an anesthetic to knock them out while they're sleeping, drag them out through the vents, and they wake up out in hold seven, isolated from the rest of the ship. There we can use the other type of drugs Dr. Johnson can get us to make up some babble juice and find out who we can trust to work with us.

"How soon can you start? And with whom do we begin?"

"Oh, I've got a list," she assured him, answering the latter question first. "Things are still kind of fuzzy, but I am sure about three of the people who put me in medbay. Goesch, McIntire, and Trendle are at the top of the roll. And Leung; Samuels in charge would be much easier to deal with. The girl's barely graduated and has no real command experience."

Aichele nodded in agreement. "At the same time, taking Young out of Engineering would leave Omundson in pretty much the same condition. He's smart enough, but it's all book learning. He's...a difficult officer to work for, too."

"He's a horse's hindquarters," Burton stated drily.

Aichele chuckled. "I agree, so I think we'd be doing more for our side by *not* taking him. Without Young to act as a buffer with the crew, and keep the work moving, things would slow down even more."

"You're right about Young's value, but I'm not so sure about leaving Omundson alone. We're already planning to take Leung. If we could grab Omundson and Samuels too, that would leave no officers to take command of the ship."

Eric sat and digested this thought for several moments. "That's a good idea, but there isn't any way to grab them all at once. At least one of them is going to be on the bridge at all times. We're going to have to break up our captures into at least a couple of nights."

"More than that, Gunny. I'm not going to be able to drag an unconscious person through the air ducts with only one good arm."

"Yeah, good point. How about this? I'll grab them and take them up to the dorsal lock. You meet me there with an extra pressure suit, and then you can haul him outside while I go back for another. Most of the trip out to hold seven, you'll be outside the gravity field, so you shouldn't get too fatigued hauling the extra mass."

Burton nodded to herself. Now that they had fleshed out some of the details, she could see that it was a very workable plan. "Okay, when do we go?"

"As for when, we still need to collect some items from Dr. Johnson, but I don't see any reason to wait, if you're feeling up to it. I can see that you are still not at the top of your game."

"It's the only game in town, coach. Keeping me on the sidelines isn't really an option. Don't worry, I won't bite off more than I can chew," she assured her superior.

"Do you need anything from me?"

"Yeah. Give me a leg up to the vent, would you? And then pass me the box of arbars. It'll be easier on my shoulder that way."

"Sure thing."

"Do you know if Dr. Johnson is in medbay or her quarters?" she asked before either of them moved toward her exit.

"Almost certainly in medbay," he responded immediately. "She told me once that she avoids her quarters as much as she can because it makes her feel guilty to see Dr. Ward's gear all the time. I offered to pack it away for her, but she just smiled sadly and said it was good for her to feel guilty. 'Better than forgetting him,' she said."

"All right, see if you can get word to her to meet me tonight in her quarters and let her know the things I'll be needing. I'll check on my hidey holes first, so give me a mark if you were able to set things up."

"Will do," he assured her.

He helped her up then, and passed the small box up after. It was heavy despite its small size, its contents being quite dense. He put the screen back in place, then said through it, "You be careful, Sarge. Sloppy gets you dead."

"I know, Gunny. If I didn't know that before, I learned it the hard way four months ago. If not for Major Chowdhury, sloppy would most assuredly have gotten me dead."

CHAPTER 47
1 October

Pum, pum, pum, went the ogre's fist, slamming into his open palm over and over. "I'm coming for you, *Captain*," the leering monster gloated. The face boasted pale green skin and a wart on its nose, but there was something recognizable about it. She had seen the ogre before, but she couldn't make her mind provide her with the information. Something about the spiky blond hair... She couldn't think. How had she come to this place?

All thought fled as the monster advanced on her, and she moved away, sprinting for all she was worth down the street. The houses she passed had that same nearly familiar feeling about them, but she had no room in her mind to ponder this. Escape was her only need, and the effort required to achieve it left no room to consider anything else.

She glanced backward as she turned a sharp corner. *Pum, pum, pum.* He was gaining on her. Suddenly, she realized that she did know this place. It was her high school. If she remembered right, there should be...yes, an unnoticed break in the hedge that would allow access to the exercise field without anyone on the other side being able to see her. She had used it a number of times in the other direction to escape from exercise period without being noticed.

Once through, she moved a few meters to her right and hunched down, trying to slow her breathing and her racing heart. She was sure the monster would hear it and be on her at once. What was going on? Why was the ogre after her? Why was it...Lamont. The monster's name was Lamont, and it wanted revenge on her for killing Teach, she suddenly realized.

Pum, pum, pum. "Are you in there, Captain?" The voice was less menacing now, and this confused her even more. She needed a weapon, something to defend herself. She checked her pocket and found the energy pistol she had started carrying after they had taken over the ship.

"We're coming in, Captain." Nice of him to announce himself. She took aim, but something wasn't right. Fog swirled around her head, obscuring the things she most wanted to see. Why we? He was only one ogre, after all.

She shot upright when the door to her cabin slid to the side and made a snick sound as it locked open. The pistol in her right hand swiveled to point at Ben Danis as he came through the door with his own pistol out. She was about to fire, her mind still not tracking events, when he abruptly stood up straight and lowered his weapon.

"Are you all right, Captain? We were concerned when you didn't answer the door, with the other disappearance."

"What disappearance?" The mental fog was lingering, and her heart still raced from the imaginary escape.

"Sorry, Captain. That was what we were coming to report. McIntire and Young didn't turn up for their shift in Engineering. We've looked through the whole ship, but we can't find them anywhere."

A puzzled look came to her face as she struggled to create sense out of the words. Finally, the import hit her and she scowled. McIntire was a solid worker, but Young was indispensable to her. Omundson might be the head of the engineering department, but it was in name only. Young was the man who knew what was what on the ship, and kept the work moving. Without him, she would have to resume supervising, keeping an eye over the ensign's shoulder. That wasn't going to make either of them happy, she knew.

Lamont could not have picked a worse person to take out.

Her nightmare was beginning to seem all too real, even now that she was fully conscious. Maybe Lamont *was* out there, plotting some kind of revenge on her.

"Young is missing? And McIntire?" she asked in a flat voice, just to be sure she was tracking. Her continued sleep deprivation gave the present scene the same almost familiar but not quite right feeling she'd experienced inside her own mind. The pain behind her eyes was the only difference she could put her finger on to say that this was reality and the other wasn't actually happening.

"Yes, ma'am. Lt. Samuels contacted the two of us at 0020 hours to report Young unaccounted for." Mention of the time made her look at her desk clock. It was now just past 01:00, and she had managed nearly two solid hours in the sack. *What a putrid mess,* she thought, not specifically about Young or her lack of sleep, but a general observation.

"When Ensign Omundson did not arrive at the bridge to relieve the lieutenant by 0015," Danis continued, "she contacted him in Engineering. He informed her that he had not been relieved by Mr. Young and so had not been able to leave his post. He reported that Crewman McIntire was also not present, but seemed to think that might have been deliberate retaliation for punishment he had received yesterday for insubordination to the ensign.

"When the XO contacted Bezates and me, we went at once to Mr. Young's quarters, but he was not there. There was no sign of anything out of the ordinary, and his bunk had been slept in recently. We found the same in McIntire's room, although there, Crewman Chin was asleep in a bunk two meters from McIntire's and reported hearing and seeing nothing unusual. We reported this to the lieutenant, and continued searching the ship. We were not able to locate them in any of the common areas, and the XO said we should wake you and report this to you."

From the look on Bezates' face, mixing panic and despair, he clearly was not pleased to be assigned this duty. Perhaps he had worked too long with that idiot, Teach, but he seemed to expect Leung to jump all over him for doing what they were supposed to do and telling her about it. Teach had been a great advocate of shooting the messenger. She was glad he was dead, even if that led her to grief from Lamont.

"Mr. Young was relieved from his bridge watch at 1600, and was seen working on control relays for the jump engines until about 1930. Crewman Trendle saw him in the commissary from 1940 to just before 2000, at which time it was presumed he was headed for his quarters. We do not have any reports that he was seen after that time. Samuels and Omundson were both on duty, with several witnesses, during that time, although Aichele was off duty," he added formally, though the tone of voice would indicate that he no longer thought there was any reason to suspect any of those three anymore.

"It might have been Burton," Bezates added. He abruptly closed his mouth again, as if frightened of punishment for speaking out of turn.

Leung ignored his overcaution, and the statement with it. Burton could not have committed the sabotage, having been comatose the entire time, and so she was not the one they were looking for. The fact that she had disappeared likely meant that she had been merely the first of Lamont's victims. What reason he might have had for killing her, she could not fathom, especially when she had been injured, immobilized, and no threat to anyone. He always had been a hothead with a fragile ego, though. He had wanted Brighton dead for some imagined insult, so perhaps he had similar reasons where the Marine was concerned. Who could tell?

What a filthy, bloody, putrid, stinking, sorry mess.

Pulling her mind back to the report she had received, she ordered, "Stop worrying about those three and concentrate on Lamont. Find out if anyone was seen going into Young's quarters. Then I want a complete sweep of the ship, every crack or crevice large enough for a person to hide in. If Young can't be found, we'll have to assume he was killed and the body spaced. There aren't any vac suits that would allow any other possibilities.

"Take whoever you need to help. Wake up the whole ship, if that seems necessary, but don't miss anything." She hated to do that, but recognized its necessity. Those available to search were going to be the ones off duty, who should be sleeping, who needed to be sleeping so they would have the energy to put in a shift or two worth of effort tomorrow.

Today, she corrected herself. It was already October.

So today, she could expect little or nothing productive to get accomplished. The routine would be broken, people would be more cautious again. More time and energy would go into watching everything else instead of focusing on what needed to be done.

Always the same, and she was getting so frustrated with the whole mess that she just wanted to scream.

Instead, she dismissed her security team and pulled her boots on. She hadn't bothered undressing before she collapsed into bed late yesterday, too exhausted to have given it even a passing thought.

She did spend a minute brushing her hair and cleaning herself up a bit. While in the head, she grabbed a stimulant and swallowed it with a drink from the faucet. She couldn't look mussed or tired; she had to go inspire the troops.

She checked her chrono on her way out her door, and decided to grab a cup of coffee as well. As tired as she was, she could use a little extra something to keep her moving. The mess was all but deserted when she entered. Crewman Green braced to attention with a broom in his hand, but she quickly waved him back to what he was doing. She never had understood that part of military protocol. It seemed too inefficient to her, always interrupting the ongoing work.

She crossed the room to a small table set against the wall, on which were two medium-sized cisterns with dispenser nozzles and a collection of upside down drinking cups. She selected one of the plastic ones to take it out with her and filled it from the left container that some joker had labeled "High Performance Naval Fuel".

She began moving toward the door and raised the steaming liquid to her lips as she went. The smell didn't really register until the fluid was already in her mouth. It didn't remain long, though. An explosive spray of coffee flew from her face and she had to double forward and breathe quickly to keep her last meal where it belonged.

Green rushed to her side at once. "Captain? Are you all right?"

"What is this?" she gasped, waving the remarkably unspilled cup at him.

"It's...coffee, ma'am," he answered hesitantly, not sure whether there was something wrong with the drink, or with the captain.

"It's sludge," she pronounced, straightening. "What did you put in it?"

"I didn't put anything in it, Captain. It's an automatic system. There's a dedicated water connection in the back, and a reservoir for grounds that Trendle and I keep filled. The coffee is the same we've always had," he explained.

"Does this smell like the same coffee we've always had?" She waved the cup again, this time close enough and slowly enough that he actually got a whiff of it.

"Ugh. No, ma'am."

Leung let out a heavy sigh and dropped the cup into the disposal chute. She went back to the dispenser and opened the hopper containing the roasted and ground beans. One sniff of the pungent stuff was enough to be sure it was not the source of the problem. That left only one other potentiality and she went into the cooking area to check that. Stepping up to the nearest sink, she turned the water on full. Within seconds, the same miasma began filling the immediate area and she shut it off.

Ignoring Green, who was tagging along like a lost puppy, she tabbed the intercom near the exit. "Bridge, Leung."

"Bridge, this is Omundson. What can I do for you, Captain?" The words were pleasant enough, but the tone of his voice made him sound suspicious. Hardly unjustified, given the other events of the night.

"Mr. Omundson, there's a problem with the water supply in the kitchen. Move it to the top of the repair list and put someone on it right away."

"Understood, ma'am. I'll have…Terry down there in five minutes."

It was clear to Leung that the ensign had been about to assign Young to the problem. As the most senior environmental technician, he was the logical choice. Now that he was missing, and Morales was dead in the takeover, that left only Martin Terry as the entire environmental department.

"Very well, Ensign. I'll see that he is not assigned to help search the ship. Leung out."

"Bridge out."

Leung turned then to Green and ordered him to close the mess hall until the problem with the water was sorted out. She left then at an almost jog. With the time she had lost in the dining area, she should have sprinted but she didn't dare. She could imagine the panic that might ensue if she were spotted running as if her life depended on it. So she tried to hurry without looking like she was hurrying.

She couldn't have said whether or not she had the desired effect. All she could really say was that no one had any negative comments to share when she arrived. Not that anyone would. The Navy's class structure was too rigid and too ingrained for that possibility.

Once she was there, Danis handed out search assignments. She knew the crew was all tired of the familiar routine, but at least no one gave voice to their feelings. The way her day had started, she didn't think she could have handled it rationally if they had.

Danis was also bright enough to assign each team of two to search an area that they had not ever checked before. This would make everyone more alert, which was a good thing. It also kept someone from helping to keep the saboteur hidden if they happened to be of a mind to.

Leung found herself grouped with Amber Sullivan and assigned to the crawlspace between the ship's outer hull and the lower deck. Amber was all business, which Leung appreciated. That was normal for her, though. She never "chatted," and in Leung's experience, ten words constituted a long conversation for her. At least she was no longer crying all he time.

They made their way forward in silence, Leung pointing at things for Sullivan to investigate, and occasionally adding a hand sign. Leung realized when they entered the area at frame thirty, just ahead of the engineering area, that this was a part of the ship she had never seen before. Previously, there had been no need. No engineering, power, or control systems routed anywhere this close to the ship's skin. *Pathfinder* had started life as a destroyer, and warships were designed to protect their vital components by keeping them out of reach of an enemy's weapons.

More than three hours later, they pulled themselves out at the frame ten access. There was no sign of anything in their area, at least nothing Leung thought was important. Sullivan had found a collection of clipped pieces of wiring, but nothing else. There was no way to know who had left the wiring there, and odds were in favor of it being a lazy dock hand who hadn't picked up after himself.

They returned to the boatbay, where the search teams were returning to report. All but one team had already reported in, and the absence of anything worth reporting was approaching unanimity. Giannini and Bezates came in a few minutes later and completed the failure.

A sudden thought had Leung issue orders to have a tech manually retrieve the access logs for each of the four air locks. Sullivan volunteered and returned within twenty minutes with all of the information in a portable reader. As expected, none of the four had been accessed at all since they had left the Minoa System except the ventral lock used to load *Vanguard* with unwanted personnel.

So no one unexpected was *in* the ship, and no one unexpected had *left* the ship. *Where could Lamont possibly be hiding?* she asked herself. Moreover, if Lamont had killed Burton, as seemed more and more certain, where was her body? Leung had assumed that the corpse had been vented to space from one of the exterior access locks, but none of them had been used. She had no answers. Her only outlet was to curse the situation she found herself in.

What a frustrating, filthy, bloody, putrid, stinking, sorry mess.

CHAPTER 48
3 October

Captain Katherine Leung laid her head down on her pillow with a sigh of relaxation. The pillow felt so good. She took a deep breath, consciously expelled the air from her lungs and took another. Finally, she felt her tensed muscles begin to relax. As the only experienced officer remaining on *Pathfinder*, she was finding the demands on her time steadily increasing. It was now halfway through third watch and she had to be up in three hours to begin her shift on the bridge. She was exhausted all the time now and she believed that her judgment was beginning to be suspect. If she had an XO she could trust, she could push some of the work down to a lower level. While Lt. Samuels seemed to be a bright and loyal officer, she had too many holes in her experience base. It was hard to remember that this girl was less than a year from the academy. She simply hadn't had the time or experience to learn the multitude of little things that went into a smoothly running ship. When Leung had given Samuels the position of XO, she had told her that she was going to dump the bulk of the workload onto her, but Leung had held back a large portion of the work for herself. She hated delegating tasks. If she did them herself, she knew they would get done properly.

With another deep sigh, Leung realized that the time had come to push some of those duties and decisions off onto the young officer, regardless of the risk. She recognized that she was drowning in the details. First thing tomorrow, she decided. And with that decision, she slid into exhausted slumber.

The heavy pounding on her hatch finally dragged her back into wakefulness after what her chrono showed was not quite two hours.

"Captain, are you in there?" came the voice of her inherited security chief. "Captain, please answer!"

Leung pushed herself up from her mattress and threw on the uniform tunic that she had discarded mere hours ago. The pounding increased in ferocity and volume.

"I'm coming!" she yelled as she ran her hands through her short hair to try to restore some semblance of order to it. As she threaded her way through the boxes and crates that littered her front office, her bare toes met the corner of the armchair with painful consequences. "Bloody damn hell!" she cried as she momentarily collapsed into the chair to rub the offending digits.

"Captain, are you all right? Let me in!" Danis yelled as he renewed his hammering on the hatch.

"Stop pounding, I'm coming," she snapped.

She opened the hatch and stood staring at Danis and Bezates who were gaping at her as if she were a ghost.

"What do you want!" she snapped.

"We heard sounds of a struggle and we were concerned for you, ma'am"

"The sounds came after your racket, you idiot. Why are you here?"

The two security men looked at each other and Danis swallowed loudly. It was obvious from their faces that they had news and it was equally obvious that the news was not good.

"Spit it out," the captain said derisively. "You can't make me think of you as any more incompetent than I already do."

"Goesch and Trendle are both missing, ma'am," Bezates said finally.

Leung stood there stunned. Since Young and McIntire had turned up missing, they had instituted new security procedures. All corridors and access areas were constantly monitored. Everyone moved around in pairs. This should not happen. This *couldn't* happen. *Except that these two are completely incompetent*, she thought.

This is Lamont, for sure. He has his bridge officer codes to defeat the monitors. Where is he hiding?

"Institute a ship-wide search. Be methodical and start at the forward end of the ship and work your way aft. Get four other crewmen and cover all three decks simultaneously."

Danis looked shocked. "Ma'am, we've searched the ship four times. Lamont has found some hiding spot that we don't know about."

"He's in there somewhere, remember the uniforms you found? Burton was probably his first victim."

"Victim? Ma'am, do you think they are all dead?"

What an idiot, she managed to keep herself from saying. "That is definitely a possibility. Why else have we found no trace of them? Search the ship for any evidence of foul play as well as evidence of someone evading the searches."

"Aye, aye, ma'am."

"Now get moving, and don't come back until you have something to report."

They both took off at a run down the central corridor.

Idiots, she thought again as she cycled the hatch closed. It's a good thing that she wasn't relying on them to protect her from Lamont. The longer this went on, the more she was convinced that her original assessment to Teach had been accurate. They *couldn't* find vacuum outside the hull. That fact had forced Leung to ensure her security for herself. If Lamont came for her in her quarters, he was in for a surprise.

She glanced at the chrono and stifled another groan. There was just enough time to shower and head for the bridge.

On the way to the shower she grabbed several rumpled uniforms from the floor and threw them into the laundry chute. She had one clean class B uniform left before she had to resort to her Dress Blacks. She stripped off her current uniform and let it follow the others down the chute. Hopefully, she could keep from losing any more people until the laundry could get them back to her.

She arrived on the bridge several minutes early, having stopped off at the galley for a large mug of coffee, she smelled it before drinking this time, to wash down her stims. Lt. Samuels turned her head at her entrance and stood to relinquish the command chair.

"Steady on course, no problems, Captain," the young Lieutenant stated mechanically.

"Very well, I relieve you."

"I stand relieved." Samuels moved to the helm and relieved Fields, who had been pilot for third watch.

The captain noticed this as she sat in the command chair and arranged her coffee within convenient reach. She reminded herself that she was not the only one on short sleep. Everyone on *Pathfinder* was pulling double shifts. Maybe it wasn't the best idea to share any more duties with the young officer. She had to be at the end of her present capabilities.

We need to get out of here pretty quickly or someone is going to make an exhausted mistake that kills us all, she thought, *or else Lamont is going to take care of it for us.*

Leung turned her attention to the astrogation screen on her right, and. activated the screen by inputting her personal code. It opened the program to the point where she had saved it at the end of her watch yesterday. She looked at the numbers with distaste. The jump engines were almost ready to test and she had no valid numbers for jump. Using the supposedly repaired astrocomp for the calculations had yielded three different answers to the complex calculation. Regardless of the number of times it ran the calculations, with exactly the same inputs, it gave back three distinct answers. Four days ago, in frustration, she had attacked the problem by hand. After four hours of calculation and studiously reviewing references, she had gotten a completely different result than any the computer had provided. Subsequently, over the last four days she had refigured the problem by hand eleven more times. She had gotten four different answers, only two of which matched the computer-produced results, although, her most common answer was also the computer's most common result. The engineer in her hated the situation. There should be only one answer, no matter how many times it was run. If you use the same numbers, you get the same answer, right?

She was beginning to panic. She had always prided herself on being able to see through all the peripheral elements to arrive at a sound solution to any problem. This problem had no sound solution available. There were choices between which guess was the closest. Operating the jump engines on a guess would most likely lead only to suicide in a grand, spectacular gesture. The only alternative, however, seemed to be to wait for death at the hands of a vengeful maniac hiding within some secret area of the ship. She had to do something before they were all dead.

Pushing down her rising panic, she began the calculations for a thirteenth time. She hoped she could finish before Lamont came for *her*.

CHAPTER 49
3 October

Eric Aichele moved quietly along the duct toward the captain's cabin. Ever since Teach's death, Lieutenant Commander Leung had been occupying the captain's quarters, which made it an easy target for the abduction. So far, he and Burton had been able to capture four of the conspirators and had yet to find any who had been going along to survive. All had been involved from the beginning, which meant that they were slowly eroding the power base of Leung and the others involved. The problem was that it *was* slow and they were running out of time. Their foray tonight had two purposes. Aichele was going to abduct Leung, which should eliminate any effective command resistance to their take-over, with only Omundson and Samuels left to coordinate the crew. Burton's assignment was to wait for Aichele to arrive with Leung, then take her out to their new holding facility in one of the external holds. They had planned to move much earlier than this, but it had taken over a week to get a suitable holding cell set up in one of the containers in hold seven.

Aichele slowed and brought his thoughts back to the job at hand. The crawl from his quarters to the captain's was a short one and he timed it to coincide with the middle of Leung's off watch shift, when she'd be asleep. Aichele slid close to the vent screen and looked out carefully. Leung was in her bunk, snoring lightly. He slid his carry sack up to his chest and pulled out a can, the contents of which he sprayed onto a rag. He carefully held it away from himself and made sure he did not breathe the fumes. With that prepared, he reached forward to work the grill loose.

Pain flared in his right hand and his back arched in a spasm. Then everything went black.

* * * * *

Katherine Leung heard a noise and woke with a start. She sprang to her feet with the pistol in her hand that had been resting under her pillow. She scanned the room for the source of the noise. She couldn't immediately see anything and crossed to the light switch and activated it with a quick slap. Still, she saw nothing. *I'm way too jumpy. I need more sleep,* she thought. Just as she was about to turn the light out again and get back into bed she saw a wisp of smoke from the ventilation grill. She moved closer and looked through the mesh. *There's definitely something in there,* she thought.

She shifted the clutter off the bookshelf and climbed up to get a better look. Seeing the back and shoulder of a fleet uniform, she let out an exclamation. *Yes! It's Lamont, I got him.*

She quickly stepped down and began to disassemble the electrical wires that she had connected to the grill surface. *I knew you had to come through the vents if you didn't want to risk being seen. I've got you!*

With the wires disabled, she removed the grill, grabbed a handful of uniform and pulled with all her strength. The bookshelf teetered under her feet and she gave one more yank. The body came free and they both tumbled to the floor. Leung stood unsteadily and looked down at her tormentor.

"Aichele!" she cried out. "Where is Lamont?"

Aichele didn't move, so she kicked him in the head. "Where is Lamont?" This brought a low groan so she kicked him again. When she got no response, she moved to her computer console and toggled the intercom.

"Security," came the drowsy voice from the speaker.

"Danis, this is the Captain. Come to my quarters immediately. I've caught one of the saboteurs."

* * * * *

Gunnery Sergeant Eric Aichele woke to full consciousness with a suddenness that spoke of stimulants having been pumped into his body. He saw Leung standing over him and realized that he was seated in an interrogation chair in the security suite. His wrists were secured to the arms of the chair and he could see Danis in the doorway.

So it was a setup, he thought. *Danis and Bezates sent me after Leung to get me caught.* His attention was snapped back to Leung as she slapped him hard enough it would have knocked him over if his chair hadn't been bolted to the floor.

"The drugs should be taking effect soon. You can't resist. Tell me where Lamont is."

"Lamont is dead," Aichele said as he started to laugh.

He was slapped again and his head snapped back. His vision darkened for just a moment and when it cleared, Leung was right there in his face. "Tell me what you know about Lamont. Where is he? Where does he hide?"

When he didn't answer, she pulled out her knife and started to make small cuts on his arms.

Aichele didn't react beyond a tightening of the muscles in his jaw. He began to recite the hypnotic trigger that he had been taught in Security training.

Aichele's last coherent thought before the cottony fog of unconsciousness swallowed him was that he was glad she was only asking about Lamont. If she ever figured out the right questions to ask, he would probably answer them eventually. You can only resist the torture and drugs for so long, even with Marine counter-conditioning and training.

CHAPTER 50
6 October

Lieutenant Samuels turned at the sound of the hatch opening.

"I was just getting ready to send PO Danis to check on you, ma'am," she said to her commanding officer as the latter entered the hatch. "Is everything all right?"

"Yes, Lieutenant, sorry to be late, but something important came up."

"Anything I can help with?"

"No, I believe I have things under control for now. Anything to report?"

"No, ma'am, everything has been quiet."

"Very well, I relieve you."

"I stand relieved," Samuels said as she stood and moved to the helm to relieve Fields who was also rising and heading for the hatch.

They were interrupted by Crystal Giannini from the Engineering console, which was currently cross-connected to Communications. Many functions had been combined because there simply weren't enough people to man all of the stations. Not that all of the stations needed to be manned right now, anyway. Some semblance of communications had been restored. The shipwide intercom was working again and incoming transmissions were available, they believed. There was no one to signal them in this system, so testing had consisted of looking for green lights on the board. They had not had any luck so far with either the short range or the long range transmitter.

"Ensign Omundson reports that the jump engines passed all simulations, ma'am."

"Very well," Leung replied and then turned her attention away from Giannini.

"XO, what is your opinion on the status of our jump engines?"

Samuels took a deep breath and continued to check all of the readouts and indicators on the helm console. "Ma'am, I think we should be very cautious. I believe the engines themselves are probably trustworthy, and I know that you have had much more actual experience with these engines than I have, but the academy courses on jump technology gave me a healthy respect for the sheer number of things that can go wrong with any jump."

"That is true, but what do you make of our overall tactical situation?"

Samuels was fairly sure she knew where this line of questioning was headed, but she couldn't believe that Leung would be willing to have this conversation in front of the remaining bridge crew. She lifted her eyes from the helm controls and surreptitiously scanned the faces of those around her. Giannini was making no effort to hide the attention that she was paying to their conversation. Terry, at the Environment board, was studiously avoiding anything that could be considered inappropriate interest. Goodwin was also pointedly ignoring them from his Weapons/Scan console. She took another couple of seconds to organize her thoughts and said, "I feel that we are just starting to get on top of the repairs, ma'am. While we are a long way from 100% mechanically, and the crew is nearly worn out, the security is being maintained and the sabotage has come to a standstill."

"Then you don't consider these disappearances to be…disturbing?"

"Yes, ma'am, of course I do. I just think that it is another sign that our security is effective. Whoever is behind this; Lamont probably," she added as Leung looked about to interrupt her, "he can't find any way to get at systems to destroy them, so he is targeting people. If we change our tactics and protect our people as well, then he will have no targets left and will truly be no threat."

"That is a well-reasoned summation. I feel that you are wrong on nearly every point, however."

"Ma'am, I don't…"

"You are right on one thing," Leung interrupted. "You do not have nearly as much experience as I do. I no longer believe Lamont alone is responsible for the disappearances. As for the shift of targets, Lamont has shifted targets not because of anything that we have done, but simply because he enjoys the chance to kill. He is not a saboteur, looking to disable the ship; he is a hunter out to kill us all for revenge over some imagined slight. The only chance that we have is to jump to a system where we can find help."

Samuels felt the tension ratchet up a notch around the bridge. She was thunderstruck by the venom in Leung's tone.

"Ma'am," Samuels began. This would have to be done carefully. She had to take the topic back to the engines and away from the explosive arena of Lamont's actions, or Lamont's nonexistent actions. The captain was not thinking rationally, and irrational people were nearly impossible to reason with. "While I am not sure that I agree with your assessment of Lamont, the fact remains that the astrocomp is not reliable and no one can accurately calculate the jump by hand. We would be doing his work for him if we decided to jump under these circumstances."

"I feel that the risk is acceptable."

"With all due respect, ma'am, I think that we should wait for the astrocomp."

"We will all be dead long before the astrocomp is finished. I think that Lamont has gotten access to the files and he is corrupting data as soon as we fix it. That was his area of expertise.

"And you are wrong in one other aspect, Lieutenant. I *have* been able to precisely calculate a jump trajectory by hand. I found the area that had been causing me problems before and corrected it. I am confident that the numbers I have worked out are accurate."

"Captain..." Samuels began, then paused. She stood from her station and faced the other officer directly before beginning again. All eyes turned her way as she spoke. "Captain, you know I have the highest regard for your ability and your authority." The lie came easily. "If you direct us to jump, I will follow your orders, come what may. But I feel it is my duty to point out that none of us are operating at 100% right now, and you are not immune yourself. Just how sure are you about those calculations, ma'am?"

Leung said nothing for some time, and Samuels could see that her words had found the mark she intended. The confidence of a few moments past was less all-encompassing now. "Thank you, XO. It is indeed your duty to point out potential problems before they arise. And I know few officers that would have had the courage to tell their captain that they may be wrong. So I will propose a compromise with you.

"The jump I had calculated was from a point that we will reach in a matter of another quarter hour or so. Let's discard that departure, and set our initial point in the equations to be our position as of 1200 on the eighth. By that time, you, Ensign Omundson and I will generate our jump vector. And we won't jump until all three of us agree. Will that ease your mind, Monica?"

It eased her mind a great deal. It would be a simple matter to introduce some minor flaws into her calculations; change a sign here, lose a decimal place there. She was sure that she could slow things down at least another four or five days. By that time, she might have found a way to move the odds into her favor.

"Yes, ma'am. I would feel much more comfortable with that arrangement. Permission to begin working on that now, ma'am?"

The captain never had a chance to respond.

"Radar contact dead astern!" Goodwin announced from the Scan console.

"What?" Leung asked incredulously. "How?" she followed up at once.

"I can't tell, ma'am. It just appeared on the scope," he replied.

"Comm, are they broadcasting an IFF?" the captain asked, turning in the chair to look back.

"Yes, ma'am. Positive ID as WNS *Yargus*," Crystal answered. Her eyes were large and her voice unsteady. "What do we do, Captain?"

"We jump immediately. Giannini, power up the capacitors."

"Yes, ma'am," she replied tensely.

What do I do now? Samuels thought to herself. *I can't take and hold the bridge by myself. I don't have any options.* If she were sure of Omundson, she might have a chance, but the rest of the crew could force their way in eventually. The hatch control panels were still jury rigged and it would require only a very small effort to open them. She wasn't even sure the locking protocols had been re-enabled. She shook her head slightly.

"Ma'am, I will, of course, follow your orders, but I beg you to reconsider this. This is more dangerous than waiting."

"You have my orders, Helm. Input the jump to Worth system by my numbers."

"Yes, ma'am," replied Samuels, hoping that she hadn't just signed the death warrant for the crew as she input the settings that appeared on her monitors. She felt the ship slow on its present course as the velocity of the ship was prepared for the value required in the calculations for the jump. The translation process tended to be more violent at higher speeds, and they needed every chance for a smooth transition they could get.

"Capacitors charged and ready," called out the contralto voice of Crystal Giannini from her engineering console.

"On course and speed for jump," added Samuels while trying to decide if further argument would be prudent.

"Very well," Leung replied, then hit the intercom button on her side console. "Ensign Omundson to the bridge," she called out. She made no further commands until the confused Omundson came through the hatch looking more rumpled and disconcerted than Samuels ever remembered seeing him.

"Take over at Astrogation, Ensign."

"Yes, ma'am," he replied. Something in her look told him it would be a bad idea to point out that the astrogation computer was unreliable and almost useless.

"Engineering, prepare for manual jump on my mark. You will find the proper calculations in the jump file." Omundson's head came up at that command and he started to rise out of the chair that he had just occupied.

"Yes, ma'am," called Giannini. Omundson sat back down with a wild, panicked look in his eyes. His look probably reflected the feelings of everyone on the bridge, save Leung herself.

The tension was palpable on the bridge as Giannini began her countdown. "5, 4, 3, 2, 1, activate jump engines."

The ship shuddered violently and Samuels felt nauseous as she struggled to hold onto her seat at the helm controls. The acrid smell of burnt wiring came from one of the abused consoles.

Omundson swore as he picked himself up from the deck and hastily began inputting commands into the astrogation computer. The view screen was still not functioning, so there was no visual representation available to show their present location.

"Position report, Ensign," called Leung shakily. There was no indication that the ship had moved at all.

All eyes were pulled to the lanky officer as he continued to work at his controls without response to the question. "Working on it," he finally said without taking his eyes from his task.

"Multiple contacts. No IDs on any of them. I make it at least ten ships - all headed this way," called Goodwin from the scan console. He stole the attention away from Omundson as the crew tried to assimilate this latest datum.

"Position confirmed," Omundson said finally. "We are in the Worth system."

"Comm signal," called Giannini in a voice very close to panic. "From FFF *Hammer*. It says: Unknown ship; identify yourself or be fired upon. The message is repeating."

Captain Leung's eyes took on a look very similar to the desperate panic that had been in Gianinni's earlier and she said the words that everyone else was thinking, "We can't answer - we have no transmitter."

ChApter 51
6 October

"Comm, sound General Quarters! Helm, All Stop!" Captain Katherine Leung yelled. "Belay that! Cut engine power, but don't fire retros!" She stood from the center seat and stared at the main view console which had been dead for some months. She looked away again, and began pacing the bridge and mumbling under her breath.

She thought furiously through her options, unaware that the desperate ideas were only partially private. A flotilla of ships were headed her way and they had already called on her to surrender. The problem was that she could not respond to them. *Pathfinder*'s vocom capability was destroyed, along with the rest of the communications room. Fight? No way to fight. There was no way to aim the lasers, and no computer to program targeting into the missiles before launch. Run away? They had too much velocity to even stop before those destroyers were on them. There would be time to charge the capacitors for another jump, barely, but certainly not enough to calculate a destination without a dependable astrocomp. Besides, where was there to jump *to*? No established system would even let them make orbit, let alone reprovision. They couldn't very well jump back to Earth in hopes of contacting Forrest there.

Maybe they could jump back to Antoc and pick up Brighton, explain that it had all been Teach's idea… She had set things up to look that way, in case things went poorly. And they clearly had. No, it was probably too late for that option now. *Vanguard*'s occupants had likely all starved to death by now, and there was already at least one Warner ship in that system looking for them.

What was left, then? This was clearly Forrest, the very people they had come to find, though where they had managed to produce warships was an enigma all its own. All Families were restricted by the Treaty of Agra into having only enough ships to defend their own territorial systems. Forrest had no such systems and therefore had no fleet. They sent enlisted crew into Combined Fleet, but they controlled no ships of their own. Where had these ships come from?

The only option she could see would be to appear as harmless as possible and hope they would try to take the ship intact instead of destroying it. Once they were on board, and she could explain, there was hope. After a few moments, with her decision made, the unintelligible words and the pacing both ceased and she resumed her seat.

"All Stop," she ordered again, in a calm and easy voice, as if several warships were not headed their way to destroy them. Lt. Monica Samuels relayed the command from her jury-rigged helm station to the engine room, saw confirmation that the message had been received there, then turned toward the center seat.

"Engine room answers All Stop, Captain." Samuels replied finally. Her voice was unnaturally calm, even to her own ears. In truth, at least half of her was rooting for the oncoming ships to fire on them. If they did, there was no doubt that *Pathfinder* would be destroyed. She had no working weapons or defensive systems at the moment. And if the ship were to be destroyed, Monica Samuels would have seen her duty successfully fulfilled. Her duty, or at least her primary duty to Warner, was to keep the technological advances on her ship out of the hands of those to whom they did not belong.

Except that such a result would leave Bybee Transstellar with the same problems from Hightower, and thus the objection of her other half. She would prefer some other way to achieve her current objective. If no other option presented itself, though, she was willing to accept death as the price she and others must pay to see it done. That acceptance gave her a sense of peace, and that allowed her to be calm in the face of mortal danger.

Leung knew nothing of the thoughts or intents of her executive officer. If she'd had the least notion, Monica Samuels would not still be numbered among the ship's complement, perhaps not even among the living. Instead, the captain was impressed at the young woman's self-possession as all others on the bridge had at least partially panicked, herself among them, she realized. Several were still shocked to the point that their military training still had not taken over. *She was a good choice for XO*, Leung congratulated herself mentally.

"Captain," Samuels broke in now, "if I might make a suggestion?" Leung nodded for her to continue. "We could decelerate faster if we flipped and used the main engines."

"No, Lieutenant. I want to look like we're stopping, not like we're trying to run away. Those are Forrest ships out there, and they've read our IFF beacon, so they know who we are. I'm betting that they know to expect us, or knew to expect us a few weeks ago." *Many weeks ago,* she admitted. Leung's voice was under better control now. It held no trace of the hammering knowledge that she was using all their lives to bet with.

"If they know who we are, they also know what this ship has on board. They're not going to want to lose it, so they are not going to fire missiles, they'll board us. When they do, we'll be able to explain ourselves to them and clear all this up," she finished, sounding much more confident than she felt.

Samuels nodded, apparently satisfied with her logic, and turned back to her station. Leung had to admit that it was a logical deduction based on what she knew. The problem was that she didn't know what the people on those ships knew or didn't know, nor what orders they might have been given. Without that information, it was not a logical proof, but merely a well-reasoned gamble. She had to wait for the dice to roll, and death awaited all of them if she crapped out.

Leung glanced at her hands and realized that they were shaking. She gripped the arms of the command chair in order to stop their involuntary movement. She could think of nothing else that she could do, and she fervently hoped that it would be enough. Their readings should be able to see that they had not raised any defenses, had not powered up their weapons, were not training targeting lasers on them. Wouldn't they?

There was no way to tell. Those ships should not even exist, so who was to say what instruments or weapons they bore?

"The message has stopped repeating, Captain." Giannini had her voice under control, but her dark brown eyes remained open as far as they would go and there was a pleading look in them. "No active signal at this time," she reported.

Leung nodded acknowledgement, not trusting her voice yet. She glanced around the bridge and found most people in similar conditions. Omundson looked to be in the worst shape, and though the ensign generally irritated her, she couldn't help granting him some of her pity. He was at the astrogation console and currently had absolutely nothing that he could be working on to take his mind off their situation.

When he turned to look at her, she noted again how much his facial features looked like a younger version of Gerald Warner, and her pity evaporated instantly. She had to bite her tongue not to simply order him off the bridge without reason. Maybe she could think of something plausi--

"Vampire!" shouted Goodwin from scan. "Hostile-1 has launched missiles! Correction, one missile inbound. Seven minutes forty seconds to impact."

"Helm, hard about!" the Captain shouted, losing in an instant her fraying emotional control. "Emergency power to engines!"

"Aye-aye, ma'am." Samuels' ice-cold tone brought Leung back to herself. *How can that* girl *be so calm in the middle of such a bloody mess?*

"Weapons free on local control, Captain?" Chandler asked from the Tactical station.

"Do we have any scanning links to the gun rooms or missile rooms?"

"No, ma'am," he admitted.

"Then there really is no point. We couldn't hit anything firing blind, and we may wind up making them mad at us instead of convincing them that we aren't a threat," she said resignedly.

Goodwin was sweating freely now, watching death speed toward them yet unable to do anything to prevent it. He counted down the approach minute by minute, then every ten seconds when it was less than a single span.

The inactivity was the hardest part of the current situation for each of them to deal with. Endless hours of training and drilling had made it second nature for them to set aside thoughts of danger, fear, even panic, in order to focus on the tasks necessary to fight the ship through an engagement. Now, though, they had nothing available to supplant the dire predictions and visions of quick and silent death which had gained free rein in their minds.

Inexorably, the count became smaller and their remaining lives shorter. The hard braking had initially added time to the estimate for impact, but the certainty of that collision had not changed.

"Twenty seconds," Goodwin announced, then, "ten seconds, nine, eight-- Vampire is changing course! No return on scan, missile destroyed!"

The release of built up tension was as sudden as it was unexpected. Leung thought to say something to the crew, then realized that she had never announced the impending threat generally. No one outside of the sealed bridge had ever known how close they had come to annihilation.

"Signal from *Hammer*, Captain," Giannini stated a bit shakily. "They are ordering us to reduce speed to forty kps and hold to our present course. We are instructed to prepare for boarding."

Relief hit Leung again, then. Her gamble had paid off and she would get the chance to sort this vomitous mess out. She nearly ordered Giannini to acknowledge the orders, before she remembered the lack that had caused the whole problem in the first place. "Helm, reduce velocity as directed, same heading," she said instead.

"Four zero kilometers per second aye, ma'am." Then, "Forward retros engaged at 90%."

Time slowed with no action to distract the bridge's occupants from the protracted advance of the Forrest ships. Leung asked Goodwin for an update repeatedly, since without a viewscreen she could not monitor their progress herself. Eventually, he began counting down the distance as he had before with the incoming missile. The continuous update kept her informed then, but did nothing to hasten the process, nor alleviate her tension.

Pathfinder was down to less than a tenth of her initial velocity before the flotilla of destroyers had moved into positions around her and matched speed and trajectory. Enough hours had passed that Leung had sent for food from the galley twice. She had decided not to relieve her bridge crew; they were the best on the ship for the stations they currently occupied, and she might yet need the best available on an instant's notice. Other stations on the ship she had stood down from General Quarters, though, and rotated fresh people in.

When the lead ship launched three assault shuttles, Leung turned the bridge over to Omundson, and brought Samuels and Chandler with her to the boatbay to await their arrival. Danis and Bezates also joined them, and they had stopped at the arms locker in Security to issue each a light rifle. Leung stressed, though, that she was not expecting trouble, and that she would flog any of her people that started anything.

The captain then led them all to the boatbay and brought them down the ladder into the connecting corridor that led from the boatbay to the lock that had once serviced *Vanguard*. Samuels felt a twinge of guilt at the reminder that whatever the fate of those on the survey launch, she was not sharing it. The thoughts were fleeting, however, given the gravity of immediate concerns. One of the shuttles had settled into the vacant berth and attached itself to the lock.

Leung waited for the shuttle to match pressure and the first Forrester to come through their end of the twin hatches before opening the inner door. "Welcome to--" was as far as she got before a heavy plasma rifle prodded her middle and she found it prudent to step back.

"Drop your weapons and surrender immediately or we will open fire!" a commanding voice boomed, sounding lifeless and inhuman coming from the battle armor's external speakers.

"Do as he says," Leung directed, suiting actions to words and laying her rifle down by the barrel. All obeyed, knowing that they had no options. The heavy armor would shrug off anything their rifles could do against them.

"Back up the ladder, double quick!" the Forrester directed next, and they readily complied. In the open area of the bay once again, they were backed all the way to the aft bulkhead while more and more soldiers rose from below to fill the available space. They deployed quickly into a formation that faced outward in every direction, but they made no move to advance beyond the spacious area of the boatbay.

"Is there a Lt. Commander Leung on this ship?" demanded the officer in charge, Captain Kerritt, she read from his breastplate, just under the green circle with brown border that showed his Family affiliation.

She took one step forward and stated, "I'm Leung."

"You're late, Commander," he observed, removing his helmet as he spoke.

Leung's anger nearly boiled over, but she managed, barely, to master it. "Yes, well, there have been some…delays. We're here now."

"I can see that," he all but sneered. "I have been instructed to escort you to the system capital. You are required to bring full engineering and design plots of the ship, as well as all active command codes. We'll leave as soon as you have gathered those items." It was clear from the way he spoke that he expected her to jump to it and race to get it done yesterday. It annoyed her. It more than annoyed her, it infuriated her. She wanted badly to put this soldier in his proper place, and finally decided that was exactly what she should do. If she appeared weak, it might place her at a disadvantage later.

"I was told to make contact with a woman named Epi Solomon, and to trust no one else."

His tone changed at the mention of the name. "Yes, ma'am. That is the woman who gave me my orders."

"Very well, Major. May I see those orders?" Her tone was pleasant enough, but the words had a bewildering effect on the Marine.

"While I appreciate the promotion, I am a Captain of the Forrest Marines. I have thirty armed troops on your ship, and six armed attack craft surrounding it. I am under no obligation to show you my orders. You will come with me, and you will do so now!"

"Major, this is *my* ship, and I am the only captain in her. If you attempt to give me another *order* while you are my guest, it will be the last word you ever utter."

Complete silence hung in the air. Kerritt towered over Leung, the powered armor adding a half meter to his already imposing height. He glared at her angrily, but she merely watched him impassively. Every other eye in the vast room was riveted to the scene being played out.

"What do you mean?" he finally asked.

"I am not an idiot, Major. Nor am I a particularly trusting person. Had I shown up here without making some...preparations...this ship might have ceased to be mine before I was ready to turn it over. Therefore, if I get the feeling that you are here to take *Pathfinder* without paying me, say, by ordering me about on my own ship, then I might think it wise to press this button." Leung raised a slender metallic cylinder, perhaps twenty centimeters in length, with a black push switch at one end. She quickly returned it to her fist and held it behind her back.

"What will that do?" he asked nervously.

"It will destroy you and everyone else on this ship. It will also deny your superior of her prize," she said gravely.

"Very well, *Captain* Leung," the Marine began in a gentler tone, "would you care to accompany me to the planet, where I will take you to see Governor Solomon?"

"Thank you, Major, I believe I would."

The air in the room seemed suddenly much easier to breathe.

"And the data I asked about?"

"Every existing copy of the engineering specs and command codes is already in my possession." She very carefully did not mention that they did not, in fact, exist anymore. Technically, what she had said was not a lie. Not exactly, anyway.

She felt as if a mountain of weight had been lifted off her shoulders. She drew in the first free and easy breath she had taken in months as she returned her magnetic tool grabber to her front pocket.

CHAPTER 52
7 October
Granada

Katherine Leung sat rigidly on the jump seat and did her best to ignore the nine people in mottled green armor who lounged all about her. They appeared to be ignoring her as well, though without apparent effort. She should be pleased that she was headed to meet her contact in the Forrest organization. It should be the first step in getting paid and leaving behind the Family and military that she had come to hate. She should be pleased that she had put herself in a better position to negotiate with a little play acting. She should be, but she wasn't.

At first, the Forrest soldiers had been a relief, but that had lasted only until they actually came aboard. Three times as many troops were still on *Pathfinder*, and they were both well protected and armed to the teeth. It was clear now that they had arrived with no intention to pay her anything at all. They held the ship, and if they wanted to turn it inside out and shake all its secrets loose, she was in no position to stop them. They *believed* that she was so situated, and that was the only thing stopping them.

Kerritt had made no effort to speak with her, not that she expected them to be on cordial terms. He had not asked why they had not communicated with him by vocom, nor had he apologized for firing at her ship. Rationally, she should be happy that it had been only a warning shot. Rationally, she should thank her lucky stars that the burly officer had not called her bluff in the boatbay. Still, the indifference with which she was being treated simply perturbed her normally logical mind, as if she had been weighed and measured and determined to be insignificant. The stress and fatigue that had built up over the previous weeks simply did not allow her to be as rational as she normally would be.

After a handful of eternities, the attack craft settled to the ground on Granada. She wasn't sure exactly where on the planet. No one had volunteered that information, of course, and she had not asked, but she assumed that it was at the spaceport of the capital city. Applying what reason she had left, she realized abruptly that Forrest must have taken over the entire system from Warner. How else could they have a military presence here? And hadn't Kerritt referred to Epi as 'Governor Solomon?' Granada had to be occupied territory now, and that made her even more uncomfortable with the situation.

There was nothing she could do about it, anyway.

The soldiers all rose as the assault shuttle settled. Leung rose with them and made her way to the rear exit. The fresh air smelled good to her, after breathing the recycled air of the ship for so long. It was clean and bore the crispness of late fall's chill. Three ground vehicles marked with the Forrest disk, dark green at the center and brown on the circumference, with a thin tan line dividing them, approached and stopped a few meters from the ship.

They were indeed at the spaceport of Levera, the capital city of this one-planet system. She recognized it from the last visit she had made five or six years before, when she had been serving on *Peregrine*.

There had been several changes that she noted immediately. The field control tower that had been little more than a foundation had now been completed, but the Warner offices to the south of the field were conspicuously absent, replaced by a large crater. A shiver ran down Leung's spine that had nothing to do with the cool air.

Kerritt remained silent, but motioned, politely, for her to step up into the truck. She did so and he followed her, placing her constrictively between the rock of the truck's driver and the equally hard place of the commander, both of whom were fully armored. She understood why Kerritt was so clad, but couldn't see a reason for the driver's protection. On the way across Levera, she got her first clues.

Conditions in the capital had certainly gone downhill. There were plenty of people moving about on foot in the crowded streets, but few of them would look their direction as they passed. Eyes were averted in nearly all cases, which felt unnatural to her. She would have expected that they would cause more of a spectacle. Those whose eyes did glance her way showed anger when looking at the soldiers, and pity when they looked at her. She glanced down and realized that they were reacting to the Warner uniform that she still wore, and assumed that she was a prisoner.

Perhaps I am.

The anger and general conditions that caused them were likely the reasons for the protective gear on the drivers.

Their destination turned out to be the Palace Hotel. The miniature convoy pulled into the covered unloading zone. Everyone but the driver got out, and the vehicles left again.

The soldiers went a different way after crossing the lobby, and only Kerritt accompanied her to the elevator. He had to duck to fit through the entry. Once inside, he removed his helmet and was able to stand straight, though his short black hair brushed the ceiling. She decided that he was not bad-looking, but his standoffishness made him unattractive. He remained speechless all the way to a room on the eighth floor, where he knocked once, opened the door, and then took up a position outside it.

"Commander! I'm so pleased to see you. I was afraid that something untoward had happened to you." Epi Solomon rose from her seat and walked around the desk to greet her visitor. The woman looked exactly as Leung remembered her from their one previous meeting. She was at least a quarter meter shorter than average, though still a bit taller than Leung, chestnut colored hair pulled back in elaborate bun, a youthful face that smiled easily, and hard greenish-brown eyes. "I had almost given up on you."

Leung seated herself in the indicated chair facing a rather plain-looking desk. She waited for her long-standing contact to resume her seat as well before responding. "As I told Captain Kerritt, there were some unexpected delays."

"Yes. I understand that is not all you told Captain Kerritt," she said icily, abruptly changing from open friendship to not quite hostility.

"Oh, my," Katherine said in mock distress. "I hope I haven't caused a stir. Last-minute changes to an operation can create such inefficiency and scrambling about, don't you think? Should I have cowered in fear in the face of his unprovoked attack and his threatening demeanor?"

"Not at all," Solomon replied, again the amiable hostess. "The 'scrambling about,' as you say, was caused by your unexpected arrival, and not by any thwarted plans of ours. Indeed, we never considered dealing with you in any way but honorably."

"I'm sure that's true, Epi. Still, the very nature of our arrangement tends to make a certain level of caution…advisable. And after all the time and grief spent getting *Pathfinder* here, it seemed prudent to have some measure of protection."

It certainly did seem prudent, now. Leung only wished that the repairs to the ship had not so completely filled her brain for so long, or it might have occurred to her in time to have an *actual* ace up her sleeve, instead of the empty hand with which she was gambling.

"Well, let's hope that we can make up for lost time, now that you're here," Epi said with an easy smile. "You've brought a copy of the full engineering designs, so let's get them to the designers and construction crews at our shipyard and start implementing them. You'll make yourself available as a consultant for the foreseeable future, of course."

The assumption that Leung was Solomon's to command and direct here and there nettled the older woman. It gave her a certain perverse satisfaction to make the next admission, knowing how Epi would take it. "I have no engineering designs for you."

The fact that there had been a Warner shipyard in this system was beginning to make sense to Leung. The occupied planet, the warships, the new designs; Forrest was certainly thinking much bigger than she had imagined before!

As expected, at Leung's response, Solomon's countenance turned from amiable to angry as if a switch had been thrown. "The reason that we have been delayed is that Brighton destroyed the central computer net before he was removed from the ship. All ship's systems were disabled and had to be rebuilt from scratch. All data files, including engineering specifications, were lost." Leung was angered all over again thinking about it, and the heat came through in her voice.

"You wanted the ship," she continued. "I could have given you the entire plans a year ago, but you told me that the plans weren't enough for you. Well, I brought you the whole ship, and I've been through hell to get it here, so just pay me the money you promised me. I'll split it with the crew, and you and I never have to see each other again."

"I'm afraid that will be impossible. Clearly you are not delivering a functional ship. We need a working model, and we need the designs in order to make copies of the jump engines. Without those, you have not met your part of the bargain. Without meeting your end, I am under no obligation to meet ours."

Exactly as Leung had feared, it seemed that Forrest was just going to take the ship and leave her with nothing. There must be something she could do to salvage the situation, but what? She thought frantically. To get what she wanted, she was going to have to give Solomon what she wanted.

"All right, I can duplicate the specifications and make the ship functional, it will just take some time. Will that satisfy you?"

"How much time?" Epi responded.

At least she's willing to negotiate. I may be able to salvage this mess yet, Leung thought. She considered carefully before answering the question. She didn't want to overcommit herself, or the crew. They were already at the end of their ropes, most of them. Instead of answering directly, she asked for information.

"Do you have any engineering staff that could assist us?"

Solomon gave her a long appraising look before she spoke. "I might be able to spare some, but our operations at the docks are in full swing, and I would have to pull people off of ongoing projects to assign them to you. Can't you accomplish what you need with the people you already have?"

"Oh, of course I could," Leung rejoined, suppressing an evil grin. In as bland a voice as she could manage, she said, "But the more help I have, the sooner I could complete the task. Unless you're not in a hurry."

"Of course I'm in a hurry! Your delay has put me three months behind!" Epi paused a moment to regain control of herself. Emotions always got in the way of good negotiating. The calmer voice was the one with power, after all. "All right, I can spare two junior engineers to help you reproduce the plans from the physical engines."

"Twelve would be better," Leung countered. "It is a complex system, and several teams could work in parallel. Plus there are repairs and rebuilding to be done. My crew has been working long hours for months now, and they need a little down time."

"Schedule them as you see fit, but shore leave will not be allowed. They, and you, will have to remain on *Pathfinder* until everything you have promised has been delivered. No payment until that time.

"And as for giving you a dozen engineers," the young Forrester continued, "that will not be possible. The most I could give you would be four. I could probably add some of the yard hands to that. They would do for the repairs you need to complete."

"Yes, they would," Leung agreed. "How many could you spare?"

"Say...four?"

"Eight technicians and six engineers," she countered.

"Hmm. By my math, that's more than the twelve you asked for to begin with."

"Different distribution of work. Twelve engineers would be the most I could use without having them tripping over each other, but a repair crew needs to cover everything on the ship."

"Still," Solomon hedged, "that's more than I can spare. I have obligations to the Family with our construction schedule. Five engineers and six technicians is the absolute limit, and even then I'm risking slipping my completion dates."

"Agreed," Leung accepted easily. It was much more generous than she had expected, and the help would be greatly appreciated by everyone on the ship. There was still one thing she needed to resolve, and that would have to be brought up and handled most delicately.

Pathfinder was not entirely hers to bargain with; it was occupied territory. Solomon *seemed* willing to negotiate in good faith, rather than dictate terms, but that could change at any time until her payment was deposited and in her exclusive control. She needed to get those Marines off her ship, or at least minimize their threat to her.

"There is one other thing," Epi broke into her thoughts.

"Yes?"

"Now that we have come to an understanding, and I am sure that you're not trying to back out of our deal, I will be pulling the remainder of the Marines off *Pathfinder*; partly as a show of faith, and partly because those troops are needed here on the planet. These Granadans sometimes need…persuading…to be cooperative."

Epi did not smile at the statement, but looked more like she had bitten into something rotten. Leung identified the sentiments immediately; she disliked using force, but she was willing to do whatever was needed to get the job done. It was exactly the way Leung felt about things herself.

It certainly relieved her of the difficulty of bringing the subject up, but it did leave her with another difficulty.

"I appreciate the show of faith, Epi." Things had taken on a friendly enough tone that she could again use the girl's first name. "I wonder if you might leave me a few of them, though. I'd prefer they not be heavily armed, I really don't want them shooting up the ship I'm trying to fix," *nor the Captain who objects to a ship being stolen from her,* "but there is a saboteur loose on *Pathfinder* that we have not been able to run to ground. Our security team has been dismantled, and so we don't have anyone with the training to get that job done."

Epi stared at Leung for a long time without saying anything. Perhaps she was trying to detect ulterior motives in the request, Leung couldn't tell. At last she said, "I'll instruct Captain Kerritt to leave a ten-man team on the ship. They will still report to Kerritt, but any polite request of them from you will be honored."

Leung could tell by the wording that Solomon's suspicions had been reawakened, if they had ever died down at all, and for that she was sorry. It made her next request even harder. "And…"

"Yes," Solomon prompted.

"I have a prisoner on the ship who has been working with the saboteur. I have not been able to get him to reveal anything useful, but then, my expertise lies in other areas. It would greatly speed up your Marines' job if we could locate someone that could…persuade…our prisoner to cooperate."

The suspicious look doubled in intensity, and Katherine regretted asking at all. It still seemed the best way to handle the problems she had to sort out. At least, it would if Epi's apparent plan of adhering to the original agreement was genuine.

Leung was kept waiting so long that she was beginning to sweat. Finally, the girl nodded once. "I'll see to it. Expect her tomorrow sometime."

"Thank you, Epi," the captain said graciously.

If the agreement was just a feint, things could quickly turn into an even bigger mess.

CHAPTER 53
12 October

"Hmmph," Ben Danis said to Cody Bezates, who lay prone under a secondary jump field emitter regulator. "Leung's going to have us shot. Today, tomorrow, next week, who knows? But it's coming, you can count on it."

"I don't know. Aichele's a pretty tough guy. Maybe he won't talk. He's lasted this long, hasn't he?"

"Oh, he'll talk. He held out a long time against Leung, but only because he told her everything he knew about Lamont, and that was nothing at all. But now there's an 'interrogation specialist' on board to break him. He can't last forever. And when they squeeze him hard enough, our names are going to pop out."

"Yeah, Ben, I see your point. But what in blazes can we do about it?" The normally easygoing petty officer nearly screeched the words out. It was a good thing that their work area was as loud as it was, or it might have brought unwanted attention their way. "In case it has escaped you, this is Engineering. We don't work in Security now that Forrest took that over. So what can we do? We don't have access to anything that can stop events from unfolding however they will."

"What if Aichele died?" Danis said stonily.

Bezates slid all the way out from under the massive machine and looked closely at his friend. There was no malevolence in his face. What he saw was closer to panic than anything else.

"Aichele doesn't deserve that. He was trying to help us gather evidence when he was caught. And even if he did have it coming, we still wouldn't have any access to do him in."

"Yeah, I know. So what do we *do*?" Danis asked plaintively.

"If we had to kill anybody, which I truly don't want to, I'd rather it were Leung," Cody stated flatly. Danis knew that to be true, after the difficulties his friend had gone through right after he'd been forced to shoot Teach.

"Hmmph. You and me both. But now that Forrest has taken over the interrogation, it's too late for that to do any good."

"True. Forrest has him now, and they'll shake the information out of him eventually, Leung or no Leung."

"And when they do, we're going to be shot." Danis said, bringing his argument full circle.

"So we need to get him out of their hands, somehow." Bezates reasoned.

"Right. And do what with him? Hide him under our bunks?"

"Well, Lamont still hasn't been found. That should prove that it's possible to hide on the ship and avoid even the Forrest Marines."

The older man looked thoughtful for several moments, and Bezates took advantage of the break to slide back under the regulator. "Can you hand me four of the B2 couplers, Ben?"

Danis retrieved the needed components and squatted down to hand them over. "So let's say once we have him, we can get him somewhere that he could hide out. You and I have seen about every likely spot there is by now. That still leaves the problem of getting him out of the brig."

"Right," Bezates agreed, with his mind and hands busy with another task. "Not likely."

"There are only two guards on duty, but they're wearing light armor. We can't sneak up and knock them out."

"Not likely," Bezates repeated.

"And we don't have any weapons that could punch through the armor."

"Nope," Bezates agreed, finishing his replacement effort and sliding out, "but Leung does."

"What do you mean?"

"Well, rumor is that Leung asked for restrictions on what Forrest could bring on board, because she was afraid of them just taking the ship and not paying us. So I would bet that she's got some bigger weapons stashed somewhere that no one knows about, like no one knew about the explosives she planted all over the ship to get Forrest to back off the first time."

"Oh," Danis said. "I thought you were talking about her having a supply of toxins or something, like she used on Teach."

Bezates stood up and stared at Danis. Danis returned the stare.

"You know…" Bezates began.

CHAPTER 54
12 October

Monica Samuels, lieutenant, executive officer, saboteur, imposter, and 23-year-old girl, augered in for a crash landing on her bunk. That act, not sufficient to display her current state of exhaustion, frustration, and helplessness, she added stuffing her head under her pillow to it. She momentarily considered a scream or two while she was muffled there, but decided to hold that in reserve in case things managed to get worse.

She couldn't imagine that being possible, but a little over a week ago, she wouldn't have thought things could get *this* bad. At that point, things had been going more or less according to plan. The ship was still in the Antoc system, where Warner knew to look for it, the astrocomp was spitting out useless data, and people were getting so overworked and overtired that they were breaking the ship for her.

Now all of those transitory positives were flipped into negatives. The ship was now in Worth, the last place Warner would think to look for it because they thought they still owned the system, which Leung's report said was no longer the case, and because Monica had not known that was where they were heading when she had launched her comm buoy, Warner had no reason to come here looking.

The fact that the astrocomp was not cooperating hadn't kept Captain Leung from plotting the course herself, by hand. She didn't have Captain Brighton's gift for rapid calculation, but she did have a thorough and meticulous engineer's mind, and given enough time, that had been sufficient.

The frantic push to get the ship working so this mad enterprise could finally end was no longer in evidence. There was still plenty to do, but the expectation to work sixteen or twenty hours a day had disappeared. Many had taken a couple days of regular duty and then gone back to twelve hour days, but that didn't take the same toll on the human body and mind as the previous unending toil had.

A lot of that had to do with Forrest taking over Security, as well. There had been a good amount of distrust and ragged nerves for the first few days they were here. Their presence, after seeing the same faces day after day for so long, felt like an invading army had come to call, but eventually, suspicions eased and people relaxed around them. Then they began feeling safer, as all the sabotage and disappearances had come to an abrupt halt on their watch.

Of course there hasn't been any more sabotage, she berated herself. *You haven't done anything, and the other saboteur is rotting away in the brig at this very moment!* The thought of what Leung had done to Sgt. Aichele, which she had noted dispassionately in one of her command staff meetings, made Monica physically ill. She dearly wanted to find some way to free him, if only to have an ally she could trust, but she knew it was a fool's hope.

She had given it her best, but that hadn't been good enough to stop Leung and the Forrest Family from getting away with stealing an entire ship. Who had she been kidding, anyway, thinking that she, acting on her own, could outwit and outmaneuver the rest of the ship's crew? She'd never stood a chance.

A wave of despair loomed up, and she made no effort to keep it away. She let it crash over her, beating and torturing her spirit with what might have been. If she'd only been better at this. If she'd only put the pieces together sooner. If she'd only thought quickly enough. If only Captain had picked someone who could do the job to send in her place.

Part of the blame was surely his, after all. He had sent her here with no help in sight, and no instructions to work from. What had he expected?

He expected me to do my duty, she answered herself. That had always been his expectation, of everyone he worked with, and most especially of himself. *But I let him down. I AM letting him down.*

She sat up and used her pillowcase to dry her eyes and cheeks. Falling apart and wallowing were definitely not among Captain's expectations. He would expect her to continue doing whatever was in her power to change. So what was in her power?

Among her assets, she could count her position as executive officer. Many things she could do now would not raise any eyebrows that she couldn't have done before. Leung would probably still hear about it, so she shouldn't get carried away; but it was still an asset.

She still had an active computer connection to the bridge, and she had the only active bridge override codes. That alone gave her more power than anyone else had on the ship, including Leung. She was an excellent computer programmer. She was well-practiced at deceiving others. She had four years of officer training. All assets.

When she looked at it that way, she actually had quite a bit going for her.

With her renewed confidence, she took a fresh look at the problem of Aichele's incarceration.

First problem, he's locked in the brig. That had an easy solution, since she held Chowdhury's access codes. She could open the lock at any time.

Second problem, he's being guarded by two Forrest Marines who were trained to fight and kill and were wearing body armor. That was not so easy to overcome.

She'd had weapons training at the Academy, and had been taught the safe use of arms before that by her older brother and father. None of that helped her without an actual weapon to wield, though. She could use her pilfered codes to get into any of the weapons lockers on the ship, but they were all in areas where it would be difficult to do so and then carry the weapon back to her quarters without being seen.

Besides, those lockers contained only small arms: pistols, light rifles, and a few small explosives. There might be one or two things big enough to punch through armor, but nothing that would make it a fair fight. She could grab some of the small explosive charges, she supposed. Those would be easier to conceal, and big enough to do the job, but in order to work, she would have to set them inside Security or on the armor itself. Monica abruptly thought of the classic line, "Who's going to bell the cat?"

None of the angles Samuels could think of for the problem bore any fruit. So, explosives were out. What did that leave her? What could she lay her hands on that could disable two Marines in armor? Her preference was to disable them, but she recognized that the way the odds were stacked against her, she would have to take whatever plan would work, even if it meant killing the guards. What could she get that would make it a fair fight?

Nothing.

Well, if she couldn't make it a fair fight, she was going to have to stop trying to fight fair.

Light armor gave its wearer some significant advantages over an unarmored opponent, but it certainly had weaknesses as well. It was not as protective as heavy armor, and it lacked the artificial muscles the heavier version had. All the motion had to be human-powered, so the extra weight slowed movements to some extent. Monica was sure the guards would be used to wearing it, though. There may not be much of a speed advantage on her side.

No, no, no. She was still looking at the problem from a direct approach, and direct conflict was doomed to fail. She had to come at them in a way they didn't expect. How could she knock out two armored guards before they saw it coming? She could probably get close to them without arousing their suspicions, being a trusted officer. At least, as long as she wasn't carrying an obvious weapon with her.

Tranquilizer? How would you deliver it? Tranquilizer gun? Samuels doubted there was one on the ship. Hypodermic injector? She could probably liberate one or two from medbay, hopefully the tranquilizer too, if she could find a time when Dr. Johnson was not there.

Even granting all that, could she deliver the necessary dosage? Would it incapacitate them quickly enough? Could she count on them having their helmets off so there would be exposed skin? How long would it take to administer one, and was it possible to do before the other one was all over her? And if the other saw her deliver the first dose, was it possible that he would let her get within striking distance?

Lots of questions, and she was fearing that the answer to too many of them was going to be "not a chance." So, scratch tranquilizer.

What about electrical discharge? There was a long history of using that as a non-lethal means of incapacitation. The armor was insulated, but if she were close enough, and if her metal leads were long enough and thin enough, she should be able to stab into one of the seams at a joint and trigger the weapon in a matter of a second or two.

She'd have to build the weapon herself, but she knew how and there were plenty of the right kinds of components on the ship, and her new rank gained her the unquestioned acccss she would need to gather them. Two weapons, actually, now that she considered what she would have to build. Even if she built a system capable of multiple uses, it would take too long to build up and store a great enough charge after the first use. She would need to have two of them, and they would have to be concealed, maybe one up each sleeve?

She'd need to get a blaster pistol out of one of the lockers, too. That would be small enough to hide in her tunic pocket. Monica had forgotten about the interrogator. She was sure to be there as well, but without armor. A simple stun blast would do for her until Samuels and Aichele made their getaway.

Monica was feeling optimistic about the chances for her plan, but thinking about getting away with Aichele slammed her headlong into the brick wall of problem three. Eric was certainly too large to fit in her pocket, so how was she going to get him out of Security and into a place of safety? She had a destination in mind already. There were four storage rooms on lower deck and two on upper deck that had obediently locked their doors when Brighton ordered them to, and had remained so ever since. Brighton's codes would open them for her, and they would be ignored during any search of the ship.

She could spoof the video bugs with an overriding signal showing empty corridors, so that wouldn't be a problem, either, but there were bound to be people walking about, even in the dead of ship's night.

Samuels wanted to beat her head against the wall. She was *so* close to having a workable plan. There was just one more hurdle before the finish line. There *had* to be some way to be sure the halls were cleared long enough for her to get into Security, deal with the guards, get Aichele out, and get him moved downstairs. But how could she get everyone congregated in one area away from her? How could she be sure the ship's forward section was evacuated?

Then she had her answer.

CHAPTER 55
12 October

"Crap!" Staff Sergeant Jill Burton swore in a fierce whisper, dropping immediately to the floor and rolling to her right. She wished she could have shouted it as loudly as the sentiment deserved, but she had grown too fond of breathing to allow that. She tried to curl her body deeper into the shadows and held herself motionless while the Forresters approached slowly through the between decks area.

Ever since that night when Aichele had failed to make his rendezvous, coming back into the ship proper was a risky business. She'd waited as long as she'd dared that night before she was sure something had gone wrong. She finally decided to go out looking for him, but he was not in his quarters and there was no message to her marked on the wall in any of their prearranged spots.

Jill was tucked into the angle made by support F16 and the recycled water line. One of the two Marines on patrol was headed in her general direction, but a few meters on the other side of the large pipe. Rather than tense up and hold her breath, which was her natural inclination, she obeyed her training and relaxed her muscles, breathing normally.

The man approaching nearest her was a bit taller than average, but she had no idea of his features. He had a full helmet as part of his light armor, and the faceplate was down and locked into position. The other was shorter and female, but there was little else she could tell. She certainly wasn't going to try repositioning to get a better look.

"No, I'm serious. I think I've got a valid grievance," the taller one said as he came within audible range.

"Frank, that is the dumbest idea I've ever heard. Even if Kerrick believed you, which I'm not saying he would, and even if he cared about your back, which I am definitely saying he wouldn't, he is not going to assign you exclusively to the cushy duty of guarding the prisoner. It's more likely he'll ship you back to Granada and put you on the front lines. Is that what you want?"

"No," Frank said sullenly. "but every time I make one of these patrols hunched over through the interstitial, it takes me hours to put my back together enough to walk erect."

"Really, and I thought you were just a natural knuckle-dragger."

"Ha flaming ha."

The rest of the conversation faded into obscurity as they moved past her and out of her hearing. They weren't the most observant of soldiers, but she wasn't going to complain. If she hadn't heard them coming soon enough to get into hiding, she would have been caught for sure.

She was less than halfway to checking the wall outside Engineering, but there was no point in looking now. There was a prisoner to guard. Aichele had not made his appointment with her to hand over an unconscious Leung. Burton could put two and two together as well as anyone.

"Crap, crap, crap!" she said again, just as quietly as before.

She'd tried once before to come into the ship, a day after she had felt the jump transition, and that foray had ended on a similar note. It hadn't been as close a call, but she had been thwarted from reaching her destination by patrolling Forrest Marines then too.

She had planned to stay outside for a while, hoping things would quiet down. Unfortunately, with four prisoners to tend, her food supply was beginning to run low. It had been necessary to make another try at retrieving supplies, and she would do what was necessary.

Now she had a new necessity to consider. She carefully raised herself up to peer over the green-colored pipe. Seeing that the pair of guards had moved far enough away to be completely out of sight, she hopped over and headed in the opposite direction. This area should be clear for a while now, with that sweep just finished.

Her priorities had abruptly changed with the receipt of this new information. Food was not at the top anymore. Her survival, and any hope of eventual success, lay now in finding some way to get Aichele out of the hands of the enemy.

If he was captured, and she had to assume he was, he was either going to be tortured or drugged for information; likely both. The information in his head included where to find Sgt. Jill Burton.

There were other options, but none of them was very practical. She could abandon her hiding spot in the external hold. That would mean, though, that she would be abandoning her four prisoners to possible starvation, if they weren't found soon. She stopped at one of the sealable hatches and peered quickly through before crossing the threshold. It would also mean constantly trying to avoid the increased security measures. Definitely impractical.

Of the guards she had seen, and she realized there were only four, all had been wearing light armor. If the guards at the brig were similarly protected, as she had to assume, she had nothing in her collection of weapons that could touch them.

She stopped moving abruptly and found a spot to sit down, her eyes still scanning for movement. Burton had been heading toward her stash of guns, but now thought better of the idea. For one thing, with as many Forresters as must have traipsed through these areas, there was a 50-50 chance that they had already been discovered. If so, a smart security officer would put surveillance on the spot, waiting for Aichele's accomplice to head there. Since there was nothing in her collection that would be able to finish her current job, there was no point in taking that risk.

So now what? *Crap!* There had to be something, anything, which could make her rescue mission anything better than elaborate suicide. Even marginally better would be enough to allow her to attempt it. What other options did she have? They didn't call these do-or-die situations for no reason.

She couldn't take the vents all the way back into the brig area; she'd have to drop out in the outer security hub. That meant she would have to fight her way through the guards.

If she were Aichele, maybe she could do it hand to hand. The light armor added no strength or speed, only impenetrable skin. You could still take them out without a gun because the joints all had free movement, and could thus be broken with the proper application of force. Aichele had taught unarmed combat in boot camp for a dozen years. If he were in her shoes planning to rescue her, she would place even odds on him being able to sneak in and break both the guards' necks before they could shoot him.

As long as she was wishing, why not wish herself Major Sheli Chowdhury? That woman could walk in the room naked, armed with a toothpick, and walk back out sporting a new set of armor and carrying both their guns.

Jill was no slouch in the hand-to-hand fighting department, but she wasn't in the same class as either of the others that had formed *Pathfinder*'s security detail with her. She'd watched the two of them spar once. It was Chowdhury's second day on the ship, and she'd wanted to take the measure of her subordinates. So they had padded up and rolled out the mats for some full-contact hand-to-hand practice. The two of them had circled warily for a few seconds, then engaged each other, the strikes, blocks, and counter-strikes flew so fast Jill couldn't follow everything. The melee lasted more than a minute, which Chowdhury admitted was her longest match in years.

When Aichele woke up, he asked her to show him what she had done, because he literally never saw it coming.

No, Burton had never been anywhere near that level, and besides, her dominant shoulder and arm were only partially healed, and hadn't made any improvement for some time. She feared that her current strength and mobility might be permanent now. Unarmed assault was out; Burton needed a gun. A big gun.

Unfortunately, everything that matched that description was sealed up in the armory. Even if she could get back to the armory door in Security, the ship-wide shutdown had made that inaccessible. She might be able to break into one of the small arms lockers, but they wouldn't contain anything big enough, anyway.

Wait, there was a big gun that wasn't in the armory. Duke. He would be in Chowdhury's quarters in Security. She might be able to sneak in there without being spotted. Maybe.

No, Aichele had said Danis and Bezates had cleared out all her stuff. That would put him in the quartermaster's storage room. That, she could certainly get into unseen.

With a new destination set, she rose and moved quickly and carefully to a point where she could climb into the air circulation ducts. She was startled by an unexpected noise on the way, but it turned out to be nothing.

Burton was lucky to even know about Duke, a DK-8515 Variable Energy Discharge Cannon. She had interrupted Chowdhury while she had him out to clean him. Burton had innocently asked why her superior was cleaning the weapon in her room, instead of in the armory where it belonged.

"Sergeant," Burton could recall the stern voice as if it were yesterday, "Duke is not an 'it,' he is the oldest and truest friend I have, and he sleeps in my room with me." Suitably chastened, Burton was about to duck back out the way she had come, when Chowdhury had directed her to take a seat instead.

She carefully placed Duke back in his case, then put the case in her foot locker. From the same locker she had pulled out a letter, an actual physical letter, printed on paper, and handed it to Burton. The letter was dated 27 March, 2781 and signed by the Chief of Naval Operations at the time. The letter was a special dispensation that allowed the large weapon, and the serial number was specified, was to be considered the "personal sidearm" of Major Sheli S. Chowdhury, and as such, she was allowed to keep it "in her personal possession, on her responsibility, under all circumstance, and such right was not to be abridged nor modified by any member of the Warner Navy or Warner Marines."

Burton had never heard of such a thing and had asked the major how she'd managed to get a letter like that. Chowdhury had taken the sheet and carefully folded it into its case before responding.

"I earned it, Sergeant. Dismissed."

That was a typical answer for Chowdhury. Especially if she was asked about herself or her history. It wasn't until a month or two later that she had remembered the date and figured out that the letter was written five months after she, and what was left of her unit, had been retrieved from Humboldt.

So, first to the storage room, and then to Dr. Johnson's to gather what intel the doctor might be able to share.

Thoughts of what it must have been like on Humboldt made Burton more grateful for the problems she had. She'd hate to have been in *that* mess.

CHAPTER 56
13 October

Captain Katherine Leung rolled over in her bunk and stretched out her arms and legs, luxuriating in the feel of waking up because her body was done sleeping. Her wall chrono showed 0942, meaning that she had slept over ten hours, and she still had more than an hour before she was expected anywhere. Heaven.

She climbed out and went into the head. A long, hot shower, followed by a clean and pressed uniform, and all was right in her personal world. She took a moment to check herself in the mirror, then left the captain's quarters, aiming her feet in the direction of the galley.

"Good morning, Captain," Green greeted her when she arrived. "The coffee's hot, if you're in a rush. If not, could I interest you in something from the grill?"

"Thank you, Alex. I could definitely go for a hot meal this morning. What's on the menu?"

"Ah, Captain, I've got just the thing. A load of fresh vegetables came up from the planet last night. How about pancakes with a Lorraine omelet?"

"That sounds heavenly, Crewman! If you can add a ham steak to that, I'll write you a promotion."

"Done! Just have a seat, and I'll bring it out in a few minutes." Green retreated back into the kitchen, where the sounds of chopping and cooking could be heard over the hum of the ventilation fans.

Leung filled a mug with coffee from the server and carried it back to an open table. She cautiously smelled it before she took a sip, but there was no sign of any problem with it. She knew she was overusing the word, but it smelled heavenly.

In fact, her life was running just about as smoothly as she could imagine. She felt liberated by all the tasks about which she no longer had to worry. Samuels had turned out to be more efficient than expected, so the crew rotations and minor decisions never crossed her mind anymore. The Forrest Marines had yet to corner Lamont, but the unpredictable sabotage had died abruptly. And Omundson…well, Leung supposed there were still a few things she could imagine improving. At least she could say that everything else that had been moved off her plate made it possible for her to direct things in Engineering herself. Truth to tell, even if Omundson were as competent as she was, or even as competent as he thought he was, she would still have taken over Engineering again. That was where she belonged.

Biltcliffe and Chin were sitting at another table with Semrad and McGough. She couldn't hear what they were saying, but the four of them erupted into laughter unexpectedly. The general good humor brought a smile to her face.

Breakfast arrived before the coffee was cool enough to do more than sip. She thanked Green and dug in. Her weight and her appetite had both suffered over the last couple of months, and she was making her first inroads to recovery now. The omelet was perfect; egg whites, spinach, onions, Swiss cheese, and a dash of seasoning. The steak was exactly what she needed to fill her craving, and the pancakes were fluffy and filling all at once.

Green appeared at her elbow as soon as she put the last bite into her mouth and dabbed the syrup off the corner of her mouth. "Alex, that was wonderful. I would order it all again if I had even a smidgen of room left in my stomach to put it in. You've certainly earned your promotion."

"If it's all the same, Captain, I'll settle for a pay raise and then retirement."

"What are you going to do after we get paid?"

"Probably travel for a while. I've always wanted to see the Copernicus Rim. But eventually I'm going to open a restaurant somewhere. Trendle and I talked about starting a restaurant. Now with his disappearance, I'll probably go it alone."

"I'm going to have to make a note of your new identity before we split up then, because that is one restaurant I'm going to visit," she replied, ignoring his silent question about the likelihood of ever finding his friend. She really had no answer for him. If they had ever gotten internal sensors working, even a simple infrared pickup, such an answer would be hers to give. But they had never found any trace of the four crewmen who had mysteriously disappeared. She assumed they had followed Burton out an airlock, despite the lack of any record on the hatch logs. She schooled her features and didn't allow any trace of her thoughts to show there.

"It would be an honor, Captain, to serve you again sometime," Green smiled.

Leung smiled back, and then rose to leave. The smile stayed planted there all the way down to the communications room, where she was meeting an engineering team at 1100. It stayed there during two hours of genial and productive work, occasionally being accompanied by a whistled tune or two.

It was still there while she was on her back staring up at what was left of a signal relay grid. Until she heard a sound that didn't belong.

Then it disappeared.

CHAPTER 57
13 October

Lieutenant Monica Samuels stood on the inside of her hatch and took a deep breath. *You can do this*, she told herself. She gripped what her dad had called a zap-gun in each hand. Growing up in a trading family, she had spent much of her post-adolescent life on one ship or another and had learned a lot of things that one would normally consider trivial or useless, but this particular bit of knowledge had come in handy. She had only been eleven when they had been boarded by pirates in the Rhodes system. Her father had hidden with her in the engineering crawlspaces. He had made one and showed her how to duplicate them. They were tricky to use against armor because they weren't very effective unless you got them close enough to pierce the armor's insulation layer before you activated them. That hadn't been a problem then. The pirates hadn't been armored and you could use the zap guns to take them out from up to two feet away. Dad had taken out all seven of the pirates, one at a time, and they had ended up adding the pirate's ship to their fledgling commercial fleet.

Samuels took another deep breath and shook her head. *No time to be thinking of happier times.* She giggled slightly. *What does it say about my situation if a pirate attack qualifies as 'happier times?'*

She tucked the two zap-guns into her tunic pockets and made sure the blaster was hidden in her waistband, and she waited. She wanted to check her vids one more time to ensure they were showing her looped feeds, but she forced herself to stay where she was. Only a couple more minutes.

She actually jumped when her chrono chirped that it was time to go. She exited her quarters and sauntered down the corridor toward the security suite. She had timed it precisely right and the evacuation alarms went off just as she stopped in front of the hatch. She quickly input her stolen security code and, grabbing the two zap-guns from her pocket, she jumped through the hatch as it slid open. She began to check for targets in the office space, and finding none, she moved quickly to the brig entrance. The security access codes again opened the inner hatch and she repeated the process she had used earlier. Again there were no targets, but this time the compartment was not empty. Both guards and the interrogator were curled up on the deck, unmoving. She moved cautiously to the first guard and rolled him over. His face was contorted and his tongue was black and hanging out. He was obviously dead. She quickly checked both of the other Forresters and found them to be in the same state.

A quick search revealed Aichele in the first cell. She input the code and moved to the side of his bunk. He was stripped to the waist and bloody all over. His face was a mass of bruises at different stages of healing. He had blood from small cuts all over his chest and arms as well as several small burns on his chest. Samuels wanted to throw up but she forced herself to grab an arm and try to lift him from the bunk. He cried out slightly at the movement and opened his eyes. He tried to grab for her throat but he was too weak to make an effective try. She batted his arm back and slapped his face lightly.

"Gunny, it's Samuels. I'm here to get you out. Can you walk at all?"

The Marine made an unintelligible grunt that might have been the yes she took it for. She tried to lift him again and he managed to help enough for her to get him off the bunk and moving to the hatch. She had to support most of his weight, which was considerable, so it was slow going.

Just before she made it to the outer hatch of the security suite, she reached into her left pocket and pulled out the zap-gun. She would rather have had the blaster, but she was too busy supporting Aichele on that side to be able to reach it.

Just as she was reaching up to key the hatch, it slid open and revealed four Forrester Marines in light armor filling the opening. She reacted instinctively and reached out with her homemade electrocution device. As soon as it made contact with the shoulder joint of the nearest Marine's armor, she activated it and let go.

The Marine was enveloped in blinding light for a fraction of a second and then he was thrown backward into his fellows. Samuels took the opportunity to slam the locking pad on the hatch. She input the emergency lock code and looked down to see Aichele in a pile at her feet. She didn't even remember dropping him.

"Damn, damn, triple damn, hell," she chanted to herself with her mother's favorite curse. "So close."

She thought she heard a chuckle from the injured Marine at her feet, but when she looked, his eyes were closed and there was only a grimace on his face. She double checked the lock-out on the hatch. Still secure, but that would only last until they brought up heavier weaponry. She pulled her blaster out and started to pace. "Think, Monica," she muttered. "Think of something quick." She punctuated each step with the slap of her blaster into her hand.

Her pacing was interrupted by a thump from behind her. She spun, raising her blaster to find the muzzle of a very large energy rifle pointing back at her.

CHAPTER 58
13 October

Katherine Leung heard what sounded like a muffled version of the evacuation alarm and threw herself up to her feet from the deck where she had been working. Every component in the communications room was brand new, and she was having a hard time getting them to fit into their proper place. This relay had been the epicenter of the blast that had gutted their communications room and nearly killed two crewmen. Once she was upright, she cocked her head to the side. It *was* the evacuation alarm. She started moving automatically to the boatbay even though she knew the evacuation pods had not been replaced. As she entered the boatbay on the starboard side, she noticed that only about half of the crew had assembled. That was all she noticed before four Forrest Marines ran in behind her and knocked her to the deck. Two of the Marines were armored, and two were not.

One of the lightly armored Marines stood with his booted foot resting on her back making it impossible to get up. She saw Sullivan hit the deck just in front of her and start crying. At the same time, others were lowering themselves to the deck before they could be knocked down.

What a stinking mess, she thought. *It has all been a trick.*

"What is the meaning of this," she yelled as loudly as she could with the weight pressing on her back.

"Be quiet," the Marine said casually as one of his unarmored partners grabbed her wrists together and secured them behind her back with binders. The other Warner crewmen that she could see were also being methodically secured. This caused an increase in the wailing from Sullivan to her left. While she watched, Danis and Bezates were shoved into the boatbay through its port hatch and unceremoniously thrown to the deck.

"Let me up, I demand to see Major Kerrick."

The Forrest Marine made no move, nor did he respond in any way. He simply continued to watch the growing number of prisoners. Each Warner who came through the hatch was immediately knocked to the deck and secured. Once all of the prisoners were under control, the boot came off her back and the Marine moved to the center hatch with the other armored trooper so that both were in a position to watch all of the prisoners.

The two unarmored Forresters began to move the Warners to the starboard side of the boatbay one at a time.

Leung and Sullivan were moved to the front of the bay near the forward hatch and the others were all separated as much as possible with such a large number of people. Leung surveyed the group. It looked like there were about twenty Warners in the bay. That would comprise the majority of the crew still aboard.

Leung turned to the Forrester nearest her and asked in her calmest possible voice. "Could you tell me what is going on here? There is no need for this. You would have gotten the ship as soon as the repairs were complete."

The guard looked at her steadily for a few moments before replying. "We might have believed that for a while, but it's pretty obvious you meant to double-cross us from the beginning."

"What are you talking about?" Leung yelled, giving vent to some of her frustration. "We've been nothing but cooperative from the start."

"Having one of your officers attack a security squad is being cooperative?" the guard spat back. "No wonder the Granadans don't know how to behave, if that's your definition of cooperation."

"What are you talking about? There are only three officers on this ship and two of them are right here. You Forrester scum planned this as a cheap way to steal my ship, but let me tell you, you won't get away with it!" Leung fumed as Sullivan mercifully went quiet next to her.

The guard laughed and casually took a step over and kicked her in the chest. Leung fell backward onto the deck and gasped for breath.

"Big talk from such a pipsqueak," the guard said dismissively.

Leung's retort was interrupted as Omundson stood up half way down the wall and began to yell at their captors. "Do you know who I am?! This conduct is unacceptable. I am the neph—"

His tirade was cut short as the other unarmored Marine took two quick steps from his position near the center of the boatbay and applied his rifle butt to the young ensign's stomach. Leung's attention, as well as that of everyone else, was drawn to the altercation, but she turned back as she sensed something move to her right. Her mind took a moment to process what was happening. Sullivan was on her feet, her hands were free. She had a glistening red knife in her hand.

After a moment, Leung realized the knife itself was not red but it was dripping blood from the guard who lay at Sullivan's feet with his stomach and throat ripped open.

I told him he wouldn't get away with this, was the only thought that went through Leung's stunned mind.

CHAPTER 59
16 October

Monica's eyes narrowed behind the sights of her blaster. The extra guard had appeared from out of nowhere, as if she had dropped out of the sky. What combat training the young officer had been through had always stressed not hesitating, yet that was exactly what she did, luckily for both of them. The uniform registered in her mind and she paused, but her next thoughts nearly made her pull the trigger anyway.

The work uniform clearly displayed the name LAMONT, N, LT(jg) and its wearer bore a short stubble of blond hair. The shock of seeing the person she had believed dead for these past months was not enough to cause her brain to turn off though, and the immediate questions that sprang into her mind allowed her the second or two she needed to realize that this person was female, and much shorter than the missing lieutenant. So who...

"Burton?" Samuels asked, lowering her weapon to point at the floor. "So I was right. You aren't dead. Have you and Aichele been working together all along?"

For her part, Burton did not lower her guard. "What are you doing here, Ensign?"

She nodded to the gunnery sergeant, propped against one wall of the main security room. "I'm here to get Aichele out. The same as you, it would appear. And it's Lt. Samuels now."

"Leung gave you a promotion. I don't recognize her authority."

"Fair enough. I don't either. Where does that leave us."

"Have you been trying to sabotage the ship?"

"Yes. I assume you have as well. I know I didn't do it all."

"Right," Burton said, and made a show of carefully aiming her rifle at Samuels' head. "So tell me what you've done to the ship, and if it matches with what I know Aichele and I didn't do, I won't shoot you."

"Fair enough," Monica repeated. "My first act was to introduce a worm into the rebuilt ship's computers that systematically destroyed databases, command lines, and sensor feeds. I built my own remote access to the bridge systems, and used it to gain access to all officers' and security files, and I blew up the communications suite."

Burton was impressed, but tried not to show it. "And you took out two armored guards on your own?" Burton twitched her gun in the direction of the prone figures just visible in the brig hallway but brought it immediately back on target.

"Well, no, not actually," she admitted. "I knew the guards would be in armor, so I made a weapon to disable them," she held up the electrical discharge rods she had cobbled together, "but I only took out one guard with this. He fell back into the corridor before I locked the door. The two guards on duty and the interrogator were down when I arrived."

Burton lowered her weapon then and moved over to examine one of the other guards. His face was purple and bloated. "Poison," Burton said at once. "Both dead," she added after confirming that neither had a pulse.

"How did you get to them?" Samuels asked calmly.

"Not me," Burton interrupted, "and there's no time to find out what happened. We've got to move, now."

"I'm open to suggestions," Samuels said. "There are at least four Forrest Marines outside that door trying to get in."

"Back up there," Jill nodded toward the still open vent cover above her. Samuels hadn't noticed it before, but it certainly explained the unannounced entrance the Marine had made.

The two women dragged one of the desks over to the spot, then went to grab Aichele. He had fallen into unconsciousness, but his head snapped up and he drew in a sharp breath as soon as they tried to lift him.

"You okay, Gunny?"

"Burton? It's good to see you, Sarge. Three ribs on the left side, one on the right. What's our exfil plan?" he wheezed through gritted teeth.

"Up to the— " Burton began, but was cut off by a loud thump at the main hatch.

"Shaped charge," both Burton and Aichele noted at the same time.

"Not big enough," Samuels said, "but they won't make the same mistake next time."

"Come on," Burton urged, "Let's get him up there."

They managed to get him as far as standing on the desk, but thereafter he couldn't help them. He couldn't raise his arms high enough to reach the opening, and it was clear he wouldn't be able to lift any of his own weight. Burton, with her injured shoulder, and Monica, with her slender build, didn't have the strength to lift him up, either.

"You two go," Eric breathed. His struggle to get as far as he did had taken a toll on him. "We don't have time to figure a way out for me, but if you two get away, we're no worse off than we were yesterday." Burton had to lean in closely to catch the last words; his volume had diminished as he went.

"Not an option, Gunny," Samuels said firmly. "They'll know who to look for, and how to find me now. I wouldn't last through the day, although Burton could still disappear." At a quick shake of the head from Burton the young officer continued, "We might as well fight it out here. There are more weapons stored here, right?"

Burton nodded off to her left. "The small arms locker has been forced open, but there's nothing in there that can stand up to even light armor. Your lightning rod won't help against multiple targets, either. The end of the day is sounding better than the five seconds it will take to dispatch us once they breach that door. The ship's main armory is right over there, but it is just as locked down as everything else since Captain Brighton hit the panic button."

"If we could get in there, we could hide in the Omega Room until the cows come home," Eric said weakly. He had seated himself on the desk, but appeared as though sheer willpower was the only thing keeping him from toppling to the side.

"What's an Omega Room?" Samuels asked, pacing over to the main armory hatch that was keeping them from safety.

"Camouflaged safe room, in case Security is under siege. The only entrance is through the armory, or an equally secure and disguised door on the lower level."

"And if it's been locked out, who's codes could get it open?"

"Chowdhury's for sure, and probably Brighton's. But both of those codes are 400 parsecs away in Antoc."

"I wouldn't be too sure of that, Sergeant," Samuels noted, punching eight characters into the pad, watching as the door slid obediently open.

Both Marines were speechless, but Jill was sporting a very predatory smile as she helped get Eric into the room. The entrance was sealed exactly as it had been for months by the time the Forresters blasted their way into Security.

They never even gave it a second look.

CHAPTER 60
16 October

"Everybody clear?" Captain H. M. Kerritt, Forrest Marine Corps, asked his troops. The two Marines in the heavy armor stood near the door to Security in flanking positions, ready to move. The other six and he, in the lightweight version of the protective gear, were stacked up against the near wall, just as prepared to move when there was an opening.

Corporal Jannson had already been moved back to the shuttle, and though she was unconscious, it looked like she hadn't sustained critical injuries.

He was thankful that he had been given permission by Governor Solomon to keep extra soldiers housed on the transport shuttle, and that he had brought at least two heavy armor suits with him. As far as Leung knew, they'd abided by the ten soldier limit, but Kerritt had felt better with an ace up his sleeve. That very large and well-armed ace was about to trump Leung's double-cross.

"Okay, Fitch, hit it," he ordered.

A heavy thump sounded in Kerritt's ears at the same time he felt the concussive pressure wave, even through the armor. Most of the pressure and energy of the blast, though, had been directed into the hatch, and the metal evaporated out of their way like so much paper in a stiff wind. They'd probably used more explosive than they'd needed, but their first effort had been short of the amount, and he did not want to keep trying until they got it right.

"Go!" The captain of Marines ordered at once, and the well-drilled troops flowed into the gap, firing weapons without having any targets in the cloud of debris that filled the room. The two in the bulky powered suits were the first ones in, and Kerritt came right behind them, looking for something worth shooting. He tripped on an unseen obstacle as he crossed into the dim room. Years of training caused him, instead of falling forward, to drop to a single knee while maintaining his assigned target sight lines.

"Clear," came the voice of Sgt. Norgaard within a second of his fall, followed shortly by several more. "All clear," the sergeant finally reported. "No sign of targets."

"Where did they go?" Kerritt asked. It was difficult to make out much in the room, though the dust was beginning to settle now. The blast had taken out the lighting in the room, but a stream was coming in from the hallway leading to the brig. Those in heavy armor had powerful lights on either side of their face shields, and they turned these on, sweeping back and forth to look for their prey. Kerritt looked back to see what he had tripped over. It turned out to be some kind of metallic rod, and he dismissed it as irrelevant. Continuing his visual sweep of the area, he saw two armored figures lying on the other side of the open entry to the brig area.

The devil take that woman. Leung was going to pay for this, in blood.

"Over here, Captain." The voice belonged to Lt. Drinkwater, amplified by the heavy armor's external speakers. Kerritt stood and followed the twin beams upward to an open vent cover. A desk or table had been shoved underneath it, and there were a dozen drops of blood on its surface.

"Hansen, Ludwig, Haeberle, peel out of your armor and get up there after them. Drinkwater and Norgaard, I want you two to stay in the heavy armor here, in case we can track them down. Drinkwater, you stay in radio contact with those in the vents and coordinate their search. Norgaard, I want you to sweep this area and find out as much as you can about what happened. The rest of you come with me." A chorus of 'yes, sirs' echoed back. Kerritt exited the room and headed aft, toward the boatbay.

Norgaard's voice came over a private vocom channel before he was halfway there. "Captain?"

"Go."

"Two Marines down, both dead. The interrogator, as well as Grant and Hale, who were on guard, were…" The voice faded out.

Kerritt stopped, causing the rest of the squad to pull up as well, though they didn't know why. "Spit it out. They were what?"

"Sir, they appear to have been poisoned. Their faces are purple with blue lips. The interrogator was back in the prisoner's area. She had also been…vomiting blood, sir."

Kerritt was a long time answering, long enough that the others with him were beginning to get antsy. "Understood, Sergeant. Anything else?

"Yes, sir, Corpsman Thorson reports that Jannson is awake now and she will be okay; minor burns from the electrical discharge is all."

"Very well, if there's nothing else to learn there, bring the big suits down to the boatbay while we…discuss…this with Captain Leung."

"Yes, sir," the sergeant replied.

Kerritt kicked the squad into motion again. Leung was *definitely* going to pay.

CHAPTER 61
16 October

Once inside the armory with the outer door sealed, Samuels and Burton half assisted, half carried Aichele to the far wall and propped him gently against it. Despite moving cautiously, he still grunted in pain as he sank to the floor.

"You okay, Gunny?" Samuels asked with a look of concern.

"A lot better just looking at that," he said, waving his hand to indicate what was behind her. She turned to take in the racks of weapons, ordnance, and powered armor.

"It *is* a sight," she said, not knowing how else to respond.

Samuels turned back suddenly at the sound of a motor running. Burton was back to help move Aichele while an entire rack of shelves, loaded with grenades and other explosives, disappeared into the floor along with the rear wall of the room. Samuels had been curious about how to get into the Omega Room, as they called it, and now she had missed how it was done. Burton was looking rather pleased with herself, and Samuels realized that the whole act had been planned for the very purpose of keeping her from knowing too much.

Samuels grinned. "Well played, Gunny."

"I don't know what you mean, Lieutenant," he said blandly.

She didn't reply, but followed Burton's lead to a fold-down bunk on the near wall, where they got Aichele seated, then horizontal. The rest of the room was relatively small for what its purpose was. It was a little larger than her bunk room, and a lot of the space was occupied with the same sort of gear: beds, lockers, mirror, head, etc. There was also a small security desk in the far back corner. Samuels assumed that, once powered up, the terminal and comm station would link into the ship's systems somehow.

In the other far corner was a circular opening with an airtight hatch dogged open. The walls of the room were filled with storage cupboards of various sizes, and each door bore a printed label describing its contents. Many were stocked with food and water, some had repair equipment, and others had medical supplies. Burton headed straight for the latter as soon as she was sure Eric would remain down. She had no trouble pulling out bandages and antiseptic for his cuts and abrasions. Even the painkillers were easily identified and retrieved, but she spent nearly ten minutes to find a rib immobilizer sleeve.

Jill knelt down by the bunk and held out a bottle of water and a handful of pills.

"What is it?" Aichele asked.

"Lodraseptamine. You're going to need it while I cinch up your new corset."

"Can you find something that won't make me groggy? We need to do some planning."

Jill looked skeptical, but rose to get something else. Samuels was already there, and handed her a bottle of quattrominophen. Aichele took several, then laid back and exhaled slowly.

Burton pulled a stool over and started in on cleaning and bandaging the worst of Eric's wounds while Samuels pulled the desk chair over close to the bunk and sat down.

"All right, then. Planning it is," Samuels began. "You two are the security experts, so where do we start?"

Aichele turned his head to look at her. "You don't already have a plan?" he asked. It was hard to tell if he was being serious or mocking her.

"Well, you know, I *did*. Funny how that saying about plans and contact with the enemy is still unchallenged," Samuels countered. "Anyway, whatever plans I had no longer apply to our current situation. I agree with you. We need a new plan."

"Will wonders never cease?" Burton gushed. Samuels had no problem catching the mockery now. "An ensign that knows when she doesn't know something. Keep this up and it's going to ruin your rank's reputation for thoughtlessness."

Samuels stiffened in her seat. "Sergeant, I will accept your greater experience, I will accept your advice, and I will accept your obedience. But I will *not* accept your disrespectful tone or your insubordination. *Especially* when I have done nothing to deserve it."

Samuels continued, "When have you ever seen me behave thoughtlessly? I have survived living under Leung's direct supervision for almost three months now because I *never* did anything without thinking about it first. Now, I don't know what I've done to get on your bad side, and I don't care. You take whatever it is and you fold it into your back pocket and sit on it until we're out of this mess! We do not have the time to deal with it now. Is that clear?"

"Yes, ma'am," Burton said quietly. "And I apologize. You are right, my comments were uncalled for."

"Yes they were, but I accept your apology. Now, since the two of you decline to offer me your suggestions—" Both Marines looked like they were about to protest, but she held up a hand to forestall any interruption. "You had your chance. Now we'll do it my way."

It was an odd scene, but Samuels didn't notice how the Marines, twice and four times her age, relaxed at the tone of command in her voice.

"First, I want a full report of what the two of you have been up to, and then what resources we have available."

Aichele let Burton give the report for both of them while he focused on breathing without causing any unnecessary pain. When Jill felt that the medicine had a chance to begin working, she put the rib sleeve on Eric and tightened it as much as he could stand. He was very uncomfortable while getting into the device, but once it was in place he found he could relax all the muscles he'd unconsciously been holding tight in his torso. Burton continued her narration throughout, and Samuels listened closely without interrupting.

For the most part, she was listening. A part of her mind was trying to work out just exactly what sort of orders she thought she was going to be giving. By the time Burton was finished, though, she had pulled herself together again by thinking of Captain and that duty he expected her to perform.

Just do what's in your power to change, echoed in her skull.

"Well, you certainly have been busy. Not as busy as I'd thought, though."

"What do you mean?" Burton asked. Samuels raised an eyebrow. "Ma'am," Jill finally added.

"Was that a complete list of the sabotage the two of you carried out?" At Aichele's nod, she continued, "Then there are still acts for which we cannot identify the saboteur. Is there any way we might identify who this person is?"

Burton responded, "That was what we were trying to accomplish when Eric was caught. We were using truth serum on our captives to see if they might be trusted. It was a good plan then, but it wouldn't work now."

"I can see why. We could cut down the numbers against us as long as we were isolated on the ship. Now that we've jumped to Worth, the Forresters can reinforce indefinitely from Granada."

"Ma'am," Aichele said, and carefully sat up to face the officer, "if I might suggest…"

"Go ahead, Gunny."

"I think we're going to have to hit them now, for that very reason. Chances are that Forrest is not going to be too friendly to Warners after this. If it were me commanding the other side, as soon as I had the immediate situation locked down, I'd be on the horn to my superiors for reinforcements, and I would take everyone else off the ship and into custody. They have communications from their shuttle even though we've been unable to restore *Pathfinder*'s own comms. If we give them time to take that step, our tactical situation will be unwinnable."

Aichele's words cast a pall over the room for several moments. Try as she might, Samuels couldn't fault the Marine's logic. Those would be her orders if she were on the other side, too.

"Does the armory contain enough firepower that two people in armor could take out the remaining Forresters and capture the remaining crew?"

"Possibly," Burton supplied, "but far from certainly."

"It could work," Aichele said. "With two of the PUMAs, we'd certai—"

"Whoa," Jill cut in, "there's no way we're going to put little miss… Ensign Samuels… in heavy armor. She doesn't have any training, and we don't have time to teach her even the basics."

"I was thinking of you and me, Sarge."

"Right. And what if you have to, oh I don't know, move? You're going to shake those ribs loose and puncture a lung."

"Sarge, why'd you put this sleeve on me?"

"Huh? To keep your ribs where they belong, and if I have to tie it to your bunk to keep *you* where *you* belong, I—"

"And how tight is the inside of a PUMA?"

"That's not the same as—"

"Yes it is, Sergeant. It will keep things immobilized long enough for whatever we have to do. Besides, 'it's the only game in town, Coach. You can't keep me on the sidelines.'"

Burton grimaced as she recognized her own words being used against her. Samuels felt like the decisions were being made without her, but in this instance, she didn't mind.

"You're sure, Aichele?"

"Yes, Lieutenant, I am sure."

Burton had to fire back, "She's not a lieutenant, Gunny. Leung didn't have the authority to promote her, which means she's still an ensign."

"Is she, or is she not, the only loyal officer on *Pathfinder*? And doesn't that make her the rightful captain of the ship? And isn't she *required*, by regulation, to promote herself to lieutenant in order to claim command authority of a WSN vessel?"

His logic was, as usual, inescapable. Burton could only scowl and nod.

"Then your attempts to demote her could be viewed as a failure to acknowledge her command authority. Is that what you intended, Staff Sergeant Burton?"

Burton's eyes grew wide at the implications of what he was implying. The formality of his words and the look in his eyes meant that the implication was intentional. If proven against her, the charge would be 'failure to acknowledge authority in the face of the enemy.' "No, Gunny, it is not," she replied at once. "I was simply…confused…about the lieutenant's status before. Thank you for clarifying it for me. And I apologize, Lt. Samuels, if you thought I was not willing to recognize your authority to command."

"The idea never crossed my mind, Sergeant," Samuels said. Sotto voce, she directed at Aichele, "Well played."

Taking a deep breath, Samuels changed the subject. "Now that that's settled, let's get back to planning. I realize I can't drive one of those walking tanks, but I do have some weapons training, and it did include the use of light armor, so we should plan on me accompanying you when we go. In fact, I—"

Samuels cut herself off when she heard some kind of tapping sound. "What was that?"

Aichele tried to stand, but then thought better of it. "Someone's at the back door," he announced.

CHAPTER 62
16 October

Smiley didn't hesitate. She was crouching on the floor of the boatbay with her back against the bulkhead. Just like the rest of the prisoners, her hands were cuffed behind her back with laminar binders. She was managing to stay in the character of her cover, but she wasn't sure how many tears she had left in her. Something was going on. She listened to Leung as the erstwhile captain ranted against the guard, but Smiley kept quiet other than her cover whimpering. It was so easy to be overlooked when you were a helpless mess.

She moved her arms slightly behind her back and twisted her right hand up inside her left sleeve. The binders cut deeply into her wrists and she felt one of them start to bleed, but she continued to twist them until she was able to pull the ten-centimeter throwing knife from its sheath. With deft fingers, she sliced the binders and waited for her opening.

As she listened to the guard, it was clear that Samuels had finally made her move. She was the only Warner officer not accounted for in the boatbay, so she had to be the one they claimed had attacked first. Something had gone wrong, however, and she must have had at least one run-in with Forrest security which had triggered this lockdown.

The rapid response by Forrest also indicated that they had this plan in place ahead of time, so their goal was clearly to get the ship at all costs. This changed the equation for Smiley. Her two primary goals were to stay covert and to protect the ship. Clearly, she could no longer do both. Nor could she delay in order to gain more information. From her interview with Colonel Valencia, it was clear that the ship had to have the highest priority.

When Omundson stood to protest his treatment, the guard in front of Smiley turned to watch the altercation. The barrel of his rifle tracked with his eyes, as it did for most people. As the muzzle moved from Smiley to cover the young ensign, she made her move. She didn't like killing, but on occasion it was necessary to accomplish your objectives or sometimes just to stay alive. Smiley had learned by sad experience that when you had to kill, it was best to do it in such a way that it gave your other enemies reason to pause or hesitate. She came up out of her crouch with her right hand flashing, closing the meter and a half with two quick strides. As she got near the guard, she swung the blade across his waist with her right hand while grabbing the barrel of his gun with her left. She pushed the gun away from herself as she stepped inside his reach and sliced across his throat with her return stroke. His finger wasn't near the trigger, so there was no shot, and with his throat opened, there was no shout to give her away.

She yanked the weapon loose from his failing grip as he slumped to the floor, where he died without a sound. Smiley did not hesitate. She sprinted to the open hatch and dove through to the sound of weapons discharges behind her. She rolled back up to her feet and moved to the stairway heading down.

As she got to the bottom step, she nearly ran down a Forrest engineering technician who was huddled in the corner of the landing. His eyes grew as large as saucers as he took in her blood-soaked uniform. With a quick step, she grabbed him by the neck of his tunic and lifted him to his feet, dropping the stolen rifle in the process.

"What is going on?" she asked in a firm voice.

"They are taking back the security office," he said shakily, tapping his earpiece.

"Whether he would have given her any more information or not became irrelevant as she heard the heavy tread of armored boots hitting the top of the stairs, starting down.

She struck him sharply on the side of the head and he collapsed to the floor, unconscious but not dead.

She grabbed her captured gun, sprinted down the cross-corridor to the port corridor and turned forward. She kept moving as she sensed the Marines hitting the bottom of the stairs and starting after her.

As she reached the far end, she tapped in her access code to the hatch on the forward missile storage room, but instead of entering the room, she lay down on the floor with her head and arms extended into the corridor and her legs in the storage room. Within seconds, the two armored Forresters rounded the corner in pursuit. She thumbed off the safety and let loose a quick high-powered burst of coherent light that struck the first guard directly on the faceplate.

Smiley was unfamiliar with the design of the weapon so she hadn't been sure whether it was powerful enough to penetrate the light armor the Forresters were wearing. Not willing to take that chance, she aimed for the faceplate on the assumption that even if it didn't penetrate, the person might be disabled; either from being blinded or from the force of the photons creating enough pressure to knock the Marine to the ground.

As it turned out, she needn't have worried. The blast went through the helmet with ease and the guard dropped in his tracks as if melting into the deckplates. The second guard returned fire, but he wasn't quick enough. Smiley shifted targets and, ignoring the incoming fire, calmly shot him as well. She jumped up and grabbed both of their weapons before sprinting back to the missile storage room and securing the hatch. She input the command override code she had been given by Col. Valencia into the hatch control to ensure no one else on the ship could enter behind her.

The rifle discharges had been quite loud and distinctive. She assumed the others would be busy with rounding up and guarding the prisoners from the boatbay, but she didn't want to take the chance she was wrong.

With that done, she moved to the forward wall and deftly removed a section of the wall surfacing. Behind its concealment, she found a one meter square opening with no handle. With the butt of her captured rifle she gave several staccato raps in the pattern of the Warner Marine March.

Then she waited, and hoped she hadn't been wrong.

CHAPTER 63
16 October

Chaos was erupting all over the boatbay. Leung watched in shock as Sullivan sprinted, captured gun in hand, to the open hatch and out into the corridor without a single backward glance.

Leung sat there stunned for a moment as the situation ran through her consciousness.

Omundson was still screaming from his position on the deck. He was curled up into a ball, but that did nothing to decrease his volume.

Two armored guards followed Sullivan out the hatch in a sprint. The only guard left in the bay fired at Omundson and the noise stopped. All of the prisoners scattered. She saw Giannini and Chandler duck behind a container that blocked the center of the bay, then she decided on her course of action. With the exception of Sullivan, Leung had been the closest to the forward starboard hatch, so she decided her best bet was to take Sullivan's lead. She stood awkwardly with her hands still secured behind her and scuttled to the hatch and out into the corridor before the single remaining guard could target her.

She turned left and headed to the galley. She was useless until she could get her hands free and the galley was the easiest place to take care of that.

By the time she was finished, she was fuming. Epi Solomon had promised her the money if she delivered *Pathfinder*. She could tell now that this had been their plan from the beginning. This was why they weren't satisfied with the plans. At least she never told anyone else about the first half of the money that was safely tucked away in her bank on Earth. She just had to figure a way out of this to be able to enjoy it.

She needed to find out how bad the damage was. Had Samuels really attacked the security troops? That seemed unlikely. It was probably just the story they were using to justify their take-over.

She had to find some way to get the ship back. There were ten Marines on this ship, well, nine now that Sullivan had killed one. *Where did that come from? Sullivan?* She must have finally snapped from all the emotional stress of the last three months. But Leung had no way to handle even one Marine. She had bluffed her way through the initial contact, but that wasn't going to work again. Or would it?

If she could get into the auxiliary bridge without getting shot, she might have a chance.

It's better than nothing, she thought. *Besides, no one knows the ship better than I do. Let's see them try to get it working without my help.*

CHAPTER 64
16 October

"Someone's at the back door," Aichele announced. Samuels wasn't sure what to do with that information, but Burton reacted without hesitation. Jill moved at once to the opening in the floor, dropping the cover into place and dogging it closed.

Eric started moving just as quickly, but his motion was slowed by his injuries. He made it to the sealed hatch after Burton had left it. Within a second, she lobbed an energy rifle to him from the storage container across the room and he armed it, standing with the business end pointed unwaveringly at the metal covering. "Eyes on?" the man asked.

"Working on it," Jill said, powering up the terminal at the desk. Samuels came up behind the Marine and peered over her shoulder. The screen came to life with an official-looking Marine emblem, but a few keystrokes from Jill replaced it with a dimly-lit room. The area within range of the video pickup was filled with enormous missiles, laid one atop another in metal racks. Against the wall, a woman with dishwater blonde hair was leaning. The figure had two rifles slung over one shoulder and another carried in both hands. As they watched, she turned back toward the wall and repeated her pounding.

"Sullivan?" both women said.

"How did she get weapons?" Burton asked.

"A better question might be: how did she know to come here?" Aichele asked, keeping his carbine aimed at the hatch, but moving back to see the screen for himself. "Or even: whose side is she on?"

"She's on our side," Samuels said with some confidence. "The only reason she's on *Pathfinder* at all is because I dragged her off of *Vanguard* with me."

"If I remember the events of that day, the only reason she was on *Vanguard* was because you dragged her *on* with you."

"That's true, I suppose," the lieutenant admitted, "but she obviously wasn't working with Leung and Teach before that."

"That's not exactly a reason to trust her, though," Jill pointed out.

"No, it's not, but either way, we need to let her in. If someone finds her out there, it would give away our location," the officer said.

"Agreed," Aichele said. "We let her in, but we don't let our guard down unless she can give us some satisfactory answers."

"All right," Samuels said. "Jill, is there some way to talk to her before we open the door?"

* * * * *

Smiley was about to start the third chorus of the march when something finally happened. Samuels disembodied voice said from behind her, "Sullivan? Is that you?"

Smiley turned to the spycam's location and smiled. "Yes, it's me. Can I come in?"

She heard the very faint hiss of an airtight seal being opened, and she quickly slung her captured weapon, which had been her improvised drumstick, over her shoulder. The square metal panel pulled in and slid to her left. Lt. Samuels stood to one side, a grim look on her face. On the other side was Sergeant Burton with a flechette pistol aimed at Smiley's center of mass.

"Amber, I want you to listen to me very carefully," the lieutenant continued. "Take the rifles off your shoulder slowly, and hand them to me butt first. Then come inside and climb up the ladder. Sergeant Aichele will meet you above."

Smiley dropped immediately into her Sullivan persona. Rather, her current approximation of the persona. After reverting back to Smiley all those weeks ago, she'd been unable to do anything more than pretend, not having the tools to reprogram herself available anymore. At least the time for Sullivan the dishrag was finally over, thank all the stars in the known universe. In the time that had elapsed, she now had a better feel for what sort of relationships Sullivan had had before the mutiny.

"All right, Monica," she smiled, "I mean, Lieutenant. I'm glad I guessed right about where I'd find you. Here are the weapons I've managed to capture."

"Yeah, come on," the officer said, reaching out to help her through the small opening. Once inside, there was barely room for Smiley to maneuver, but Burton managed to keep the weapon trained on Sullivan and out of reach at the same time. Samuels indicated the ladder along one edge of the constrictive metal cylinder they were inside. "Up you go. I need to arrange the storage room again so no one sees anything out of place."

"Yes, ma'am," Sullivan acknowledged. She clanked up the rungs, followed closely by Burton, while Samuels reached through and picked up the piece of wall paneling from the floor. Some thoughtful designer had provided retractable handles on the back side, so it was possible for her to lock it back in place easily, then close and latch the interior access hatch.

When Samuels arrived at the top of the ladder, Burton already had Sullivan in a chair with a cup of water. Sullivan was in the process of confirming that almost none of the blood on her was her own, and she would not need medical attention except for her wrists.

Jill asked her bluntly from across the room, "So how did you know to come here, Sullivan?" Smiley could tell the two Marines were paying very close attention to her response.

Smiley was glad she had a cover story already prepared, and she launched into it without pause as she pulled her stringy blonde hair away from her face. "When the Forresters grabbed me and put me in binders, I thought they were finally onto me as being one of the saboteurs. Then, when I saw that they were rounding everyone up and pushing us into the boatbay, I thought that the ship was finally close enough to being completed that they were done with us, and it was time to kill us all instead of paying for the ship.

"Then, they said that an officer had attacked them in Security, and I knew it had to have been you because Leung and Omundson were already in the boatbay, so I looked for a break in the guard's attention, which Ensign Omundson provided. I managed to wiggle out of the binders, cutting my wrists a bit, and I broke the nearest guard's nose, which bled on me, and I slipped away.

"As for why I came to the Omega Room, I figured since Security is where Forrest lost track of you, there was at least a chance you'd made your way in here. I didn't have any better ideas, anyway, and roaming the halls looking for you was a great way to cross paths with armed enemies.

" I know about the Omega Room because I used to be a Marine. I finished boot camp and one posting before I realized I really wanted to be in space and transferred to the Navy." That part was the truth, as far as Sullivan's record went. Not that anyone was in a position to check at the moment.

Smiley waited expectantly, looking from Burton to Samuels and back again. Both looked satisfied, but Aichele's face was as unreadable as a statue's.

"Well, it's good to have another ally," Burton finally broke the silence, "especially one who's been working against Leung all along. In fact, Lieutenant Samuels and I were just talking about sabotage. Could you help us out by letting us know which acts you were responsible for?"

The request might have fooled a three year old, but not anyone in the Omega Room. Subtlety was not one of Staff Sergeant Burton's skills. Smiley knew she was being tested, and her tone let everyone know that she knew it was a test, but she wasn't particularly worried.

"Sure, Sergeant. My first act was disabling the cooling monitor station in Engineering. I sprayed the acid on the control runs. I wired in the power amplifiers in the Astro lines. I reversed the tracking inputs for the laser guidance system. And I was responsible for the gravity plate malfunction. I hope I didn't injure any of you with that one," she said honestly.

Burton and Samuels exchanged glances and relaxed just a bit. Sullivan's list exactly matched those items for which responsibility was still unclaimed, with the addition of the guidance system, which apparently had yet to be discovered.

"All right, then. Let's get back to our planning," Burton said, effectively closing that investigation. "That accounts for all of the sabotage we know of. I suppose that means that Lamont is not hiding out somewhere working on our side."

She had said it as a joke, but Smiley's reaction wasn't one of amusement. Samuels and Burton both noticed, but misinterpreted the reason behind it. "I can explain that," Samuels said, at the same time that Burton said, "I know why people think that." They looked at each other again and Samuels said, "You first."

"Well, when I started sneaking out of Medical, I was in a hospital gown. That was hardly the proper attire for crawling around the ship, so I needed something different to wear. I couldn't get to any of my own uniforms because they were in Security, so I broke into the laundry room to take some. The only ones that fit, and that belonged to someone who wasn't going to report them missing, were Lamont's." She pointed to her left breast pocket, which still bore his name. "Anyway, I had some of the uniforms in one of my hidey-holes that Danis discovered."

"I was going to say that I had caused all the confusion by logging Lamont's command code into random doors throughout the ship. I know Leung believes he's still hiding out somewhere," Samuels added.

"I wonder what really did happen to him." Burton mused.

"We may never know at this point," Sullivan observed blandly. Aichele's eyes opened slightly wider, the only reaction he'd shown at all. He finally crossed to the bunk he'd occupied before and very gently sat down on the edge.

"Doing all right, Gunny?" Burton asked.

"Yeah," he said. Then after a pause, "Could you bring me that bottle of Marine candy, and help me loosen up this sleeve a little?"

"Sure."

Aichele swallowed the painkillers while Sullivan and Samuels put their heads together to get reacquainted.

"It's this section here," Aichele said, raising his right arm and drawing his finger across his lower ribs. Jill leaned in to get a closer look and Aichele quietly told her, "Don't react."

"I see it," she said in a normal voice. "Turn to the side and let me get at those laces." She undid the clips and started loosening the strings along the back.

"Something is off with Sullivan," Aichele whispered. "Keep an eye on her."

Burton leaned closer while adjusting the slack evenly. "Why do you say that?"

"Ever heard Omega Room mentioned at boot camp? Or anywhere outside of ship security, for that matter?"

There was a long pause while she tightened the laces from the bottom up. "No," she finally admitted. "Missed that. Sorry."

"And when she talked about Lamont, her voice was off. She knows something she's not sharing. And there are two other problems. When the lieutenant spoke, Sullivan turned to the camera, knowing where it was, even though that wasn't where the sound came from. She also hasn't explained where the three rifles came from. She might have pulled one off the guard whose nose she claims to have broken, but she didn't say for sure, and didn't mention collecting the others."

Burton spared a casual glance Sullivan's direction. "Crap. I've been out of the security game too long, if I missed all that," she said quietly, turning back. Aichele nodded. "Should we lock her up?" Burton asked.

This time the long pause was Aichele's. "No. She appeared to be honest about the sabotage, from her voice and posture, so I think she's on our side, but…keep an eye on her."

"Copy that." Burton stood up straight and continued in a normal voice again, "How does that feel?"

"Better, thanks."

"All right, *now* let's get back to planning. Lieutenant, do you have a plan for us?" Burton turned back to the others as she spoke.

Samuels stood and leaned against one of the cupboards. She looked like she was about to speak twice, but finally she said, "Honestly, Sergeant, if we were planning a ship to ship engagement, I could say I had some idea of what to do, but this is not my kind of fight. I don't have the training or experience to have the first clue about details. I know we need to hit them hard and fast, preferably one or two at a time. I know we've got to keep them from calling up reinforcements, and I know that we're going to have surprise on our side, at least to begin with."

Samuels took a long breath. "I'm sorry if that statement undermines your confidence in me, but I really need for you two to plan the tactics of a shipboard action for me."

Aichele launched his lopsided grin at her. "Truth to tell, Lieutenant, I think I have more respect for you now than I did before. It's a rare officer that can admit to not knowing everything.

"Ma'am, here's what I would recommend. Sullivan stays here to monitor communications, and make sure the armory does not fall into Forrest hands. Burton and I load into our PUMAs and take medium weight weapon loadouts. You get into light armor and accompany Burton. We sweep fore to aft level by level. If they don't know we're armored, they will be spread out looking for us, so we should be able to catch them isolated."

"Is that it?" Samuels asked.

"Yes."

"Heck, *I* could have come up with that!"

"I know. I still appreciate the trust." He grinned at her again.

Sullivan piped up, "I've had combat training in the Marines, and our odds will be better if I come out with you." Inwardly, Smiley was grateful that her cover identity made her request logical. This was one fight she was not about to sit out. Protecting the ship was still her top priority.

"She's got a point," Samuels noted. "Our odds are going to be pretty short even with her."

"Granted, ma'am," Aichele said, "but even outnumbered, with the medium-weight weapons, we'll have the firepower advantage as long as we catch them one or two at a time, which I expect we will. The biggest weakness in our plan, then, is to make sure they don't have a parity in weapons. Since the only place they could obtain heavy weapons is here in the armory, we need someone to guard it.

"You and Sullivan are the logical choices, but I didn't think I could convince the ship's captain to stay out of it." Aichele was hoping that Samuels would accept those reasons at face value. She didn't want to confront Sullivan directly until he knew more of what she was after, but he would if he had to. He was not going into combat with anyone who might decide to shoot him in the back.

"All right, I can see that, but why not take the heavier weapons with you?" Samuels responded.

"Well, ma'am, it's basically for the same reason. They are all in light armor, so we will take heavy enough firepower to overwhelm those systems. But if, stars forbid, we should lose one of our weapons, I don't want to give them something heavy enough to damage our PUMAs." Aichele was speaking with less and less force as he outlined his plan. Samuels noticed this, and felt she needed to address it.

"OK, I approve your plan, with one modification. I go with you instead of with Burton."

"Ma'am, I was a drill instructor for 13 years, and I have taught armored combat to thousands of Marines. Burton can use the backup more than me."

"Noted. And you've got four broken ribs, so my orders stand."

"Yes, ma'am," he acknowledged. "When do we go?"

She checked her chrono. "In one hour, we go throw the barbarians back out the gate."

CHAPTER 65
16 October

Captain Kerritt led his half squad down the portside corridor while the other half of the squad went to the starboard. He needed to corral the rest of the Warners as quickly as possible. The more time they let pass with free moving entities in the ship, the more problems they could cause. He was directing his men to search the various rooms and berths they were coming upon when his comm chirped and he heard the report from the boatbay team squad leader, Sergeant Norgaard, that Lt. Commander Leung was among those that had not been recaptured near the boatbay.

The good news was that almost all the rest were accounted for, either dead or recaptured. There was a part of him that wished he could just wipe them all off the ship, since it would be so much easier to maintain order without them aboard.

"Burrows," he said into his comm.

"Copy. This is Burrows, go ahead Captain," Burrows replied over the comm.

"I want you to search room by room, look in every nook and cranny on this boat if you have to, but we need to find them all, especially Leung," Kerritt ordered the lance corporal he had placed in charge of the other half squad.

"Roger. We'll find her, Captain. Burrows out," came the confident response.

As Kerritt moved with his men, alert for movement or possible hiding places, he began to realize this was going to take a while. Obviously, the Warners knew the ship better than his men, so it was going to be laborious to find them all if they gave them time to hide.

The longer this took, the more potential issues they would face, and the more that could ultimately go wrong.

"Drinkwater, Kerritt," he said into his comm next.

"Drinkwater," came the immediate response.

"Lieutenant, pull those men out of the vents and get them to help round up runaways."

"Yes, sir."

As much as he disliked the idea, he knew he needed to report this to Solomon. It could represent more than just a setback.

However distasteful it was to report that they had failed to maintain full control of the crew and officers, Solomon needed to know to be able to prepare to respond appropriately, if needed.

He moved to a small doorway out of the way of his men, motioning for them to continue the search, then commed a request to be patched through to the planet and to Solomon specifically.

He waited, observing that his men were following protocols in their search and were checking everywhere he would have while the connection was made.

"Sergeant, this is Epi Solomon, what's your status?"

"Ma'am, we have a small situation aboard and we are getting it under control, but I wanted you to be aware," he began, and recounted to her what had transpired, ending with, "and Leung is among those few we are attempting to round up at the moment."

"Leung is missing, then?" she asked with a touch of annoyance in her voice.

"Unfortunately yes, ma'am, she is," he replied.

"Very well, Captain, I expect you to round them all up, especially Leung. I want regular reports from you, at least every hour, but preferably on the half hours as well until every crewmember and officer is accounted for," she ordered.

"Yes, ma'am," came the pat reply.

"In the meantime, I will bring the fleet to alert status and we will have them standing by just in case anything else goes awry. But Captain, for your sake and your team's sake, it had better not." With that, she dropped the comm channel before he could respond or acknowledge.

He didn't like threats, veiled or open. In his opinion, you didn't threaten, you just committed and acted. Straightforward, blunt, and tactless. It annoyed some people, but it was always the best approach. Maybe that was why he had always felt like he belonged in the Corps.

There was no hiding your understanding or knowledge of things when it was spelled out for you.

Obviously, Solomon wasn't of the same opinion, but he doubted that he really wanted to test her on this, either. He had already seen that she was one of those who would follow through on her threats. One week on Granada was enough to show that to anyone's satisfaction.

He now had another reason to despise this crew and this ship. The best thing now would be to end this quickly by recapturing the missing crew and avoid any further problems with Solomon. He set his jaw again, more to keep himself from grinding his teeth in frustration than any other reason, then he moved back up the corridor to rejoin his men in their search.

CHAPTER 66
16 October

Captain Leung slid into the Auxiliary Control Bridge buried under Engineering on lower deck. It was shocking to see the pristine bridge after the chaos of the ship under repair. Leung moved quickly and surely to the computer control circuitry at the rear of the compartment.

She had the beginnings of a plan, but it all depended on whether she could get access to the scuttling charges. She had to work fast. The truth was that this was something she should have thought of doing before they ever transited into the Worth system. She had been so worried about Lamont and Teach that she had forgotten to worry about the Forresters.

That omission had cost her. The Forresters were moving through the ship and eliminating any resistance they encountered. Her impromptu bluff of wiring the ship to blow had obviously ceased to be effective and her only choice at this point was to make good on her threat. Of course, there was no guarantee this would work either. They had called her bluff once and she had nothing to back it up so they would be even less inclined to back off now.

That didn't make any difference in the long run, however. She was down to her last play. The only choice she had left was to take the ship back to Warner and convince them that Teach was at fault and she was not involved. Maybe taking word to Fleet of the takeover of Grenada would help redeem her situation.

As she refined her plan in her mind, she slid under the console and opened the panel, exposing the control runs. Luckily, she knew just where to go to bypass the command lockout. One good thing came out of being forced to rewire the bridge controls several times.

As she redirected the complicated jumble of wires, her mind continued to work on her plan. The only thing she could think of to force the Forresters off the ship was to threaten to blow it up if they didn't evacuate. *Would they be willing to do that after they had taken over the ship? Probably not. What would be a credible threat?*

Even if she threatened to vent the atmosphere, that would do more damage to her crew than to Kerritt and his bunch. At best, she might catch a few of the Forresters out of their suits but not all of them. And her crew had no suits available. They still hadn't been replaced.

With that cheery thought, she realized that her job was complete. She had wired in a direct input to activate the scuttling charges that bypassed the computer control completely. She took a few moments longer to wire it to a manual switch on the console surface so she wouldn't have to crawl back under to activate it.

What if I separate the charges? she wondered. *I might be able to set off one or two charges to convince them to evacuate without actually crippling the ship too badly.*

How do you cripple the ship and then still get away? she thought. *Then there are the destroyers in the system.*

I could blow up their shuttle, or better yet, threaten to do so. That might work.

CHAPTER 67
16 October

"Okay, I think it's time to move," Gunnery Sergeant Eric Aichele said to his troops. "Lt. Samuels, I want you to stay right on my six. That light armor will help protect you to an extent, but not completely. The particle beam weapons that the Forresters are using will punch through it if you get hit squarely, so stay behind me and cover my back." With that statement, he reached up and sealed the helmet to his personal armor. Though he turned his head away, all of the others in the Omega room could hear the slight groan that escaped from his lips with the movement. Burton ignored it with a glance at Samuels to make sure that she didn't say anything.

"Gunny, I think we should use the lower exit just in case they put surveillance in the security suite," Burton said to distract him from the pain.

"No, the lower hatch is too small for the heavy suits."

"All right, but we have to move fast, in case they are alerted."

"They're going to know you're coming," Sullivan added. "They're already actively searching for you."

"We'll move fast and stay in contact," Aichele said as if he hadn't heard Sullivan's remarks.

"Sullivan, I need you to monitor our comms as well as the Forresters. See if you can guide us to them and keep us out of any ambushes."

"Aye-aye, Gunny."

Aichele turned to Samuels and Burton to indicate that they should follow him before turning to unseal the hatch to the Omega room and finally the armory hatch itself. He cautiously extended the vid probe around the corner before moving out into the Security suite. It was empty of personnel, alive or dead.

He followed the same procedure at the outer hatch, even though it was bent and incapable of being closed. He quickly extended his vid probe and seeing no one, moved into the corridor. He motioned Burton aft and signaled Samuels to follow him forward.

They both changed their pace to move more quietly as they closed in on the last stretch before the corner that would take them into the bridge corridor. They paused at the edge while Aichele snaked a finger around the corner and checked the video pickup on his heads up display.

A quick hand signal had them both sprinting down the passageway straight at two very surprised and unprepared Forrest Marines posted directly before the bridge hatch.

Aichele took the one on the left, Samuels the one on the right, and both lightly armored Marines dropped before they had even brought their weapons to bear on the two Warners.

Aichele spared a glance to confirm both were indeed down for good before allowing Samuels to unseal the bridge. While she did this, Aichele relieved both of the dead Forrest Marines of their weapons and moved them out of the way of the hatch.

Just as the hatch was sliding open, the external audio sensors on Aichele's armor picked up a sound coming from the nearest corpse, so he turned and moved toward it to investigate.

When Samuels turned her attention back to Aichele, still hovering over the dead man, she found him with an earpiece pressed to his armor's mic. She realized he was listening to Captain Kerritt, and the last of the Forrest Marines on the ship.

"The bridge is still secure. It looks like no one has been able to break my lock-out," Samuels reported to Aichele.

"Good. Reseal it and let's get moving. We need to hunt these Forresters down before they figure out what is going on and work out some way to get into either the comm room or out in the assault shuttle," Aichele said in a tone that was a suggestion only by the broadest of interpretations.

"I agree we need to move fast, but I need to take five minutes here," Samuels said. "I can lock the boatbay down with the command overrides so that no vessel can detach or launch, then we can get these guys off our ship in a permanent manner."

"What if we undock it remotely instead? That would still keep the transmitter aboard out of their control," Aichele suggested.

"True, but if anyone is already aboard when we kick it loose, they'll report in right away. If there isn't, those destroyers are going to notice a shuttle drifting aimlessly away from us and start asking questions. Locking it down and jamming their comms seems the best option."

"Aye aye, ma'am," replied the Marine. "We can spare a few minutes. I'll go secure the comm room while you do that. Seal yourself in and don't open for anyone but me."

"Right. There were Forrester engineering techs working in the comm room before the evacuation alarms, trying to get the vocom equipment working. I don't know if they're still there or not, so be careful," she said before she sealed the hatch between them.

Aichele continued to listen to the small comm of the dead Forrester for a few moments, hoping for information about the areas the Sergeant and the other Marine were searching. He was happy that he had decided to pull the bodies out of the hallway and into hiding as he caught someone named Sergeant Driscoll saying to Major Kerritt that they had swept the starboard corridors past Medical and the other Marines should focus on the lower deck while he finished the upper deck and went over to check on the Marines on main deck once he finished. He was clearly agitated that none of his other men were responding, but it sounded as though he believed some sort of ongoing communications issues were at fault. *Thank heavens for that, at least,* Aichele thought as he moved around the corner to the comm room to make sure they couldn't use it to contact the planet.

"Comm check, Cobra Two," Aichele said into his armor's internal pickup almost without thinking as he headed toward the communications room.

WSMC Powered Universal Mechanized Armor, or "big cat" as the Marines called it, for obvious reasons, was equipped with the latest version of encrypted micro-burst transceivers. It allowed for clear communication virtually anywhere on a ship (short of something generating an EM scrambling field) that was incredibly secure. It was one of the only systems WSN or WSMC made that was designed to function completely outside of a normal shipboard comm system, mostly because a PUMA was primarily used to assault unfriendly ships, bases or hostile planets, and you didn't want to rely on the hosts' comm systems for your use.

"Five by five, Cobra One, what's on the news?" Burton replied. He quickly outlined the changes in plans and the information he had gotten from the dead Marine.

"My jamming seems to be working sporadically," Sullivan cut in. "I'm only getting a few of the Forresters. Do you want me to up the power? It might interfere with your suits."

"Let's leave it the way it is for now. It seems there have been intermittent comm issues for our uninvited guests over the last few days, thankfully, and they are not as suspicious as they should be," Aichele answered her quietly as he leaned slowly into the ladderway to check it both up and down

"I'm headed down to the lower deck. I'll sweep from the Engineering bulkhead forward." Burton called.

"Roger that. Sweep down the central corridor and come back on the port side. I want you to come back up and secure the comm room when you're done. I'll gas it on my way by if the techs are still there. One clear," Aichele said as he pulled a sleep gas canister from its external rack and tossed it in among the techs in the comm room before heading back to retrieve Samuels.

Burton moved quickly through the ship, keeping her eyes sharp for any sign of the remaining Forrest Marines. She saw none, and made it quickly back up to the comm room. She accessed the hatch with her new code, provided by Samuels, knowing that while the gas would probably be fully dissipated in the room, it didn't really matter to her in her sealed armor. PUMAs had their own air scrubber unit and did not pull in any of the outside air. Being inside a PUMA was as good as being inside an EVA suit. Better, really, since all sorts of things could puncture an EVA suit. Not much could hurt a big cat.

The room still held a slight haze of the knockout gas hanging low to the floor. The Forrester engineers were sprawled randomly around the room. In assessing and securing the compartment, there were several factors to consider. First and foremost, these five engineers could not be allowed to wake up and get any kind of transmission off *Pathfinder*. That meant she needed to secure them, either away from the room or in such a manner that they could not possibly gain access to anything in here. The dose of gas that they had been given would keep any normal person out for several more hours. Marine Security had taught her that you did not trust people to be normal, so she had to assume that any of them could awaken at any time.

The second factor to consider was that this room was not very secure. Even with locking codes, there were ways in. The equipment available in this room could completely jeopardize their ability to take back the vessel. She couldn't destroy it either, though, since they would need it to get back in contact with Warner when the time came, and she had to assume that anything she broke in here would stay broken. She seriously doubted that the Forresters had brought enough spare components to rebuild this suite again.

Also, the way these systems were being rebuilt interlaced them with other core ship's systems that she didn't have a firm grasp on. The main ship computers were back online, so communications was fully integrated to the bridge.

She decided to focus on the things she knew and could control. That meant these five Forresters needed to be elsewhere, locked up tight, and this room had to be locked down in a way that would prevent Kerritt or his other goons from getting in through any available method.

Burton paused while she considered. She had six pairs of lock cuffs with her still, but she also had about 25 meters of high tensile stranded cable in the left arm of her powered suit.

She quickly spooled out her line from the deployment assembly, and rigged together a series of loops. She then put the five of them inside the loops and cuffed the hands of one engineer to the feet of another, so that they alternated heads up to feet up. She ripped one of their uniforms and made each of them a tight gag, which she stuffed in each mouth and secured. She tied off the loops of cable so that she had a neat "barrel" made up of the five men, the last man's hands secured to the first one's hands to complete the circuit. Once she was done, she went to the ship's comm board and punched up the bridge.

"Samuels," came the response. Burton was pleased it was working. She hadn't been sure that would be the case.

"It's Burton. I am going to disable the external pad on the comm room hatch. Can you ensure the hatchway stays sealed?" she asked, knowing that if any hatchway pad was damaged the main computer should still be able to open or close that hatch.

"I can lock it down with my command code and the ship won't let anyone but me in," came the confident reply from Samuels.

"Thank you, ma'am. Give me about 25 seconds and then lock it down, please." Samuels was rapidly becoming a commanding officer.

Burton looped another length of line through one end of her bundle of five men, then used that to drag them into the hall. She was surprised to find that even with her jostling, all of them were still out cold. The gas they had used was a stellar anesthetic.

She keyed the hatch locked from the outside, then blasted the entry pad into a smoking mess with the blast rifle.

Burton dragged her cargo to an access hatch not far aft from the comm room. Once there, she opened the hatch, and shoved them in. The Marine wedged the five techs into the crawlway, careful not to break any bones with her enhanced strength, but making sure there was no wiggle room around them. There was no way these men were getting out without assistance from another party; probably several parties.

"Cobra One, communications room and former occupants secure," she said into her comm as she pulled the access cover shut.

"Roger that. Samuels is sealing the bridge and I am moving in on Sergeant Driscoll. Tango is still on active comm, so I will have to be quick. Going comm silent," Aichele responded to her.

* * * * *

Smiley finished donning a set of light armor, locking the left gauntlet into the wrist connector with her already gauntleted right hand. She started the automatic system check and watched green lights appear in the heads up display of her face shield.

Fortunately for her, the connecting door back into the armory did not require a passcode. The secrecy of the room's existence was its protection. On his way out, Aichele had made sure she was facing the wrong direction to see how the portal was opened, but, like the fact of the room itself, it was a secret Merissa already knew.

That Aichele was hiding the information was troubling. It might have just been ingrained habit, or it might be that he suspected something was off. He did work security, after all, and so he was paid to be paranoid. There was also the fact that her story had holes big enough to walk a PUMA through. Samuels seemed won over, and Burton had as well, at least to begin with. Aichele, on the other hand, was clearly keeping a wary eye on her.

That was almost certainly the reason he had left her behind during this foray. He expected her to remain locked away where he knew exactly where she was, and limited in what she could do should she want to betray them. Asking her to monitor communications would also keep her tied to this location. That is, it would have if she were not able to get into the armory and take her communications links with her.

The smart play for her would have been staying put and doing what was expected in order to gain the trust of the others. Well, smart play or not, she was about to do the unexpected. There was no way she was leaving the fate of *Pathfinder* in the hands of others without doing a thing to help. The ship *had* to be retaken, even if it meant that her cover would be exposed.

Once the diagnostic finished running, Smiley began tying in all the communications she had been monitoring. This was a simple matter of designating frequency sets to the internal comm menu of her suit. Once she was finished, she resealed the Omega Room, tabbed open the side hatch of the armory, and went hunting on her own.

The ship was the highest priority. She probably hadn't dropped her cover with the others and she would protect it to the best of her ability, but *Pathfinder* must stay in Warner possession. Any risk she had to take to make sure that happened was an acceptable one.

She went aft to avoid being seen by Burton or Aichele and headed down the aft stairs into the lower deck.

This was one fight she was not sitting out.

* * * * *

Aichele had determined approximately where on upper deck Sergeant Driscoll was, and the apparent search pattern he was using up here, so he had moved ahead of him to wait. He asked Samuels to guard the starboard main ladder as a precaution. Mostly he was trying to keep her safe and out of his way. He would have preferred to go after Kerritt, but the captain was being very cagey about his position, so he decided to take out the sergeant first and then look for the officer. Aichele had stopped moving, so there not even the muffled sound of servo motors to give him away.

Aichele waited; his many years of experience allowed him to do so without impatience or nervousness.

Before long, he heard faint approaching footfalls. Driscoll's footsteps were very irregular, with occasional long pauses between. It sounded like he was checking every hatch.

Time seemed to stretch out for Aichele, waiting for the enemy to walk into his ambush. Eric could track the man's position by the light steps, and he was ready to act as Driscoll paused out of sight, then suddenly came around the corner.

Aichele fired his blast rifle the instant he saw his target, but Driscoll was already rolling sideways. The two pulses passed harmlessly into the bulkhead behind his target. Driscoll came up firing, and it was no fletchette gun, but a blast pistol.

"Mech armor! Somebody in mech armor!" Driscoll screamed into his comm, and Aichele heard the fierce cry both from the man and from the earpiece he had attached to one of his external mics. Aichele heard a reply from Kerritt, "Repeat, Sergeant. Armor?" Aichele didn't focus on that. He was already moving toward his quarry and firing his rifle. As Aichele's second barrage bore down on him, Driscoll tried to move back around the corner and out of Aichele's range. He wasn't fast enough this time, though, and he suffered two hits before escaping.

"Delta four, delta four..." Driscoll cried weakly into his comm. Aichele accelerated down the distance and was checking Driscoll within the space of three heartbeats. Driscoll was not moving. A quick sensor scan showed that he was already dead.

Aichele now refocused on the comm he had taken from the dead Forrest Marine at the bridge, and he realized it was dead quiet. There was no questioning Marine on the other end. There was only the white noise of an open channel, a light static.

"Cobra Two, target is down," Aichele said to Burton through his own comm. "Suggest rendezvous, starboard main ladder."

"Roger that, Cobra One, standing by in one-point-five," she said as she moved aft down the main deck corridor she was in. She turned left to reach the stairwell on the starboard side of the ship to wait for him. When she arrived, Samuels was already there, looking nervous.

Aichele arrived shortly thereafter. Not wanting to waste precious time, he had not done anything with Driscoll's body, knowing that no one else was on the upper deck.

"They clearly have some sort of contingency plan in place," Aichele said as soon as he spotted her while coming down the ladder. "He wasn't very happy about seeing me in armor, but something about that delta four command he issued suggests to me they had previously planned some sort of response for it."

"Well, we know the other Marines are searching on lower deck, let's get down and take them out before he has any time to put this delta plan in motion, Gunny," Burton suggested.

At Samuels' nod, Aichele turned back to his fellow Marine. "Agreed, let's move." He turned, heading down to the lower deck with the other two trailing after him.

CHAPTER 68
16 October

Aichele and Samuels moved smoothly through the lower deck, searching for any Forrest Marines. They came across two bodies lying prone near the port aft stairwell, just forward of the cross corridor, as if they had been shot down as they rounded the corner. They were the fourth and fifth bodies they had encountered, but they had yet to find a single live Forrester. These two had been dispatched with a heavy energy weapon. Both sets of armor had a thirty centimeter hole in the torso, the ceramics and ablative metals charred around the circumference. One of the others was taken out with the same type of weapon, but two were killed with shots to the face; probably with a lighter weapon, or a variable output gun on a lower setting.

Aichele had almost completed his self-assigned search area, so he took extra time with this scene to evaluate what it all meant. He knelt next to the Forresters while Samuels continued scanning the area. The two corpses had only a single wound each. The angle of the damage was different for the two women, also. One had been hit at an angle, and the energy bolt had burned into the downed soldier from left to right. The other had been hit squarely in the chest.

He stood then to check the surroundings. The nearby walls bore no marks at all, but there were two burned spots against the wall at the other end of the hallway. The two still held energy carbines in their cold grips, and they matched up with the marks. The last one had also still carried a weapon, but the first two had been missing theirs.

So, someone had waited at the other end of the hall for both targets to be visible, even while taking fire, then dispatched both with a single shot each as soon as target two came into view, but before she could turn to engage. And it was someone carrying a big gun, maybe a PF-27, or something equally large. Aichele had given his team weapons that would punch through the light armor, but these two might as well have been wearing nothing.

Eric knew what weapons Burton was carrying, and he knew he and Samuels had not taken these soldiers down. He further knew what weapons the Forresters had been allowed to bring onto the ship. There was no guarantee that's what they *had* brought, but even so, they had no reason to attack their own men. So who did that leave?

Aichele wondered for a moment if Major Chowdhury had somehow made it back aboard. She could have made those shots, having been through sniper training, but Eric doubted he could have duplicated that feat. He certainly couldn't with a PF-27, or anything in the same class. Guns with that kind of power were not noted for their accuracy.

That had been another reason for his weapons choice, though he hadn't told Samuels that. Firearms with that level of discharge were designed to punch through defensive armor. When you miss your target, which invariably happens, you tend to put holes through parts of the ship you're in; sometimes vital parts dedicated to keeping you alive.

They were just starting to move forward when Aichele raised his arm to signal a halt. Samuels turned to watch their backs. Eric activated his comm.

"Position check," ordered Aichele.

"Copy," came Burton's reply. "Just cleared room L-4. Moving to L-6." That put her location in the forward cross corridor on lower deck.

"This is Sullivan. I'm right where you left me."

"What was that sound?" Aichele asked. The sound was faint, and indistinct, but it set Eric's hackles on edge. He couldn't identify it, but it didn't belong, somehow.

"I'm listening in on multiple communications right now, Gunny. It's hard to say what you heard. Anyway, from the comm traffic, it sounds like all the Forresters have fallen back to the boatbay with the prisoners. There's some griping about not being able to launch the assault shuttle, so it would appear they've discovered what Lieutenant Samuels did," she explained.

Eric wasn't sure. The account seemed reasonable, and Sullivan sounded sincere, but what other explanation was there but that she was the one taking out bad guys?

Wait. He was sure. Aichele still had his captured radio affixed to his mic in order to monitor their comms himself. Ever since that 'delta four' message, there had been absolute silence from Forrest. If they had called troops back to the boatbay, he would have heard it.

"Well, then I think we know where our missing Marines are," Aichele said, turning with Samuels to head to the boatbay. Sullivan was lying, but he didn't know for sure why. He kept puzzling at it as he moved, but decided that he didn't have any time to waste trying to gather information now. The ops plan called for a rapid strike, and that was their only chance of success. "All right, Burton, meet us at the port entrance to the boatbay. Sullivan, let me know if you hear anything else we need to know."

"Copy that. On the move," Burton said. There was a brief pause, then Sullivan also acknowledged her orders.

Aichele and Samuels made good time moving back up to main and over to the boatbay. Burton came up the far stairway from the lower level only moments after they arrived. Aichele threw Burton the hand signal for 'stay alert' and he turned to touch helmets with Samuels.

"Ma'am, it might be best for you to go back to the bridge and take control. We need to make sure the Forrest shuttle can't launch. If it gets to the surface, we won't be able to hold the ship even if we successfully take it back. If they find a way to break free, I would advise destroying the shuttle with the belly guns."

The young officer nodded her understanding but didn't move.

"Gunny, I don't think we can trust info from Sullivan until we verify it," Samuels said. "There's a couple of things that aren't adding up for me."

Good girl, Aichele thought. "I know. Can you access the security feed from the bridge?"

"Yes."

"Then when you get there, find out where our targets are. If they are all in the boatbay, like Sullivan says, give me two clicks. If they're not, give me three, and Burton and I will join you on the bridge to make a new plan."

"That should work," Samuels said. "Keep your heads down, you two." She turned on her heel and headed off at a fast trot, keeping her weapon ready just in case there were still Forresters outside the boatbay or hostile Warners who had managed to arm themselves.

Once the officer was out of sight, Aichele opened his helmet and motioned for Burton to do the same. In that way, he could talk to her without the conversation going out over the radio.

"What did you find down there, Sarge?" Aichele asked.

"Not much, Gunny. One Forrester was already down. I assume I have you to thank for that?"

"Nope. Nor do I think I need to thank you for the five Samuels and I found."

Burton's eyes widened appreciably. "So Sullivan—?"

"It has to be Sullivan," Aichele confirmed. "But I'm not sure Sullivan is Sullivan."

"Say again?"

Eric ran a hand over his brush cut. "Okay, Sullivan is the only one who was in a position to have taken out those Forresters. She could have put on light armor and used that to link herself into the comm net. But the Sullivan we know about should not possess the skills demonstrated by whoever hunted down those armed Forresters. Seriously, I'm not sure I could have done what she did. Whoever Sullivan really is, she's in a class with Chowdhury."

Burton let out a low whistle. "So, who is she? And why didn't she tell us she had skills we could use?"

"I've thought of several possibilities; none of which I like."

"Such as?"

"What if she's not working for Forrest, but she's not working for Warner, either? Remember Jhonsruud? He turned out to have been a plant by the DaGamans. And Sullivan transferred aboard just after Jhonsruud was arrested and taken off the ship. Maybe she's his replacement."

"That doesn't explain how she knew about the Omega Room, though."

"Doesn't it? Jhonsruud was here to steal secrets, wasn't he? We don't know for sure how much he got and how much of that he was able to get off the ship. The Omega Room is just one more secret and one that is known by nearly all Marines who have worked security."

"Okay," Burton said, "I'm not sure I buy that last part, though I suppose it's possible. But if she is working for DaGama, why is she helping us by taking out Forresters? Six was more than we had expected downstairs, and who knows if we would have gotten the drop on them or them on us."

"Because she needs to get both Forrest and Warner off the ship in order to take over. So she uses us to help her get rid of Forrest, gaining our trust, then turns on us to eliminate any resistance. For all I know, she's the one who poisoned my food, and took out my guards."

Burton suppressed a shiver. She didn't want to believe it, but it seemed to be the only story that would cover everything they knew about the situation. "Crap!" she finally said with some feeling. "Okay, so we head straight for the armory, and when Sullivan isn't there, we'll know for sure she's been lying to us."

"We don't have the time," Aichele countered, "and it's unnecessary. You know how air scrubber three has that odd rattle because it's not quite in alignment?"

Burton raised an eyebrow. "I can't say I've ever noticed. You're the one working in Engineering these days."

"Let's just say it took me a while to realize it, but I know that she was on the lower deck of Engineering when I called you both a few minutes ago."

"Okay," Burton summarized, "we know she hasn't been straight with us, but we don't know for certain why. Without knowing that, we can't be sure whether to treat her as an enemy or not."

"I'm not sure we can afford to take any chances, Jill. With this girl's skill, we may have to shoot first and ask questions later."

"Great. I nominate you, as the senior noncom, to tell Samuels all about why we shot her friend without giving her a chance to explain herself."

Both heard two clicks on their comm channel.

Eric's face was stone when he replied. "If it comes to it, I'll pull the trigger, and I'll tell the captain why I did." He locked his helmet closed again, then signaled 'let's go.'

CHAPTER 69
17 October

Samuels hurried down the port corridor, eyes and gun barrel constantly moving. When she reached the forward cross corridor, she turned and headed right past the bridge to her own quarters. After she'd left Aichele, she'd realized that to get into both the ship's and security's systems, it would be easiest to use her remote hooks from her quarters.

Plus there were currently two dead bodies on the bridge, and she'd had quite enough of that creepiness while she was locking down the Forrester's shuttle and blocking external comms. Not that she would have mentioned that to the Marines, of course.

She tabbed the door to her quarters open and hurried to her seat. Fortunately, no one had thought to search here after she was stuck in the Omega Room. Or, if they had, they'd missed her illicit equipment in their sweep.

As she sat, she pulled off her helmet and gauntlets, throwing them both on her bed, along with her rifle. Otherwise, she made no move to get comfortable. She moved as quickly and efficiently as she knew how, and had her connection active in record time. Her first image to view was an overview showing every active spy bug the system was tracking. She needed to check all the feeds in the boatbay, but a glimpse of Aichele and Burton talking with their face plates up caught her eye.

She settled on a split screen view, with the Warner Marines to the left and a constantly changing rotation of the views from every other bug on the right.

"... took me a while to realize it, but I know that she was on the lower deck of Engineering when I called you both a few minutes ago," Aichele was saying once she connected the audio feed. What was this?

They had to be talking about Sullivan. Apparently, Aichele had also been suspicious of several things that didn't add up with the girl. No, more than suspicious, he *knew* something was not right about her.

She thought about comming him and ordering him to...well, she wasn't sure what. That reminded her of both the need for comm silence and her assignment. She scanned the remaining channels and learned two things.

The first was that Sullivan had not provided an accurate picture of the current situation. Everything forward of the boatbay was clear, but there were as many armored enemy in Engineering as there were in the boatbay. Where were all of them coming from? By her count they had already accounted for almost double what they had been led to believe was their number. They had to be sleeping on the shuttle.

The second thing she had learned was that Sullivan was in Engineering, moving quickly and cautiously in search of targets. Should she send three clicks, and rendezvous for a new plan? No, what she should do is to keep pressing the attack. Once the three in the boatbay were handled, she could get word to Aichele and Burton to expect more. She reached up to where she had clipped her comm and pressed the transmit button twice.

Unless there were no more by that time. While she watched, Sullivan silently lay prone on the decking and shot a Forrester as he came around the corner. He was dead after the single shot. Sullivan rose to her feet just as silently as before and resumed her hunt.

"If it comes to it, I'll pull the trigger, and I'll tell the captain why I did," Aichele said from her screen. She wasted no time entering a few commands to grab the rest of this conversation as well as all of Sullivan's movements from the Security server to study.

After hearing it all, Samuels could not fault Aichele's reasoning. He had come to a logical conclusion; undoubtedly the most probable, too. It was certainly borne out by Sullivan's current activities. But her father had always told her that logic could only get you so far. Sometimes you needed to trust your gut instincts. Right now, her guts were telling her...well, okay, so they weren't telling her anything. But Aichele's conclusion was only one possibility, and Sullivan at least deserved the chance to explain herself before he took matters into his own hands.

Unless Samuels did something to head her off, Sullivan was going to finish in Engineering and walk right into the middle of Aichele's fight, and Aichele might decide to remove Sullivan from the equation. It sounded like he had already decided on that very course of action.

Samuels was not going to let that happen. She was going to go down there herself, and make sure things went as they should.

That also meant that she was not going to let Sullivan walk around loose without some very good answers. Surely, there must be satisfactory answers.

After all, if anyone knew that things were not always as they appeared, Monica Samantha Bybee was that person.

* * * * *

Aichele nodded to Burton once she'd sealed her armor and they both moved cautiously through the port hatchway into the boatbay. According to Sullivan's report, all of the remaining Forresters were here, and Samuels confirmed that. Aichele was sure that if Sullivan were attempting an ambush, Samuels would have used three clicks to have them pull back. That didn't mean Sullivan wouldn't try later, though.

Once inside, he saw that the prisoners were not in the immediate area, but that was all he could see for sure. Eric cursed the recent change to the boatbay. Over the last weeks, the Forresters had brought in containers of spare parts to aid in the repair work. The once open bay was now a congested mess with numerous spots for the enemy to hide. In truth, it also covered their approach, so maybe it wasn't the worst development after all.

They moved into the bay, shifting carefully around cargo containers, some opened and half full of parts and supplies, others unopened, and still others completely emptied. When they got into position, they could see three Forresters guarding eighteen prisoners. The former Warners were seated against the wall with their arms behind them. The three Forresters were all in light armor.

We've accounted for far more than the allotted ten Marines plus an officer. They obviously smuggled in more troops on their shuttle than they were supposed to have, so they probably did *plan to double-cross Leung all along,* Aichele thought.

There was one Warner halfway down the row who was laying face-down in a small pool of blood. The officer's uniform made him easy to identify as Omundson, but there was no way to tell if he was still alive. Eric scanned the other prisoners from cover, trying to assess their condition. As his vision passed over Hilary Calvi, he could see that she was staring directly at him. His attention snapped back to the guards as he heard her begin to yell. The guard directly in front of him spun back to face Calvi who was trying to stand up. She was screaming obscenities at the guard and making a break toward the forward hatch. Aichele wasn't sure why she would do this, but he wasn't about to waste the distraction she offered. His first shot took the guard high in the back. He purposely aimed at the neck joint of the armor hoping to hit a weak spot. He needn't have worried. They had known going into this fight that a medium-weight energy weapon should easily deal with the lightly armored Forrest Marines, and it penetrated without difficulty, cutting a clean hole through the unfortunate trooper's neck and dropping him in his tracks.

The soldier near the hatch fired at almost the same time, but his target was the escaping prisoner. Calvi fell to the deck like a ragdoll.

Aichele heard Burton's rifle fire behind him, taking out the third guard, while he shifted his target and put a blast into the guard who had just shot down Calvi. The guard went down just as the man squeezed the trigger on his own weapon. It let loose with a burst that was also directed toward the prisoners and Aichele heard another scream from the Warner group as the Forrester went down.

"The others went to the shuttle a few minutes back," called Giannini from behind him. "We've got this. You two go."

"Okay," he called back. "Get everyone moving out of here and into the galley or medbay."

The old Marine paused long enough to see that they were going to listen to Crystal without his help. When Giannini and the others started moving, he motioned to Burton to head inward to the shuttle access.

There were more targets, but they were holed up in their assault shuttle. That was going to make them twice as hard to get to and root out.

Good strategy, Eric thought. *The shuttle has independent comms and a working engine. Running away or calling for help would seem very attractive, if I were them. That's probably their 'delta four' plan.*

He motioned to Burton to move around to the left and circle toward the hatchway where *Vanguard* had been docked all those months ago. He circled right, ensuring that there were no Marines waiting to ambush them from behind the containers.

Before either of them had made more than half their circuit, an armored head popped out of the hatchway.

Aichele dropped to one knee and opened fire with his blast rifle. As the Forrester exited the shaft, it was all too clear that this was bad news. The head that emerged from the hatch was enclosed within a thick helmet, part of the Forrest version of heavy powered armor. The blast rifle that Aichele was firing had been specifically selected because it was not capable of penetrating that level of protection.

A quick glance told him Burton had already registered the same fact. She made no attempt to fire, but moved forward to one of the containers to give herself some cover. As the armored Forrest Marine turned his similar light blast rifle at Aichele and returned fire, a second man began emerging behind him, in a matching heavy armor assembly.

Two? Not good, thought Aichele as his mind raced through his tactical options. *Are there any more on the shuttle?*

The Forresters had broken the bargain they made with Leung and had smuggled heavy armor and extra troops onto their shuttle. Surprise was about all he and Burton had going for them at this point, and it was beginning to look as if the surprise was about even on each side.

Both Forresters were up now, and advancing on Aichele's position. Since Burton had a container between her and the Forresters, she tried to distract them. While she fired, Aichele moved in closer and found a spot among the limited cover available. As he slid into position, he thumbed his blast rifle up to its highest setting It still wouldn't be able to penetrate the heavy armor, but it had a chance if they could put multiple shots into the same spot. It also slowed his rate of fire considerably while the weapon built up a greater charge.

While Aichele took aim, he continued to scan the shuttle hatch, expecting to see more armored Marines coming up. Who knew how many more were hidden down there? His ribs were aching and his stamina was just about depleted.

There didn't seem to be any more forthcoming, so he turned his attention to what he hoped were his last two targets.

Burton popped out from behind the container and opened up on the nearer of the two Forresters with a barrage from her light assault rifle on rapid fire.

Aichele fired on the one closest to him as both targets turned to return Burton's fire. The heavy pulse hit the Forrester in the back of his armored head and he was thrown forward by the blast. His compatriot threw himself behind the only container on his side of the bay and shot back at Aichele, completely ignoring the lighter fire from Burton.

Burton took advantage of the temporary lull in the action to thumb her rifle to its highest setting as well.

Aichele waited for his rifle to hit its full charge before risking a view of the scene. He was rewarded with another blast that struck the container just above his head. Apparently, the Forrest weapons had a quicker recharge rate.

He was satisfied to see that his first target was still down, but Aichele had no shot at his head to try to rupture the spot he had weakened with his first hit. Instead, he targeted the servo junction at the base of the back where all of the relays should be concentrated. He swung out of his cover and took his shot. Unlike the inexperienced Forrester, Aichele didn't miss. His shot struck squarely on the junction. A second shot hit the same spot less than a second later as Burton added her firepower to the equation. Their target was still alive and they had not penetrated his armor, but it was evident that they had done some damage as the Marine struggled to sit. He was having difficulty getting his legs to move.

Unfortunately, both he and Burton were still waiting for their weapons to cycle, and had no option but to let him recover. After he finally reached a sitting position, he turned his rifle on Aichele. The speed of his fire meant that he had not adjusted his power setting. While the low power setting was highly effective against unarmored opponents, it was less than an insect bite to Aichele's heavy armor.

Aichele's power level finally hit its peak, and he moved into the lighter fire in order to send a blast directly into the armored faceplate. Burton moved out of her cover to add her fire to his when she was hit with a blast from the other Marine. The shot hit her in the right shoulder and threw her back behind her container. It didn't look to Aichele as if the shot had penetrated her armor, but it had hit her considerably harder than his own shot had hit his target. She was not moving.

With Burton out of action, Aichele made a quick decision and locked his blast rifle into its appointed slot on his back. He jumped out of his hiding spot and sprinted toward the injured Forrest Marine sitting on the deck. PUMA armor can build considerable speed in even a short distance.

The Forrester got off several low powered shots as Aichele crossed the distance, but then Aichele lowered his shoulder and planted it squarely under the immobile Marine's helmet. The armor kept the Marine's head from snapping back, but it didn't keep him upright. His armored head slammed into the deck as Aichele rolled over the top of him.

Aichele picked up the Forrest Marine's fallen rifle and pulled it to his chest just as the other Forrester fired a blast that hit him with a glancing shot on his left side. The blast knocked him back over a meter and set his ears ringing. His side erupted in pain from the concussive force of the blast on his injured ribs. He felt something give way.

Now that constriction that was keeping his ribcage in its proper shape felt like it was squeezing the life out of him. He had to concentrate just to take in air, and his whole body was awash in torment when he did.

Darkness closed around the edges of Aichele's vision, but he pushed it back. He did his best to ignore the pain and lunged for cover before his opponent could get off another shot. He immediately switched to his own rifle and let off a shot at the just emerging Forrester and knocked him back into cover with a partial impact on his right shoulder. He should have been able to hit him squarely, but he couldn't hold his arm steady enough to do the job. He moved the captured rifle to his right hand and worked to make his next shot count. The gun's design was an exact match of his own rifle, which was a relief. He thumbed the power up to its highest setting and let his own rifle droop in his almost nerveless left hand. He held his breath while the captured weapon built up a charge and slid down to sit behind the shipping container, letting his breath blow out of him. The motion caused a jolt of pain in his chest.

He just needed to rest a moment to gather his strength.

CHAPTER 70
17 October

Merissa Smiley knew already that her cover was not going to last to the end of this mission. She had left too much evidence in her wake for any of her three allies to miss.

There had been four patrolling around the lower deck of the forward section, and the two she had dispatched as a pair had nearly taken her head off. That meant that there were six bodies down there, including the two she had killed during her escape from captivity, for Burton and Aichele to find.

From the tone of voice, subtle as it was, it seemed like Aichele suspected something. The very fact that he was checking on her position was proof of that. She had continued playing her role with him on the comms, but it was an empty gesture at this point. She knew that, and accepted it as the price of doing business, but she figured she would have a chance to explain things to them after this was all over.

More and more, she was glad she had chosen to fight rather than wait it out. The number of enemy combatants she had already seen meant that the original plan had drastically underestimated the enemy's strength. If she hadn't made herself part of the fight, things would have gone differently for the good guys, she was sure.

Smiley was almost done clearing out Engineering. Her plan now was to finish here, then sneak through the boatbay along the catwalk that connected the upper levels of Engineering with the main area of the ship farther forward. If she could do that before everyone else was done, she could be back where she belonged before anyone could check on her.

It wouldn't fool anyone, but it would give her a chance to answer questions without appearing to be a threat. And, truth to tell, it was hard *not* to look like a threat walking around with the weighty gun she had selected. She absently wished she had considered how much of the ship she was going to have to cover first. Smiley had kept herself in top physical form, but the energy cannon was getting heavy.

Upper and lower decks were cleared, and Smiley moved through the main deck without noise, peeking around the edges of machinery she only partially understood to check for danger. Sullivan had known everything about these mechanical contraptions, but all that knowledge was gone now.

That was all right. She hadn't needed it to do the basic repairs she'd been assigned the last few months, and the knowledge inside Smiley's mind was much more applicable to the current situation.

The last section Smiley came to was the engineering control hub. Hearing voices, she lay on the floor and eased her head slowly out, then just as slowly back. There were nine people there, but only two were soldiers. The others were either engineers or technicians who had been sent to decipher and repair *Pathfinder*'s systems.

"Haeberle, what's the count?" one of them said.

"Forty-nine minutes since they ordered delta four," Haeberle answered.

"We've got to leave now, Sanderson," the first soldier said. "They won't wait any longer, and if we're still on the ship when they leave, they'll blow us up along with it."

"Forty seconds," Sanderson said, "and we'll have what we came for. That should be worth the wait."

Smiley risked another slow look. She could get to one of the soldiers, the one in charge, she thought, but the other had all the noncombatants and part of some machine in the way of a clean shot.

She'd taken too long sizing up the situation. The first soldier had spotted her in his constant sweep of all the approaches, and aimed his rifle at her. Smiley pulled back before he squeezed the trigger, but not quite far enough. The machine took almost all of the directed energy, but enough bled through to make small bubbles appear in part of her face shield. The polymers would be more brittle now, and any sort of repeat impact would go right through.

The enemy knew where to hit her now, and Smiley took the prudent action of immediate relocation. She dropped back two bays, and maneuvered for a different approach. She had to swing her head farther to the side now to take all her surroundings in. Everything in the upper right part of her field of vision was too blurry to make out, thanks to the near miss.

"We're moving now!" she heard the one in command direct from behind her.

"I've got it!" Sanderson responded. Smiley could just make out the sounds of movement over the running machinery. She doubled her pace to circle back before they slipped away from her. She was prepared to fire as she swung her energy cannon in line with where her targets were.

But they weren't. Hot plasma hit her in the back, burning into her armor and throwing her forward into the console she had just come around. The pain should have been incapacitating, but pre-planted hypnotic directives moved it to some distant corner of her brain for later study. She twisted her body around as she fell and her big PF-93 coughed out two rounds of blazing power.

Projected Force was a company that made solid weapons; simple, accurate, and well-designed. But even a good weapon can't aim itself. Smiley's shots went well wide of their intended target.

They were impressive shots, though, and perhaps their size contributed to the soldier's decision to leave at once, without making sure Smiley was finished.

She wasn't finished, but her half spin, that had brought her weapon to bear, also meant that her injured back was what slammed into the decking when she hit. That walled off pain was getting more and more insistent that it required Smiley's attention. Immediately.

Smiley could see a first aid kit on the floor under one of the consoles. She tried to roll over to go retrieve it.

She couldn't move.

* * * * *

Damn, damn, triple damn, hell! Samuels swore to herself. She had delayed her departure only long enough to connect the video feeds to her portable unit, the way she had done whenever sneaking around, and also connecting an alarm in case the Forrest shuttle managed to disengage from the ship. She was almost to the boatbay when she saw that Aichele and Burton were facing a couple of enemy Marines with the same kind of heavy armor they themselves had, prompting the creative language. Samuels was not going to be of any help as she was.

She turned to head back to the armory to get a gun with more throw weight, when a herd of people broke around the corner. Samuels' weapon snapped up as if it had a mind of its own, and Crystal Giannini screamed and tried to scramble back the other way.

"It's okay, Crystal," Monica soothed, gun pointing down and her other hand raised placatingly. "I'm here to help."

"Lt. Samuels?" she asked, not able to see the officer's face clearly through the shield.

"That's right. Get these people moving again, into the galley," Samuels repeated the orders Aichele had already given them, which eased Giannini's mind.

Between the two of them, with Danis and Bezates helping, they were inside the mess hall in no time. The large room quickly filled with the sounds of panic, and Samuels moved quickly to squelch it.

"Belay that racket!" she ordered, just loudly enough to be heard. "Do you want to give away our position?" The noise ended as if all the air were sucked out of the room.

"Dr. Johnson, you're going to have your hands full in medbay. Do you need anyone here to help you?"

"We had to leave our wounded behind in the boatbay. Is there any way we can retrieve them?"

Samuels consulted her hand unit again. "Oh, hell!" she breathed, surveying the conflict going on at that moment elsewhere. The buzz in the room started up again. Samuels didn't try to stop it this time. "Maybe," she finally decided. "The fighting isn't in the immediate area of our downed people right now, but no promises it will stay that way. I won't order anyone to go, but I'll allow volunteers," the officer said.

"I'll go," Bezates said at once.

"I'm in," Giannini followed.

"I'll go, too," Morrison added. Those nearest turned to look at him. "What?" he asked of all of them, but no one responded.

"Fine," Monica said. "Doctor, you take these three to medbay. Gather what you need, and wait for me there."

"Aye-aye, Lieutenant," the medical officer said. "But where are you going?"

"If I'm going to provide cover, I need to pick something up first. Now, move out," Samuels ordered. She really didn't have time to explain everything.

All four of those addressed could hear the command in her voice, tinged with annoyance. They moved out quickly.

"Danis, front and center," Samuels ordered next.

"Yes, ma'am?" Danis pulled himself to attention in front of her.

Samuels sized up the older noncom and hesitated, not sure if she was making the right move here or not. She didn't have time to weigh the pros and cons. Burton and Aichele needed backup on the bounce. Finally, she decided to trust him and hoped she wouldn't regret it.

"You're Security, and this is an emergency, so I'm leaving you in charge. When I go, I'll be able to lock the hatches shut. I'll only give the unlock code to someone I trust. If the door opens, it'll be okay. If the door is forced open, you shoot first, understood?" She handed him the energy weapon.

He accepted it, then took a close look at it. "Where did you–?"

"Understood?" she repeated.

He pulled himself back to attention. "Aye-aye, ma'am."

"The Forresters have heavy armor on the ship." Danis' eyes grew large, and the rest of the room became still and quiet. "If one of those comes in, your only chance is to set this to maximum and hit the same spot two or three times. But your best defense is going to be to lay low until help comes."

She stopped and took a deep breath. "I'm sorry, PO, but that's the best I can do for you all right now."

"I understand, ma'am," Danis said softly. When she reached the hatch, he added, "Good hunting, ma'am."

"Thanks, Danis. You keep these people silent," she said forcefully. Then, more quietly, "You keep these people safe." The hatch door sealed behind her, and after a few seconds, the metallic sound of the pressure locks engaging was heard from within.

$$* * * * *$$

Burton came to her senses shortly after landing. She realized immediately that her right shoulder had been hit by the blast. It was on fire with pain and the servo motors in her suit arm were unresponsive. She *would* have to get hit in the same spot where Morales had shot her four months ago.

Burton bit back the cry of pain that threatened to escape her lips, blinked away the tears that came unbidden to her eyes, and she tried to move her arm. She had to sit for a few seconds to gather her breath again.

As soon as she could, she rolled over and took a good look at her right shoulder and side. It was definitely a mess. The blast had hit her directly on the shoulder plate and had partially fused the joint. The dark polymer was lighter in color and looked thinner, as if part of the armor had evaporated away.

She forced the PUMA into a half roll to get her legs clear and under her again, then used her left arm to extricate herself the rest of the way from the debris where she had landed. She searched for her weapon and found it laying a few feet to her left. She realized that it must have taken at least a portion of the blast as well. It was set to half power and the control would not increase its setting, no matter how much she tried to force it.

She heard weapons fire coming from the other side of a nearby container, and knew that without help, Aichele would not be able to hold them off forever. She started back toward the fray, her teeth clenched to wall up the pain in her right shoulder.

She carefully leaned out around the edge of the container to assess the scene. Aichele was just firing a blast at the farthest Forrester and the other target seemed to be motionless in the middle of the deck. Something was wrong with Gunny. He wasn't moving well at all; too slow to last much longer. The mobile Forrester was taking advantage of the break in Aichele's fire to come out of cover and advance. Burton needed to provide something else for the Forrester to worry about. She shouldered her damaged weapon with her left hand and pulled the trigger.

Nothing happened.

CHAPTER 21
17 October

Samuels entered Captain Brighton's authorization code into the control panel and selected SECURITY, then EMER. LOCK from the menu. A satisfying click-whirr-click sounded, indicating that the pressure locks were engaged to keep one set of enemies out, and another set in.

She deliberately reminded herself that the people inside the room were not victims she had rescued, but thieves and traitors she could only trust so far. Behind locked doors, though, they were a problem to deal with another time. She needed to get a weapon with enough juice to take out a PUMA, or its equivalent, and get it and her to the boatbay before it was too late for her to do any good.

It was a relatively short trip to the security bay, and Monica ran the entire way. The outer door was no longer there, so she didn't need to pause to enter a passcode until the armory door. Once inside, her available options daunted her. She was in a hurry, and wasn't about to take the time to study out all the benefits of one selection over another.

She walked down the aisle of racks and pulled out the biggest gun she could see. She left it lying on the floor. It was too heavy to get back in its cradle. Backtracking two types, she found one that she could carry, though probably not for too long. It was easily twenty kilos, but the rated number of megajoules of output made it just what she was looking for.

She turned to go and made it as far as the end of the aisle, then turned back. She collected three of the same Phuleproof Munitions light assault rifles Aichele had handed out and slung those over her back as well.

She hurried as fast as she could under her load down to Medical, and found all four waiting for her in the corridor. She handed out the LARs to the three volunteers, who already had medical gear to carry, then directed them aftward, toward the starboard entrance to the boatbay. Giannini and Morrison took theirs without comment, but Bezates was about to ask Samuels a few things. Once he looked at the set of her jaw, he decided that perhaps any questions could wait until later.

They all stopped outside the hatch, while Samuels took out her pad. Her three armed companions divided up the approaches to watch without any command from her, and they carried their weapons like they weren't about to shoot themselves in the foot. More of their basic training must have stuck with them than she had feared might be the case.

Samuels pulled up the video stream from the bay and scrolled between the three bugs with a view of the area they were about to enter. From over her shoulder, Bezates said, "Wait, isn't that—?"

"Yes," the officer cut him off. Bezates kept quiet.

"Okay, here's the plan. Once inside, we split up into two groups. Bezates, you take Dr. Johnson and Giannini and head straight for the injured. The doctor will start working on them and you and Giannini cover her.

"There's an antigrav pallet sitting next to the hatch to hold nine. That will be my objective. Morrison, you and I stay tight together, move to the wall, and follow it down to hold nine. We grab the pallet, and you maneuver it back to where the wounded are. We retrieve them, Johnson rides the pallet with the wounded, and we head straight back to medbay.

"Once you pass the hatch, you shouldn't have any problems. There aren't any bad guys forward of that bulkhead. I'll stay behind in the boatbay and join Burton and Aichele. Clear?"

"Crystal," Bezates said.

"What?" Giannini responded. Bezates grinned at her.

"Can't you ever be serious?" Morrison asked.

"Can't you ever take a joke?" Bezates countered.

"Let's get to work," Samuels said, ignoring them all. She could tell they were nervous, but she didn't have the time or the words to do anything about it. She locked her face shield into place, effectively conveying the fact that the time for talking was done.

Sullivan unsealed the hatch and moved through, the others trailing after her. The various shipping containers made it difficult to see very far in any direction within the room. Once all were inside, Samuels watched the first three move to the right, then she went diagonally to the left and followed the starboard wall aft once they reached it.

Sounds of fighting could be heard from Samuels' right, but she did her best to focus only on what was immediately around her. At least it wouldn't be hard to find the Marines once she took care of this task. *If they last that long,* she worried. They passed hold eight without any problems, and visibility was better here than it was nearer the center of the bay.

Just as they reached the antigravity platform, the nearest hatch leading to Engineering burst open, and people started spilling out. The first one through was both armed and armored, and he spotted Samuels and opened fire on her all in the same second.

Samuels had been facing toward the center, and had only turned at the sound of the Forresters' entrance. The enemy's first shot missed her to the left, and Samuels let her military training take over. She dropped to one knee, narrowly avoiding a blast just over her head, and brought her weapon's sights into line with the chest of the soldier. She squeezed the trigger.

Her face screen immediately darkened to compensate for the sun-bright flare of her PF-27's discharge. The energy was more than she'd expected, but she'd never actually fired a weapon this large before. The bolt had travelled completely through her intended target and into the others behind him. Three bodies were down, but her mind, still locked into the pathways trained into her, did not register them as anything of note, while she continued scanning for threats.

There were none to be found. The rest of the group had fled back the way they had come, looking for an easier way.

"Morrison, get this pallet moving while I cover you," she ordered. Not hearing a reply, she tore her eyes away from the hatch long enough for a quick look back, keeping her weapon aimed at the enemy.

A quick look was enough. Morrison was dead.

* * * * *

Stassia screamed.
Why does it hurt? Make it stop!
Hush, little one. Go back to sleep, and let me take care of it for you.

I can't sleep now! Oh, it hurts, Merissa!

I know. I feel it too. But I can't fix it while you're in control.

Please, Merissa! Just make it stop!

Calm down, Stassia. I can't do anything. I've already tried. You have to let me take control so I can help us.

But, Merissa! I can't calm down! I don't understand what's happening. What do I do?

Let me have control.

No! You got us shot! I remember now. I'm not letting you drive now!

Stassia, be reasonable. You don't know what you're doing, and those people that hurt us might come back.

Don't try to fool me, Merissa. They're leaving the ship. I heard them.

And that would be even worse, sweetie. If you heard their plans, then you know that once they're away, they're going to destroy the ship we're on.

Oh.

It was a small sound that Stassia made, but suddenly, Merissa found that she could move again. Stassia was still there, watching instead of sleeping, which felt different to her, like someone peering over her shoulder, but she didn't have the time to worry about that now. She rolled over onto her knees, and the jolting pain nearly made her collapse again. She didn't have time to satisfy that urge, she knew. The decking where she had lain was smeared with red slime.

Smiley disconnected her helmet and dropped it. She crawled over to the medical kit she had spotted before and opened it up. She took a handful of melting pain tablets, and went to work while they took effect. Her armor came off easily, until she got to the torso shell. The clips at the shoulders wouldn't disengage until her fifth try, which included the use of a pry bar from a nearby tool bag.

She tried to be gentle about peeling it off, but it hurt anyway, and time was critical if she wanted to live through this. Even more important keeping the ship from being blown apart, she had to stop those Forresters from making off with whatever data they had gathered. Protecting the ship was the highest priority.

The front piece was disconnected now and laying in front of her, but the back piece was stuck on still. Warm blood trickled down her legs as she stood there. Time was critical in another way. That was too much blood flowing out of her for it to stop on its own, and a few more minutes of that would lead to her unconsciousness and then death. She put the pry bar over her left shoulder, took a deep breath, clenched her jaw, and shoved the bar backwards.

Merissa kept her jaw tight, but somehow Stassia managed to scream anyway.

"What was that?" a voice asked from somewhere to starboard.

"Quiet!" another voice insisted, and Smiley heard nothing else. She reached into the kit and pulled out the wound sealant, grabbed her gun, and ran to port as fast as she could manage.

* * * * *

Crap! Burton shouted in her mind. Her weapon had been hit worse than she'd thought. At least the power cell hadn't ruptured and taken her whole arm off.

Burton thought frantically. She had to do something to slow down or stop the Forrester or Aichele would be dead. The enemy was in full armor, and she knew it was a wasted effort, but she did the only thing she could think of.

She threw her rifle at the mountain of metal and polymers and popped her sidearm out of its slot. The rifle bounced harmlessly off the armored figure and landed a meter away. The man inside didn't even notice the impact, but he did notice the first shot from her blaster, which splashed glowing energy across his face shield.

While the shot was useless as an offense, it did accomplish two things. First, it caused the Forrester to stop and look for the new threat, and second, it bought Aichele a few moments to recover. Unfortunately, Aichele couldn't make his body respond. He exerted all his strength but couldn't raise his arm to the level. He dropped to his knees, unable to stand or defend Burton as the other's shot took her dead center in the chest. She was thrown back into the front of the same container where she had crashed before and she did not get up.

Aichele screamed in fury, and pressed a red button on his control board twice. A needle slipped into his right thigh and injected a double dose of adrenaline. Strength flooded into him, but he could see at once that it would be too late. The Forrester had heard him and was turning back to finish him off.

Aichele looked up at the man who would kill him and caught a brilliant flash of light reflecting off the armor he wore.

The Forrester turned in the direction of the light and said, "Holy–"

CHAPTER 72
17 October

Samuels set her jaw and advanced in a crouching walk to the still open hatch. She couldn't afford to focus exclusively there, though, and kept her eyes scanning left and right; and up as well, checking the catwalks of the upper engineering deck.

She approached the hatch obliquely, letting the open door shield her as she neared. She peered inside, saw nothing, then she jumped completely in, sweeping all around for targets. There were none.

She backed out, and slammed the hatch closed, keying the command for emergency lock into the controls. That avenue of approach secured, she did the same cautious duck walk back to hold nine. When she arrived she moved as quickly as she could, still watching her surroundings suspiciously.

She slung her gun across her back, then grabbed Morrison by the legs and dragged him onto the pallet. She tossed his carbine next to him, then thought better of it. She couldn't manage her gun one-handed while she steered the antigrav unit, it was too heavy for that, but Morrison's lighter weapon was a different matter. She made the switch, and powered up the platform, maneuvering it quickly through the containers that were spread all around the floor.

Bezates nearly shot her when she arrived, but he recognized her in time. Neither he nor Giannini commented on Morrison's state, through Crystal looked like she might be sick. Johnson didn't bother to check for a pulse, either.

"Ensign Omundson is still breathing, Lieutenant, but I have to get him into surgery right away. Calvi and Fields are both dead," the doctor reported evenly.

The news was accepted by her mind but she didn't really feel it. She knew she would later, but for now, her heart was isolated from the rest of her while her brain worked to finish the next step, and the next after that.

"Okay, Giannini, you drive; Bezates, cover the starboard flank. Let's move," she directed, exchanging weapons with the dead Morrison once again. When they arrived at the hatch to the forward section, she called them to a halt. Bezates stayed watchful while she consulted her portable data unit. All clear.

"Bezates, you lead. When you get to Medical, seal the hatch and you and Giannini stay on guard."

"Aye-aye, ma'am," the security man replied. No other words were exchanged, and then they were gone. Samuels turned back to locate the Marines. She checked her pad before she put it away, but it didn't have a view of where Aichele and Burton were. It did have a distant view of the ladder leading to the ventral dock, currently occupied by the Forrest attack shuttle. That view showed that two more Forrest Marines were coming out in suits of heavy armor.

Samuels put her data pad away. She had run out of swear words for today. Directing her gun in a sweeping motion, she advanced quickly toward where she knew she'd find Aichele and Burton. She needed to get a warning to them before reinforcements arrived for the other side.

An excruciating blue flash followed by a concussive sound shook the whole ship and knocked her from her feet. She feared it was already too late for a warning to do any good.

* * * * *

Smiley knew she was leaving a trail behind her. She needed to stop that, for multiple reasons. She was already starting to feel lethargic from the loss of blood. Adrenaline was making up for some of that, but it wouldn't last. It wouldn't be long before those familiar voices were on her trail, either.

She ducked into a narrow alcove formed by two massive machines and dropped to her knees. Pulling the cap off the bottle, she sprayed the contents as well as she could over her back. The numbing agent went to work at once, and the synthetic skin covered the area well enough that she could no longer detect any blood still flowing down her back. That was all she was going to be able to do for herself until she could get medical treatment, and that was going to have to wait.

She dropped the bottle and got back on her feet, pulling her weapon back up along with her. She was beginning to regret her choice now. The powerful gun had been nice to have for offensive reasons, but it was going to slow her down now that she was weakened and injured.

After a few dozen meters, she looked back and was pleased that she was no longer leaving a trace for the enemy to follow. Her immediate instinct now was to find a good vantage point and wait for them to come. She knew they would follow the trail of blood, and knowing where they would be made for a perfect ambush. She looked all around her and then headed to port as swiftly as she could move. She took one of the port ladders up to the overhead catwalks and then moved back to starboard.

Her progress now was not as rapid as she took time to be less noticeable. Within a minute or so, she could again see where she had treated her wounds; where the trail ended. They hadn't reached that point yet, so she continued moving, cautiously stalking her prey.

She made it all the way back to the central hub before she found them. One soldier was arguing with the technician who had been pulling data from the computers. Smiley couldn't make out what they were saying over the noise in Engineering, but whatever it was, they were both being insistent about it.

Finally, the soldier aimed his rifle at the other's head. The arguing ended abruptly.

There were seven of the technicians and just one soldier, but they all began moving in the direction he indicated, toward the center door leading forward to the boatbay. Smiley lined up the shot to take out the single armed man, who she now saw had corporal's stripes on his collar, but she waited instead of pulling the trigger.

Once she fired, the others would scatter, and she wouldn't be able to contain them. She didn't want any of them to slip away with the information they had. Besides that, if she had counted right the first time she had seen this group, there were three of them already missing somewhere.

She considered dropping back down to the main level to retrieve her damaged armor, which would have protected her from the front, but decided not to take the time and risk losing this group again. Instead she moved out on the catwalks, staying out of sight as much as possible, and taking quick looks from cover to stay in contact with the enemy. It wasn't hard to stay out of sight; they never looked up at all.

A few minutes brought them to the limits of the engineering area, and Smiley again had to decide whether or not to act at once or allow them to continue. The lack of a clean sight line made her decision for her. She knew that there was a large door used to move machinery into and out of Engineering on this level, just above the hatch whereby her quarry would be leaving. Once opened, it would give her a perfect sniper's nest, with a view of most of the boatbay and thick steel to provide cover.

She moved quickly to that spot and opened the sliding bay door a few centimeters. She had to disengage the motor and push it open manually in order to avoid giving away her position. It was a heavy door, and moving it even the short distance she had was difficult. Even worse, though, was that it reawakened the pain in her back which the numbing agent in the synthetic skin spray had masked. This needed to end shortly if she wanted to be around to see it finished.

Smiley stayed back in the shadows, but moved about to get a clear picture of everything visible before the Forresters came out. At the far end of the bay, a small group was gathered near the forward hatch. They were leaving, it seemed. Near the center, there were two Forresters in heavy armor just coming out of the entrance to the shuttle dock. She should be able to take them out from her current position without catching any return fire.

She finished her scan on the port side, and that's where she saw Burton hit hard and knocked backward into one of the crates. It happened too far away to be sure, but it could have been a fatal shot.

Aichele was in a tight spot as well, but his opponent was blocked from her view. She couldn't take him out directly, but maybe she could distract him and give Aichele a chance to fight back. But what could she do?

Her mind raced to find an answer. She heard the group she had been following emerge below her. One of the two armored Forresters had come to meet them and escort them to their escape vehicle. Either they hadn't tried to leave yet and didn't know the shuttle had been locked down, or else they knew and had found a way around the obstacle.

She had to stop the information from leaving the ship, she had to take out a fully armored Marine, and she needed to distract another one. When she saw that the short convoy of Forresters was about to pass a stack of Turin power cells, her thinking was done.

She put a shot into the fuel cell closest to her and the mixture of hydrogen and helium-3 exploded with the fury of a demon. For Smiley, it was like staring into a new sun, and she had no face shield to block the photons, nor armor to blunt the force of the shock wave.

CHAPTER 73
17 October

Aichele saw his opportunity and took it. There was a colossal boom on the heels of the light, great enough to momentarily throw the massive armored form off balance. Eric heaved to his feet and brought his weapons to bear. His left side screamed in agony, and he found that he could not raise the blast rifle in his left hand at all.

The Forrester recovered his balance all too quickly, and before Aichele could fire, his enemy's rifle swung into his and knocked it from his grip. Aichele used the force of the blow and added it to a spinning kick that connected with the other's wrist, disarming him as well.

Eric had no chance to use his right hand to take the gun from his left. The Forrester rained a barrage of blows on him that were more than he could block one handed. Hand to hand combat inside what was essentially a tank might seem pointless, but there was still a human being inside, and the added strength and speed a PUMA afforded you made it a viable option, if you knew what you were doing. The man he faced clearly did, but Eric would have been more than a match for him under normal conditions. It was obvious that Aichele was disabled on one side, and the other Marine was taking full advantage of that fact.

Without being able to block any of the incoming blows to his left, Eric tried angling his body to minimize the impacts. The fifth shot, though, connected solidly. Aichele screamed in pain as the battle steel deformed and pressed against his broken ribs. The boost granted him by the adrenaline was dissipating now and the agony overwhelmed him. He fell to his knees once again, struggling just to fill his lungs with air.

The Forrester could see that Aichele was through fighting, but he wanted Eric finished. He stepped back several paces and looked around him for one of the weapons that had been knocked loose in the brawl. He hoisted the first one he found and aimed it at Aichele's head. Eric didn't look up this time, barely aware of anything beyond his own suffering. The man pulled the trigger.

Nothing happened.

Confused, he held the weapon sideways to get a closer look.

Burton knelt groggily from her position near the container and, seeing the Forrest Marine standing over Aichele, snapped a shot in his general direction. Her shot hit the Marine's gun in the stock, igniting the exposed power pack and setting off the second such explosion in the boatbay; albeit considerably smaller than the massive one moments before.

Still, it was large enough to do the job. When Jill's vision cleared, the Forrester was down, a smoking crater near the center of the armor's chest plate. She wasted no more time on the dead man, but hurried to save Aichele. The blast had knocked him over onto his back, but there didn't appear to be any further damage to his armor from the explosion.

Burton knelt down next to him and peered into his face plate. She couldn't see through the scorching, so she tabbed it open and then did the same with her own. "Gunny, can you hear me?"

Eric tried to speak but coughed up frothy blood instead. Burton reached under his arms and pushed left-right-left in the emergency unseal sequence. The seams on the right popped in response, but the ones on the left barely moved, and she had to pry them apart with her metal fingers. Once the chest plate was folded down, she gently extracted Aichele, cradled him in one arm and raced for Medical.

* * * * *

Samuels picked herself up and struggled to her feet. The extra weight of her protective gear and weapon, when added to her having been blasted to the ground, made it a slow process. She'd managed to keep hold of her gun, so she didn't need to track that down.

What she *did* need to track down were answers to what had happened, and what she should do about it. Monica pulled the data unit out from its sleeve and started looking through the video logs.

Within a minute, it was clear what had exploded, and where the shot had come from that caused it. A different log would have shown who had fired, but she knew who it must have been without looking. Instead, she shifted to a view of Aichele, just in time to see Burton take out his opponent. Gunny appeared to be in good hands, though critically injured. She hoped he would make it, but she couldn't spare him any more of her thoughts.

Returning to the view of the aft end of the bay, she pushed the timestamp back and froze the image. She couldn't see what she wanted to learn, so she switched feeds again, this time to one that had ended abruptly. This had a clean shot of the area just before the blast had occurred. A heavily armored foe had been adjacent to the Turin cells when they went up. The entire group of Forrester techs were close enough that she didn't see how any of them could have survived either.

Blast that woman! Here Monica had been, trying to keep Aichele from killing Sullivan without giving her the chance to answer for herself, and yet she goes and takes out seven unarmed civilians without giving them the same opportunity.

And no 'collateral damage' defense was going to hold water. Sullivan had already demonstrated the ability to hit exactly what she aimed at, as Aichele had pointed out. Had the woman been sniping at the armored Marine, Samuels would have had no problem with what she'd done, but this was not right!

When she caught up to her, she was going to—

"Lay your weapon on the floor and kick it over here," a deep voice said. "Don't try anything," the voice continued, in response to Samuels' tensing up.

Samuels turned slowly toward the man, then did as he directed, ending with her hands above her shoulders and away from her body.

Stupid girl! Her combat instructors would be ashamed of her now. One of the first rules of any engagement was never to lose track of an enemy. She had seen two armored figures coming out of the shuttle dock, and she had seen one killed in the explosion. Doing the math too late was no comfort.

Captain Kerritt picked the gun up from the floor and held it in his left hand. "All right, Lieutenant. Now order whoever you've got in that sniper's nest to throw down his weapon and come out."

Kerritt must have seen where the shot had come from. He was carefully keeping a shipping container between him and the 'sniper's nest.' Samuels thought about telling him that she hadn't sent anyone up there, that she wasn't sure whoever was up there would take orders from her, even thought of saying a few things that weren't true, but she knew he would never believe any of it.

She walked out to where both Kerritt and Sullivan could see her.

"Sullivan," she yelled upward, "Kerritt here would like you to throw down your weapon and come out."

"That's right, Sullivan," Kerritt shouted, without leaving his cover. "Ten seconds, and then I put a hole in the lieutenant, here."

Samuels looked around her, but there was no cover within three of four running steps, not near enough to reach before Kerritt shot her. She'd risk it, of course, when the countdown reached about one, and she didn't have a choice left.

If Aichele was right, Sullivan would probably let her get shot. There was only one Forrester left, unless there were still more hiding on the shuttle, and with Samuels dead and Burton and Aichele injured, that one was all that stood in the way of Sullivan having complete control of *Pathfinder*.

"Five seconds, Sullivan," Kerritt reminded her. "Fo—" was as far as he got before a light touched him, flowed into his armor, and made an explosive fountain on the other side of him.

"Are you all right, Lieutenant," Sullivan asked, walking over and pointing her PF-93 in the other direction. A PF-93! She must have had the flaming thing powered *down* earlier. How could she even carry that without power assisted armor? The weapon was far thicker than any of the woman's limbs.

Samuels kept her hands in the air. Now *she* was the only one in Sullivan's way. "Fine, thanks. And you?"

"I got shot in the back. It stings like I've been whipped, thanks for asking…Why are your hands in the air?"

"Because you still have a gun, and I assumed I would be your next logical target, since I don't have a weapon at the moment." Monica said the words calmly and levelly, but inside she was as scared as she had ever been. It was even worse than hiding from the pirates on her family's ship.

"What? Whatever gave you that idea? I'm not going to shoot you. I take orders from you."

Samuels dropped her hands. "Orders like, 'stay here in the Omega Room and monitor communications?' Those sorts of orders?"

"Well, you have to admit, you *did* need my help out here."

"Maybe so. No, yes, we did need your help, but that's not the issue. Who are you really, and who do you work for?" Samuels demanded.

Sullivan tried smiling, but she could see that Samuels wasn't joking. "My name is Amber Sullivan, Specialist 2, Warner Space Navy, a division of Warner Gateway Interstellar."

"Care to try again, 'Amber?' And how the blazes can you carry that gun? It must weigh almost as much as you do!"

"It is heavy, but it's not that bad for someone raised on Abernathy. I had almost half again Earth-normal gravity until I was sixteen, which does good things for developing muscles," Sullivan said.

Samuels folded her arms across her chest. "Except that during our trip out to *Pathfinder*, you told me you grew up on Idyll."

"I did?" She had no recollection of talking to Samuels about her youth.

"Who are you, really?" Samuels pressed.

Merissa almost raised her gun again. Her orders were to stay covert, no matter what. She'd blundered into letting Samuels have doubts because part of her memory was missing. Her first reaction was to lock Samuels up, or remove her somehow, to keep her secret hidden.

But she also needed to keep this ship in Warner hands, and to do that, *Pathfinder* needed an officer. Of the three on the ship, one was a thief and a murderer, one was in medbay and couldn't take command anytime soon, and the last was as curious as a cat.

Smiley sighed and left her gun aimed at the floor. "I'm afraid I am not at liberty to answer that question at this time, ma'am."

The abrupt formality made Samuels feel that she was getting somewhere, but the brick wall Sullivan was hiding all the answers behind made her want to reach out and strangle her. Probably not a good idea, since Amber was the one with the gun. But, how to know if she could trust her?

"Are you working for the DaGamans?"

The question surprised Smiley. Hadn't she just been helping them rid the ship of intruders? "No," she responded.

"Who are you working for then?"

That was another tricky question, but maybe a general answer would suffice. "I am a Warner citizen," Smiley said simply.

"What if I said I didn't believe you? Where would that leave us?"

"*Do* you believe me?"

"I'd like to, but…no, I don't think I do."

Smiley sighed again and came to a decision. "All right, how about this? First, we need to secure that assault shuttle and make sure there aren't any more surprises," Sullivan began. "After that, assuming we both survive, I will turn myself over to your custody and answer any question you want to ask. Will that satisfy you?"

"No," Samuels said bluntly. "I don't just want answers, I want truthful answers."

"My word on it," Smiley grinned.

CHAPTER 24
18 October

Samuels sat in the command chair on the still and now silent bridge of *Pathfinder*, once again a Warner Naval Ship, and thought about Amber Sullivan, aka Merissa Smiley.

They had found the Forrest shuttle to be empty, and as promised, the woman had explained everything she knew about her current mission, and then sworn her to secrecy. If it were all true, it filled in many of the missing pieces to Samuels' puzzles. For one, Smiley knew what had become of Lamont.

As part of her investigation into the deaths of Capt. Vanderjagt and Lt. Sepulveda, the agent had found evidence leading her to Lt. Lamont. When she had confronted him, he had attacked her. She had suffered a head injury, but managed to lock him inside one of the life pods. She had discovered what he, Teach, and Leung were planning, and was headed to warn Chowdhury, when she had passed out from the blow she had taken to her head. She had awakened while being dragged to the boatbay, and for several weeks, she had had difficulty remembering details of the time surrounding her injury.

What was more, Smiley worked for the Warner Internal Counter-Intelligence Unit, the group you heard all sorts of rumors and conspiracy theories about, but few, if any, facts. They were supposedly always watching but never seen. The saying you always heard was, "You won't see us, but WICIU."

She had no proof that she could offer, of course. Undercover agents didn't carry anything to identify them as anyone but their cover identity. But, again, it would explain the level of her combat skill, and how she was aware of the Omega Room's existence.

Tentatively, Samuels had agreed to accept her explanation until and unless evidence arose that contradicted it. Not that she expected she would find any such thing. Not that she would have time to look for any such thing. She had left Smiley, after getting new clothes and seeing to her wound, to help guard the galley while she started on the thousand and one details she needed to take care of now.

The ship was secure in friendly hands, Omundson, Burton, and Aichele were in medbay to have their injuries treated, and it was time for her to seal the bridge and move onto the next step, figuring out how to get back to the Antoc system and collect her rightful commanding officer, Captain Brighton.

In order to do that, Samuels needed the jump engines functioning and accurate data coming from the Astrocomp. Even more, she was going to need to get the ship running before a report to the planet was overdue and those destroyers came to investigate.

In order to do that, everyone that was currently on the ship was going to have to pitch in and work as if their lives depended on it, which they did.

In order to do that, she was going to have to offer the crew something to convince them to side with her, probably amnesty. Could she do that? Maybe an offer to testify in their defense would be sufficient. She hoped so, for all their sakes. What about Leung? Would she surrender to the reality that Samuels held the ship? Was she even still alive?

She sat down in the command chair, an awkward feat with the unpowered armor she still had on, and brought up the main command system. She had to disconnect the gloves and fold them back to lock onto the forearms to be able to type in commands. Voice recognition wouldn't help, because then the system would know she was impersonating Captain Brighton.

Her first step was to unlock all the piracy protocols, plus the extra measures Captain had added. Brighton's codes were all that was needed to permanently deactivate the locks. Next, she moved the system into a different mode. When she had the change of command screen up, she entered in Brighton's codes, transferred command to her name, and entered her new captain's codes.

It seemed odd to do so, and something of a betrayal of Captain to take his placc in the ship's logs, as if she were giving up hope of him returning to resume command. She'd waffled back and forth about taking that action, but finally decided that it was what the regulations specified, and therefore, what Captain Brighton would expect of her. That necessary step done, she moved to the hatch and began entering her code to open the door.

Samuels stopped with her finger on the last key. Out of the air came the voice of Captain Leung. Lt. Commander Leung, now, she corrected herself.

"Attention, Forrest personnel. This is Captain Leung speaking. You have attempted to seize this ship in violation of our agreement. As of this moment, I have control of the ship's scuttling charges, and I will use them if you do not immediately lay down your weapons and report to the boat bay. If you do as I say and turn over all your weapons, I will allow you to exit the ship with your lives. You have five minutes to comply."

"That...idiot!" Samuels exploded. Why couldn't she just fade into the woodwork and let her get busy saving them all? Why, for once, couldn't the universe stop rearranging itself between the time she made her plans and had the chance to implement them? Just once, was that too much to ask?

Apparently so.

Monica took a deep breath and tried to get her mind to engage on this new problem. Okay, first step, deactivate the scuttling charges and lock Leung out of their control. Piece of cake.

She retraced her steps and sat at the center console. Once there, she brought up the appropriate system. When she entered the command to disable them, though, she found that the central computer was no longer connected to the controls for the charges. That was bad, and her deadline was coming closer.

Okay. Leung must have taken local control of the charges. Where could she do that? Anywhere the control lines ran. And Leung would know where every single one of them was.

So how could she figure out where the woman was hiding? And in the next four minutes? Ah, communications logs. Samuels pulled those up and checked the last entry. AlHnds—AuxCon.

She was in auxiliary control, the backup bridge.

Samuels raced to the door, keyed it open, and sprinted aft. She thought about grabbing Smiley for backup, but decided not to. For one thing, she didn't have time to stop anywhere, and for another thing, Smiley's responses to threats against the ship tended to be lethal. If it would be possible to keep Leung around to help repair the ship, she would take that option.

It looked like it was just Samuels, and time was ticking away from her. She continued her mad dash toward the engineering area. through the hatch and into the boatbay. Around the containers, trying to ignore the images of dead comrades and soldiers around her.

It had been a busy day, and she was completely winded before she had crossed into Engineering. The added weight of the protective armor wasn't helping, either. Once in the engineering section, she dropped down a level, unslung her blast rifle as she ran, and pulled up short outside the hatch. She greedily sucked in two deep breaths, then entered her override code into the keypad.

Leung was turning at the noise of the opening door while Samuels strode in with her rifle sights centered on Leung's head. "Ma'am, you need to step away from those controls, right now."

"Samuels? What are you doing here? And no, I can't do that. We have to keep this ship out of Forrest's hands. Either they leave and we take the ship back to Earth, or I blow it up. If you try to stop me, I'll detonate it now."

"There's no need for this, ma'am. All of the Forresters are neutralized."

"All of them?" she asked in confusion, her resolution wavering a bit.

"Yes. Now put down the gun, surrender peacefully, and we'll get the ship back to Warner."

"All right," she said. She set her weapon on the console and began disabling the charges. Samuels was surprised that there was no argument, but perhaps, after she had steeled herself to commit suicide, the reprieve had left her numb.

"I never wanted any of this," Leung said. "Teach forced me to go along."

"Why didn't you turn the ship around after Teach died, then?" Samuels left out the fact that she knew exactly who was responsible for that death. She didn't trust her enough to lay all her cards on the table yet.

"Because of Lamont! I had to stick to the old plan until I could find Lamont in order to be safe. Lamont and Teach were working together, and I had to be sure I had him contained before I could take on the rest of the crew."

"What about Aichele?"

"I thought he was working with Lamont when he tried to break into my quarters."

"What are you planning to do now?" Samuels asked after a thoughtful pause.

"We have to jump back to Antoc and collect Brighton, then get back to Earth and report all this."

That was exactly the answer Samuels was hoping for. If Leung and Samuels were after the same thing, Samuels could let her remain in command, and all of these heavy decisions would belong to someone else. Leung could figure out how to finish fixing the ship before Forrest came back to retake it. She had the experience to do it right. Brighton would understand that, when that day of reckoning arrived and she had to account to him all that she had done in his name.

Right?

The answer crystallized deep in her soul, and it galvanized her to the action she had to take.

She tightened her grip on the rifle she had never lowered and made sure it was steady. "Ma'am, I certainly understand your reasoning, and I hope that this matter can be cleared up. But under Article IX of the Warner Naval Code, I am required to relieve you of command until and unless your actions and loyalties can be vetted by a military court. Please step away from the controls and the weapon and precede me back to Security."

Leung was shocked at this turn, and thought furiously to find a way out. She was sure she had convinced the naïve girl of her innocence, exactly as she had planned. What could she do now? Her pistol was only a step away, lying on the surface of the control board. Samuels could be counted on to hesitate before firing at a live human being, since she was just a kid who'd never even had to contemplate killing someone. Was it enough time, though?

The armor was worrisome, until Leung saw that the face shield was locked up and out of the way of their conversation. That gave Leung a perfect target, easily hit from the short distance between them. Still, the sudden motion needed to make the shot might panic the girl into firing without thought, and Samuels' weapon was already aimed and at the ready.

"I don't understand," Leung said, stalling for time. Samuels advanced, but moved to one side to allow Leung a path to the hatch.

"We need to get to the security bay to get this sorted out. Please move in that direction, ma'am."

"What are you talking about, Lieutenant? I need to get to the bridge and take control."

"No, ma'am. I have control of the ship and I'm not going to turn it over to you until you are cleared by Security."

"That's ridiculous," Leung said. The demands of the girl had steeled Leung to act. There was no way she could allow herself to be taken into custody, or to stand trial. As quickly as she could move, she reached for her dropped pistol. "I'm going to the bridge. If you want me in Security, you'll have to drag--" Her voice cut off as Samuels' rifle butt connected with the side of her head, just as her hand was closing on her pistol.

"Aye-aye, ma'am."

CHAPTER 25
17 October

Monica Samuels, Acting Captain of WNS *Pathfinder*, stepped over the motionless form of the ship's former commander and collected the gun from the control board, where it had proved such a temptation for the other woman. She dropped the weapon into a cargo compartment in the left leg of her armor, then tried to think of what to do next, now that the immediate situation was resolved.

Well, *this* immediate situation was resolved...temporarily, she admitted to herself. Leung would not stay unconscious forever.

Then there was still a flotilla of destroyers out there, ready to take *Pathfinder* back with little or no difficulty, once the ship's status became known. There were all the things on the ship which were still not functional, keeping them from escaping. There was *Vanguard*, Captain Brighton, and all the other officers and crew that were depending on them for rescue.

To balance all those pressing needs, there were only five people she could count on to help her, including herself. It wasn't enough, she knew.

Monica took a deep breath and sat on the floor with her back against the control board. She held it in for a long moment, and then let it squeeze out of her loudly. She undid her helmet and shook out her hair, which had matted to her scalp with the exertions of her long day, then gathered it back into its accustomed ponytail.

For a moment, she welcomed the immobility and chance to collect her thoughts. Too much had happened too quickly for her of late, and none of her planning had taken her beyond this point. To be honest,

Samuels hadn't expected to make it this far. Rather, the young officer believed that she'd wind up dead, but knew she'd had to try anyway.

So far, so good, she thought. She was still breathing at least. She hoped to keep it that way for as long as possible.

Back to business, then, Monica. Where do you want to get to?

Antoc. She needed to get back to Antoc A-3 as fast as she could, to rescue Captain Brighton and the others stranded with him. But to get there, she needed the jump engines working and reliable astrogation data. Did she already have that? *Pathfinder* had jumped into Worth. Shouldn't they be ready to jump again? Depends on how much the Forresters have torn things apart to study the system. *Probably not,* she decided, *but it shouldn't take too much to put things back together.*

I think.

She kicked Leung in the hip, though not hard enough to cause any damage. She wished that Leung had given in and accepted Samuels' authority, because she was the only one left that really understood the engines as a whole. Although, Samuel wouldn't have been able to trust her anyway. Monica had not forgotten that Teach's death was caused by the woman.

What about data? Originally, she had thought that would be the easiest to fix; simply a matter of turning the worm off. However, the worm had been corrupting the astrogation data files for a while now. What if some of it was unrecoverable? Hopefully, Brighton's codes would be enough to unlock the old system, and there would be a backup copy of the data stored somewhere she could get to.

So that was doable, almost certainly. And putting the jump engines back together was possible too, just time-consuming. The regular engines would also need to be functional, in order to reach the minimum transit velocity. With all the things torn apart to be mapped and studied, Samuels was not sure what state they were in at the moment. But again, it was reparable—given enough time.

What sort of manpower could she throw at the work? If she assigned Aichele and Burton to guard all the prisoners—

Wait, *could* she? Both of them were injured in the fighting, and she didn't know exactly how badly. Aichele had not been in good condition before the fighting, and Samuels' last image of him was being carried off the field by Burton. They were both in medbay at that moment, having their wounds tended to. So, at least for now, that left herself, Sullivan, and Dr. Johnson—who knew nothing at all about ship's systems and repair.

Really, there was only herself and Sullivan, and, since there were more prisoners than would fit in the brig's lockdown, one of them would have to be on guard duty at all times. When the two Marines were recovered, they could take over that duty, but that would take time.

Time, time, time! There was nothing beyond their ability to arrange, but there was nowhere near the time available that they would need! Damnation!

Well, what if she came at the problem from the other angle? How much time would she have? She didn't know what Kerritt's reporting schedule had been. He might be overdue already, and the Forrest destroyers could be sending Marines to retake the ship right that instant. She was sure that Governor Solomon or the Marines' commanding officer would expect to hear at least every day. So, if a report was made just before any trouble started, then another report would be due in…seventeen hours.

That was the maximum time she could expect before they were discovered. It was impossible. There was simply too much to get done for one or two people to manage it that quickly.

Monica sprang to her feet and again kicked Leung, a great wallop to the ribs.

"This is your fault!" she screamed, "you and that greedy ogre, Teach! Why don't you join him in hell!" She pulled the pistol back out and aimed it at the woman's head.

Stop it, Monica. That's murder! Some piece of her whispered. But it wouldn't be. Leung was a traitor and a murderer, and Monica was in possession of proof. Samuels was the rightful captain of a WNS ship. As such, it was within her power to execute Leung for either of those offenses. And she wanted to, oh, how she wanted to. The grief and pain this woman had caused surely warranted her death.

The fact that Monica had never killed anyone like this held her back; not intentionally. With as inaccurate as her cobbled together weapon was, she might have killed the guard when trying to break Aichele out of the brig. She certainly had killed the soldier in the boatbay, and the two men standing behind him; but he was armed, and the others had been in the wrong place at the wrong time. A cold execution was very different to her.

Still, she was the enemy; of that Monica was certain. Leung deserved to die; of that, too, Monica was certain.

The thought that stopped her, though, and had her putting the gun away, was that Leung was the only one on the ship that was really qualified to put *Pathfinder* back together. If she gave in to what she wanted to do, it would make all that knowledge forever inaccessible.

If she wanted to use her, though, she would have to get Leung to cooperate, which wasn't likely. Once Forrest came back and took over the ship, Leung would be back in the pilot's seat, mapping out the ship's secrets and collecting her blood money.

Or would she? Samuels paused to consider, then began pacing among the control stations as she thought.

Leung had been about to destroy the ship rather than give her to Forrest. There was no way Forrest would be paying her now, and Leung had to know that bridge was burned. From her view, then, what options were left? Get out of the system before Forrest caught her, that's what. And it just so happened that exactly coincided with what Samuels needed.

In fact, everyone onboard was in the same position. If Forrest came back, they would be unlikely to leave anyone alive, except their own scientists and technicians. Would that be enough to convince them to throw in with her and work together to get the ship working? Was there anything else she could offer? She didn't have money. She couldn't offer amnesty, could she? The captain of a Warner ship had quite a bit of latitude in dealing with crimes committed on her ship. In most cases, captains could execute judgment themselves, without turning the matter over to a military court. Treason was a serious crime, though, and there was enough proof of that to convict at least the ringleaders, and probably everyone who had signed up before the takeover. She was sure she couldn't simply drop the charges in exchange for their help now.

It was a gray enough area that she might be able to offer the *chance* of amnesty. Perhaps that would suffice.

What else?

She needed them united. And she needed them to accept that she was in charge. How was she supposed to manage that?

The question made her think immediately of her father. He moved from ship to ship every few months, and each time he worked with a crew he was unfamiliar with, he made sure that each understood that he was "the boss" for that run. How had he done it? Usually, the fact that he was a company officer was enough, but occasionally he'd needed more than that. There was that time they'd boarded the

Coromandel. Her dad had known going into it that there was likely to be some resentment and insubordination there, so he had come prepared. Boy, did he knock their socks off right from the start.

She stopped her pacing back where she had started and looked down at Leung. Monica decided that's what she needed to do. She needed some sort of display to demonstrate her authority.

Monica used her boot to roll Leung over onto her stomach, grabbed hold of the woman's belt and hefted. Hngh. She was heavier than Monica had expected such a short woman to be.

Samuels dropped her unceremoniously and went aft to collect a null-g pallet jack.

* * * * *

Jill's vision slowly refocused itself and she could see Dr. Johnson leaning over her.

"Welcome back," Johnson said, followed by, "Don't move." Contrary to orders, Burton turned her head to look at the carnage of her right shoulder.

"I said, don't move. Neck muscles connect to the collar bone, and I'm trying to keep them that way."

"Sorry. I had to see for myself, though. Okay to turn back?"

"Wait," she directed, sealed off whatever she was working on, and then held both hands above and away from her patient. "Go ahead."

Burton turned away and spent the next few moments trying not to vomit. She'd seen her share of wounds in her time, but none of them had been on *her* body, and the sight of someone else's fingers poking around under her skin and slimy with her own blood was almost more than she was able to handle.

When her brain was able to stray outside of gastronomical control, she asked, "How come I'm not out?"

"You were bleeding out, and I didn't have time for a general anesthetic to take effect. I had to start before the local had much chance to take hold. Fortunately, you passed out."

"Fortunately," Burton repeated. She kept her eyes fixed on the ceiling after that, but the sounds of wet bits of something being tossed in a basin made it hard not to think the worst of what was happening.

"What about Aichele?" Burton asked.

"You don't remember?"

"No."

"Hmm. Not surprising, I suppose. I was giving you a report on him when you passed out. I hadn't realized how badly you were injured when you came in, because you were still inside that walking tank." Johnson fell silent again as she concentrated on her work.

"So, what about Aichele?" Jill prompted again.

"Hmm? Oh, yes. Aichele. He's going to be awhile in recovering, but he'll pull through. He had a punctured lung and eight broken ribs. I stopped the internal bleeding, reinflated the lung and then knocked him out for a while. He's in your old bed right now, and when I'm done with you and Omundson, I'll go back and set the ribs."

Burton took a while to process this information, then ventured, "What's my prognosis this time, doctor?"

The doctor kept right on working, and was a long time responding. Finally, she said, "Not as good, Jill. I'm afraid there's no chance you'll get full strength or range of motion back, even when you see a specialist on Gateway. Likely, you won't have more than 40% of either one until then. After the specialists look at you, well, it's hard to say, but what I'm doing to keep you alive is going to make it impossible for them to heal you completely. I'm sorry. Can you feel that?"

"No." She felt the weight of her future crumbling onto her, but nothing in her shoulder.

"That?"

"No."

"Hmm. We'll try it again when the local is all the way out of your system. Just let me seal this…no, don't turn to look. Don't move at all, if you can help it."

"For how long?"

"I'd tell you a month, if I thought you'd listen. Just give me a minute."

Jill kept motionless until the doctor was done. After cleaning things up, Johnson slid Burton's right arm into a sleeve, then magnetically locked it to her side. "That should keep you out of trouble for a while," the surgeon noted.

"Now, normally I would leave you immobile for the next few days, but I need you out of O. R. as soon as you can move. Do you think you can sit up? The blood loss has been replaced."

"I'm not sure. Help me up?" Doctor Johnson was quick to comply, and after several minutes and the doctor doing most of the work, Burton was able to lie down on a cot set up in the medical suite's hallway.

Johnson immediately went into the recovery room and wheeled a gurney past Burton and into the operating room. The gurney contained

Ensign Omundson, lying on his stomach, his uniform charred and peeled away from a blast burn in the center of his back. The wound was severe, and it was a wonder to Jill that the man was alive at all.

Looking down at herself, she wished she had asked Johnson for a blanket. It wasn't that she was cold, she just wasn't dressed.

You couldn't wear a uniform inside powered armor; the pressurized interior would turn any wrinkle into a wound. So she and Eric were wearing a special sort of black conductive material to interface with the armor which fit like a second skin; and looked like it. Burton had learned to get over her modesty issues long years back whenever her duty demanded it of her. But that was always around other Marines. She didn't feel the same way then, a meter from the door leading out of the medical suite, where anyone walking by could get an eyeful. There was nothing she could do about it without getting up, and she was sure Johnson would come out to yell at her if she did. Omundson needed Johnson's attention more than Jill did, so she stayed put.

And staying immobile left her with lots of time to think. Thinking led to evaluating her current state, which led to feeling sorry for herself.

She had already been planning retirement from the Marines at the end of this assignment, but retirement to do something else on Earth, with Diego, her husband. What was she fit to do now? Desk work was really not her thing. She could deal with it easily, in small doses. But all day? Every day? Not her.

Her thoughts strayed to the plans they'd had. They would have to change certainly, but they would figure things out. It wasn't the end of the world; not even the end of her arm and shoulder. She could still use it, just not as much as before.

She tried to convince herself, but it didn't cheer her at all.

The local anesthetic was wearing off, adding to her foul mood. In an effort to avoid thinking about herself, she began to consider the current tactical situation, which made her feel just about as low as it was possible to be.

If the ship didn't get moving soon, reinforcements would be dispatched, and then how to deal with the pain in her arm and shoulder, and what to do after retirement would become moot questions.

She needed to get up and help, she decided, and tried to do something about it. Sitting up was awkward, with one arm immobilized, and each motion causing an echoing throb of pain in her shoulder. She managed to sit up, turn sideways and drape her legs over the side of the cot. The effort made her start to sweat, more from the pain than anything. The world spun for a few seconds, and Jill feared she would pitch off the cot face first. She leaned back against the wall and waited until the sensation of motion left her.

Her first item of business was going to have to be finding something to put on. She thought she knew where the doctor kept surgical scrubs, but it would mean getting up and walking to the supply room. Burton wasn't sure she could manage it yet.

As she sat there a figure dressed in unpowered armor strode past with an unconscious Leung draped over one shoulder.

Something was going on, and Jill moved to grab some clothes and follow. The internal call to her duty had overridden any complaints her body had lodged.

"Where do you think you are going?" Johnson's voice brought her up short as she came back out of the supply room.

Burton turned to answer. The Marine was ten centimeters taller than the medical officer, and outmassed her by a good twenty kilos. Still, Burton felt as if she'd been caught stealing cookies by her mother. She fought against the feeling before she answered.

"I am going to get back to work, ma'am," she said.

"Oh, no. You get back on that bunk right now."

"No, ma'am." The answer shocked Johnson, and left her speechless long enough for Burton to continue. "Look, Doctor, I am the first to admit that staying immobile for the next month is probably the best thing for me; would give my shoulder the best chance to heal. But *Pathfinder* is in a precarious spot. If we don't get her out of this system right away, these halls are going to be full of vengeful Forrest Marines and all of us will be dead. Given those options, I'll trade in my recovery time for whatever I can do to help."

The doctor seemed to deflate all at once, and she waved the soldier off to finish what she'd been doing.

"Besides, Doctor," Burton continued, "You've got a patient in there who needs you more than I do."

"No, Jill. Stuart doesn't need anything anymore."

* * * * *

Monica Samuels marched into the galley and roughly shouldered Amber Sullivan out of her way. She hadn't wanted to, Amber was just fulfilling her assignment by blocking the exit and watching her prisoners within, but Samuels had to get Leung off of her before anyone noticed how much effort it was taking to put one foot in front of the other.

As it happened, the unannounced shove added to the aura of command she was trying to convey. Monica strode into the large room in her battle gear, exactly as if she owned it, bounced an obstacle out of her way, walked to the nearest table, and dropped an inert Leung onto it like a sack of potatoes.

Every set of eyes in the room was fixed on her, and most were widened in shock.

Samuels didn't wait for them to regain any of their lost equilibrium, but started speaking immediately. "Let's get one thing clear right now, people: I am in command of this ship."

The eyes looking back at her grew, if it were possible, even wider.

The newly minted captain considered asking if anyone wanted to challenge that, then decided she didn't really want to know. Instead, she confidently met each person's gaze and looked for any sign of defiance. There was none.

"Good," she continued. "Now let's get down to business. Here's where we stand: There are no Forresters on this ship that are not either dead or locked up. As soon as those Forresters fail to report in, someone is going to come to find out why; probably several heavily-armed someones. *Pathfinder* is not in any condition to escape the system. The plan to sell the ship is not viable now, if it ever was. Clearly, they had no intention of paying anyone. So, where does that leave us? The only place we can take this ship is back to Warner.

"Each of you has exactly two options. You can get locked up in the brig as mutineers or you can help me get *Pathfinder* moving again. If you opt for the brig, before too long a Forrest Marine will be along to execute you. If you help me, I will do everything in my power as captain of this ship to dismiss the charges against you. Chances are, the Navy is not going to want any of this secret ship being discussed in a public court. If they have *Pathfinder* back, I think they'll let me drop the matter entirely.

"Are there any questions before I ask you to choose?"

The group's attention drifted for a moment, and Samuels turned to see Sergeant Burton arrive dressed in her combat fatigues and carrying an assault carbine over her left shoulder. When she saw Monica notice her, the Marine came to attention and saluted left handed. Her right arm was locked to her side. Samuels returned it, and all eyes turned back to her. Dr. Johnson hovered behind Jill, expecting her to collapse at any moment.

"Ma'am," Danis said, "about Captain Leung, is she...you know..." He couldn't quite bring himself to finish.

"I'm not dead yet," came a voice from behind Samuels. Leung raised only her head then and said, "Could you help me up, Captain?"

Samuels turned to extend an arm to the older woman, at the same time wondering what she was playing at. Samuels had brought the woman as an object lesson, but she hadn't considered the impact if Leung woke up before the end. What could she do? She momentarily regretted letting the traitor live, but it was too late to change her position on that.

Leung sat up on the edge of the table, but did not attempt to go any further. She leaned forward and rubbed her temples with her thumbs.

"Captain Samuels is exactly right in everything she said," Leung continued. Samuels barely noticed the murmured reaction while she fought to keep her jaw from dropping. "We were just discussing it when I was ambushed and she came to my rescue. You see, the only place we can go now is back to Earth, to turn the ship over to Warner. If we do that, it can't be with me as the captain, since I was part of the theft. The only way it will work is if Lt. Samuels takes command.

"I urge you to decide to support her, as I am. We need all hands if we're going to make our way out of this system."

Samuels couldn't believe it. How hard *had* she hit Leung in the head? Where did that story come from? Ambushed? Rescued? That devious woman was definitely up to something.

The others didn't bat an eye at the falsehoods, though. Danis was the first to say "I'm in," but everyone else in the room followed suit within a few seconds. They all *looked* sincere. She hoped they were, because she didn't have the time or attention to spare to make sure they pitched in.

Suddenly, the enormity of what had just happened sunk in. Yes, Samuels was acknowledged as the captain, but the crew might not be following her at all. Leung had stolen Samuel's thunder, and suddenly, Samuels was the captain not because they had accepted her authority, but because Leung said so.

Monica wanted to scream in frustration, but held it all in beneath an impassive mask. Why couldn't the woman stop meddling?

She'd have to figure out what to do about that later, though. Immediate threats took priority.

"All right, then. Commander Leung will take charge of engine repair. The rest of you will receive assignments from her. Sergeant Burton will oversee our prisoners. I will see to getting the bridge working properly myself. We've got, at most, a few hours to get this done; certainly not more than a day. Let's all get to it, then," Monica finished, by way of dismissal.

The younger woman hated giving the viper any freedom or authority at all, but what choice did she have? Their best chance of escape lay with the most competent engineer putting the ship back together. She would have to assign Sullivan and Aichele to keep a close eye on her.

Samuels realized then that Aichele was not there among the group. She quickly moved to where the doctor and Burton still stood. "Doctor, could I get your report now? Is Gunny Aichele all right?" Samuels asked.

"I expect he'll be fine, though I haven't had a chance to finish treating him yet. His ribs are immobilized, the internal bleeding is stopped, and he's sedated. And that's about all the good news I have," Johnson sighed.

"Omundson, Calvi, Fields, Morrison, and Biltcliffe are all casualties. Giannini received a gash on her left arm that will make it difficult to use for the next few days. Aichele was close to death when Burton brought him in. And Jill almost died, again. I kept her from bleeding out, but the damage to her shoulder is severe. She probably won't be able to use it at all for a week, and then it will be limited in range of motion."

Burton looked uncomfortable in having her condition discussed in front of her, but she didn't try to interfere.

"Will you be okay with the assignment I gave you?" Samuels asked.

"Yes, ma'am." Jill responded at once. Amber Sullivan had walked over to join the discussion. Jill eyed her warily, but said nothing.

"Good. Then would you pass along orders for Aichele when he's back on his feet?" At the Marine's nod, Samuels continued, "Tell him that he and Sullivan are to watch Commander Leung at all times for any signs of trouble."

"Are you expecting some?" Burton asked.

"I know that her best move is to get *Pathfinder* out of the system and look for leniency in the courts, but somehow I suspect she's going to look for another option. We have a lot of work to do, and not much time to do it, so I need her skills, at least for the moment."

Samuels turned her gaze toward the topic of discussion, who was just leaving the room with Giannini and De Saumserez. The others turned to watch her as well, but there was nothing out of the ordinary to see.

"But I do not trust that woman. She would kill us all, if it got her what she wanted."

"Yes, ma'am. But that is a problem for another day." Burton responded.

"You're right, Sergeant, let's get this ship moving."

Hey, Reader.

So, you got to the end of our book. We hope that means you enjoyed it. Whether or not you did, we would just like to thank you for giving us your valuable time to let us try to entertain you. We are truly blessed to have such a fulfilling occupation, but we only have that job because of people like you; people kind enough to give our books a chance and to spend their hard-earned money buying them. For that we are eternally grateful.

If you would like to find out more about our other books, then please visit our website for full details. You can find it at:

www.7csbooks.com.
Also feel free to contact us on Facebook, Twitter, Goodreads, or email (all of the details are available on the website), as we would love to hear from you.

If you enjoyed this book and would like to help, then you could think about leaving a review on Amazon, Goodreads, or anywhere else that readers visit. The most important part of how well a book sells is how many positive reviews it has, so if you leave us one then you are directly helping us to continue on our journey as writers. Thanks in advance to anyone who does this.

It means a lot. Thank you for your support!!

ABOUT THE AUTHORS

Jeffery L. Cheney

Jeff is the second of the seven Cheney brothers. In the past he has worked as a heavy equipment mechanic, a high school teacher, and a high technology manufacturing technician.

He enjoys coaching Basketball, working on cars and woodworking when the time allows.

Jeff has been writing science fiction and fantasy stories for enjoyment for over thirty years but Day of Reckoning is only his second attempt at a published novel.

He lives in a small town in NW Oregon with his wife of 31 years and their children.

Craig J. Cheney

Craig is the fourth of the Cheney sons.

He holds degrees in both Accounting and Computer engineering. He has worked as a disk jockey, put on trade shows, organized a circus, and currently solves other peoples engineering problems.

Craig volunteers to teach Shakespeare to 12-16 year olds and serves on the school board.

He was the runner-up for the 2009 Next Mark Twain Award.

Craig lives in the Portland, Oregon area with his wife and their five children.

Jared L. Cheney

Jared is the youngest of the brothers. He has worked for many years as the director of Information Technology for a Fortune 500 company.

He loves to travel and has lived and worked all over the US and in over 10 different countries.

Jared and his wife also live in the Portland, Oregon area with their children.

The authors all graduated at or near the top of their respective classes at the same High School on the Oregon Coast. All three are Eagle Scouts and volunteer their time to support The Boy Scouts of America.

www.ingramcontent.com/pod-product-compliance
Lightning Source LLC
Chambersburg PA
CBHW070344260626
47161CB00001B/2